PALACE *of* JUSTICE

PALACE *of* JUSTICE

Susanne Alleyn

MINOTAUR BOOKS

A THOMAS DUNNE BOOK

NEW YORK

THOMAS DUNNE BOOKS.
An imprint of St. Martin's Press.

PALACE OF JUSTICE. Copyright © 2010 by Susanne Alleyn. All rights reserved. Printed in the United States of America. For information, address St. Martin's Press, 175 Fifth Avenue, New York, N.Y. 10010.

www.minotaurbooks.com
www.stmartins.com

Library of Congress Cataloging-in-Publication Data

Alleyn, Susanne, 1963–
    Palace of justice : an Aristide Ravel mystery / Susanne Alleyn.—1st hardcover ed.
        p. cm.
    ISBN 978-0-312-37989-6
    1. Ravel, Aristide (Fictitious character)—Fiction.   2. Private investigators—France—Paris—Fiction.   3. Serial murder investigation—Fiction.   4. Paris (France)—History—1715–1789—Fiction.   I. Title.
PS3551.L4484P36 2010
813'.54—dc22   2010035766

ISBN 978-0-312-37989-6

First Edition: December 2010

10   9   8   7   6   5   4   3   2   1

To Erika Vause and Frimousse, who generously
shared Aristide's apartment with me;

and to the memory of Don Congdon, agent extraordinaire

ACKNOWLEDGMENTS

A big thank-you goes to the following scholars who helped me with various details: Professors Suzanne Desan, David A. Bell, and particularly Albert Hamscher. Also to Johanna, to Berenice, and to my agent and editor, Cristina Concepcion and Katie Gilligan, for hanging in there with me through the first draft; and to Pamela Thrasher, reader and treasured neighbor.

PREFACE

Palace of Justice takes place in October 1793, seven years after the events of *The Cavalier of the Apocalypse* and three years before *Game of Patience* and *A Treasury of Regrets*. Readers familiar with the Aristide Ravel novels should be aware that Charles Sanson, the executioner who appears in these pages, is "Old Sanson," the father of the younger Sanson featured in *Game of Patience*.

I have followed general European practice in the naming of floors in buildings; the first floor is one flight up from the ground floor, and so on.

Many of the tiny medieval streets in the heart of Paris disappeared during Baron Haussmann's extensive rebuilding of the city in the 1860s. Other streets have had their names, or the spelling of their names, changed during the past two centuries. To make matters even more confusing, many street names still in use today had been temporarily changed or altered by 1793 to eliminate references to royalty, aristocracy, or Christianity (Rue Royale became Rue de la Révolution; Rue St. Honoré became Rue Honoré). All streets and street names mentioned in this novel, however, existed in the 1790s.

TERMS

Bourreau (plural *bourreaux*): A hangman or professional torturer. Used as a derogatory term for any executioner, including the master executioner who, by royal appointment before the Revolution, held a largely ceremonial office; he was a title-holder and officer of the court, and rarely performed the dirty work of executions himself unless the victim was of noble birth.

Commissaire: After 1790, a local police official, in charge of a section (administrative district) of Paris; the commissaire combined the approximate functions of precinct commander and chief investigator.

Commissariat: Police headquarters for a Parisian section.

Commune: An all-purpose term, adopted during the Revolution, for any municipality, whether a small village or a major city. It could also refer collectively to the members of a local government.

Faubourg: A suburb or, less precisely, a neighborhood at the edge of the medieval center of a city; areas of Paris such as the faubourg St. Germain, the faubourg St. Marcel, and so on, were so named in the Middle Ages, when they were parishes lying outside the twelfth-century walls, but by the eighteenth century they were well within the city limits.

Hôtel: Can mean a hostelry, a large public building (*hôtel de ville*, city hall; *hôtel-Dieu*, charity hospital), or a large private town house or mansion (*hôtel particulier*). I have used the French form, with the circumflex over the *o*, whenever referring to a mansion or municipal hall, and the unaccented English word when referring to public accommodations.

Inspector: After 1790, a low-level police officer roughly corresponding to a uniformed sergeant or senior "beat cop" in a modern police force.

Jacobin: A member of the longstanding, left-wing political club which, from 1792, called itself "Society of Jacobins, friends of Liberty and Equality." In Paris, it met in the former monastery of the Dominican Brothers (nicknamed Jacobins, from their mother house on Rue St. Jacques). The term grew to include any radical republican.

Money: The most common standard unit of eighteenth-century French currency was the livre, although there was no one-livre coin. Twenty sous (which were further divided into the small change of copper deniers and liards) made up a livre; six livres a silver écu; twenty-four livres a gold louis d'or. In 1790, the National Assembly introduced paper currency, the assignats, which promptly plummeted in value and incited people to hoard coinage. The franc was not introduced until 1795.

Mountain: The most radical members of the republican government were called the Mountain, or Montagnards, because their habitual seats, at the far left of the chamber, were the highest ranks of benches in the hall where the elected assembly met.

Notary: The equivalent, in France, of a British solicitor: an attorney who deals in contracts, transactions, wills, property, legal issues, and the like, but who is not licensed to plead in court in criminal cases.

Palais-Égalité: In the 1780s the Duc d'Orléans built the Palais-Royal, an enclosure of elegant buildings with ground-floor shopping arcades, to surround the extensive gardens of his family's Paris mansion, and opened it to the public. It was temporarily renamed during the Revolution, first "Palais-Égalité" (Equality Palace, after the ex-duke, who had renounced his title and renamed himself Philippe Égalité), and then the more plebeian "Maison-Égalité" (Equality Hall), to follow republican fashion. Though quiet today, in the eighteenth and early nineteenth centuries the Palais-Royal was the center of racy, fashionable social life, chic shopping and dining, and expensive debauchery.

Parlement: Under the ancien régime, the supreme court of a region, which served as a court of appeal against judgments rendered by the lower royal and nonroyal courts in both civil and criminal cases; they sometimes also tried important cases of high treason, and criminal cases with aristocratic defendants. The chief parlement was located in Paris, with others in the provinces. The National Assembly abolished the parlements in 1790.

Police: The duties of the police of eighteenth-century Paris extended far beyond the prevention and investigation of crime and the maintenance of public order. Essentially city administrators, they supervised all kinds of public affairs which today, in a large European or American city, would be managed by various departments of health, sanitation, public welfare, housing, trade, the fire department, and even public morals.

President (of a court): The chief or presiding judge at a trial, during both the ancien régime and the Revolution.

Republican calendar or French Revolutionary calendar: Used officially in France from 1793 to 1809. It consisted of twelve months with three ten-day weeks in each, and five additional festival days (six in leap years) completing the calendar. The republican year began on September 22 of the Gregorian calendar and was dated from September 22, 1792 (the day the French Republic was established), though it was not put into official use until October of 1793, a month into "Year II."

Sansculotte: A member of Paris's artisan or working class, so named because the workers wore loose trousers as their everyday dress, rather than the knee breeches (culotte) worn by the middle class and aristocracy.

Section: One of forty-eight administrative areas of Paris, replacing the numbered districts of the prerevolutionary regime, consisting of a few square blocks in the heart of the city, and a wider area in the more sparsely populated outer quarters. Their names frequently changed during the Revolution, as personages or political movements grew popular or were disgraced; the Section du Palais-Royal, for example, became Section du Palais-Égalité in 1792, after the fall of the monarchy; then Section de la Butte-des-Moulins in 1793; then Section de la Montagne, within the year; and then once again Section de la Butte-des-Moulins in late 1794, after the decline of the "Montagnard" faction. Neither the sections nor the numbered prerevolutionary districts bore any relation to the modern arrondissements.

PALACE *of* JUSTICE

1

Paris
October 7, 1793

*G*od *help me*, Désirée said to herself, as she tried to ignore the dull, persistent ache of her empty stomach, *I cannot even earn a living as a whore.*

The fashionable hurried past her, eager to escape the chilly night air, toward the bright lights of the cafés, restaurants, theaters, and brothels of the Palais-Égalité. Along the stately length of the stone arcades, the lamps burned overhead, illuminating the restless swirl of humanity in its never-ending pursuit of amusement.

The women lurking beneath the rows of sculpted lime trees were banished from the light. Patient as the poor who once had formed lines before church doors to receive bread and soup, they waited, unsmiling, their eyes vacant, until some solitary figure from the milling crowd might fade away from the glitter and join them in the shadows.

She had waited hours in the dark, since before the twilight had fallen on a gray, wet October day, and seen the other women come and go, while only one man had approached her.

"You," he had said, out of the darkness, plucking her sleeve. "You've a pretty figure. What's your price?"

She had jerked about, surprised. He was middle-aged, stout, his neat frock coat cut in last year's fashion: a bourgeois from the provinces enjoying a holiday in Paris.

"What's your price?" he repeated.

That, at least, she knew; she had asked some of the other women what the going rate was. Those who had not laughed at her, snickering about amateurs, had been friendly enough. "Th-three sous, and the price of the room."

"If they rent by the hour, then. I'm not looking to spend the whole night with you."

"Yes, citizen." She turned and gestured at the arcades, toward a small hotel that charged lower prices and turned a blind eye to what might go on behind closed doors (as did all hotels in the Palais-Égalité, even after the pleasure gardens had been "officially" purged of prostitutes). The man followed her.

They had nearly reached the hotel when abruptly he thrust his face in hers, squinting in the bright lamplight shining through a café window.

"No wonder you women skulk in the shadows. How old are you?"

"I—twenty-nine." She had shaved five years from her true age, but evidently no one wanted anything over twenty-five or, better, twenty—

"And new to this line of work, from your manner. Well, I'm not paying for mutton dressed as lamb."

She had gazed after his retreating figure for a moment, speechless. At last she had heaved a long sigh, half in regret, half in relief, and fingered the coins in her pocket. Her last two sous—less than the price of a single meal. She had preserved her virtue for another half hour, and soon would virtuously starve.

Of all the misnamed folk in the world, she mused, not for the first time, *I am the most absurd. Désirée . . . but no one desires me, even as a whore.*

"How much?" said a voice, a different voice, close beside her. "Not too much, I hope—you're a little long in the tooth to be charging full price."

"Two sous," she muttered.

"Two sous for you? I don't pay two sous for any trollop who's past sixteen." He ran his hands over her, snickering as he prodded her. "Not much meat on those bones. Half a sou for a quick one in the alley." His hand was on her breast, clutching and kneading at her. "What do you say, little chicken?"

"I say you keep it to yourself until you've paid," she said between clenched teeth, her cheeks burning, as she attempted to push him away. "And don't paw at me in public."

"Don't paw at me in public!" he repeated in a high-pitched voice, with a sneer. "Dear me, how modest we are." His other hand slid down and grabbed at her through her skirt, between her legs. The prodding, grasping fingers fumbled and groped and would not, would *not* let go of her. She wrenched her arm away and slapped him.

"You little bitch!"

Suddenly her ears were ringing, and a sharp pain was creeping along the line of her cheekbone to the back of her skull, and the world was spinning about her. She was sitting—no, lying—on something cold and wet. As she struggled up to a sitting position, through a dim haze she saw him dust off his hands and saunter away.

"Bastard," said one woman, a shabby one near her own age, as another laughed drunkenly and swayed off in pursuit of a customer. "All bastards, all of them." She reached down and offered her hand. "Here."

Désirée lurched to her knees, gritting her teeth in an attempt to swallow back her despair. The skirt of her green gown, her last dress, was dripping and smeared with mud.

"Mademoiselle?" said a man's voice beside her. "Are you all right?"

She squeezed her eyes shut for a moment, opened them, and found herself gazing up at a tall, lean man in a shabby overcoat. "Are you all right?" the man repeated, bending toward her. "That was quite a blow he gave you. Better you should sit down—you don't want to faint. Someone might seize his opportunity to rob you."

"Rob me—" she exclaimed, and all at once, to her hideous embarrassment, she burst into violent, gasping sobs. "Oh, dear God, if only there were something in my pocket to steal!"

The stranger shook his head and offered her a hand to help her to her feet. "Come, come, it can't be all that bad—"

"Yes, it *is* that bad!" she screamed, no longer caring who might hear her. "What do you know about it? Look at me! Just a useless woman whom no one wants, not even as a whore, and with two sous to call her own!"

"Here, now," he said, handing her a handkerchief and drawing her aside, away from the other women. "Dry your eyes, squeeze out your skirts, and let's get something warm inside you. You've not eaten, I suppose?"

"Eaten . . ." When had she eaten last? "Not since yesterday morning. Some bread."

"Come with me."

Dazed, Désirée followed him. He strode along with the easy step of one who was accustomed to walking, leading her out of the Palais-Égalité to the narrow side streets west of the gardens, at last pausing before a food stall whose owner had not yet hung up his shutters. "Here, some soup will do you good."

She glanced up at him as he pulled out a few crumpled assignats for the soup seller. Her companion was a lean, dark-haired man of forty or so. A broad-brimmed, low-crowned round hat shadowed a long, stern face, which she could just make out in the gloom, though she caught the glitter of eyes in the feeble glimmer from the soup seller's lantern. The man's clothes were less than impressive; he wore an old, well-worn black worsted suit that might have belonged to a lawyer's clerk, and hanging open over that, a dark overcoat of indeterminate color, which once had been of good quality before moths and the passage of time had ravaged it.

"You're very kind, citizen," she said, avoiding his gaze. "After what I said to you. Anyone else would have pushed me into the mud again for such insolence."

"Such men are swine. You've not been long in your trade, have you?"

"Only today. I had no more money, and nothing to eat, and the rent is due. And there's no work in Paris, at least nothing I know how to do."

The soup seller put a bowl and spoon before her. She seized the spoon and began wolfing down the soup. Oh, the exquisite feeling of having something in her stomach at last, vegetables, a little tough meat, and plenty of thick broth! The tall man watched her, smiling.

"Better?"

She glanced up at him, wishing she could scrape the bowl out with her finger to get up the last few drops. "Thank you."

"My pleasure, citizeness. You're well-spoken," he added, turning away from the stall. "Who and what are you, for God's sake?"

"My father was the second son of a gentleman and owned a little land, but we never had two sous to rub together, and we lost the few dues from the property when the Revolution abolished them. Then my father died, two years ago, but not before he'd gambled away most of what we had; and I had to sell our property to settle his debts. I had a fiancé, but he jilted me in the end, because I had no fortune." An old, monotonous story, one everyone had heard a dozen times before. She paused, but he merely nodded.

"So I came to Paris as companion to my mother's cousin, who's married to a rich man. Then her husband made advances, and when I—when I kicked him, he threw me out. That was four months ago. I can't get any work. I don't know any trade besides sewing, and half the dressmakers have shut up their shops and the other half aren't hiring anyone new. I've sold everything I had, my bits of jewelry, my books, even my clothes. So at last I came here, to offer the only thing I had left to sell, but it seems I'm no good even for that." Her stomach rumbled and she clasped her hands over it, embarrassed.

"I think your appetite wants more than some soup," her unexpected savior observed. "There's an eating-house nearby. Come along."

She blinked away tears, so weary she had no strength left to resist. "A favor for a favor—that's it, isn't it? Do whatever you want. You can have me for the whole night if you like. At least the room will be warm."

"You misunderstand me. I'm not looking for a whore. Let's say," he continued, as he steered her down the street and gestured to a narrow alley, "that I think you've had more than your share of ill luck. The least I can do, out of Christian charity, is to give you a hot meal."

"Thank you, citizen," she whispered, wondering how many months it had been since she had heard the word "Christian" used without derision. Many of the brutalized, bitter sansculottes, day laborers, and prostitutes she now saw every day had little love for the Catholic Church, which, for centuries, had taxed them and dictated to them while its cynical, worldly bishops flaunted their wealth. Though the Church, in its present state-sanctioned, revolutionary form, was still tolerated, anti-clerical feeling had been swelling of late.

"This way—it's not far now."

He gestured her onward and she preceded him into the empty alley, feeling her way along. The closest street lamp was far behind them and the chinks of light from behind barred shutters, and the tiny new moon above, cast only a meager light, barely enough for her to see her groping hands.

"Are you sure this is the way?"

"It's a shortcut. Keep going."

She stumbled on a loose cobble, hearing it clatter like a pistol shot in the silence, and stopped short, heart pounding. She was all alone here with him, isolated and helpless, just as he wanted her.

Fool, she told herself. *You credulous little fool.*

She was going to be raped in an alley, by a degenerate with unnatural desires that a decent woman should not even know of, for the price of a bowl of soup.

She twisted about, but in his dark coat and broad hat he was invisible in the murk.

"Please—please don't hurt me. I said you could do whatever you wanted. Just don't hurt me."

Now she could hear his breath, close by in the darkness. His arm slid about her from behind, clutching her to him until she felt the warmth of his body.

"I told you," he murmured, "I don't want that from you."

"Then what—"

He whispered a few words. She thought they might be "May God forgive me" in the last instant before the knife was at her throat.

2

The woman lay on her back in a narrow alley a few steps beyond the Palais-Égalité, sprawled in a great splash of her own blood, which had stained her sodden, mud-blotched green gown and trickled away, dissolving beneath the rain, along the channels between the rough cobbles. The stump of her neck looked as raw as cuts of meat at a butcher's stall in the sullen gray of a wet morning.

Aristide Ravel stood in the alley, bareheaded, hands clasped behind the back of his shabby black redingote, and stared at the mutilated corpse. All around them, the fine autumn rain dripped down.

"Death of the devil," Commissaire Brasseur said, beside him, hat in hand. "I've never seen anything like this."

Aristide could well believe him. He had been working for Brasseur as a freelance police investigator for seven years now, but even the brutality and vice of Paris had not prepared him for such a sight.

"Have your men found—" He was about to say "the head," but using the definite article seemed cruelly impersonal, reducing the pathetic corpse before him to nothing more than a lump of flesh. He sucked in a breath and began again. "Have they found her head?"

"Not yet." Brasseur was silent a moment, then spoke again, choking on hoarse fury.

"What sort of monster would do this?"

Aristide could not see that a decapitated corpse in an alley was much different from the decapitated corpses that the executioners now carted away from the Place de la Révolution two or three times a week; according to yesterday's *Moniteur,* some of those guillotined during the past fortnight had been sentenced to death for minor infractions against authority that once, before the Revolution, would have meant no more than a public whipping or a month or two in prison. The Law of Suspects, passed three weeks before to preserve the struggling young Republic in a time of political and economic crisis, had abruptly transformed petty offenses into crimes and indifference into treason.

"You mean," he said, "what sort of monster would do, in the street, what they often decree at the Revolutionary Tribunal?"

"That's different," Brasseur said, groping for words. "It's—"

"Sanctioned?"

"This," said Brasseur, ignoring his bitter sarcasm, "this is just— obscene." He donned his hat, cramming it down against the chill rain, and puffed out a long sigh. "Dr. Prunelle's on his way. What do you make of her?"

Aristide looked over the body, thinking how much one depended on the face to make such judgments. "Not young, but not yet old," he said, eyeing her bony shoulders and veined hands. "I'd say thirty-five or forty. You?"

"Yes." Brasseur knelt beside her and lifted her arm, moving it back and forth. "Killed sometime after dark last night. I don't need a police surgeon to tell me she's just beginning to go stiff, so I'd guess she died between dusk and midnight."

Aristide nodded. In the congested center of Paris, a bloody, headless corpse could not have lain on the cobbles in daylight, even in the tiniest alleyway, without being stumbled upon within ten minutes. The side streets, however, swiftly emptied with the onset of darkness and the pickpockets, ruffians, bandits, and housebreakers that the night brought out.

"Who discovered her?" he inquired. "Do we have any idea who she is?"

"Not an inkling. The fellow who found her was a local on his way to work. Sells brooms on Rue St.—" Brasseur paused, annoyed with himself, and continued, avoiding the dubious word "Saint." "On Rue Honoré. As to knowing her, what am I supposed to say? Without a face, all we can go on is the clothes and effects." Brasseur bent once again over the corpse. "Try her pocket; she might have a civic card."

Aristide knelt opposite him, taking care to keep out of the puddle of blood and the ever-present manure and refuse, and felt in the dead woman's right-hand pocket. "Two sous in small change. A clean handkerchief, a bit thin and frayed. A copper thimble. A twist of thread and—damn it!—a needle folded inside a bit of old paper. A key, ordinary-looking, presumably to her lodging, and a smaller one to a case or a trunk. Nothing else. No identity card. Anything on your side?"

"Only a soiled handkerchief. And she's not wearing a wedding ring."

"That might have been stolen before we got here."

Brasseur shook his head. "You're a bachelor, Ravel. My wife claims the dent on her finger began to show after a couple of years of wearing her ring." He raised the corpse's hand. "No mark. No sign she's ever worn a ring there."

"I defer to your greater knowledge." Aristide stared at the woman's bloody gown a moment, brow puckered in thought, and then examined her hands, which often provided useful clues to identity.

"Well?" said Brasseur, after a few minutes of silence.

"She's not a peasant. Nor a laborer, but not a woman of leisure, either. Her hands don't have the hard calluses of a lifelong worker, though she's done some manual work in her time."

Her modest gown, what he could see of it where the blood from her severed neck had not flooded all across the fichu, bodice, and sleeves, was of green calico, sprigged with small blue flowers. A great smear of mud soiled one side of the skirt and dirty water had stained much of the cloth. It was not the plain homespun of a peasant newly arrived in the city; nor did it show signs of multiple alterations or seem shabby enough to be a second- or third-hand piece of clothing purchased from the *fripiers*, the old-clothes dealers whose carts and rundown stalls were ubiquitous in the poorer quarters. It tallied with the image he had formed of a once-respectable woman now forced to support herself in any way she could.

"Her gown's a decade old at least, well-worn but carefully mended; it might be secondhand, but more likely one she'd owned for years. And it looks loose, as though she'd grown a good deal thinner lately and had not yet taken it in. I'd say a woman of the modest bourgeoisie, or perhaps a small landowner, who's fallen on hard times and has had to shift for herself."

Brasseur grunted. Food shortages and high prices, brought on by the war, continued to plague the city that troubled autumn, while rising unemployment, particularly in the luxury trades that had once catered to the wealthy, made the situation even worse for Paris's poor.

"A woman with what might have been her last two sous in her pocket usually doesn't have a fixed address," he said. "That'll be a treat, it will, trying to put a name on her."

"Yes, I expect she was alone, to be in such straits. And who takes notice if a solitary woman disappears—one with no husband and no money?"

"Nobody," said Brasseur. When the rent for her seedy furnished room came due, and his tenant was not present to pay it, a landlord would seize her effects as payment, advertise a room to let, and forget about her. "Well, I'll send a couple of inspectors out to inquire at cheap lodgings."

"Could she be local?" Aristide continued. "Any recent reports of missing women in the section?"

"None, so far."

"Well, if it turns out she wasn't from the neighborhood, then what would bring her here to this quarter? Not shopping—the poor stick to their own sections. We're just a few steps from the Palais-Égalité—"

"The Maison-Égalité."

"What?"

"That's what some of my men are calling it now. Palaces aren't in fashion, you know. Better to go with the flow."

Aristide sighed. Soon so many suspect names from the bad old days of the ancien régime would be changed to good republican ones that no one would be able to find his way around the city. "If you like. The Maison-Égalité. As I was saying, what would this woman be doing there? It's mostly high-priced luxury shops."

"The ones that are still open, anyway."

"A woman who appears to be down on her luck and starving would scarcely go to the Palais—the Maison-Égalité—to buy anything; she'd be there to sell."

Brasseur snapped his fingers. "Offering herself to any man who'd have her. The girls, the ones who still hang about the arcades—they all know each other. They'd notice the amateurs."

"Describe her gown to them," Aristide said. "And don't forget the fresh mud on her skirt. That's more than a splatter from a passing carriage; it looks as if she had a bad fall recently. Perhaps one of the girls will remember."

Brasseur glanced at his watch and stifled a yawn. "Well, I don't doubt they will, but it's far too early in the day to go looking for the whores yet. Any other ideas?"

At that moment Dr. Prunelle, the local police surgeon, hurried up. "What's this you have for me, Commissaire?" he inquired, closing his umbrella and shaking hands with Brasseur. "The lad who fetched me said it was a beast of a case, but wouldn't elaborate. He looked a little pale."

"It's a beast of a case, all right," Brasseur said, gesturing. "See for yourself."

"Oh," said Prunelle, as he knelt beside the corpse. "Oh, my. Dear me. Where's the head?"

"Your guess is as good as ours. Ever seen anything like this?"

"Oh, no. That's to say, not as a case of murder. Of course I've seen more than enough decapitated corpses lately at the Place de la Révolution."

"Don't tell me you're a connoisseur of executions," Aristide said. Prunelle scarcely seemed the type of citizen who had gleefully taken to attending the free entertainment of trials for counterrevolutionary activities at the Revolutionary Tribunal, and their frequent, bloody aftermath at the public scaffold.

"Hmm?" said Prunelle, without looking up from his examination of the corpse. "Oh, executions. No, I don't attend for the sake of amusement, dear me, no. But my colleague Dr. Beaumont and I are conducting a series of experiments, you see, in order to determine whether or not execution by guillotine is as quick as we've been led to believe. Beaumont's grown concerned about the question ever since the rumor began to go around that the Corday woman blushed after some brute of an assistant executioner slapped her severed head."

"Swine," grunted Brasseur. "Sanson sacked him, you know. And he got thirty days in lockup for it."

"Did he?" Prunelle echoed him, peering at the stump of the neck. "Glad to hear it. So," he continued, "from time to time, we obtain permission to stand close by and observe the corpse immediately after decapitation. Personally, I suspect the idea of Corday's head blushing is complete nonsense. Nothing I've seen indicates that consciousness survives for more than a second or two after the great vessels of the neck are severed. The corpse may twitch a moment, but so does a chicken on the block. See here, for example," he added, rising and dusting off his knees. "This unfortunate creature's throat was cut. She would have been dead within a few seconds."

"She didn't die of . . . from . . . beheading?" Brasseur said.

"Oh, no. That came soon afterward. That is, I suspect the murderer caught her from behind—the angle of the cut indicates as much, assuming he's right-handed—and slit her throat, opening the vein here, below the left ear, where the slash would have begun. I could show you, if the head were present. Much easier than attempting to hack the head off a living victim. Then, within a minute or two, I'd say, he went to work with a large, sharp knife of some kind, or a cleaver, perhaps. It wouldn't have taken long, if he was strong and knew something of anatomy."

"I saw a field surgeon in America take off a leg once," said Brasseur. "Must have taken him less than a minute."

Prunelle shook his head. "Ah, but this wasn't done with a bone saw. I would need to dissect the cadaver to be sure, but the looks of the visible bone seem to indicate a heavy cutting blade, hacking at the vertebrae, rather than any kind of saw."

"Brasseur estimates she was killed between dusk and midnight," Aristide said. Prunelle nodded.

"Quite right. Soon you won't need me at all, Commissaire! Well, is there anything else I can tell you?"

"Only if you can deduce, from looking at her corpse, who killed her," Brasseur said, "and why, and why he hacked her head off and took it away with him."

"That, I fear even I can't tell you," said Prunelle, with a hint of a smile, which he quickly suppressed. "But you've considered, of course, that this is the work of a madman?"

"Of course."

"Such men—it's rare, but one hears rumors—such men sometimes mingle rape with murder. I shouldn't like to make an examination here—we have to preserve the decencies, after all—but I'll instruct the attendants at the morgue to examine her for signs of assault, if you wish."

"I'll tell them myself," Aristide said. "It's on my way home."

"Well," Brasseur said as Dr. Prunelle departed, "let's get this cleared away. Didier! Bring over the litter. Careful, now, be sure she's covered up. Nobody needs to see something like this. You, there, find a house with a well and fetch some water."

Brasseur, Aristide knew, would have to return to his office at the nearby commissariat to write his report of the murder and the initial investigation. Aristide followed the litter bearers out of the alley and waited while they loaded the corpse onto a waiting cart, then climbed up himself beside the driver. The man was a taciturn sort, as it proved, and Aristide was in no mood for talking, so they proceeded in silence down Rue de la Loi and along the busy, noisy length of Rue Honoré to the Châtelet.

Paris's morgue had, for centuries, been situated in some lower chamber or other of the Châtelet, the medieval fortress on the Right

Bank, close to the river, that now housed jails and police courts. Victims of accident or suicide in the water, as well as unidentified murder victims, invariably were delivered to the Basse-Geôle de la Seine, a dank cellar hidden beneath the court chambers. There they would remain until their bodies and effects were claimed, or until the municipality bestirred itself to pay for a pauper's burial in one of the common graves of the city's numerous cemeteries.

Aristide left the cart waiting in the public passage beside the magistrates' stairway and went in to fetch the concierges, a pair of gloomy individuals named Daude and Bouille, and their assistant who performed the menial tasks of sweeping and carrying. Together the assistant and the carter lifted the litter from the cart and lugged it through the antechamber and down the stone stairs to the cellar.

"I expect you've seen worse," Aristide began, for Daude and Bouille were in charge of inspecting and inventorying all the remains, including the swollen, putrefying corpses dragged regularly from the river. "But you ought to know that this cadaver has no head."

"No head!" Bouille echoed him, looking more like a doleful bloodhound than ever. He took a quick swallow from his pocket flask. "But—"

"That's nothing new these days, is it?" Daude said hurriedly. "But why didn't it go straight to the cemetery nearest the Place de la Révolution?"

"This one was murdered, not executed."

"Tch." He made a small sound of annoyance and shook his head. "What's the world coming to?"

"Be sure to examine her for signs of rape," Aristide added, as he followed Daude down the stairs to the chilly cellar where the corpses were kept, recoiling at a particularly noisome odor that met him at the bottom. "And get the blood out of the gown as best you can—Brasseur may need it to identify her—"

"It'll have to wait," Daude told him, pausing at one of the stone tables and lifting a corner of the sheet draped over a still figure. "They fished two corpses out of the river yesterday near the grain port, neither in good condition, and we'll have to tend to those first, before they decay further. Come back tomorrow or the next day."

"As you wish," Aristide said. The examination and inventory would be done when they were done; he knew, from seven years of investigating murders with Brasseur and others, that there was no hurrying the meticulous morgue attendants. He hurried up the stairs, thankful at least to get away from the stink of decaying flesh.

3

The eating-house a few steps from the Pont-Neuf had once been called the Evergreen Gallant, after King Henri IV, and its hanging sign had boasted a crude portrait of a crowned head. Now, fourteen months after the abolition of the monarchy, even the splendid equestrian statue of France's most beloved king was gone from its pedestal at the middle of the bridge, where the Pont-Neuf crossed the western tip of the Île de la Cité, and the eating-house's sign was painted over and bore the good republican symbol of a liberty tree. But the food at the Liberty Tree, despite climbing prices and shortages brought on by war, inflation, hoarding, and the general pigheadedness of the peasants who grew grain and vegetables for the Paris markets, was still nearly as good as that in far more expensive establishments.

Aristide had been a regular at the Liberty Tree, which the locals continued to call "Michalet's" after its talkative southern-born proprietor, since moving to the Latin Quarter in 1786. Brasseur had left their familiar ground of the former Eighteenth District in 1791 and moved to the Right Bank, to a larger apartment that would accommodate his ever-growing family; he had, shortly afterward, been elected police commissaire of what had then been the Section du Palais-Royal. The raffish and informal atmosphere of the Latin Quarter, however, suited

Aristide and he had chosen to remain on Rue de la Huchette, in the center of the city.

Having had no messages or orders from Brasseur for the past day and a half, he took his time finishing his midday dinner. The cassoulet (a southern dish that was one of Michalet's specialties) was rather poorer in meat and richer in haricot beans than in previous months, but that was to be expected, when times were so lean and disordered. He broke off a lump of dark bread from the slab in the basket in front of him and wiped absently at the thick gravy.

A pair of men from the neighborhood just to the south of the Seine, judging from their plain, serviceable coats—the clothing of the master artisan or *petit bourgeois*—slouched at the far end of the long table where he sat. They had apparently worked their way through a second carafe of cheap red wine, for their voices rang out, louder than they needed to be, despite Aristide's presence nearby. A solitary, taciturn diner wearing black, the traditional color of civil servants, the police, and often their spies, invariably invited distrust; few of the local regulars, unless they were tipsy, would dare to let a potential informer overhear their conversation.

"The Austrian bitch is going to get it in the neck, did you hear?" said the man in the green coat. "Jaquet who lives upstairs, his wife told my wife. His brother's a jailer at the Conciergerie and they're saying she'll be up before the Tribunal soon. Good riddance, I say! Too bad they can only cut your head off once, even if you're royalty."

"M'wife won't be happy 'bout that. Thinks Antoinette's a saint or summat."

"Women! What do they know? Me, I'll go and watch her get shortened and drink to the Republic, and so will my Jeannette. Jeannette never misses it when they've got somebody famous on. 'S always a good show."

Aristide stifled a yawn and glanced at the glistening windowpanes. Perhaps, when the rain let up, he would take coffee at the Palais-Égalité after stopping in at the morgue to collect the report on the corpse, and delivering it to Brasseur. Meanwhile, despite the disagreeable conversation in the background, Michalet's was at least warm and dry.

"Oh, once or twice a month," the man in the green coat was saying. "Like I said, Jeannette never misses somebody important, but I've got the workshop and the men to look after. Can't be sailing off to the other side of town whenever I hear the Tribunal sent another one to be shortened."

"You let your women go there like that, whenever they please, and they'll get all kinds of morbid fancies," his companion in the slate-blue coat warned him, and burst into tipsy laughter.

"Here, what's the matter with you?"

"It's not just the women who're making up wild stories, see! One of my journeymen, he was telling the lads yesterday some foolishness 'bout a dead body without its head."

"Nothing new about that," said Green Coat, belching, "not lately."

"No, but this wasn't Madame Guillotine's leavings. Or if it was, it'd got up afterward and took a walk for its health and got lost in the alleys, see?"

Aristide twisted in his seat, wondering how rapidly the rumor mill could possibly work; the murdered woman in the Section de la Montagne, on the other side of the river, had been found only the day before. Green Coat went on, unaware of his scrutiny.

"That's mad. A body in the streets, you mean, without its head on?"

"That's 'zactly what I mean. Headless corp . . . corps . . . corpuses," Blue Coat managed at last. "Now you can find 'em around the city. How's that for a tale?"

"That's rubbish, that is. How'd a headless corpus get onto the street?"

"Some madman *left* it, didn't he, for you or me or my old mother to find?"

"You're cracked if you believe that." Green Coat shot a quick, suspicious glance Aristide's way and gave an artificial and unconvincing laugh as he dragged their three-quarters-empty carafe of wine away from his companion. "That's enough gossiping. You'd better lay off the sauce."

The rain had dwindled to a fine drizzle. Aristide paid his bill and left the eating-house, shaking his head at the feverish rumors that war, an unstable government at odds with itself, and a general mood of fear and uncertainty could provoke. A damp wind beat at his face as he tramped, head down, along the narrow street toward the river.

He collected Daude's report at the Basse-Geôle and went on to the Right Bank to deliver it to Brasseur. "I doubt it will tell you anything new," he said, passing it to his friend. Neither the scanty medical details nor the meticulous description of every piece of the corpse's well-worn clothing had provided him with any clues. "She wasn't molested, by the way."

"No?"

"In fact, she was probably the only virgin in Paris."

Brasseur snorted, then added, with a logical sequence of ideas, "I haven't been able to spare anyone yet to talk to the girls who work the gardens. Want to do that? They like you . . . well, at least more than they like the average inspector."

Aristide shrugged. Questioning the whores at the Palais-Égalité— curse it, the *Maison*-Égalité—seemed their best option. He left Brasseur in his office and strolled over to the gardens, where the girls were beginning to appear beneath the trees as the sun slipped westward.

One recalled a woman in a green gown who had hung around them, two days ago, and who had had "no notion of what she was about, the silly bitch." The seventh he interrogated, a weary-looking woman of thirty whom he had seen before, answered his questions in a monotone until he mentioned the mud on the green gown.

"Mud?" she said. "Faith, you're right! Two nights ago, an amateur in a green gown—"

"Know her name?"

"Not likely. Didn't look like she half wanted to be here, but you could tell she was desperate. And then one of the bastards knocked the poor little cow into the mud, got it all over her skirt. But she went off with another of them a tick later."

"Who? Who'd she go off with, Fanchette?"

"Didn't know him. Not a regular here."

"Describe him."

She eyed Aristide sadly. "I got my living to earn. How long's this going to take?"

"A quarter hour of your time," he told her, holding up a few coppers. "Look—coin, not paper. Tell me what you can. What happened?"

"All right," she said, shuffling over to a scarred marble bench, "some bastard knocked her into the mud, like I said, because she talked back to him. But a man comes up behind us and gives her a hand up and asks her if she's all right. Then all of a sudden she busts out crying, and says something about being no good for anything, and how she's got only two sous left in the world."

"Two sous?" he said, remembering the pathetic bits of copper in the woman's pocket.

"Yes, and then he takes her off a ways, but I hear him asking her if she's eaten, and she says no, and he says come with me, and she goes off behind him, that way toward the Montpensier passage. That's all."

"Fanchette, you have to tell me anything you can remember about this man."

"Oh, the poor cow," she exclaimed. "Was it her that they found, cut up in an alley? What a hell of a life," she continued, as he nodded. "A hell of a life, and then get yourself butchered. Did he rape her, then?"

"Evidently not," Aristide said. "What did the man look like?"

She shrugged. "It was dark. I didn't get much of a look at him. Tall, thin."

"Clothes?"

"Not a workman. Good clothes, though they'd seen better days. He had . . . he had a dark overcoat, and boots . . . and a hat that hid his face."

"Did he wear a wig?"

"Who wears a wig anymore? No." She sighed, trying to remember. "Dark brown hair, like yours, almost black, that's what it was. Long, dark hair, with a bit of gray in it, pulled behind him. Could have been you," she added with a flicker of malicious amusement, "savin' the hat, of course; and you wear your hair any old way, don't you?"

"How did he speak?" Aristide said, ignoring the remark about his lank, gray-threaded hair, which, save for special occasions, he rarely bothered to dress properly. "Like a gentleman? Or did he have a rougher manner?"

"Like a gent, I think. What I could hear, he was talking to her polite. Sounded like he was sorry for her, the lying swine."

"He asked her if she had eaten?" he said, glancing over his notes. "And then they went off in the direction of Rue Montpensier? You're sure about that?"

"Sure as I'm sitting here. 'Cause I said to myself, he'd better hurry if he wants to catch old Jacques before he closes up his stall. S'pose that's where they were going. It's the closest place to get a bite that don't cost you a week's earnings."

The soup seller's stall lay between the passage out of the enclosure of the Palais-Égalité and the alley where the wretched woman's body had been found. "Thanks, Fanchette."

Jacques at the soup stall could tell him little that Fanchette had not already told him, though he confirmed her opinion that the stranger had spoken well, like an educated man. Aristide returned to Brasseur's commissariat to find him irritably dealing with the petty day-to-day business of policing a section of Paris. He scribbled a signature on an order, thrust it at his waiting secretary, and turned to Aristide.

"Any luck?"

"No one knew her name," he said as Dautry, the secretary, retreated to his own tiny room. He pulled out a chair. "But one of the girls remembered her going off with a tall, lean man in a dark overcoat and a hat, presumably a wide-brimmed one if it shadowed his face as she said. Jacques, the soup seller, remembers them both. The man paid for a serving of soup, which she wolfed down as if she hadn't eaten for days, and that seems to be the last anyone saw of them."

"That alley's not too far from Jacques's stall," Brasseur said. "You think that was the man, then? Tall, lean, dark overcoat, and a wide-brimmed hat . . . could be plenty of folk. Could be you, for that matter, though I know you're not partial to low-crowned hats."

"A stranger in the quarter, it seems; of course, he may lodge somewhere else entirely."

"Well, I'll set my men to asking around the neighborhood. I suppose I'd better ask right away for their help at Piques and Le Peletier and Halle-au-Blé, too," Brasseur said, with a glance at the vast map of Paris that was pinned to the wall, referring to the sections that bordered on the Section de la Montagne. "*And* Tuileries, *and* Gardes-Françaises! That's the worst of this new system," he declared, elaborating on a theme Aristide had heard many times before, during the past three years. "Everything's decentralized now and nobody knows what anybody else is doing! You could have a crime in your own section, and another two streets away committed by the same culprit, but since it's in another section, you never hear about it! Before the Revolution, everyone in the district reported to the commissaire, who was somebody with some real authority, not just a petty supervisor like me with a handful of streets to cover. . . ."

Aristide smiled at Brasseur's habitual, half-serious complaint. "Yes, and *he* reported to the Royal Lieutenant of Police—"

"And information got shared among the districts quick as lightning, and things got done!"

Aristide waited until Brasseur had run down, like an unwound automaton. He seized the moment to fetch a pack of battered playing cards from a drawer of the cabinet where Brasseur kept a discreet bottle and glasses, together with the folded tricolor sash, designating Brasseur as a commissaire of police, that he donned when official occasions demanded it.

"Let's not waste our efforts until we've thought this through a little more. Daude's report says the woman wasn't raped. Why, then, did he kill her and hack off her head, if it wasn't part of some hideous perversion?"

He began to lay the cards out on Brasseur's desk. *Gain, jealousy, revenge, self-preservation, love,* he said to himself, repeating the five essential reasons for murder that Brasseur had taught him when they had first worked together. "Surely not robbery; she had nothing to steal. And I don't see how jealousy or revenge could come into it; she was a stranger to him by all accounts, just a woman to be picked up."

"Self-preservation?" Brasseur inquired, crossing his arms and leaning back in his protesting chair. "How could a shabby woman down on her luck be any threat to him, or to anyone?"

"Love?" Aristide said, swiftly moving various cards to their foundations. A round or two of patience, he had found, occupied his hands and helped him think.

"Well, he didn't love *her*. Damn it, Ravel, it seems so . . . so random. If he wasn't a pervert, and he had no motive to kill her that we can see, then why the devil did he do it?"

"I don't know. But it must be one of those reasons." The round of patience ended unsuccessfully, as it usually did, and he swept up the cards and returned them to their drawer. "My brain's in a fog; perhaps some coffee will clear it. Care to escape for half an hour?"

"Can't," Brasseur said, gesturing at his desk. "Too much to do. But you go. Stop in on your way back."

4

The Palais-Égalité had lost much of its previous luster during the past year, since the monarchy had been abolished and luxury had come under suspicion. The Café Février, at least, remained the same, an oasis of elegance in a city growing ever more shabby and unruly as it became prudent to deplore all manners and fashions that might link one to the vanished ancien régime. Almost no one but the most elderly and conservative still wore a powdered wig unless he could claim baldness as an excuse (Maximilien Robespierre himself being a notable exception), and even the vogue for a layer of pomade and powder on one's own neatly dressed hair was fading, to the hairdressers' despair. *Sansculottisme*— dressing down to the comfortable, practical, everyday trousers, belted blouse, short jacket with or without plain waistcoat, woolen cap, and sometimes even wooden sabots of Paris's laboring classes—was the new fashion, usually achieved with only middling success.

Aristide glanced with some amusement at a few pseudosansculottes as he strolled down the broad staircase into the café. Despite their amateurish efforts to appear like simple workingmen, evidently these comfortably-off bourgeois and professional men still could not bear to be parted from their daily demitasse of mocca or glass of fine liqueur in congenial company beneath a crystal chandelier.

He himself, he feared, catching sight of himself in one of the mirrored panels on the wall, would look ridiculous dressed as a sansculotte. Indifferent to fashions and with too modest and irregular an income to employ a servant, he invariably wore a redingote or frock coat, waistcoat, and culotte of unadorned, shabby black above top boots in the English style—a costume that did not soil easily and spared him the nuisance of making decisions about his meager wardrobe. And, though he would admit such trifling vanity to few, he believed it rather suited his lean frame.

He moved in on an empty table just as the previous occupants rose, leaving their well-thumbed newspapers behind, and settled down to learn what was happening in the rest of the city and abroad. The news in the *Moniteur* was not encouraging, though the armies at least were beginning to drive the Prussian and Austrian invaders off French soil in the northeastern provinces. He glanced past the bulletin from the Revolutionary Tribunal—he had no desire to gloat over the wretches who had fallen afoul of the new laws that, with the flourish of a pen, had made so many citizens suspect of trivial crimes against the Republic—but came to a halt at a small announcement beneath it.

> By decree of the National Convention, the Brissotin traitors whom the nation expelled from its bosom on the illustrious 2nd of June, since that time held under arrest, have been transferred to the prison of the Conciergerie. The ex-deputies will appear within the month before the Revolutionary Tribunal to answer charges of conspiracy against the Republic, One and Indivisible.

Mathieu. Oh, God, not Mathieu.

Mathieu Alexandre, whom he had known from boyhood, his best friend. Mathieu, who had gone into politics when the Revolution had brought France a representative government, who had been elected a deputy to the National Convention at the fall of the monarchy. Mathieu, who had thrown his lot and his political destiny in with the moderate republican deputies whom most people called "Brissotins," after Jacques-Pierre Brissot, one of their most famous leaders, or "Girondins," after the *département* whose capital was Aristide's own home city of Bordeaux, from which several of them came.

"Your coffee, citizen."

He came to himself with a jerk and stared at the waiter.

"Your coffee. Sugar, citizen?"

Sugar, since the price of imported goods had risen astronomically with the British blockade of the ports, now cost an additional sou. Aristide had chosen to learn to like his coffee unsugared.

"No." He pushed three sous across the table and continued to glower at the newspaper.

Mathieu . . . and Ducos, Boyer-Fonfrède, Vergniaud, Gensonné, old friends whom he had known in Bordeaux, and the rest—soon to fight for their lives before the Tribunal, which was not known, lately, for its leniency.

Only recently it had seemed as if the National Convention, or perhaps the Committee of Public Safety under Robespierre's restraining influence, had been content to keep the most notable Brissotin deputies immobilized under house arrest in Paris. Immobilized, powerless, but unharmed. Only the most fanatical of Jacobins and street rabble truly believed that Brissot and his associates were traitors within the Convention; rational people knew it had been no more than a political quarrel between the conservative republican Brissotins and the more radical Montagnards, a furious difference of opinion on how best to govern France in a time of war and crisis, that had led to the Brissotin deputies' expulsion from the government.

Unfortunately, in the autumn of 1793, it seemed a difference of opinion might be fatal, for the Revolutionary Tribunal pronounced only one sentence for the guilty: death, without appeal.

His hands were icy. He dropped the newspaper and fumbled with the coffee cup; it had cooled while he had been staring at that impersonal paragraph. He swallowed the tepid liquid without tasting it.

"The devil with the Brissotins!" someone exclaimed nearby. Aristide turned, not meaning to eavesdrop, but wondering how the patrons of the Café Février—many of them prosperous, middle-class professional men of the same sort as the Brissotins themselves—were view-ing the present state of affairs.

The speaker was a well-dressed, middle-aged man in a brown coat and striped yellow silk waistcoat who, with a companion in blue, was settling himself at an adjoining table. "This damned war just keeps go-ing on, and on, and we don't gain a thing," he continued. "Those cursed Brissotins should never have shouted for war. Just wanted to cover them-selves with glory, they did."

"Some glory. They almost lost Paris!"

"You needn't tell *me*! My wife was all for running home to Nantes. But I told her I'd face the Austrian army any day over her mother."

"At least that danger's done with," said the other, chuckling.

"But now it's executions. Every few days you see some poor sod being carted off to the Place de la Révolution. How many forgers and spies and royalists can there be, for God's sake?"

"Oh, you'd be surprised, I expect. And it looks as if the guillotine'll soon have more work to do."

"What d'you mean?"

"You don't think the Brissotins will escape the Tribunal, do you? Why, if they got off, then Robespierre and Couthon and Billaud-Varenne would have to admit that the Brissotins might have been right, at least about some things, and that would never do. . . . I wonder," the second man continued, when his companion said nothing, "if it would be worth taking time off to see the trial. Half of them are lawyers, I hear; it should be a good show."

"Show?" the man in the brown coat echoed him, as Aristide gulped down the last of his lukewarm coffee. "You're talking about men's lives here, Vilneau. They don't deserve death just for being foolish, and we all know it. My God! How many are they, two dozen? Imagine the carnage! In the old days it was something if they executed more than a couple of dozen a *year*."

"It's the fault of the war, I tell you. Dangerous times."

"Bah—always back to the war! Is it the fault of the war, I ask you, when they find a headless body on a rubbish heap?"

A headless body? Aristide echoed him silently, raising an eyebrow. How fast a lurid rumor could speed through Paris!

"Headless? Where did you hear that one?"

"My neighbor's son-in-law's cousin is in the police," said the man in the brown coat, "inspector at the Section de l'Arsenal, and he says they found a decapitated corpse in a back street near the old Visitandines' convent, though they're keeping it quiet."

The arsenal? Aristide said to himself.

The arsenal was near where the Bastille had once stood, halfway across Paris from the Palais-Égalité.

What was their decapitated corpse doing in the Section de l'Arsenal?

5

You're sure it's not some morbid fancy brought on by all those executions, and their precious guillotine?" the second man continued.
"That thing would give me nightmares, I don't mind saying. Headless
corpses! Saints alive! You think someone's digging them up?"

"God knows."

"You!" Aristide said, rising, crossing to their table, and pulling out
his police card. "Say that again."

"I beg your pardon?" the man in the brown coat said, indignant.

"I am an agent of the police, and I'd like to know what it was you
just said about a decapitated corpse."

The man seemed to shrink a little into his chair. "I was only repeating a rumor I'd heard. Something my neighbor said."

"Go on. A relative of his is in the police?"

"Yes—"

"In the Section de l'Arsenal? You're quite sure?"

"Of course, citizen."

"And your neighbor repeated a rumor to you about the police of
the Arsenal section finding a headless corpse—finding it in their own
section?"

The man nodded. Aristide could see the sweat beginning to bead on his forehead.

"What's your name, citizen?"

"Ogereau, Citizen Inspector—"

"I'm not an inspector," Aristide said, cutting him off, his thoughts racing.

A *second* headless body?

"I want you to come with me to the commissaire of this section, right away."

"But—what have I done?"

Aristide sighed. "You've done nothing, Citizen Ogereau, except repeat a rumor. I assure you, you'll be back here within the hour. But," he added, "if you're not cooperative, then Commissaire Brasseur will have to assume you're hiding something."

The bluff worked, as he knew it would. Ogereau trotted along beside Aristide, eager to stay on the right side of the police. Aristide led him to the commissariat, pushed past the crush in the antechamber of milling informers and locals waiting to make statements or file complaints, and took him straight to Brasseur's office.

Brasseur was closeted with a voluble middle-aged lady, who was clutching the arm of a miserable-looking girl. Aristide recognized the woman; she had brought in a complaint against her daughter's sweetheart, who had taken advantage of her and now refused to make an honest woman of her.

"Citizeness Panequier will have to wait," he said as he stepped inside. "Commissaire, you need to hear this."

Brasseur gratefully dismissed Madame Panequier and her daughter and turned to Aristide. "Well? Who's this?"

"M-my name is Ogereau, Citizen Commissaire—"

"Go on," Aristide prompted him. "Tell the commissaire what your neighbor said."

Ogereau tugged out a handkerchief and mopped at his face before continuing. "My neighbor, citizen, his son-in-law's cousin is in the police and he told us that he—his son-in-law's cousin, I mean—he'd said they'd found a headless body in an alleyway somewhere."

"What the citizen hasn't mentioned," Aristide said, when Brasseur merely looked irritated, "is that the cousin in question is an inspector at the Section de l'Arsenal."

"*Where?*"

"The Section de l'Arsenal," Ogereau said, paling.

Brasseur exchanged a glance with Aristide, then took up a quill. "What's the name of this inspector at the Section de l'Arsenal?"

"I . . . I don't recall."

"What's your neighbor's name, then, and his address?"

"Citizen Vaillant, the grocer, on Rue des Vieux Augustins, Halle-au-Blé section."

"There, now," said Brasseur, scrawling down the address, "that wasn't so terrifying, was it?"

"Do you think it can be true?" Aristide said, after Ogereau had hurriedly left them. "*Another* headless corpse?"

"And halfway across Paris . . . it bears investigating." Brasseur scratched his head. "Well, I've got three men out asking about a woman in a green gown and a stranger in a dark coat and a wide-brimmed hat. If I spare any more inspectors, the pickpockets'll get too bold—and I think I'd like to keep this quiet, if there's anything to it. I suppose we'll have to find this talkative inspector ourselves. Coming?"

Rue des Vieux Augustins was only a few minutes' walk away, east of the gardens, and they found Vaillant's shop without difficulty. It proved to be a specialty grocery, selling imported foodstuffs and spices from the East and West Indies. Vaillant, getting over his alarm at seeing a strange police commissaire walk into his shop, was eager to be of help. His son-in-law's cousin was Citizen Tiffrey, Inspector Tiffrey of the Arsenal section. Had young Tiffrey been wagging his tongue a bit too much?

"Why do you say that?" Brasseur inquired, with a hungry glance at the tempting glazed sweets displayed on the counter, and a deep, appreciative sniff. Despite the half-empty shelves, owing to the naval blockade, the shop was redolent with a heady aroma of pepper, coriander, and cinnamon.

"Why, he does like to spin a good tale, and the more outlandish, the better. But there's no harm in him, indeed there isn't, though as a young, thoughtless fellow, perhaps he talks a bit more than he ought to. Some candied almonds, Citizen Commissaire?"

They left the shop, with a handful of sugared almonds each, and proceeded to the police commissariat of the Arsenal section, bordering the river and south of the former location of the Bastille. Inspector Tiffrey was gone for the day, the inspector on duty at the reception desk told Aristide, but could probably be found at the wine shop around the corner. They went on to the wine shop, where a glance along the long, crowded tables near the fire quickly revealed a plump young man wearing a telltale black suit. A trio of jovial friends surrounded him.

"Citizen Tiffrey," Brasseur said, thrusting his police card under the inspector's nose, "I'd like a word with you." He guided the young man to a solitary table on the colder side of the smoky common room. "Now, what's this about a headless corpse?"

Tiffrey's mouth sagged open. He glanced from Brasseur to Aristide and back again before straightening in his chair and swallowing.

"What about it?"

"You thought you would entertain your friends and relatives by telling them horror stories?" Aristide said.

"I—all right, maybe I got a little tipsy and talked too much. But where's the harm? Everyone in the neighborhood's heard about it by now."

Brasseur lowered his voice to a soft rumble. "Tell us about this corpse. When and where was it found, and who was the victim?"

"Janneteaux found it. A week ago. Well, some vagrant scavenging in the alleys found it, and came yelling out and Janneteaux was first there."

"Well? Where was it?"

"On a rubbish heap beside the wall of the Visitandines' convent, a bit south of the square." He shivered, despite the stuffy heat of the wine shop. "It was horrible. I'd never seen a dead man before, except laid out proper in a coffin, of course, and—"

"Man? The victim was a man?"

"Yes, citizen."

"Who was he?" Aristide said, with a glance at Brasseur.

"Nobody knew. The—there wasn't a head. But he wasn't from this section. Nobody the right age has gone missing lately, and he looked like a beggar—ragged and filthy. A few people came to take a look before it went to the morgue, but you . . . you can't tell much from just a body, without a head. Nobody identified it, or the clothes, and I don't know any more about it."

"But your commissaire would, wouldn't he?"

Bouille and Daude were just locking the grille to the cellars as Aristide arrived at the Basse-Geôle de la Seine for the second time that day. "Aren't you rather late, Ravel?" Daude grumbled. He glanced through the gloom at the nearby clock, whose hands pointed to ten minutes to nine.

"Sorry." Aristide made sure the door behind him was shut and strode forward, keeping his voice down. "But this can't wait. What the devil is going on?"

"Going on?" Bouille inquired, surreptitiously reaching for his pocket flask.

"Why the devil didn't you two ghouls breathe a single word to me about another decapitated body?"

They exchanged glances, but said nothing.

"Citizens," Aristide continued, "it's not the sort of thing one neglects to mention! Did they, or did they not, bring you the headless corpse of a man from the Arsenal section? And yet, when we send over a murdered, decapitated woman from the Section de la Montagne, do you pipe up with 'Dear me, how peculiar—this is the second headless murder victim we've had in a week!' No, you don't. And I'd like to know why."

Daude retreated to his desk, slumped in the chair, and balanced his chin on clenched fists. "Citizen . . ." he said at last, and paused.

"Well?"

"We've had strict orders not to talk about it. I wouldn't even be telling you that much, if I didn't know you could be trusted."

"Orders!" Aristide echoed him. "From whom?"

"High up. He said he came from the Committee of General Security."

Aristide digested that. The Security Committee oversaw secret, delicate matters related to ferreting out traitors and foreign spies, and, it was said, sent far more people to the Revolutionary Tribunal and the guillotine than did the Committee of Public Safety. When the Committee of General Security issued an order, one obeyed it.

"All this because of two mysterious murders? What's going on, Bouille?"

"Not two," said Daude, after another stretch of uncomfortable silence.

"Not two? What do you mean?"

"Yours isn't the second," Bouille said. "It's the fifth."

6

The fifth!" Aristide exclaimed.

"Fifth in a fortnight."

Aristide stared at him. "*Five* victims found murdered and decapitated in the streets?"

"Yes. All in different sections. That's how they've managed to keep it quiet, I expect."

"Not so quiet. You can't keep a secret for long in Paris, Bouille; don't you know that by now?" Aristide turned about on his heel, looking from one to the other of the concierges. A faint whiff of decay rose from the cellars beyond the iron grille. "The Committee of General Security," he repeated, trying not to breathe too deeply, "has ordered you to keep quiet about this?"

"We had a letter from the Committee after the third one, the one from the Arsenal section," said Daude. "It told us, in no uncertain terms, to tear up our reports, keep our mouths shut, and tell anyone who'd seen the bodies to do the same."

"They want to hush it all up." Aristide shook a loose strand of hair away from his face and continued, thinking it out as he spoke. "Commissaire Roche at the Section de l'Arsenal would barely speak to us.

He probably received the same letter. And if the commissaires of the other sections where bodies were found . . ."

"The first was just over in Section Révolutionnaire, next to the gendarmes' stables in back of the Palais de Justice," said Bouille, when Aristide paused. "The Maison de Justice, I should have said. The second—"

"If the commissaire of the Section de l'Arsenal has also received one," Aristide continued, interrupting him, "telling him to shut up, and so have all the others, then they're not going to be comparing notes, are they? Any lurid rumors that people may hear on the street can be dismissed as embroidered accounts, with the facts distorted, of one, particularly gruesome, individual crime. Bouille, if you were an ordinary citizen living in the Arsenal section and knew about the headless corpse found a couple of streets away from your house, and then later you heard a juicy rumor about a headless corpse being discovered in the Section Révolutionnaire or the Section de la Montagne, wouldn't you assume it was just a garbled account of the murder in your own section and think nothing more of it?"

"I suppose so," Bouille said gloomily.

"Five bodies." Aristide pulled out his notebook. "Section Révolutionnnaire was the first. The woman found in Brasseur's section was the fifth? And the one in the Arsenal section was . . ."

"The third."

"What about the others? Where were they found? What became of them? And you must have compiled reports on all of them."

"The first corpse," said Daude, "had a distinctive birthmark on his breast. His wife, or his common-law wife, rather," he added primly, "identified him."

"The third corpse was never identified," Bouille said, "and it went to the mass graves within the week, like all our unclaimed cadavers. The other bodies were claimed by their families."

"Fine," said Aristide. "I need to see your reports on the first four."

"Are you sure you want to butt in, Ravel?" said Bouille. He rubbed at his nose, his lined face crumpling into a clownish mask that, at some other occasion, would have been comical. "Someone's trying hard to keep this quiet. I should have said, the third corpse went to the mass graves—as far as we know. The day after we received that letter from the Committee, you see, a couple of strangers came by, waving official orders, and took away the body for burial. But it's not routine to bury them quite so quickly; someone wanted that corpse out of sight. The men were dressed like crows," Bouille continued, using the popular slang term for an undertaker, "but one of them, whom I'm certain I'd never seen before—and I know most of the crows of Paris at least by sight—enjoined me to hold my tongue if I knew what was good for me."

"And they told you to tear up your reports?"

"Yes."

Aristide eyed him. Both Bouille and Daude, he knew, were scrupulous, fussy record-keepers; destroying a report and disarranging their records would have caused them acute pain. "Did you?"

"Indeed not," said Daude, with a sigh. "But we said we would, and that appeared to satisfy them." He smiled, without humor. "I like to keep my records in order."

"Obviously they don't know you as well as I do. Might I see the reports?"

"Certainly." Daude disappeared into the cellars and returned a moment later with the papers. "I hope I can trust you to be discreet? I didn't like the look of that fellow; the genuine crows are more agreeable than he was."

"You ought to know me by now, Daude." Aristide leaned against the edge of the desk and scanned the reports.

First victim: Male, identified by his mistress, Citizeness Lépinay, as Louis-Michel-Rémy Jumeau, age sixty-seven, man of property and former chief court clerk to the Grand' Chambre of the former Paris Parlement; born in Paris, residing in Paris at No. 38, Rue du Faubourg Honoré, Section de la République. Victim's head was severed from the trunk; head unaccounted for. Discovered early morning of 29 September, near the Maison de Justice, outer clothing and personal effects missing (see full inventory below). Victim apparently met his death by acute hemorrhage and suffocation, namely, severing of the great vessels of the neck and of the windpipe in the course of decapitation by several cuts or blows.

Second victim: Female, identified by husband as Jeanne-Louise Houdey, age forty-six, ink peddler; born in Paris, residing on Rue du Petit Lion, Section de Bonconseil. Well known to residents of the Section des Piques where she sold ink on the corner of Rue Honoré near the Place des Piques. Decapitated corpse discovered 2 October at dawn near the foot of the statue of Liberty at the Place de la Révolution. Victim apparently met her death in the same manner as the first, but severed head present (found lying away from the trunk, near the scaffold erected in permanence in the square). Clothing in poor condition (see full inventory below).

Third victim: Male, approximately fifty to sixty-five years of age, unidentified. Decapitated corpse, head unaccounted for, discovered 5 October in an alley off Rue de la Cerisaie (Section de l'Arsenal). Appearance undernourished, and clothing and general appearance that of a pauper. Identifying marks: warts on left thumb and middle finger, dark birthmark near left elbow, large mole on right buttock. Clothing, of worse than average quality and in poor condition, provided no clues to the murderer's identity or motives. Conclusion: The victim is presumed to have been an unknown vagrant. Victim apparently met his death in the same manner as the two previous.

Fourth victim: Male, identified by his servant, Citizen Gros, as Marc-Antoine Noyelle, age seventy-three, ex-army officer; born in Tours, residing in Paris at No. 96, Rue de Vaugirard, Section de Mucius-Scevola. Victim's head severed from the trunk; head unaccounted for. Discovered at dawn on 7 October, before the doors of the cathedral of Nôtre-Dame, outer clothes and personal effects missing, presumably stolen (see inventory below). Victim apparently met his death in the same manner as the three previous.

"Fifth victim," Aristide scribbled down, beneath the notes he had taken, "unidentified woman in thirties or forties, found in alley in Montagne section, near Palais-Égalité, morning of Tuesday, 8 October. Presumed to be a bourgeoise reduced to selling herself to survive. Decapitated in same manner, no head found, no clues to murderer in her clothing or effects."

He gazed gloomily at his notes. Nothing, save the manner of their deaths, seemed to connect the five victims.

On the other hand, that might be the beginning of a pattern after all. Why had only two of the five, seemingly random, victims been part of the vast majority of Paris's teeming population, the working poor: the hundreds of thousands of artisans, domestic servants, day laborers, street peddlers, and ragged paupers?

So what sort of lunatic went about beheading respectable citizens and leaving their bodies strewn about like so many dead rats?

One answer flashed into his thoughts immediately. People spoke, now and then, of "Revolution fever"; it was the collective, panic-driven madness that had impelled otherwise ordinary, peaceable men and women into some ferocious acts of bloodlust and cruelty during the first summer of the Revolution and, later and even more dreadfully, during the September Massacres of 1792. Had a new sort of Revolution fever driven some unbalanced ultrapatriot into exacting the Republic's revenge on people who had, at least in his own warped mind, escaped revolutionary justice?

Oh, Lord . . .

7

The message arrived well after dusk, in the wet, windswept autumn darkness when Aristide's spirits were at their lowest ebb. He had not expected callers and automatically glanced toward his window as he heard the tapping; a neighbor's pet cat, nimble on rooftops and ledges, often pawed at the glass and wound itself, purring, around his ankles while he foraged for scraps from the remains of his latest meal.

But there was no small white and brown figure at the window, and no plaintive mew. The tapping sounded a second time, louder. At last he muttered "Hell" under his breath and swung long legs to the floor from the bed where he had been lying, head pillowed on folded arms, staring at the grimy ceiling of the alcove.

"Citizen Ravel," the porter said, scowling at having had to climb three flights of stairs, and handed him a note. The note, Aristide realized, had to be urgent, or the porter would have waited to deliver it until the next time Aristide passed the front door. He retreated into his room, bolted the door, and cracked the wax seal.

Citizen Ravel: You are kindly requested to present yourself at my domicile on the Cour du Commerce, at the corner of Rue des Cordeliers, at ten o'clock this evening, on a matter of the greatest importance and deepest secrecy. I know from our past transactions that I can depend upon your discretion in this and all subsequent affairs.

It was signed with a scrawl Aristide knew well, though he had not seen it for months: *Danton.*

He stared at the note. What on earth could Danton, former Minister of Justice, elemental guiding force within the uncertain republican government, the man who had toppled the monarchy, want with him now?

Though he had worked for Danton, on and off, for several months in 1792, Aristide had rarely visited his home, and had not called there since Danton's first wife had died in childbirth eight months before. Luckily, the house was only ten minutes' walk through the thinning rain from his own lodging on the outskirts of the neighboring Latin Quarter.

A curtsying, middle-aged woman servant admitted him to the apartment and led him through three stylishly but comfortably appointed rooms, in one of which a young girl—Danton's sixteen-year-old second wife, he supposed—was lounging by the fire and plucking at a Spanish guitar as a small audience of guests applauded. He recognized a few faces, among them the radical journalists Desmoulins, Fréron, Robert, and their wives, as well as Delacroix and Hérault-Séchelles, both Montagnard deputies to the National Convention.

The maid gestured Aristide to a door beyond the salons and opened it a crack to announce him. Aristide entered, at a roar from within, and found himself in a snug, book-lined study dominated by the robust, untidy figure sprawled at the desk in its center.

"You look a mess," Danton said, raising his eyes from the papers in his hand and measuring Aristide with a sharp glance. "You haven't turned to drink, have you?"

"No, citizen," said Aristide, thinking that his host should speak for his own appearance; Danton's clothes, though of excellent quality, were rumpled and creased, as if their wearer had more important matters than tidiness on his mind.

"Then have a glass. You look like you could use one. You're still dressing for a funeral, I see."

Aristide said nothing; Danton knew perfectly well that he wore only black. He raised a hand as Danton reached for the decanter of brandy that stood on a silver tray nearby. "Thank you, no."

"You're not a teetotaler like Robespierre, are you, Ravel—immensely complacent with your own abstemious virtue?"

Aristide cared little, one way or the other, about the morals of drinking alcohol, but he did not care to drink it often himself. Coffee, he believed, was far superior as a stimulant to one's mental processes. "If you insist, I would prefer wine, with water."

"As you like. Have a seat."

He studied his host as he rose and rummaged in a cabinet. Danton, he knew, was only thirty-three or -four, a year younger than Aristide was himself, but overwork, the hectic pace of revolutionary politics, and, Aristide suspected, frequent overindulgence in good food and good drink had combined to age him until he seemed closer to forty-five. His broad, scarred face, never handsome at the best of times, now seemed lined and faintly blotchy, while the big, muscular body, too, was growing fleshy and his hair looked unkempt beneath a flyaway peruke.

"Here," Danton said, pushing an oversized glass of watered red wine toward him. "A drink first. You think I don't know why you're looking like death?" he added, as he poured out a splash of brandy for himself.

"Pardon me?"

"Your friend—Deputy Alexandre—I know he was among the Brissotins who were just transferred to the Conciergerie. You know some of the deputies from La Gironde, I think, coming from Bordeaux as you do?"

Aristide stiffened. Was that why he had been summoned?

"Yes."

Danton waved a dismissive hand. "That's not my concern. I know where your loyalties lie, and I don't give a damn about your private connections, so long as you go on providing me with the same level of service you always have."

"Thank you." He relaxed a little. Evidently his patriotism was not in question after all.

"I'm sorry, Ravel," Danton said abruptly. He poked at the fire and returned to his chair.

"Citizen?"

"I did what I could—even Robespierre tried, you know—to keep the Brissotins out of the Tribunal, but a man can do only so much before he runs headlong against popular opinion and begins to risk his own head. You understand that, don't you—or you ought to."

"Quite well."

"You're close to Alexandre?"

Aristide nodded. "Mathieu Alexandre is the best friend I ever had. More like a brother than a schoolmate."

"Then I am truly sorry. After Gorsas's ten-minute trial the other day—you heard about that?—it looks as though the Tribunal isn't disposed to be lenient to anyone labeled a Brissotin."

"But Gorsas was already declared outlawed, was he not?"

"Yes. Yes, that's true."

"So the rest, not being outside the law, are entitled to a perfectly fair trial before the Tribunal."

"They are, if you believe that."

"I'll continue to cherish the hope that they'll be acquitted, then."

Danton grunted, bent to a paper on his desk, and scrawled a few lines, while Aristide stared hard at the nearest shelf of books, a row of eminent English authors and playwrights bound in fine gold-stamped leather. Word had it that Danton, despite his rough, blustering, rather uncouth public image, could read at least three languages.

He came out of his abstraction to find that the other man was watching him.

"Read English?"

"After a fashion."

"Read as much as you can in a foreign language, and you'll learn it well enough. I taught myself English and Italian that way. Take one, keep it as long as you like. Go ahead. I've already read them all." Danton turned back to the papers on his desk and reached for his sand shaker. Aristide glanced over the bookshelf and, not wishing to seem unappreciative, picked out a worn octavo volume of English plays from the previous century.

"Citizen Danton," he said, after a moment, "I doubt you summoned me here merely to tell me how remorseful you were about the Brissotin deputies being committed for trial." He slipped the book into a coat pocket and took another sip of wine.

"I like a man who can get down to business without dancing around a subject," Danton said. "First of all: here." He pushed the sheet of paper across the desk. "I don't know if you'll care to use it or not, but this should get you through some doors if you wish it to."

Aristide glanced over the paper. *The bearer of this letter*, it read, in bold, slanting handwriting that he did not recognize, *the citizen A.-C.-M. Ravel, shall be admitted, at his request and at any time, to any and all prisons of the Republic, and shall be granted private access to any and all prisoners (save the widow Capet and the Capets, also known as the ex-royal family, held in the Temple) for the purpose of questioning them. A.-Q. Fouquier, Public Prosecutor, the 11th October 1793.*

Beneath it, in a different and more familiar hand, was written: *Citizen Ravel is an excellent patriot, known to me personally. He is to be tendered all courtesy. Danton, this 11th October 1793, 4th Year of Liberty.*

"In case you should ever need to interrogate someone who's already been locked up," Danton said blandly, as Aristide looked up, startled, and began to stammer a few awkward words of thanks. Danton drank down his glass of brandy and leaned back in his chair, his bulk making it creak alarmingly. "All right, then, Ravel; here's what I want from you in return. Tell me what's making the rounds of the cafés and the chop-houses."

"The general opinion, do you mean?" Aristide said. "Or rumors?"

Danton began to pick his teeth, in what Aristide thought was rather too offhand a manner. "Whatever comes your way. What are they saying these days?"

He thought for a moment, wondering why Danton was asking him about tittle-tattle that could be learned from any common *mouche*, an informer for hire to anyone with a little silver. Spies, at all levels of society, had been unsavory fixtures of the old, absolutist regime, and now were used just as frequently by the equally mistrustful republican government.

"They're cautiously optimistic about hearing good news from the front, for a change," he said, "although they know the enemy is still occupying French soil; they laugh at Chaumette's attempts to banish prostitution; they complain about food prices, of course, even with the maximum on the cost of bread, and they grumble about the scarcity of bread and mutter threats against hoarders, grain profiteers, and dishonest bakers; the rising price of soap is putting laundresses out of business; I myself have stopped sugaring my coffee because I can no longer afford the sugar."

"Go on."

"Word is circulating that they're going to put the queen on trial soon—the widow Capet, if you prefer—and some people are delighted that the Austrian is going to get what's coming to her, while others try to hide their distress."

"Nothing new there," said Danton, expressionless. He paused, working something out of a molar, and continued. "What else? Anything out of the ordinary?"

"Only a rumor so bizarre that people seem to dismiss it as a morbid fantasy, conjured up by folk who have attended too many executions. So would I, if I didn't know it to be true."

"Yes?"

"The other day I overheard a couple of men discussing a rumor that dead bodies are turning up here and there around Paris . . . left in corners and alleys . . . not the usual paupers and vagrants dead of starvation or disease or cold, but dead headless bodies—"

"Holy—!" Danton growled, pounding a massive fist onto the desk and setting the inkwell and brandy glass to rattling as Aristide started. Danton, in his experience, presented a genial, vigorous front to the world, behind which lurked a shrewd, calculating, practical politician.

Anything that could cause him to purple and lose control of himself so quickly must be disturbing and dangerous indeed.

"So it's already in the wind," Danton added, as if to himself.

"Yes."

He gave Aristide a hard stare for an instant. "That's right, one of them was found in your friend Brasseur's section, wasn't it?"

"Yes, a few days ago. And I've learned from the concierges of the Basse-Geôle de la Seine that the woman found in the Section de la Montagne was actually the fifth victim found decapitated. Also that someone in the government doesn't want it known, and is doing his best to hush it up."

Danton sighed. "Well, you've confirmed my fears, Ravel, nothing more," he said, his wrath subsiding, and poured himself another splash of brandy.

"About what? The fact that there seems to be a madman on the loose?"

"More than that."

"More?" Aristide echoed him, wondering what might be worse than a murderous madman at large in Paris.

Danton tossed back the brandy and was silent for a moment, drumming his fingers on the desk. "All you need to know is that there's been a certain amount of secret correspondence with England."

Aristide opened his mouth to speak, but thought better of it. England, since her declaration of war shortly after Louis XVI's execution nine months previously, was then (and traditionally) the enemy.

"That doesn't go beyond this room," Danton continued, "or your head won't be worth a sou. You can keep your own counsel, can't you?"

Aristide nodded, curious, and said nothing.

"The heart of the matter is that I, and others, with the tacit approval of some of the Committee of Public Safety, have been attempting to cobble together some manner of peace treaty with Pitt. The last thing we need is war with England, as well as with Prussia and the Empire, and some of the liberals in Parliament still sympathize with the Revolution. But these fanatical fools who've been howling for Antoinette's head are going to muck everything up—they can't see beyond their own hatred, and their Jacobin dogma, that she's much more useful to us alive, to bargain with, than dead. It's a damn stupid thing to do, but they're going to do it. Her preliminary interrogation'll start within the next day or two, if it hasn't already."

"If Antoinette is guillotined, though, I assume you're going to try to persuade the English that the public execution of an Austrian princess and queen of France is actually quite unimportant in the scheme of things?"

"I'll do my damnedest. But you understand, I think, that we don't need any other vile rumors floating about. First Antoinette—and if you think they won't find her guilty, you're a fool—and now this fresh barbarity, which will ruin any credibility we might have with Pitt, and which could turn even liberals like Fox against us." Danton took up a newspaper, which Aristide could see was in English, and read a paragraph aloud.

" 'It has come to our attention, from an observer across the Channel, that new outrages are to be found every day in Paris. Not content with massacring their anointed king and keeping prisoner their wretched queen, the French people, if capricious Dame Rumor is to be believed, now daily harden themselves to such frightful horrors as decollated corpses, which are often to be found not only on the public scaffold but also at every street corner of the capital.' " He slapped down the paper. "You see? Every overstated, inflammatory scrap of news that the émigrés smuggle over is one more bit of evidence that the French are now sacrilegious savages."

"The English needn't be so self-righteous," Aristide said. "It's only a century and a half since they cut off a king's head themselves. The reality of politics and diplomacy might soften any of these blows, might it not?"

"Oh, it might. But what the average Englishman thinks is, 'How can a race of people be anything but barbarian, and unworthy of being parleyed with like a civilized nation, if it butchers its king and queen and keeps on chopping the heads off people for trivial offenses?' And now this might be the last straw," Danton continued. "The royalists who took off in 'eighty-nine and 'ninety-two would like nothing better than to tell the rest of Europe that illiterate louts and bloodthirsty fanatics are governing France. What are the English, even the most sympathetic of them, going to think when they continue to hear these rumors of beheaded corpses lying like dead dogs on the streets of Paris?" He lowered his voice to a whisper, which for the stentorian Danton was still a rumble. "And you and I know they're *not* rumors, Ravel. That's why you're here."

"You fear," Aristide said, "that the truth will come out, and that the actions of this murderer, lunatic, whoever he may be, will horrify the English so much that any hope of peace between England and France—which is already fragile, at best—will be destroyed."

"I always knew you were a damned astute fellow, Ravel."

"And where do I come into this?" he inquired, fearing he already knew the answer. Danton's scarred lips twisted into a sardonic smile.

"Where do you think?"

"You want me to investigate these murders, and find and stop the killer."

"Naturally. You can begin with the latest."

"Brasseur and I are already—" Aristide began.

"The *latest*," Danton repeated, and reached into a drawer. "The sixth."

"Sixth? Already?"

"Found this afternoon, with the head nearby, in the burial trench at the Madeleine cemetery. The executioners knew right away that it wasn't one of theirs."

Frowning, Aristide looked over the report Danton handed him. The corpse had already been identified as one Pierre-Marie Echelard, water seller. It had, as usual, been transported to the Basse-Geôle.

The gilt clock on the mantel chimed and he glanced over at it. Half past ten. Far too late to begin questioning witnesses.

"All right," he said, "I'll need money . . . and a room or two, somewhere central, that I can use as a base. My own lodgings certainly won't do."

"Fine."

"And I want any reports of future corpses of this nature—any murder that's out of the ordinary, in fact—to go straight to me, in care of Commissaire Brasseur of the Montagne section, until further notice. The individual commissaires don't need to hear about what's going on in other sections and get ideas, but I need to know everything, *everything,* as soon as possible after it happens."

"You'll have it. All of it. Find rooms to suit yourself, whatever you need, and it'll be paid for."

What have I gotten myself into?

Aristide's hand drifted to his lips, but he willed it away; this was no time to betray weakness or nerves by biting his nails.

"I'll start tomorrow."

8

Aristide walked across the Seine to the Right Bank soon after first light, grateful once again that Rue de la Huchette, while somewhat seedy and damp—it was only a few paces to the quay and the stony riverbank below—was wonderfully convenient to the Law Courts, the Châtelet, their attached prisons, and the morgue. Bouille, yawning at desk duty in the antechamber, waved him past the gate to the rank, chilly cellar, where Daude glanced up from examining a tattered shirt, waistcoat, carmagnole jacket, and pair of striped canvas trousers spread out in front of him.

"I thought I'd be seeing you soon." He smiled, without humor. "I expect you're here about the corpse they found at the cemetery of the Madeleine? The crows," he added, lowering his voice, "already came for your woman's body yesterday evening. Gone without a trace."

"Are those the clothes?" Aristide inquired, with a glance at the items Daude had been looking over.

"Yes, I'm just writing up the inventory. Want to see him? At least, this time, you have the head." Daude moved to one of the stone tables that filled the room and lifted away the sheet from the corpse.

Despite the smell in the cellar, to which he had grown somewhat accustomed over the past years, Aristide found that the sight before him was not as horrid as had been his first glimpse of the murdered woman in the alley. Perhaps, he thought, it had been the blood. Here, no great pool of blood was splashed about, polluting the stones; the thing before him was merely the naked body of a muscular man of early middle age, its head detached but propped up against it with wooden blocks. A few flies buzzed sluggishly around the stump of the neck.

"What's this white powder?" The pallid, bluish skin looked absurdly as if it had been floured, like a lump of dough at the baker's.

"Oh, that's quicklime; they scatter a layer on the corpses, you know, to speed decomposition, before they add a few inches of earth. I understand they found the cadaver in the grave pit, lying on top of the shrouded bodies."

Aristide stood over the corpse and gazed at it for a long moment while Daude fetched his report. Despite the man's burly arms, he seemed in only passable health; spider veins crisscrossed his long nose and his skin was coarse. Aristide pulled up an eyelid just far enough to see that the man's eye was bloodshot and rheumy.

"I gather the commissaire of the Section de la République," Daude said, "when he was called to the scene, recognized him right away."

"Hmm?"

"An old acquaintance who'd spent plenty of time in the local lockup for drunkenness and disturbing the peace," Daude continued as he handed over the report to Aristide. "Pierre-Marie Echelard, native of the Auvergne and resident at Rue de l'Égout: water seller, habitual petty criminal, and general nuisance. I doubt anyone will miss him, especially Commissaire Conchon."

"His throat wasn't cut," said Aristide, looking from the report to the corpse. "That is, not before he was decapitated."

"No, this one was stabbed. A single lethal wound in the chest, up under the ribs, made, I'd guess, by someone who knew what he was doing."

Aristide lifted one of the corpse's hands. The palm was callused and the fingernails broken and dirty, but the fresh scabs on the knuckles drew his attention. "What about this fresh cut here on the wrist, and the torn knuckles? Do you think he was trying to protect his head or face from his attacker?"

"Most likely."

He gazed again at the corpse and at last shrugged. It was conceivable that a personal enemy or a greedy partner in crime, rather than the elusive headsman, had murdered Echelard; but that was a matter for the commissaire of the République section, who knew his local criminals and local feuds. If an enemy had stabbed Echelard for private reasons, and then hacked off his head and dumped him in the open to make the murder resemble the lurid accounts that were undoubtedly swirling about from the Parisian rumor mill, the commissaire would soon hear of it from some underworld spy.

"Clothes and effects?"

"Only what you see here."

Aristide glanced over them. Carmagnole jacket, shabby waistcoat, trousers, fetid body linen that probably had not been washed in a month, a greasy and ancient woolen stocking cap with a limp tricolored cockade pinned to it, and a pair of wooden clogs encrusted with the usual filth of the Paris streets. The collection of effects nearby consisted of a battered metal pocket flask, empty but reeking of cheap brandy; a pipe and dirty tobacco pouch; an all-purpose knife with notched blade and well-worn handle; a small tinderbox; and a few deniers in copper together with a crumpled, soiled five-livre assignat, worth perhaps a few sous in trade. There was nothing to give him a clue about the man's killer. He shook his head and turned away.

"The sum of a life. Well, since we already know who he is, I think they can hurry him away as soon as they wish." He shook hands with Daude and departed.

Danton had told him that the staff of the Revolutionary Tribunal and the executioner's men were under orders to cooperate with any investigation into the matter. Aristide went next to the Law Courts, bracing himself for an interview with Fouquier, the public prosecutor. A diffident secretary met him at the bottom of the spiral staircase that led up to the prosecutor's office between the two medieval towers of the Conciergerie.

"He's not in a good mood today, citizen," the secretary muttered to him, with a glance up the stairs behind him. "Can't this wait?"

"I fear not."

"Well, if he skins you alive, don't say I didn't warn you." He led Aristide upstairs to an ill-lit, whitewashed chamber in which two clerks sat writing at their desks, studiously ignoring the angry voice shouting in the next room, whose door stood ajar.

"—not to free enemies of the Republic but to do away with them!"

The reply came in a quieter voice, which Aristide could not make out. The first voice, which he guessed to be that of Fouquier himself, continued, though less loudly. The secretary, seeing Aristide's quizzical expression, gave him an apologetic shrug.

"Citizen Fouquier's feeling snappish these days. That's one of the jurymen from the Tribunal with him. It seems that Citizen Sauvade, yesterday, once again persuaded the other jurors to find a certain suspect innocent of the charges."

"What's reprehensible about that?"

"The prisoner was once a police commissaire, back before 'eighty-nine. When you're a former servant of the old regime, it's pretty much assumed that you're an enemy of the Republic, unless you've taken pains to prove yourself otherwise."

"And Fouquier was priding himself on bagging a royal official?"

"Just so. And then Sauvade convinced the others that the fellow wasn't guilty of counterrevolution after all! I ask you!"

"Well," said Aristide, "was he guilty or not?"

"How should I know? But the citizen prosecutor gets testy when he doesn't get his way. And he's starting to lose sleep over the trial coming up."

"Antoinette?"

The secretary nodded. "I'd tread lightly, if I were you."

"Thanks for the advice." He pulled out his notebook. "Perhaps you can tell me: The cemetery where this corpse was found, it's the one closest to the Place de la Révolution, isn't it? The parish cemetery of La Madeleine, the same one where the k—where Louis Capet is buried?"

"Yes, that's the one."

"Isn't it guarded? To ensure that no one turns it into a place of pilgrimage or—or tries to collect relics?"

"To be sure. A twenty-four-hour guard at the gate, and at night the local patrol makes a quick tour through, once every hour or so. Nobody's getting in to dig Louis up, I assure you. Anyway, the grave's unmarked and the coffin's buried ten feet deep. The gravediggers," the secretary added, with a wry glance at an account book, "charged extra for that."

"But it's just possible that someone could have climbed the wall to dump a corpse without being seen."

"Yes, I suppose you could get in; the difficulty would be in avoiding the patrol if your business kept you in there for any length of time. You could climb in easily enough if you used the northern or western walls, where there's nothing but farmers' fields, and the barracks about a quarter mile away."

The door to the public prosecutor's private office swung open and a smartly dressed man strode out, nearly colliding with Aristide. He checked himself, murmured a polite "Excuse me," and continued to the outer door.

"We'll be seeing you for the widow Capet's trial, Citizen Sauvade?" one of the clerks inquired as the juror passed him.

He paused for an instant as he reached for the door handle. "Despite his bullying, Citizen Fouquier understands that I'll always follow my conscience. Isn't justice always our goal here?"

Aristide learned little more from the secretaries, or from a disagreeable five minutes with Fouquier himself, and left the prosecutor's office with a sense of relief. Even questioning the executioners, he decided, no matter how distasteful the thought of conversing with a *bourreau*, would be preferable to an interview with the public prosecutor.

9

Aristide emerged from the tower staircase into a small courtyard and paused a moment in the fine rain, pondering his next move. A few steps would bring him to the doors to the Conciergerie, the medieval prison that lay below, and served as an antechamber to, the Palais de Justice—though, naturally, they were calling it the Maison de Justice these days, he reminded himself, now that palaces were a thing of the unlamented, aristocratic past.

And some, he knew, were now calling the Conciergerie the antechamber to the guillotine. At least half of those tried at the Revolutionary Tribunal returned to the prison only to leave it within twenty-four hours, in the executioner's cart.

At last he sighed, squared his shoulders, and strode around the corner to the Cour du Mai, the wide, busy courtyard of the Palais de Justice, and down a few steps to a small, sunken yard beyond. "I wish to question a particular prisoner," he told the elderly turnkey who answered the bell at the door. He held up the pass that Danton had given him, hoping the man could read. The turnkey stared at it a moment with filmy eyes before bobbing into a slight bow.

"Of course, citizen. Which prisoner were you wanting?"

"Deputy Alexandre. He's here, isn't he?"

"Yes, came in a few days ago with some others of the deputies. Very agreeable gentlemen, very well mannered. You'll want to question him in private? Come this way, if you please."

He followed the turnkey into a broad hallway littered with straw, past some ragged prisoners who huddled together in corners or lounged morosely against the walls. The man led him to a series of small, dark offices and gestured him into the nearest. "The clerks use these rooms, but Citizen Orrieux won't be in today; you can use his office."

He hurried out, returned with a lit candelabrum, which he placed on the absent clerk's desk, and vanished down the hall. Aristide pulled a stool away from the wall and perched on it, half amused at the turnkey's obsequiousness. No doubt the man had been a jailer for thirty or forty years, all but the last few of them under the monarchy; the king's titled officials, prosecutors, and magistrates would have expected groveling deference from their inferiors when their business took them to the royal prison.

Footsteps sounded in the passage and he turned from idly glancing over the massive, leather-bound registers on the shelf behind the desk. Mathieu stood in the doorway, hands in pockets, regarding him with a tilt of the head and a raised eyebrow.

"Robespierre?"

Aristide stared for an instant before coming to himself and recalling the ironic nickname Mathieu had often used during the past two years.

Faith, Ravel, I swear you're as solemn as Robespierre. Don't you ever enjoy yourself?

"My God, you're not here . . . I mean, you're not a prisoner here, too, are you?"

"No. I have a pass." Aristide held up the letter signed by Danton and the public prosecutor. "I can get in anywhere, at least for the present."

"And why the devil would you choose to visit this rat-hole?" Mathieu inquired, with a broad grin. He crossed the space between them in two long strides and flung his arms around Aristide. "Faith, it's good to see you. What are you up to? Why this special treatment that allows you a pass to interrogate us dangerous criminals?"

"I'm investigating something for Danton," Aristide said, when he had caught his breath and returned his friend's embrace. "But I didn't come here about that. I just . . ." He stepped back and looked Mathieu over. Mathieu looked uncharacteristically tired, he thought, and a little unkempt for someone who normally took care of his appearance. He wore no cravat. His coat and waistcoat seemed rumpled and needed to be brushed down, and the wavy dark hair was unpowdered and gathered carelessly back with a limp ribbon, but his eyes were as lively and bright as ever.

"You look like hell," Mathieu said, echoing Aristide's thought. That, at least, was no different from the Mathieu he knew, who had never minced words among friends.

"No worse than you."

He smiled unexpectedly, the same impish smile Aristide had known from boyhood. "The Conciergerie isn't ideal for keeping up one's appearance. Though the ladies here somehow work miracles."

"Ladies?" Aristide said. Men and women, he knew, were kept separate in the Conciergerie, as in many of the prisons, so that women would have little opportunity to get pregnant and, if condemned to death, demand a temporary reprieve from their judges.

"A grille, at one corner of the women's courtyard, adjoins a corridor we're allowed to use. A lot of kissing goes on through the bars, and, of course, the ladies try to look their best."

"You seem like an old hand here already. I heard you'd been sent here just a few days ago."

"Yes, several of us arrived at much the same time," Mathieu said, referring to the chief Brissotin deputies. "Do you have time to spare? I'm sure Ducos and Boyer would be delighted to see you."

"Ducos and Boyer," Aristide repeated. "I still can't believe that the three of you were expelled from the Convention. I thought you were quite popular."

"And yet," Mathieu said, with an expressive shrug. "They often voted with the Mountain, as I did, but it seems, in the end, that we're all tarred with the same brush. Brissotins, federalists, moderates . . . it all equals 'counterrevolutionary' these days. And I expect it will end the same way for all of us. . . ."

"Don't say that," said Aristide, with an attempt at an encouraging smile. "You can't know that."

"Can't I?"

"The Tribunal has freed plenty of prisoners."

"It's freed plenty of inoffensive nobodies," Mathieu corrected him. "A couple of dozen notorious federalists, whom the Jacobins hate almost as much as they hate Antoinette—have you heard that they're going to try her in a couple of days?—is something else again. Oh, I cling to hope as best I can, but I'd rather not delude myself into believing that it's all been a terrible mistake and we'll soon be released, like Marat, to the cheers of the populace. You and I both know that's not going to happen."

"But—"

"What's this affair you're investigating?" Mathieu said suddenly.

Aristide eyed him for a moment. Mathieu, he realized, did not wish to speak about himself, think of his possible fate; any distraction would be welcome.

"Murder. More than one."

Mathieu balanced himself on a corner of the clerk's desk and gestured Aristide to the stool. "A good juicy problem you can sink your teeth into?"

"That's understating it." He debated with himself a moment, decided that Mathieu and his friends were in no position to spread rumors throughout Paris, and lowered his voice. "Some madman—it couldn't be anyone but a madman—has been murdering people, hacking off their heads, and leaving them about in the streets."

"Hacking off their heads?" Mathieu echoed him. "Rather in the spirit of the times, isn't it?"

"Alexandre, it's not funny." Though, he thought, it was typical of Mathieu to cheer up a friend by delivering endless sarcastic comments about a dire situation, until all you could do was laugh.

"I never said it was."

"He's murdered at least half a dozen people, and we've no reason to believe he'll stop there."

"And you're supposed to hunt through the half million inhabitants of Paris and finger him before he kills again?"

"That's about the essence of it."

"Got a lot of faith in you, haven't they?"

Aristide sighed. "For some reason, of all the people Danton probably has working for him, he trusts me to take care of it. He said that, as an experienced police spy—"

"He used the word 'spy,' did he?" Mathieu said, with a grin. Aristide loathed the average *mouche* as much as anyone did, and preferred to call himself an investigator, or simply an agent of the police; Mathieu was among the few people who could get away with calling him a spy to his face.

"Danton can use any word he wants, and who's going to stop him?"

"Well, go on."

"He said that, as I'm an experienced—agent—and have a reputation for discretion as well as for solving crimes, I was the logical person to be set to untangling the problem. But I'm proceeding here with nothing more than headless corpses, most of them already buried; I scarcely know where to begin. In the end, though, if I don't succeed, Danton will probably have *my* head—and that's not meant as a joke."

"I doubt it would come to that," Mathieu said, unsmiling. "You've proved yourself competent in that sphere more than a few times. Look here, Ravel, will you be able to come back?"

"I don't see why not."

"Can you bring me some books? I've read everything I brought with me."

"Of course. Whatever I can do."

"And why don't you bring me any notes and information you have on your mad headsman and his victims? Perhaps I'll see something you've overlooked."

"If you wish," said Aristide. The detailed descriptions of the decapitated corpses were the last thing he would want to know about, were he in Mathieu's position; but perhaps, with the shadow of death looming so near, perhaps there was something to be said for hardening yourself by reading a dispassionate account, inoculating your mind against the terror of it, like being inoculated against smallpox by taking a small, harmless dose of it into yourself. "There's not much."

"Never mind. I'll read it with interest—hell, I'd read *anything* with interest right now—even Fabre d'Èglantine's poetry," Mathieu added with a wink, referring to the popular author who was a friend of Danton and a bitter enemy of the Brissotins. He slid off the desk and stood up. "Come on. Ducos and Boyer'll want to see you."

He led the way down the corridor, through some fetid passages, and up a narrow, twisting staircase to the second floor and a cell whose heavy, ironbound door stood open. Within, it was far less disagreeable than Aristide had feared; though ill-lit and narrow, otherwise it resembled the average chamber in a shabby roadside inn. The walls were whitewashed and it was furnished comfortably enough with a bed, a writing-desk, a small chest of drawers, a washstand, a table on which a breakfast tray held an assortment of used crockery, and a screen behind which, he assumed, was a closestool or chamber pot. It had to be Boyer-Fonfrède's cell; the son of one of the richest merchant families in Bordeaux, he could easily afford to pay for comfortable prison accommodations, to have his own furniture carted in, and to have a caterer send in his meals.

"My word, if it isn't Ravel!" a young man cried, springing off the bed on which he had been lazing and seizing Aristide's hand. "Boyer, look who's here!"

"You're not a prisoner, I hope?" said a second young man, who had been leaning against the wall, staring out the small window at the rainy sky.

"No, he's got a magical bit of paper that allows him to pass all barriers," Mathieu quickly assured them. "Signed by Fouquier himself."

"Gods! How'd you get *that*?" Ducos exclaimed.

"A . . . a police affair," Aristide said, as he shook hands all around. "I work for them, you know," he added, when Boyer cast him a dubious glance.

"Well, no matter," said Ducos. "My, it's good to see you! A familiar face from home . . . it's almost like family." He shook Aristide's hand again, clasping it in both of his own. Aristide summoned a smile, thinking that Jean-François Ducos had changed little in the past eight years since they, together with Mathieu and a few dozen other scions of the merchant and professional classes of Bordeaux, had argued the new philosophy in the local coffeehouses; he was still the slight, eager boy with a mop of unruly black hair and an engaging grin. With a pang he realized that Ducos could not be more than twenty-eight or twenty-nine, and Boyer-Fonfrède—Ducos's best friend and also brother-in-law, he now remembered—was scarcely older.

He glanced at Boyer, who gave him a quick, tentative smile and returned to the window. Boyer—the quiet one of the pair—was less willing to flout convention than was his capricious, talkative friend, and had never been entirely easy with Aristide. Boyer had never quite forgotten that Aristide was the son of a man who had murdered his wife and died on the scaffold for it, and had always treated him with distant, self-conscious politeness, without the genuine warmth that Ducos displayed.

And yet now they're the ones in prison, while I, the son of a felon, shunned all my youth, walk free and serve justice as best I can . . . though I wish with all my heart I could do something, anything, to get them out of here. . . .

"Want to drop in on Vergniaud?" Ducos said. "His room's not far."

"He was busy writing something when I looked in half an hour ago," Boyer said, leaving the window. "He may not welcome interruptions."

"Another time." Vergniaud, the unofficial leader of the delegation from Bordeaux, was several years older than the others, and Aristide was not as well acquainted with him.

"So do you think we can assist you in your present investigation, Ravel," Ducos inquired, "or are you just shamelessly exploiting that pass to visit your friends?"

"The latter, I fear," Aristide said with a wry smile, "unless you can give me any insight as to why—keep it to yourselves, all right?—why a madman should be murdering people who seem to have no connection to each other whatsoever, hacking off their heads, and leaving the corpses in plain sight."

"Well, gracious, what's another headless corpse, more or less?" Ducos said, with an airy shrug, as Boyer paled and turned away. Ducos and Mathieu had always shared an ironic sense of humor, which had apparently grown darker with their experience of imprisonment and revolutionary politics. "Paris seems to be full of them."

Mathieu gave him a sour grin. "That's what I said."

"Say that again," Aristide demanded, turning to Ducos.

"What's another headless corpse, more or less?" the young man repeated, puzzled.

"Yes. 'Paris seems to be full of them.' "

"And we intend to try our best not to join their ranks," Mathieu said coolly, during the silence that followed, and leaned against the door frame. "What's the matter, Robespierre? Get an idea?"

"Perhaps. What was it you said earlier? 'It's in the spirit of the times, isn't it?' "

"Something like that. Why?"

"Because I'm wondering if this killer is really a madman after all, or if he's as sane as we are."

"Sane?" Boyer broke in. "Nobody's sane these days, at least not in Paris."

"Exactly."

"Ah," Mathieu said, after a moment's thought. "A fanatic. Sane in the strictest sense of the word, not a candidate for the madhouse . . . but someone who 'executes' people who he believes have betrayed the Revolution. Doing Madame Guillotine's work for her. Have you thought of that?"

"Yes, that had occurred to me."

"On the other hand," Ducos suggested, "what about a royalist fanatic? Someone who's concluded that these murders will make France look even worse than it is."

Mathieu laughed. "A political plot? Robespierre—the genuine article, I mean, not you—" he added with a nod to Aristide, "Robespierre's been talking himself hoarse about plots for months. I'm sure he'll be thrilled to know that one might actually exist."

"Keep us abreast of it," Ducos told Aristide. "This is as good as a play; I want to know how it ends."

"I'll visit again soon—every day, if I can." Aristide glanced at his watch and shook hands with the three of them. "And you—you keep your spirits up, all of you."

10

A visit to Brasseur was in order, he decided, emerging into the court-yard of the Palais de Justice from the dark corridors of the Conciergerie. The morning's damp, gray weather had scarcely brightened, though the rain had ceased. He walked to the Palais-Égalité and on to the commissariat on Rue Traversine, just a street beyond, where he found Brasseur alone in his office with a bottle and a heap of reports.

"Busy?"

"Just give me an excuse to think about something else," said Brasseur, straightening in his chair and stretching. "What's up?"

"We're going to be busier than we'd like."

He had already shared the truth about the number of the headsman's victims with Brasseur, and now he swiftly brought him up to date about his meeting with Danton. "So we're stuck with it, I fear," he concluded. He paced to the window, watched the hurrying passers-by for a moment, turned about, and stared at the city map on the opposite wall. "I imagine there are three possibilities. One: He's a genuine madman, with motives we can't begin to comprehend. Perhaps a mad-doctor could help us, though I'm not optimistic. Two: He might be a fanatic whose head has been turned by the Revolution. A man, perhaps not too balanced to begin with, who is passionately devoted to the Republic and who believes that the Revolutionary Tribunal isn't doing its work quickly enough—"

"Someone who's decided to become his own judge, jury, and executioner?" Brasseur said, brightening. "Going after people he thinks are enemies of the Republic, and who are on the run from the authorities. . . ."

"Or whom the Tribunal set free, even though he thinks they shouldn't have been." Aristide paused. "Earlier this morning, I crossed paths with a juryman at the Tribunal who, evidently, has been responsible for a couple of questionable acquittals. I should look into those. Doubtless there have been others. If we can match any of the victims with prisoners who were tried at the Tribunal and released, that would be a sign that we're moving in the right direction."

"And the third possibility?" Brasseur said. "The opposite of your fanatical republican—somebody who hates the Revolution with all his heart?"

"Yes, he could be a passionate royalist with a political motive, to make Paris look like a slaughterhouse and turn people—and England—against the Revolution."

"Or simply to terrify the populace and stir up trouble. If you were an ordinary, harmless, patriotic citizen, Ravel, wouldn't you honestly be less frightened of being arrested for incivism, than of being singled out by a killer who murders at random from the shadows, who might get you any time you stepped outside your door?"

"Unhappily, if that's the case, it'll be no easier to find him than if we're hunting for a genuine lunatic."

"Well," Brasseur said, "whatever I can do to help you, officially or unofficially, I'll do. After all, I saw that poor woman's body, and it would give me a good deal of satisfaction to catch the bastard who killed her."

Aristide nodded, pondering the best course of action. First he would have to question the executioners and gravediggers, he decided, and learn what else he could about this latest victim; the unclaimed corpses, Danton had told him, had already been quietly disposed of in a cemetery beyond the city walls.

"Got a newspaper?"

Brasseur handed him that day's *Moniteur* and he glanced through it to the bulletin with the heading REVOLUTIONARY TRIBUNAL. One death sentence, passed the previous afternoon, which would be carried out that day. Executions usually took place at about three o'clock; undoubtedly Sanson, the master executioner, and his men could be found at the Madeleine cemetery after the day's bloody business was over. Aristide sighed. Despite his varied experience with violent death over the past seven years, mutilated bodies and not-so-fresh corpses still made him queasy.

"Can you get away from here this afternoon and meet me at half past three, then?" he said. "Outside the Madeleine cemetery—no, we'd better not be seen hanging around outside, it might give rise to curiosity—how about in front of the Benedictines?"

A look of distaste, quickly hidden, flickered across Brasseur's face as he filled his wineglass. "You want me to go to the cemetery to question the *bourreau?*"

Centuries of superstition had left the average Frenchman with a deep-seated aversion to the *bourreaux* who served the law by disposing of criminals. Everyone detested executioners, although, for the past few months, as the guillotine efficiently dispatched the Republic's enemies, they had acquired a certain perverse celebrity.

"I told you, old Sanson's men found the latest corpse. We'll have to talk to them."

"Well, if we must."

"Commissaire?" One of Brasseur's inspectors knocked at the office door and peered in. "I've a message for Citizen Ravel."

"For me?" Aristide said, puzzled.

"Yes, the messenger says he was sent to you and is to deliver the letter personally, and he's to stay until you've read it."

A moment later a young man wearing a shabby army uniform strode into the office and gave them a smart salute. He was an extraordinary-looking fellow, Aristide thought: a powerfully built youth with a thick bull neck, pugnacious chin, a mop of disheveled light brown hair spilling from beneath his battered hat, and keen gray eyes.

"Citizen Ravel." He thrust a crumpled, sealed letter at Aristide. "My letter of introduction."

> *Citizen Ravel* [it read],
>   As I expect this letter will find you, despite my instructions to you, already with your friend Commissaire Brasseur, you may share all information with him, and him only. I know of nothing against Citizen Brasseur and I understand that you've worked together many times before. I hope I may trust his discretion as I trust yours.

Aristide paused. "Apparently Danton has spies watching his spies." "Who doesn't, these days?" said Brasseur.

> *Perhaps you've been thinking that I've not only burdened you with this task but also that I expect you to rely solely on your own resources. Never fear. The bearer of this letter is sent to you to assist you in whatever manner you may think proper. I think you will find him useful. He's something of a rogue, but he's also a clever young fellow, sharp in his wits, a fine swordsman, with an excellent record on the battlefield and an equally excellent opinion of himself. You may trust him, I believe, though you should trust first in your own judgment.*
>   *You will also find, enclosed, a bank draft for five hundred livres to cover your expenses. Come to me for more when you need it. I suspect that you're a moderately honest man, and that you will not appropriate more than a reasonable portion of these funds for your private use.*
>   *I expect to hear of your progress shortly.*
>
>   *Danton*
>   *This 12th October 1793*

"Well," Aristide said, folding away the letter. "This puts a better light on things. An aide-de-camp, and our expenses paid. What's your name, citizen, and what are you good for?"

"You may call me François."

"François? And is that your given name or your family name?"

"Whichever you prefer," the young man said, with an engaging grin.

"Oh, d'you have a reason for concealing your name?" inquired Brasseur.

"A few scrapes that I got myself into at home, and then in the army, citizen."

"Scrapes?"

"Impersonating an officer. On the field," he added, upon seeing Aristide's dubious expression. "My talents were wasted as a common soldier, as cannon fodder. I proved myself at Valmy, and they promoted me—to corporal! I knew I was worth more than any damned corporal. So at last I deserted from my regiment, went elsewhere, rejoined the army, and posed as a lieutenant. And acquitted myself honorably."

"Until you were found out?" Brasseur said.

"Well, yes. But evidently I made such a marvel of myself, in my masquerade, that Citizen Danton interested himself in me and had me recalled to Paris, and here I am."

"How old are you, François?" Aristide said. "You seem rather young to have had so many adventures."

"Twenty-five."

"Oh, come now. Every young man claims to be legally of age."

"Twenty-two," said François hastily.

"I doubt it," Aristide said, but with a faint smile.

"I may be young, but I know Greek, Latin, rhetoric, astronomy, philosophy, and physics. I'm an experienced swordsman. And I've also spent some time as an actor—"

"Enough, enough!" Aristide exclaimed. "I'm convinced of your usefulness. Sit down, then, and we'll tell you what we're about."

"You need someplace you can use as a headquarters," Brasseur said, after Aristide had given François a swift summary of the case. "Want to use the back room where we question people? If messages come for you from other commissariats around town, they can be sent here without raising any eyebrows."

François, though apparently willing to do almost anything else, flatly refused to go near an executioner, so Aristide sent him off to Rue de Vaugirard to learn what he could about Noyelle, the fourth victim, and took an early dinner at the nearest inexpensive eating-house, well before the midday crowd of workmen and junior clerks came clamoring in. He would walk to the Madeleine, he decided, in order to remain as unobtrusive as possible.

The ruins of the old church of La Madeleine, half demolished in the decade before the Revolution and never rebuilt, stood at the head of Rue de la Révolution—once Rue Royale—with a clear view down to the Place de la Révolution. One could easily see the scaffold and guillotine that were now permanently erected near the plaster statue of the goddess Liberty in the center of the square.

Aristide swiftly turned northward when he reached the Madeleine, avoiding the sight of the guillotine in the near distance. Liberty, enthroned on the pedestal that once had held a fine equestrian statue of Louis XV, now gazed coldly down at the almost daily executions of a miserable counterfeiter here, a profiteer there, now and then a luckless general who had lost too many battles, or—more often—merely an unfortunate fishwife or layabout who had tipsily insisted on shouting "Long live the king!" in front of a fanatical patriot. The number of prisoners held under suspicion of "incivism," which encompassed everything from active treason to expressing dissatisfaction with the Republic, had doubled since the Law of Suspects had been passed. Now, merely to have shown insufficient enthusiasm was enough, sometimes, to send you to prison until the end of the war (and it looked as if the war was going to stretch on with no end in sight), or until some fussy clerk decided that your case ought to be tried before the Revolutionary Tribunal.

In such conditions, he thought bleakly, even a careless word, or foolish idealism and impractical politics like that of the Brissotin deputies, became crimes. And it seemed more and more likely that the

Brissotins, surely guilty of such faults though the truest of patriots, were going to have a hard time of it at their impending trial. The Tribunal, though it had freed a respectable number of suspects over the past seven months, was not likely to let so many enemies of the Mountain out of its clutches.

Would Mathieu and his friends soon be traveling that same route to the Place de la Révolution?

11

Brasseur was waiting for him outside the shuttered, deserted Benedictine monastery, now national property. Aristide glanced about them, on the lookout for prying eyes, before gesturing his friend a quarter mile farther up Rue d'Anjou, toward the parish cemetery that lay near the edge of the city, surrounded by a high stone wall. Here, owing to its convenient proximity to the Place de la Révolution, all the guillotine's most recent victims were buried, including the king, back in January, and the young provincial Charlotte Corday, who, for the sake of her Brissotin heroes, had bravely but foolishly murdered Marat three months ago, setting off a furious wave of reprisal against them. Aside from those famous names, there were, he knew, several dozen—fifty or sixty, perhaps?—forgotten unknowns as well, executed during the past six months for sundry crimes, major and minor, against the Republic.

He shivered, from more than the damp breeze and overcast sky. He found his pace had slowed as they arrived within sight of the cemetery gate, a sturdy new one designed to keep out royalists and the curious, and impatiently quickened his step. A uniformed National Guardsman moved forward to meet them at the gate. "Citizen Ravel? Might I see your card, please."

He silently extracted his card of civism, which served as identification and proof of good citizenship in such uneasy and disordered times, from his pocket-book and handed it over. Brasseur held up the card that identified him as a commissaire of police and the man hastily nodded.

"The citizen prosecutor sends his compliments," the guard continued, "and says we're to allow you—and you, Citizen Commissaire, I'm sure—every liberty. The site's that way, halfway through." He pointed the way along a muddy path rutted with wagon wheels.

The cemetery, Aristide guessed with a glance at the weathered wall, had been in service since early in the century, when its parish had been a small village outside the city. Now Paris's bourgeois neighborhoods and comfortable private houses of the prosperous western quarters were creeping outward to engulf it. The distant upper stories of a few fine stone houses were visible to the south and east, but beyond the high walls to the west and north of the burial ground lay only gray sky and a handful of small market farms and muddy fields. A few gnarled trees, almost bare of leaves, stretched their bony fingers heavenward like the dead rising from their graves.

He caught the first faint whiff of the smell as he neared the northern wall across an unkempt stretch of coarse grass, still slippery from the previous night's heavy rain. Beneath the usual October scents of chill air, damp earth, and falling leaves hovered a different odor, ranker than that of the Basse-Geôle, a faint, foul charnel-house odor of spoiled meat and old blood.

"Citizens?" said a tall, sober, middle-aged man in a dark green coat, approaching them. "Are you the agents I was told would question us about this unfortunate discovery?" Aristide nodded and he continued. "This is a terrible business, citizens. I assure you that none of my men had anything to do with this dreadful affair. I have my standards, and I do my best to choose my men wisely."

Charles Sanson, the master executioner. Aristide recognized him immediately, having seen him from time to time in the Palais de Justice, though of course they had never formally met. He gave Sanson a polite little dry bow—even now, when all men were equals, he found he could not bring himself to shake the hand of an executioner—and clasped his hands firmly behind his back. "Citizen Sanson. If you please, tell me everything you can."

"It's my assistant Hamelin to whom you must speak. I wasn't present at the discovery, and know little more than do you."

The corpse stink grew stronger as Sanson led them toward the long trench. Aristide turned his head for a breath of fresher air and Sanson, noticing, gave him an apologetic nod. "Naturally, we cover the corpses with quicklime, but the sheer numbers of late—three or four fresh bodies from the scaffold added nearly every week to the usual parish burials, and sometimes more—often overwhelm our resources. Though, to be sure, it's hardly as bad as Les Innocents was, ten years ago."

If you only knew, Aristide said to himself. The Cemetery of the Holy Innocents, Paris's oldest, busiest, and foulest burial ground, which had been receiving the corpses of the city's poor since the thirteenth century, had been closed in 1780 for the sake of public health. Its clearance, six years later, had revealed more than a few long-hidden secrets among the ancient bones.

He stepped forward and, a macabre curiosity taking hold of him, gazed down into the trench. Near a ladder that leaned against the edge of the pit, a layer of powdery white lime lay like new snow over shrouded shapes twelve feet below him, though it did not entirely mask the faint traces of dull brown bloodstains on some of the shrouds. He turned back to the master executioner.

"Who discovered the extra corpse?"

"I did," said another man, hurrying to Sanson's side. He might have been any inconsequential *petit bourgeois*, a solidly built man of forty-five, plainly dressed in brown broadcloth and well-worn boots, hat in hand. "I'm Hamelin, one of Citizen Sanson's chief assistants. It was I and the gravediggers who discovered it. We were bringing a body here from the square as we're supposed to do—"

"How long have you been burying the executed here at this end of the ground?" Brasseur interrupted him. "Your trench looks pretty new."

"You're right, citizen. A ditch like that holds a couple of hundred bodies—not anything like the size of the trenches they used to have at

Les Innocents, of course. This parish isn't thickly settled, and the sexton was digging individual graves as he always did, until . . . well, until the Revolutionary Tribunal got busier last month, and then we decided that we'd better have a regular grave pit to take them all, like in the bigger cemeteries. So this is a new trench that they began digging at the beginning of the month, and already we've put sixteen bodies down. Sixteen executions in less than a fortnight—I ask you! A dirty business."

"Go on," said Aristide. "What's your usual routine?"

"We bring the body here in a wicker basket—in those," Hamelin added, gesturing at a pair of long coffinlike baskets lying a little distance away. Aristide had not noticed them at first, for they were almost the same color as the yellowed horse-chestnut leaves littering the ground, but for the dark reddish-brown smears at the baskets' lower edges. "Two to a basket if we have more than a couple in one day, like we had on the second of the month; five of them, we had then. Dirty business.

"Here we hand the body over to the gravediggers," Hamelin continued, "though we stay to make sure that everything's done proper, so that that bast—so that the public prosecutor can't fault us for neglecting some detail in his precious official procedure. Then the body's stripped to the underlinen and goes in a shroud, together with the head, and they sew up the shroud and lay it in the ground and scatter lime just like a regular burial, and a priest comes by when he can, to swing some incense and mutter a bit of Latin. We take inventory of everything that's been found on the body, and I take charge of any valuables or money and deliver it to the Hôtel de Ville, while Fermin arranges for the clothing to be sent to the charity hospital. That's all."

"No coffins?"

"It's not usual, especially since they started sending us more and more patients—"

" 'Patients'?" Brasseur echoed him, startled.

"The customary term," Sanson murmured. " 'Clients,' if you prefer."

"The government pays the gravedigger's bill," Hamelin continued, "and the nation's not about to spend a sou more than necessary for the bodies of criminals and traitors. We did have a coffin for the king—for Capet, that is," he corrected himself, with the briefest of glances toward the gate through which Aristide and Brasseur had entered. "Nailed down well and buried deep, so nobody can get to it, royalists and such hoping to get relics. But the rest, they're given the usual pauper's burial—a priest, a sack for a shroud, and a place in a common grave."

"Though the spot was badly chosen," said Sanson quietly. "The earth here is full of clay and doesn't absorb well. We need much more quicklime than we ever did in the ground at St. Jean-en-Grève."

"How did you discover the body?" Aristide said.

"Couldn't have missed it," said Hamelin. "It was lying right on top of the others. You see, we'd brought the cart with the body from the square and we began to open the trench. We cover it with planks over-night to keep the rain off and the animals out.

"Well, even before we had the planks up, Fermin says to me, 'Hamelin,' he says, 'there's something not right about this. These boards have been disturbed since last night.' And damned if they hadn't been. At first we thought something—stray dogs, perhaps, for they come to lick the blood at the foot of the scaffold if we don't fence it away—had been at the corpses, but of course no stray dog would have put the planks back on afterward. Then we thought it might have been some of these peasants hereabout. There are market farms just a short ways away," he added, jerking his thumb over his shoulder to the northwest, "and these farm folk have their superstitions, you know."

"Superstitions?"

Sanson stirred. "Many ignorant people have believed for centuries that a magical salve, which cures all ills, can be made from the fat of a hanged man."

"I remember an old woman just outside my hometown who claimed to work magic," Brasseur agreed. "She claimed she climbed the gallows to take dead men's fat and bones. A hanged man's finger bone was worth twenty sous at least, as a good-luck charm. And plenty of our neighbors swore by her concoctions."

"They used to come to my father and grandfather to buy such a salve," Sanson continued, "and also to me, in the old days. Old superstitions die hard among common folk; some may believe that the guillotine imparts as many magical powers as does the rope."

"And what did you tell the people who used to ask you for this salve?" Aristide inquired, fascinated despite himself.

"Nothing we could have said about foolish superstitions would have convinced them that their beliefs were nonsense. We sold them the salve as they asked us to. I daresay it may have cured a few of them."

"Sold them the salve! Don't tell me you—"

"Never fear, citizen; it was nothing more than an ointment made from medicinal herbs and pork tallow," concluded the executioner, with the faintest hint of a smile on his lips.

"I'm relieved to hear it," Aristide said. "Pray continue, Citizen Hamelin."

"Well, as I said, we thought perhaps someone had climbed the wall to fiddle with the bodies, to get a bit of hair or bone or such. So we open up the pit, and what do we find but sixteen bodies instead of the fifteen we'd already buried—an unknown dead man, without his head, lying right on top!"

"But you're sure that this unknown man was not guillotined?" Aristide said.

"Certain of it. *We* didn't bury him, not without a shroud and all. And between us, we and the parish sexton keep good records. This one was just pushed into the trench after he was dead and left where he fell. Besides," Hamelin added, "you can tell at a glance, when you look for it; the guillotine—well, the guillotine leaves a clean cut. But this one, he wasn't guillotined. Far from it. Rough cuts, and several of them. Messy work. If he'd been beheaded right here, the blood would've spouted all over and stained the shrouds below."

"He certainly wasn't murdered down there," Brasseur said, with a glance into the pit. "No stains worth speaking of. Any sign that he was killed nearby?"

"No pool of blood, if that's what you mean, Commissaire," said Hamelin. "We had some rain, remember; it might have washed it away."

"And also washed away any signs that might have told us whether the murderer did his work here, or did it elsewhere and got the body in somehow," Brasseur grumbled. "Where did you find the head?"

Hamelin pointed to a corner of the burial pit. "It'd been shoved down into a gap under one of the bodies, like they didn't want it to be found. But we noticed right away that some of the shrouds at that end had been disturbed, were showing a bit through the quicklime. A layer a half inch or so thick it should be, to keep down the stink, and around that corner, it was no more than a dusting, as if someone had shook it off. Fermin says, maybe someone's hidden something there, for who knows what filthy reason: an unwanted baby or such. And so we go down into the trench and look more careful, and what do we find but that poor fellow's head, shoved down tight and well limed, like the killer was trying to keep it from being found or recognized—"

"Citizen Ravel, have you already examined the corpse?" Sanson inquired. Aristide nodded.

"You'll have observed the state of rigor mortis, then," said Sanson. "The rigor was still advancing when my men found the corpse yesterday afternoon. Rigor, I expect you know, sets in upon a corpse from six to twelve hours after death, and usually lasts for a day and a half to two days."

Brasseur and Aristide could not help staring at him.

"I have had some small medical training," he added gently. "And, in my profession, one unhappily comes to know more than a little about corpses."

"To be sure," Aristide said, feeling himself on uncertain ground. This articulate, dignified individual, in his respectable, well-cut green frock coat, round hat, and spotless mousseline cravat, was not at all what he had expected of a *bourreau*.

"The corpse could not have been left here before the afternoon of the eighth of October, of course," Sanson continued, "when Hamelin and the others last handed over a corpse to the gravediggers; they would have seen it straightaway. And judging from the rigor, the man died no later than early yesterday morning. Possibly sometime late on Thursday the tenth, near midnight, or in the small hours of the eleventh."

Aristide scrawled a few notes. "That's helpful. Now why," he continued, thinking aloud, "would you bring your victim in here to murder him, when the place is so well guarded? And if he didn't kill the man here, then how could the person behind this mischief have deposited the corpse here? He couldn't have slipped past the gate, not with the night guard and the local patrol. Was there any sign he'd tried to tamper with the lock on the gate?"

"None."

"More likely he got in over the wall," Hamelin suggested. He pointed to the high wall at the northern perimeter of the burial ground. "Some of it's not in good condition. He could have climbed that more easily than the new wall to the south."

"And what of the corpse?"

"Why, he could have used our ladder, I suppose, if he was strong."

"Let's see. Help me with it, will you?"

Together they heaved the ladder out of the burial trench and leaned it against the stone wall. Aristide glanced at Brasseur, who shook his head.

"Better you than me!"

Aristide climbed the ladder and looked over the wall, into a small field of cabbages and turnips, and searched for any sign of disturbance. At last he saw, faint in the grassy perimeter directly beneath him, a few marks that might have been traces of footprints. He climbed to the top and picked his way along the wall until he found a small area where the long grass below seemed more trampled.

The wall was, indeed, somewhat deteriorated at one point, and he easily found footholds down to the other side. The faint footmarks ended not far away, but neither the grass nor the earth of the turnip field held any washed-out vestiges of wheel tracks or hoofprints.

He climbed to the top of the wall again, looking for recent scrapes, chips, dislodged mortar, or other evidence of an intruder's passing, but found none, and at last returned to the cemetery. Unburdened with the weight of a corpse, he thought, anyone of an athletic build could have scaled the wall, using the jutting edges of carelessly placed stone blocks and the gaps where old mortar had fallen out; but how on earth had the murderer brought his victim's body here, climbed the wall, fetched the ladder, and somehow hauled the dead weight of the corpse up the ladder and over the wall without leaving any unmistakable traces behind him?

It implied a murderer of extraordinarily powerful physique . . . or else more than one man, and probably a well-thought-out plan. But the faint marks in the grass did not seem to indicate more than one pair of footprints.

Sanson approached him as Hamelin and Fermin lugged the ladder back to the grave pit.

"Will that be all, Citizen Ravel? My men are done for the day, and I've no doubt they'd like to go back to their families."

"Yes—yes, that's all, I think." Aristide scribbled a few brief notes and thrust his notebook in a pocket, with an involuntary grimace at the idea of a woman who would want to bear the children of an executioner.

12

"Imagine being born to a trade, a detestable trade, and growing to manhood knowing that, all your life, you'll never have another," Aristide said as he and Brasseur walked back to Rue Honoré past servant girls gossiping as they swept the front steps of the elegant houses on Rue d'Anjou. "Sanson's father, and grandfather, and great-grandfather were all master executioners before him, weren't they?"

"So I've heard," said Brasseur. "My previous secretary grew up in the quarter where they live, in the parish of St. Laurent; he told me a bit about old Jean-Baptiste Sanson, father of Citizen Sanson whom we met today. Old Jean-Baptiste was a godly and charitable man, people said. He tried to make up for his trade by giving great sums of money to the poor and curing their ills. But the poor fellow fell to an apoplexy and so his son had to take his place young. He was still in his middle teens, I think. He's been executioner of Paris, man and boy, for near forty years now."

"In his teens," Aristide echoed him. "Good God. To be obliged to torture and kill men—or at any rate to oversee it—in the name of the king's justice, while still a boy . . . it doesn't bear thinking about. To spend your whole life bound to that . . ."

"He has the guillotine now, at least, rather than the wheel and the gibbet," Brasseur said, unsuccessfully waving at a passing fiacre. "And torture's gone for good."

"Yes, but I suspect he executes as many men and women in a fortnight, now, as ever he did in a year, before the Revolution. A poor bargain, I'd say." Realizing that he was close to being indiscreet—for in the autumn of 1793 informers were everywhere, even among the loafers at the street corners, always ready to repeat an imprudent remark to the vigilant guardians of the Republic—he changed the subject.

"We need to know more about our madman's victims. I saw the body from the cemetery already, at the morgue, though it didn't tell me much more than that the man was a sansculotte of the more uncouth variety. Perhaps you could pay a semiofficial visit to the local commissaire, Conchon, and ask him about this Echelard." He pulled out his notebook. "The first victim, Jumeau, lived not far from here. I think I'll call at his address and learn what I can about him."

They shook hands and parted. Aristide turned westward and proceeded along Rue du Faubourg Honoré, which began at the Madeleine and continued the east-west axis of Rue Honoré toward the western edge of the city. No. 38 was a handsome apartment building with, he guessed, the usual distribution of tenants in a prosperous neighborhood: well-appointed shops on the ground floor, the well-off on the first and second floors, the modest on the third and fourth, and the genteel poor on the fifth, with servants and perhaps a few artists, writers, or seamstresses living hand-to-mouth in the top level of attics, where the air was fresher and the light good, but the daily climb up six or seven flights of stairs was punishing.

The resident porter directed him to the second floor, adding, "But I don't know if they'll see you, citizen; poor Citizen Jumeau died last month—murdered, they say—and Citizeness Lépinay's taken it hard."

"So I hear," Aristide said. He jingled a few coins in the pocket of his redingote. "I came to pay my respects to the family. Who is Citizeness Lépinay? A relative?"

"Oh, no," said the porter, with a wink. "Citizen Jumeau was a widower, you see. I expect the lady's been his mistress for some time, and they've been keeping house together since Citizeness Jumeau died three years ago."

Aristide took a seat, still absently jingling the coppers in his pocket. "A friend sent me to Jumeau, but I'd never met him. Was he as agreeable as my friend said?"

"Yes, citizen. Always with a 'good day' when he passed me, and inquiring after my family, and a generous tipper. A pleasant gentleman all around; he'll be missed."

"Indeed? What a misfortune for his family." He leaned back, accepted the offer of a cup of wine, and entered into small talk. After twenty minutes, he had learned everything the porter knew or guessed about his former neighbor, which was unrevealing; the late Jumeau, a bureaucrat from a family of upper-middle-class bureaucrats that had aspired to minor noble status before the Revolution, had evidently led a contented and blameless life.

A pert, pretty, fair-haired maid answered his ring at Jumeau's door. "Police," he told her, showing her his card. "I have some questions for Citizeness Lépinay."

"But I'm sure that was all done with a fortnight ago," she said. "What—"

"More questions, I'm afraid. Is the citizeness at home?"

"I'll see if she can receive you, m'sieur—I mean, citizen."

She led him into a small antechamber and disappeared. He glanced about. It was simply furnished with two small, somewhat worn, armchairs in the rococo style of the last reign, perhaps the taste of the late Madame Jumeau. The widower's mistress had not yet taken it upon herself to redecorate in the newer, more classical style of the past decade.

"Citizen? What is it you wish from me?"

He turned. "Citizeness Lépinay?"

"What is it? I already told the police everything I could. I don't know what else I can tell you."

"It's not my wish to distress you," he said, measuring his words carefully in order not to give away too many details, "but someone— there has been another murder similar to that of Citizen Jumeau, and we're trying to find the connection between them, if any."

He saw her pale. "Oh . . . how horrible." Her gaze, which had been suspicious, softened. He swiftly took her measure. She was quietly elegant in a black taffeta gown that was fashionable but not ostentatious. Though not young by any standards, she was still a handsome woman and, he thought, had once been remarkably beautiful. He would have guessed her age to be somewhere between forty and forty-five, but as he looked more closely he realized that, beneath the careful application of rice powder and a light touch of rouge that gave her a fashionably pink and white complexion, she was probably a few years past fifty.

"Please—who—who has been murdered? It was like Jumeau? His throat was cut?"

"Throat? No, they were—" Aristide began to correct her before realizing that the concierges at the Basse-Geôle, out of consideration for a woman's delicate sensibilities, must have made an effort to conceal the true, even more gruesome, manner of Jumeau's death from her when she had gone in to identify the body.

She had identified him by means of a birthmark on his chest, he recalled. Yes, it would have been possible to disguise the fact that he had been decapitated—and to conceal the missing head, in fact—by swathing the corpse in sheets, telling her that Jumeau's face had been disfigured and could not be viewed, and then hurrying the headless cadaver into a sealed coffin as soon as the undertaker arrived.

"They were—what?" she said sharply. "What do you mean?"

"They—their . . ." he began, cursing himself for his carelessness and wondering how best to answer her without horrifying her into hysterics.

"Are you trying to tell me that Jumeau—that this murderer did *not* cut his throat?"

"No, citizeness," he said, not knowing what else to say. "His throat was cut."

"But you were about to say something else. That's not all. How did he die?" She reached for his arm and clutched at it, her fingers digging into his flesh. "What are you keeping from me?"

He laid a hand over hers and said, as gently as he could, "They—the morgue attendants—they would have wanted to shield you from the ghastliness of it. It could be of no help or consolation to you to know how he died."

Her voice was steady, though she still clutched at his arm with a fierce grip. "Please tell me the truth. They owe me the truth."

Crude, ugly words, but there was no way to soften them.

"He was found decapitated," he told her, his voice low, praying that no talkative servants would overhear and spread the lurid rumor throughout the quarter.

She stared at him, speechless. He could see the blood draining from her already pale face. At last she whispered, *"Decapitated?"* An instant later she let go of him and took a swaying step backward. Aristide caught her before she fell and, supporting her, shouted for the maid.

The girl hurried in and fussed over her mistress, chafing her wrists and loosening her bodice. After a few minutes of such ministrations, and a swallow of brandy, Mademoiselle Lépinay recovered herself and smiled weakly at the maid. "I'm all right. Thank you, Margot."

"Clearly you've had a terrible shock, citizeness," Aristide said. "If you wish me to leave and return when you're better—"

She shook her head. "No, no. I'm well enough. You must do your duty, of course. Help me into the salon, and I shall be quite able to answer your questions."

Between them, Aristide and the maid assisted her into the next room, a small salon with a harpsichord in one corner. "Now," she said, after seating herself on a well-cushioned sofa and dismissing the lingering maid. "What can I tell you that will help you?"

"Your name is Marie-Clarisse Lépinay," he said, consulting his notes, "condition spinster—"

"Why not say 'kept woman'?" she said, with a sad smile and a shrug. "Perhaps 'aging courtesan'?"

"'Spinster' will do, I think. You reside here, at this address?"

"Yes; though I doubt I'll reside here for much longer."

"Tell me about Jumeau, please. Everything that comes to mind."

"He was a kind, charitable man. He enjoyed music. He treated his wife well and loved his children."

"Children?"

"Two daughters, both married, and a son who died as a child." She paused, a wistful smile on her face. "He was . . . well, in short, Jumeau was a good, decent, conventional, rather unimaginative man, who loved God and his king. It's like a cruel joke," she added. "I feared for his safety, these past few months, because he would keep on insisting that he was a loyal subject of the king, no matter what, and I wouldn't have been surprised if they'd arrested him. I was sure he'd been arrested that awful night, when he didn't come home."

Aristide glanced at his notes again. The corpse had been found near the Law Courts, which would have made perfect sense if only Jumeau had still been an habitué of the Palais de Justice, where the Paris Parlement had once sat in judgment in the Grand' Chambre, the chamber—now officially renamed, without a hint of irony, the Hall of Liberty—in which the first and most important division of the Revolutionary Tribunal now sat. "Jumeau was chief clerk to the court of the Grand' Chambre, wasn't he?"

"Yes, he began as a junior secretary, when he was little more than a boy, and worked his way upward to chief clerk. He had nothing to do with the Parlement's judgments, of course," she added, "nothing at all, but still they troubled him sometimes, when he felt that the matter had been . . . been somehow unjust." She paused and pressed her fingertips to her temples, closing her eyes. Aristide watched her, concerned, but at last decided that she could endure a few more questions.

"Did he lose his position when the parlements were dissolved, three years ago?"

"Yes. But he decided it was time to retire, in any case, and live on the income from his property. He wasn't rich, but it was enough to live comfortably."

"So why would he have been in the Cité at all, that day?" The Île de la Cité, the legal and spiritual heart of Paris with law courts, cathedral, and charity hospital, also boasted the oldest and seediest neighborhood in the city on the eastern half of the island; most of the decrepit houses that huddled about Nôtre-Dame and the Hôtel-Dieu dated back to the Middle Ages. Two streets east of the stately Palais de Justice, one could easily be swallowed up in the Cité's medieval squalor and vice-ridden anarchy. "It's not the most savory of neighborhoods, particularly after dark. Do you know of any reason why he would have been there in the evening?"

"He sometimes went to the Palais de Justice to see friends or former colleagues, of course."

"You think, then, that he must have been meeting someone?"

"Possibly."

"Perhaps this friend he was meeting also had royalist sympathies?"

"Perhaps—perhaps." She turned her great kohl-rimmed eyes to his, as if pleading with him. "But Jumeau was no fanatic. And he was not, after all, arrested for his loyalty to the king, but murdered by some madman for no reason that I can make out! It makes no sense!"

"Why do you say that?"

"He had no enemies. None at all. How could he have? He was a perfectly inoffensive civil servant, no different from a thousand others. But he had the kindest of hearts. Why, sometimes, in the past, he would come to me very upset, because the Parlement had . . ." She passed a hand over her eyes as if to shield them from the pallid sunshine that suddenly spilled into the salon windows. "Because the Parlement had confirmed a death sentence," she continued, her voice shaking a little, "and that often distressed him."

"Did Jumeau welcome the Revolution?"

Clarisse nodded. "Oh, yes. He embraced it at first, because he believed that the laws and the courts would be reformed, and judicial reform was much on his mind. It wasn't until last year, after all those horrible uprisings, when they deposed the king and then judged him, that he began to say it had gone much too far. Jumeau was a good patriot, citizen, though he always believed that the king meant well and knew what was best for the nation; I suppose he was too old, and had lived too long as a servant of the monarchy, to change his ways much. He always drank the king's health at dinner," she added, as if in a daze, "and went to Mass as often as he dared." Her voice trembled and she fell silent.

"I was very fond of him," she said, a moment later, when she had collected herself and dabbed at her eyes with a handkerchief. She was not too faint or distracted, Aristide observed, to be careful of her appearance. "We were happy together, just like an old bourgeois married couple. We enjoyed walking together in the Champs-Élysées on Sundays and festival days. He had asked me to marry him, in fact, now that a decent interval had passed since his wife died. He said that society's silly rules were all different now, and he would marry his mistress if he wanted to, and damn people's opinions. *Why* would someone have murdered him?"

"It might have been simply because he was a royalist," Aristide said, watching her. "Did he make his opinions known?"

"No more than anyone else. I tried to hush him as much as I could. He wasn't a fool; he knew it could be dangerous to speak one's mind in front of strangers."

"Do you know if he ever knew anyone named Echelard, Noyelle, or Houdey?"

"No, I don't believe so," she said, after a little thought. "Who are they?"

Aristide did not reply and Mademoiselle Lépinay fell silent for a moment, hands clasped in her lap, her somber gaze drifting about the room and its comfortable appointments. "I wish I could help you," she said at last.

"Who inherits Citizen Jumeau's fortune?" Aristide said, more for the sake of keeping the conversation going than in the hope of learning anything useful.

"His daughters. Though of course they've already received much of it in the form of their dowries."

"Do they live in Paris?"

"One is married to a shipowner in Marseille, and the other lives in Besançon. But it's absurd to think that they might have murdered him," she added. "They're both quite well-off. And Jumeau wasn't wealthy; he had his pension, and income from various investments and annuities, so we lived well enough, but I'm sure no one would have murdered him for his money. . . ." After a moment she raised her head, looking at him with an impassive, direct gaze.

"You'll forgive me, I'm sure, for not rising. Good day."

It was a firm dismissal. "Good day, citizeness," Aristide said, and bowed and left her. The pretty maid showed him out to the landing.

"Citizen?" she said as he reached the head of the stairs. "Please don't blame mad—the citizeness for being a little short with you. She's really the best of ladies."

"Did you hear our entire conversation?" he said, amused.

"Yes, a good bit of it, after she took faint."

"Ear pressed to the keyhole?"

"It's my business to know what's upsetting her," she retorted. "She may not know it, but she doesn't have any secrets from me, and that's the way it should be, 'cause I care about her. And she's not herself, what with poor M—Citizen Jumeau dying like that, so sudden, and now his daughters want her out of the apartment within the fortnight."

"Understandably." Grown, respectably married children were unlikely to continue to maintain their late father's mistress.

"It's a hard burden for her, and her such a kind lady and all. The Lord knows she doesn't deserve such trials. But there!" she added, with a shrug and a pert, wry smile. "Anyway, citizen, if you have any more questions, you come to me first, and like as not, I can answer them without troubling her."

"Thank you." Aristide felt in his pockets and parted with a double sou. "What's your name?"

"Marguerite: Margot to my friends."

"Thank you, Margot. Well, you overheard my questions: Have *you* ever heard of a water seller named Echelard, an ink peddler named Houdey, or an old soldier named Noyelle?"

"No, citizen. Our regular water seller's name is Jacques Lavallée, and he's a terrible flirt," she added, with a complacent smirk.

"I don't blame him." Margot was a charming creature, with a slender figure, delicate features, a fresh complexion, and lively hazel eyes. "Tell me," he added, wondering how he was to find Clarisse Lépinay if he should have more questions for her in the near future. "If your mistress has to leave this apartment, where do you think she'll go?"

She thought for a moment, pouting. "I couldn't say. She's mentioned the country, but if she goes to the country, then she can find herself another maid, 'cause as much as I love her, I'm not going."

"Don't you like the country?"

"Lord love you, what's there to do, besides picking flowers? I've been with her to m'sieur's little cottage that he rented once or twice for the fortnight during the summer, and I nearly died of boredom. No, give me Paris. She can hire some lump of a country girl if she wants a maid. Now maybe," she added, "maybe her son could do something for her."

"The citizeness has a son?" Aristide said. Illegitimate, no doubt— the fruit of some past liaison.

"He's grown-up now. She was just a girl, still in the opera chorus, when he was born."

Aristide tried, unsuccessfully, to imagine the sedate Clarisse Lépinay wearing a flamboyant, exotic costume on the stage of the opera house as Margot continued. "She talks about him once in a while, though she hasn't laid eyes on him more than half a dozen times since he was a boy. If you were a respectable gentleman, you wouldn't want a lady with a shady past hanging about, would you, letting it be known that she's your mother and all? She understands that. But he might set her up in a little flat somewhere, discreet like, if she approached him. Sounds like he's a decent enough gent, and doing well for himself."

"Well," said Aristide, parting with another coin, "let me know where Citizeness Lépinay goes, won't you? You can always leave a message for me—Citizen Ravel—at the commissariat of the Section de la Montagne, on Rue Traversine near the Palais-Égalité."

She pocketed the coin, with a smile. "Yes, citizen, anything you say."

13

I've some good news, for a change, along with the bad," Brasseur said when Aristide called at the commissariat on Rue Traversine late Monday morning, two days later.

"Let's have the bad first," Aristide said with a sigh, throwing himself down into the nearest chair in his friend's office.

"Well, I never did get to see the commissaire of Section de la République. He was out when I arrived, and I didn't have time to linger. You'll have to talk to him yourself."

"That's easy enough," said Aristide, making a note to himself. "What about the good news? Come on, out with it. I could use some good news."

Brasseur grinned. "First, Didier's found our female victim. Though you won't find it very enlightening." He consulted a page of notes on his desk. "Désirée-Anne-Marie Marquette, age about thirty-five. Three months ago, more or less, according to her landlord, she took a wretched little attic room on Rue Froidmanteau, behind the Louvre, but he hasn't seen her for a week."

"Is that all?"

"I said it wasn't very enlightening." Brasseur pushed the notes to one side and shouted for his secretary. "Dautry! Fetch Didier, will you?"

"Commissaire?" Inspector Didier said, arriving a moment later from the front room where local inhabitants waited to speak to authority. He caught sight of Aristide and gave him a chilly nod; they had disliked each other from their first meeting, over two years before.

"Brasseur tells me you may have identified our female murder victim," Aristide said. "Are you sure?"

"The landlord told me she'd gone missing. His description fit her well enough."

"People disappear without warning all the time from seedy lodging houses, Inspector."

"I'm perfectly aware of that," Didier said, "but if she did take off to avoid paying the rent, she didn't disappear with any of her belongings—not that much was left to take. Citizen Pageot—the landlord—described her as a skinny piece, a bit long in the tooth, no wedding ring; and he said he'd seen her going out with parcels under her arm and coming back with nothing but a little food that wouldn't keep a dog alive."

Probably selling her possessions one by one. "Any friends or visitors?"

"None that he saw."

"Does he recall what she was wearing the last time he saw her?"

"He knew right away. Said she'd been wearing the same green gown for the past fortnight—had most likely sold the rest of her clothes."

"Any hint at all that she might have had trouble with the local authorities? Suspicions of royalist sympathies, or anything of that kind?"

"The landlord said nothing about that."

Brasseur dismissed Didier and leaned back in his chair. "Well. Think she's the one? Past her youth, underfed, down to her last few sous, and the green gown to top it all off."

"Oh, yes, you've convinced me," said Aristide. "A woman without a friend in the world . . . and, I imagine, without an enemy, either, including her section committee." He sighed. "It looks as if nobody cared enough about her to want to kill her. So where does that leave us?"

"Nowhere, I expect. Though if we can find out who the third victim was, the one from the Arsenal section . . . Want me to put François onto it?"

"I doubt it's worth our time, if the man was a vagrant not known in the district. I'd rather keep him asking questions about Noyelle, the fourth. The report didn't say much." He shook Brasseur's hand and left the office. As he passed through the antechamber to the street door, a young woman jumped to her feet at the sight of him.

"Citizen Ravel!"

He stopped, recognizing her. It was Clarisse Lépinay's maid. He picked his way past Didier's desk and the benches where a handful of local inhabitants cooled their heels, together with a few shifty-looking individuals, police spies from various walks of life. "It's Marthe—no, Margot—isn't it?"

"Yes, citizen. Margot Simon." She gave him a perfunctory curtsy and continued before he could ask her what she was doing there. "It's Mademoiselle—Citizeness Lépinay, that is. She's gone."

"Gone?"

"Up and left, without hardly a word. That's to say, yesterday morning, after she'd had her breakfast, she called me in and told me she was leaving Paris, and likely not returning, and she was sorry to lose me and Louise and Henri—that's the cook and the valet—but that's the way it was. And then she gave us each a week's wages and packed a trunk and a valise with whatever she could carry of her own clothes and such— she's honest, she didn't take a thing that ought to have gone to poor M'sieur Jumeau's daughters—and had me fetch her a fiacre and off she went."

"How peculiar."

"Yes, m'sieur—citizen—I thought so, too."

"Why don't you come back to the commissaire's office with me and tell us everything you can?" he said, gesturing her down the hallway.

"The commissaire?" she echoed him, looking dubious. "But this isn't our section. Should I have told our commissaire in Section de la République?"

"It's not his concern. Commissaire Brasseur is working with me. Don't worry, he won't bite you."

Brasseur listened to Margot's story in silence, drumming his fingers on the desk when she had finished. "Any idea where she went?" he said.

"I overheard her telling the hack driver that she wanted the Place des Victoires. That's all I know."

"The coaching station," Aristide said. "So she meant what she said, that she was leaving town. Have you any idea at all where she might go? Has she relatives or friends outside Paris?"

"I don't know. She never talked about her past much—though I think she mentioned Rambouillet once or twice, that she'd been a girl there. Maybe she still has some family there."

"Could be sixty miles away by now," grunted Brasseur. "Why didn't you come earlier and tell us all this?"

"Well, I was that surprised!" Margot said, indignant. "She up and tells me she's leaving town and taking no servants, and two hours later she's gone, and what am I to do with myself? She said, stay in the apartment if you wish, until you find another place, for the rent's paid through the fortnight, though Citizen Jumeau's heirs will be sending for his furniture before then. And so I did; Louise and I stayed the night, and got to talking, and I thought I'd better come find you, Citizen Ravel, and tell you what was what. And here I am."

"Didn't you tell me, the other day," Aristide said, "that Citizeness Lépinay had a grown son?"

"Yes, I asked her about him, and she said she'd decided it was better this way. Truth is, of course, they hardly know each other."

"Well, that's neither here nor there," said Brasseur. "I expect you'll be staying at the late Citizen Jumeau's apartment for a few more days, till you find yourself another place?"

"Yes, Citizen Commissaire."

"Let us know immediately if you have any word from her—or of her."

"Yes, citizen."

"Wait a moment," Aristide said, as Margot turned to leave. "You're a clever girl. How would you like to help us catch the person who murdered poor Citizen Jumeau?"

"*Me?*" she exclaimed, the great hazel eyes widening in excitement. "Help you? Oh, yes, please. I liked monsieur, and I'd like to catch the monster who killed him." Abruptly she frowned. "This wouldn't mean that I'd be a police spy, would it? 'Cause I wouldn't want it known that I'm a spy. I'd never get another good situation if that came out."

Aristide exchanged an ironic glance with Brasseur before saying, "No, helping us doesn't make you a police spy."

"Now what was that all about?" Brasseur said, after Margot had laboriously written down her name and address and left them.

Aristide shrugged. "I thought she'd be a useful ally. People tell things to pretty girls. And now," he added, "I really must have some dinner. You'll find me at Michalet's if you need me."

14

The eating-house was crowded that day. Aristide slouched the length of one of the long tables, looking for a spot not too close to the workmen loudly discussing politics while devouring their midday meal, but few places remained.

One of the men at the next table, a sturdily built man of forty or forty-five, had swung about from his seat on the common bench and was eyeing him curiously. Aristide recognized him after a moment; they had met only two days before, at the cemetery of the Madeleine. Hamel . . . Hamelin, that was the name.

Hamelin seemed to be making up his mind whether or not to address him. It would be unpardonably rude, Aristide decided, to turn his back on him, when it was clear they had each recognized the other. He tipped his hat and inclined his head a fraction.

"Citizen Hamelin."

"It's Citizen Ravel, isn't it?" he said. "Of the police?" He grinned and edged sideways, gesturing to an empty space beside him at the table. "Taking your dinner here? Won't you take a glass with us?"

Aristide hesitated. He rarely drank wine in the middle of the day, when he drank it at all. Hamelin, interpreting his hesitation as reluctance to be seen with an executioner, continued, a little defensively, "We all serve justice here. Do you know Sauvade?"

Hamelin's companion was a grave, good-looking man of about forty, attired in a smart striped cutaway and waistcoat, a restrained version of the newest, raffish fashions that had become popular among those who found the trend toward *sansculottisme* absurd. "I think we ran into each other a couple of days ago at the public prosecutor's office," Aristide said. Sauvade nodded, with a faint smile, as he rose.

"Or rather, I nearly ran into you. My apologies."

"Sauvade's a member of the jury at the Revolutionary Tribunal," Hamelin continued. "A good fellow and a good patriot. And generous with the wine," he added, with a wink at the jug between them on the table.

"You flatter me," Sauvade said. "At the Tribunal, I'm simply doing my duty." He turned to Aristide as they took their seats on the bench. "You're in the police, Citizen Ravel? In what capacity?"

"I often work for them," he said, wondering why Sauvade had walked over to Michalet's when he could have dined at the private dining room in the Palais de Justice. Perhaps Sauvade was merely frugal, or else he had a taste for cassoulet. "Though I have no official position—"

"Police spy?" Sauvade said, unable to hide the scorn that flickered across his face. Evidently even the company of an executioner's assistant was preferable to that of a *mouche*.

"I'm not an informer. I assist the police with investigations. At other times I take on clients, now and then, as a private inquiry agent."

"An all-around busybody, eh?" Hamelin said, with a loud guffaw, signaling to a server for another glass.

"Something like that. But, as you said, we all serve the law in our various ways."

"That we do. Why, Citizen Sauvade here, he's an educated man. Yet he gave up a good position in a notary's office to serve as a juror. Not many professional gentlemen would do that."

Aristide privately agreed with him. Most of the jurors of the Tribunal's four divisions, handpicked from a large selection of applicants for the job, were of the lower middle class—tradesmen, artisans, and two or three mediocre artists—men who could be relied upon to view all aristocrats and servants of the monarchy with suspicion and not a little resentment. Sauvade, however, from his demeanor and his dress, seemed a cut above his colleagues.

"I felt it was my duty," said Sauvade. "You, of all people, Citizen Hamelin, ought to know that nothing is more important than justice for all." He consulted a small watch and rose to his feet. "And, speaking of my duty, the dinner recess will be over soon. Hamelin, it's been a pleasure. Citizen Ravel."

"Citizen," Aristide said, rising and following him through the swarming crowd of midday customers, "I wonder if I might have a word with you at your convenience? I'd like to learn more about the Tribunal, and what goes on inside the jury room."

Sauvade stiffened. "If you're curious about the widow Capet's trial, I have nothing to say."

"It's nothing to do with Antoinette," Aristide assured him, recalling belatedly that the queen's trial was to have begun that morning, according to the *Moniteur*.

"A police affair?"

"Yes."

Sauvade thought for a moment. "I imagine I'd be permitted to discuss other matters, within reason. Perhaps this evening, after the session is over, around ten o'clock? You might come to the house where I lodge," he continued, "with Lemarchant, the notary, on Rue Baillet. North of the Pont-Neuf, near the Louvre, first floor, above the office."

"Pleasant fellow," said Hamelin, filling Aristide's glass from the jug as Aristide resumed his seat at the long table. "There's not too many professional gentlemen—citizens, I mean—who'd take a glass with a—a man like me."

Aristide was not overpleased, himself, to be seen drinking in public with an executioner, but held his tongue. "What did he want?"

"Don't know. We got to talking about Sanson, the father, that is. The boss. Sauvade was curious."

"Citizen Sanson seems to be a most respectable man," Aristide said, remembering his encounter with him at the cemetery.

"That he is. A decent fellow, and a good enough employer. If you're born to the trade like me, and haven't any choice, then, well, Sanson's the man to work for. The pay's passable and he's a fair man, treats you right. It's a wonder more folk aren't applying for work with him."

"Perhaps they foresee more work than they'd like," Aristide said as he added water to his wineglass, "or they don't relish the idea of executing royalty."

"Mm-hmm."

Aristide glanced about him. The crowd of diners was growing and the tables were packed. He lowered his voice and leaned forward across the scarred, wine-stained table, assuming that no one within earshot knew Hamelin worked for the executioner, and that Hamelin would prefer that no one did.

"They're trying Antoinette today."

"Aye, Sauvade said they began questioning her this morning."

"And there's still the king's sister and the children. What does Sanson think of the prospect of cutting off more royal heads?"

"Oh, he's closemouthed, the boss is," Hamelin said, lowering his own voice and taking a long swallow of his wine. "Doesn't often let you know what's on his mind. But it was pretty clear how he felt about guillotining the king. Old Sanson, see, he doesn't smile much at the best of times, except when he's safe at home with his family, but when he's particularly distressed over an execution, he just goes silent and formal and polite, like he's hiding behind a mask."

Suddenly Aristide felt a pang of kinship between himself and a man whom he would have thought the least likely in the world. How many times had he, too, hidden his fury or pain behind an impassive mask?

"The less emotion you see," Hamelin continued, "the more he's feeling, as a rule. And that day, with the king, he was as stiff and correct as I've ever seen him—and I've been working for him for almost ten years now."

"He's a royalist?" Aristide said, surprised.

Hamelin shook his head vigorously. "I wouldn't say that. He was pleased as anybody about the Revolution, back in 'eighty-nine. Equality for all, including executioners—it was important to him. It's more like, he's got a bit of a sentimental attachment to the royal family, just like most folk. You go all your life—and he's fifty-four—saying 'Long live the king' and meaning it, and it's a bit of a shock when all of a sudden the king's not the king and the government's telling you to chop off his head. Mind you, at least he had the guillotine. If he'd had to use a sword, like in the old days, I don't think he could have done it. Too much chance of something going wrong—and when your patient's the king himself, you're going to be extra nervous, aren't you?"

Aristide nodded. He did not want to imagine "something going wrong" with an aristocratic execution of the past—with the victim kneeling upright, awaiting the blow from a heavy, razor-sharp sword swung horizontally at the terrifyingly minute target of his bare neck.

"Because sometimes it did go wrong, you know," Hamelin continued, oblivious to his discomfort. Aristide suspected that several glasses of wine with Sauvade had made him more talkative than usual. "Even a hanging can go wrong. Most of the time it would be a good clean hanging, and the patient didn't suffer, but once in a while it didn't go as it should." He hunched his shoulders and bent toward Aristide. "I saw how Sanson would take it; why, he looked like death for a week, a few years back, after some wretched woman we strung up took half an hour to strangle, because we couldn't get her neck to snap when she dropped. Thank God for the guillotine, I say. Why, if you don't set the rope properly around their necks, or if you swing the sword just an inch too high or too low—well, it's a pretty horrible scene."

He gulped down another swallow of wine. "Thank God for the guillotine," he repeated. "Sanson doesn't like executing women, first of all—nor do any of us—and when it's the queen of France herself or a royal princess . . ."

"Surely he can't refuse to do it."

"Oh, he'll do his duty, all right, because it's his trade and because he has no choice—but he won't like it. That's to say, he never likes it; but it'll be worse than usual with Antoinette." He sighed noisily. "It's peculiar times we're living in. First they cut off the king's head, and now it'll be the queen's soon enough; and they're saying that those

Brissotin fellows from the government, even though some of them voted to cut off the king's head, that they'll be up before the Tribunal themselves before the month's out. Seems a right mess to me. Who's next, I'd like to know." He tossed back the last of his wine and wiped his mouth with the back of his hand.

An executioner, Aristide thought suddenly, *is a man who wouldn't have qualms about hacking off a corpse's head. They've seen far worse than that, in their time.*

Might one of Sanson's men have been seized by Revolution fever?

"And do you think we get extra pay for the extra work?" Hamelin continued, with a mournful glance at his empty glass. "No, we do not." He feebly thumped his fist on the table. "It's all one, whether we chop off one head in a month or half a dozen in a week. I ask you, is that fair?"

15

Aristide was just finishing his dinner, Hamelin having long since slouched off, when Brasseur appeared at the other side of the table. "You're still here. Good. We've got another one."

"Death of the devil." He bolted the last of the ragout and gulped a few swallows of watered wine. "Where?"

"Somewhere near the Bastille, they said."

"The Bastille?"

"Been there lately? Debris scattered about still, especially down in the dry moat. You could leave a corpse and it might not be found for days. Done? Come on, then."

The Bastille had been demolished almost three years ago, but Aristide could not help remembering his first visit inside the medieval fortress, a few years before the Revolution; as an author of seditious, banned pamphlets and, temporarily, a suspect in a baffling and gory murder, he had been in danger of becoming an unwilling lodger there himself.* Now all that remained of the Bastille was the trace of foundations in the vast empty square at the end of Rue Antoine, and the long, broad defensive

---

* *The Cavalier of the Apocalypse.*

ditch at its eastern edge, where the gatehouse had once stood. He and Brasseur alighted from their fiacre near the ditch, where a pair of uniformed National Guardsmen and a black-clad police inspector waited impassively.

"Down there," said the inspector, with a jerk of his head. "Good luck getting to it. A local roofer should be coming with a ladder any minute now."

"He was killed down in the dry moat?" Brasseur demanded, dubious.

"Looks like he was killed right here," the inspector said, gesturing the guardsmen aside to reveal a muddy stain in the trampled earth not far from the rampart. "Killed here, sometime in the small hours of the morning, and then tumbled over the edge. That's why nobody noticed him until midday."

Aristide leaned over the low parapet and stared down into the ditch. Twenty feet below him, a huddled, crumpled, blood-drenched thing lay amid the last of the rubble from the demolished fortress and assorted refuse from nearby houses.

The roofer soon arrived with his ladder. Aristide gingerly descended into the dry moat, the two guardsmen behind him. "The same amateurish hacking to take his head off, from the looks of it," he called up to Brasseur, after peering at the stump of the neck. "Dead about twelve or fourteen hours; he's quite stiff."

"What about the head?"

"Don't see it." He sent the guardsmen off to search among the nearby debris while he made a cursory examination of the corpse. The man was middle-aged or more, and wore no coat or cravat. His clothes and shoes seemed of good quality, though worn.

"Nothing," one of the guardsmen said, approaching him, "though we did find this." He held up a crumpled and muddy coat. "There's a notecase in an inner pocket."

Aristide seized the notecase and found the identity papers within. The name, Louis-Pierre-Auguste Deverneuil, meant nothing to him, nor did the address on Rue de Sèvres, on the Left Bank.

"Citizen, if the head is here, it's well hidden. Want us to go on looking?"

"Do your best." He gestured at the corpse. "But let's get this out of here." He clambered back up the ladder and rejoined Brasseur. "Are you up for a visit to the faubourg Germain?"

A frail, wizened manservant answered their ring at the substantial house at No. 87 Rue de Sèvres. He confirmed that Monsieur Deverneuil had not, indeed, been seen since late the previous evening, when an unexpected summons had called him out—one of the many odd-job men who haunted the street corners had delivered a note. No, he did not know who had sent it. He shook his head mournfully when Aristide inquired whether or not any other family members lived within.

"No, messieurs. All the rest of the family emigrated a year ago or more, after they abolished the monarchy. But monsieur refused to leave, no matter how madame and his son and the rest would try to persuade him that they could do more good working from outside. . . ." His voice trailed off and he shrank back, avoiding their gaze.

"Deverneuil was a royalist?" Aristide said.

"I fear your master is dead," said Brasseur, when the old man hesitated, fearful of saying too much, "and with the absence of other kin, you'll have to identify the body. But his political opinions are none of our affair. Was he a royalist?"

The old man lowered his voice. "A most devoted royalist, monsieur. He wouldn't leave his home to go off to Germany or England while his king and queen were still prisoners in Paris." He bowed them inside and gestured at the bare, chilly vestibule. "Very little is left, messieurs. They sold all they could. What with monsieur's position disappearing and—"

"What position was that?"

"Deputy royal prosecutor to the Parlement, monsieur. Deverneuil d'Estauran was his full name."

"You don't say," said Brasseur, impressed. A *procureur-général-substitut* to the high court had been, before the parlements were abolished in 1790, a wealthy, influential, and titled personage. "Now no salary, no fees, and no royal pension, eh?"

"No, monsieur. And monsieur's private income was reduced considerably by the loss of revenue from his property. In truth, messieurs, I am the only member of the household staff left. Monsieur Deverneuil and I were living here alone, in two rooms on the first floor; the rest of the house is empty."

Aristide shivered, thinking of the two old men huddling beside a meager fire in an empty room, as the elegant furniture, decorative objects, and *boiseries* were sold piece by piece, most likely in order to send gold secretly abroad to the royalist cause—an action that, if discovered, would have promptly sent the aristocratic old lawyer to the Tribunal and the guillotine.

"Did Citizen Deverneuil have any personal enemies?"

No, monsieur had had no enemies, so far as the old manservant knew; no enemies, now that the times had passed him by and he no longer swayed the courts as he once had. He brought a handkerchief to rheumy eyes. No, no one would have killed monsieur for his property, for there was little property left to inherit, and the young master, the sole heir, was across the frontier in Coblentz with the other émigrés, raising a royalist army for the Comte de Provence.

"Just one thing more, Vivier," Aristide said, as they left the house. "Was your master ever arrested and tried by the Revolutionary Tribunal?"

The old man stared at him, astonished. "No, monsieur. He lived quietly; not attracting any attention, you might say."

Well, it was worth a try, he thought glumly as they flagged down a fiacre. Perhaps Sauvade could tell him more, that evening, when they met as he had promised.

"All we know," Brasseur said, as they snatched a late, hasty supper of rolls and gristle-laden sausage from a street vendor near the Châtelet, after old Vivier had identified the body and returned to the empty house, "is that our headsman didn't just pick a random victim off the street this time. It looks like he deliberately sent a messenger to Deverneuil's house and lured him out. Wish I knew what the message had said."

Aristide nodded, his mouth full. "It's possible that Deverneuil might have had an enemy from his days at the Parlement, long before the Revolution; but why would such an enemy wait so long to take his revenge?"

"I suppose he tried to remain inconspicuous," Brasseur said, "but you know Paris; he might have had a local reputation as a royalist."

"And if so, then our idea that the killer is murdering enemies of the Republic may still be valid."

They parted and Aristide went on to Rue Baillet, a few steps from the northern span of the Pont-Neuf. A plumpish man of Sauvade's age, with a round, cherubic, good-humored face, opened the door to him at the apartment above the notary's offices.

"Citizen Ravel?" he inquired. "Sauvade sent word that you'd be calling," he continued. "Do come in. I'm Bernard Lemarchant. It looks as though Sauvade'll be late tonight—he's already missed supper—but he told us to take good care of you. Will you take coffee with us? Julie's just preparing it now. Do have some—she makes excellent coffee."

A little dazed by the rush of words, Aristide followed him through the spacious apartment and into the salon, where a pleasant-looking lady of sixty-five sat knitting on the sofa by a crackling fire. Lemarchant introduced Aristide to his mother, adding, "Julie's my sister. She'll be in with the coffee in just a moment."

"And Citizen Sauvade?" Aristide said. "He said—"

"Oh, Sauvade'll be along soon. He never knows how long the session at the Tribunal will last, of course, and since they're trying the queen—the *former* queen," he added firmly, as his mother made the sign of the cross, "you can imagine it'll be rather late. He sent word that we were to entertain you until he arrived. Ah—here's Julie. Julie—our guest, Citizen Ravel."

"Good evening, citizen," Julie Lemarchant said, as she set down the coffee tray on a nearby marquetry table. "Will you take some coffee with us?"

She resembled her brother, Aristide thought, glancing from one to the other of them, though Julie was the younger by about ten years or more; they shared rosy cheeks, an easy smile, and apparent endless good spirits. The family, judging by their comfortable apartment, well-maintained furniture, and fashionable clothing, seemed quietly prosperous. The notary's office was evidently thriving, even in the midst of revolution, as well as it had under the monarchy.

"Sauvade lodges here with you?" he said, accepting a cup. Julie nodded.

"Yes, he's lodged with us for years, on and off, since Bernard and he were at school together. He's an orphan, so he would spend the school holidays with us. He has a house and a little property of his own just outside the city, in Montsouris, but it's much too far to go when the Tribunal has a late session, so he comes here to stay the night whenever it's necessary."

"And of course he's always welcome!" Lemarchant added, as he threw himself down on a well-upholstered armchair.

Madame Lemarchant cleared her throat. "When Monsieur Sauvade—"

"Citizen Sauvade, Mother."

"Yes, dear. When Citizen Sauvade finished school and took his law degree, my late husband, who was a notary, took him into his office, along with Bernard. And we expect him to propose to Julie any day now," she added, with a fond glance at her daughter, "and you'd think that Bernard was marrying him himself, the way he goes on about it."

"Oh, come," Lemarchant said, with a grin, adding a heaping spoonful of sugar to his coffee. Evidently the Lemarchants could afford their little luxuries. "I'm merely pleased—no, I admit it, delighted!—that he could truly be part of the family."

"Bernard and René were best friends at school," Madame Lemarchant added, with a smile at her son's ebullience, "ever since they were ten years old, and they've remained close."

Aristide glanced from brother to sister. The talkative Bernard Lemarchant seemed an odd contrast to what he had seen of the grave Sauvade.

"They were always that way, even as boys, I'm told," Julie said, as if reading his thoughts. "Bernard was always the noisy one of the pair, and René the quiet one."

"Quiet but deep," said Lemarchant, laughing. "Terribly grown-up for his age and extraordinarily conscientious."

"He said to me that he felt it was his patriotic duty to serve on the jury," Aristide agreed. Julie smiled.

"If you take a look at the other jurors, you can imagine that most of them—the majority are shopkeepers and craftsmen, you know—applied not only because they're serving the Republic but because, in their eyes, it's a soft job that pays eighteen livres a day—considerably better than their usual line of work."

A soft job indeed, Aristide reflected; eighteen livres a day, the same as deputies to the Convention were paid, was about five times what the average skilled worker earned in Paris.

"René, on the other hand," Julie continued, "would certainly be earning a more lucrative living, and would have more time to himself, if he'd continued to practice law. But he insisted. He has a strong sense of justice; it's one of the things I love about him."

"Oh, yes," Lemarchant said. "He was always like that, almost from when I first knew him. It got so that by the time he was fourteen or fifteen, the other boys at school would come to him with their quarrels, and he'd resolve them. They knew he would be absolutely impartial. If we were still at school," he added, with a chuckle, "we'd be calling him 'Robespierre the Incorruptible' by now."

Aristide glanced at him sharply and his broad grin faded.

"I'm sorry, have I said something I shouldn't?"

"No, you couldn't know. A—a dear friend of mine often calls me 'Robespierre.' A friend who will probably soon appear before the Tribunal," Aristide added, feeling he had to explain himself.

"Do you think he's been wrongly imprisoned?" Julie said.

"I don't think he's done anything to warrant arrest and trial," he said, feeling it would be wiser not to mention that his friend was one of the imprisoned Brissotin deputies.

"Then you can be sure he'll receive justice from René. Often he's the one who sways the other jurors into bringing a verdict of 'not guilty,' you know; most of the others aren't inclined to be as lenient."

"Do you recognize the name Saint-Silvestre?" Lemarchant inquired. "A judge from the old Paris Parlement," he continued, when Aristide shook his head. "He was up before the Tribunal a few weeks ago. Sauvade did his best to save him—said that being a magistrate in a royal court ten or twenty years ago was no crime in itself, and that the man hadn't done anything to warrant prosecution for crimes against the nation. They overruled him, in the end, and Saint-Silvestre was guillotined, but Sauvade fought like the devil for him. That's the kind of man he is."

"He's really very gentle," Madame Lemarchant said unexpectedly, from the sofa. "Why, once, long ago, when they were boys, Bernard and young Sauvade were naughty and played truant from school—"

"Oh, Mother, no!" Lemarchant exclaimed. She smiled indulgently and went on.

"They played truant to sneak away and watch an execution at the Place de Grève, because they were curious, as boys are . . ."

"And a bit bloodthirsty, as boys are," Julie said.

". . . and Monsieur Sauvade actually fainted; he didn't have the stomach for it. I imagine he's more sensitive than he would wish to admit."

Lemarchant snorted. "I nearly fainted, myself. But please, don't you go bringing that up in front of Sauvade—he won't thank you for it. Nobody wants to be reminded of something like that. Here's Sauvade now," he added, at the sound of a distant bell. A moment later the juryman joined them, bowing to Madame Lemarchant, bestowing a chaste kiss on Julie's cheek, and heartily shaking hands with his friend.

"You're here, Citizen Ravel," he said, turning. "Please pardon my lateness; the session ran much later than I'd predicted."

"No need to apologize. Your friends have been showering me with kindness."

"Well . . ." Sauvade glanced about the room, taking the coffee cup that Julie handed him, and turned back to Aristide. "You wished to ask me about the Tribunal. Perhaps we could go into the other room and not weary the ladies."

Aristide followed him into an adjacent room that was set up with a dining table, a pair of matching marble-topped buffets, a linen press, and a tall china cabinet. "Now," said Sauvade, seating himself in the nearest chair and gesturing Aristide to another. "How can I be of service to you?"

"I heard that you . . ." Aristide began, hesitating as he realized the question he was about to ask might be construed as insulting. He had no desire to question Sauvade's integrity, though he found the juror, despite his courteous manner, just a trifle disconcerting. Perhaps, he thought, he instinctively sensed a steely revolutionary fanatic beneath Sauvade's otherwise commendable pursuit of justice.

"I understand that—when prisoners have been acquitted at the first division of the Tribunal—that you've sometimes been the member of the jury who's persuaded the rest that the prisoner was innocent and ought to be set free."

"Yes, I suppose that's correct."

"Was the prisoner . . ." Aristide checked himself. "Forgive me, I mean no disrespect—but was the prisoner, in these cases, truly innocent of any crime against the nation—of any taint of treason or incivism?"

"Certainly," said Sauvade, raising a quizzical eyebrow. "I, at least, was convinced of it. Since the Law of Suspects, you see, it's become far too easy to denounce an enemy on all sorts of absurd charges."

"Such affairs, under normal circumstances, would never have come to trial?"

"Precisely. In all of those cases," he continued, after a swallow of coffee, "the law was clearly being abused, and there was no evidence beyond, perhaps, the dubious testimony of a witness who had a quarrel with the prisoner over some personal affair and who clearly wished him or her ill. A few of my colleagues on the jury are sometimes too dull-witted to discern a genuine case of incivism from a matter of private animosity. Antonelle and I are usually the voices of reason among them. Why do you ask?"

Aristide reached for his own cooling coffee, debating with himself how much to reveal. "I hope I can trust you, as a member of the Tribunal, to keep this to yourself."

"Word of honor."

"Have you heard the rumors of decapitated corpses—random victims of some deranged murderer—turning up in the streets?"

"I've heard a few whispers," Sauvade said. "Harmless beggars and laborers? It's abominable. You said you worked for the police; are you pursuing this murderer?"

Aristide nodded. "I've wondered if, perhaps, the killer is an unbalanced, fanatical patriot who believes that his victims have escaped revolutionary justice." Sauvade opened his mouth to speak but shook his head and gestured to Aristide to continue. "And that's why I came to you; I thought you might be able to tell me if, in fact, any of the murder victims had recently been tried at the Tribunal and released, and if you believed these prisoners were actually guilty or not. Do these names mean anything to you?"

He pushed his notebook across the table to Sauvade, who looked over the list of names. "Nothing," he said, stifling a yawn. "I don't recall any of these. I'm sorry I can't be of more help." He paused, staring at the notebook as he handed it back, and added abruptly, "These atrocities—the murder of innocent people for no reason whatsoever—this is appalling. It has to be stopped. And since none of these people have appeared before the Tribunal, I would suggest that these murders are the work of a madman or a royalist agitator, rather than a Jacobin fanatic."

"At this point," said Aristide, "I'm ready to consider almost anything. Thank you, and good night to you."

16

Distant shouts in the street below woke Aristide two days later, on the morning of the sixteenth of October. Grateful once again that his room was in the rear section of the house, and not directly on busy, clamorous Rue de la Huchette, he pulled himself up onto an elbow and listened, at last making out the word "guilty."

So Marie-Antoinette's trial was already over. Well, nobody would be surprised at the verdict.

He dressed, bought coffee and a roll from a stall on the street, and made his way to Rue Traversine, devouring the roll as he walked. François was waiting for him in the back room of the commissariat, leaning back with dusty boots on the table as he finished his own meager breakfast.

"I think we'd better find out anything we can about Echelard," Aristide told him, consulting his scribbled notes, "and get that out of the way. François, I don't fancy staring at the soles of your boots. What have you learned about the fourth victim—Noyelle?"

"Not much," said François, swinging his feet to the floor with a sheepish grin. "I went to his address, but they'd already cleared out his rooms and let them to someone else. All the porter could tell me was that he was an old retired army captain, a widower who lived alone on his pension in furnished rooms, with one servant. Fought in the Seven Years' War and the American war, without much distinction, I gather. No family but a middle-aged niece who he didn't see above once a year."

"What could the servant tell you?"

François shrugged and followed Aristide out of the commissariat. "He was long gone. I suppose, once he'd identified the body—it would've been easy enough to identify, because they told me Noyelle was missing a couple of fingers from some battle—once he'd done that, and collected the pay owed him from the niece, he was off to find another situation. Noyelle wasn't especially well-off, and the niece sent his traps to be sold as soon as they'd finished the inventory. She said he had a few friends of the sort you play chess with in cafés, and no enemies. You can talk to her yourself, if you want, but I doubt she can tell you anything useful."

"Perhaps another time. That line of inquiry doesn't seem very fruitful, does it? Well, come on."

The commissariat of the République section was just beyond the Madeleine; the quickest route was westward along busy Rue Honoré. Aristide had intended to flag down a fiacre, but the street was more than usually crowded with milling, chattering pedestrians of all sorts, from bourgeois in fashionable cutaways to chimney sweeps and herring women, who seemed in no hurry to be on their way. After staring about him for a moment, annoyed, he gestured François onward through the crush.

They heard the procession approaching behind them just as they passed Rue de Luxembourg. François, squinting in a sudden ray of pallid sunshine, peered over the heads of the crowd and elbowed Aristide.

"It's her."

"Who?"

"Antoinette, of course!"

Aristide would have walked on, but François hung back, going on tiptoes and stretching his neck for a better view. "They put her in a cart, just like everybody else!"

"Why shouldn't they?" a nearby artisan in smock and dirty leather apron demanded, overhearing. "If it's good enough for people like us, it's good enough for her."

The procession neared them. A dozen mounted gendarmes led the way and surrounded the horse and cart. Aristide recognized Sanson's tall, black-clad figure, standing in a corner of the cart; he had removed his hat, as had a tall young man who resembled him—Sanson the younger, Aristide guessed.

Marie-Antoinette sat staring straight ahead, rigid as a primitive statue, her back to the driver and the ambling horse. She seemed unaware of what was happening around her. The priest beside her bent toward her, reading from his prayer book, but she ignored him. Aristide could not decide whether she was numb to her surroundings or so terrified that she had been reduced to immobility.

He could not help muttering, "The poor creature." François shot him a glance.

"You think so?"

"Don't you?"

"No, I don't. To hell with her." He shrugged and stood glowering at the cart as it inched past. "That woman had the best of everything all her life, pampered and fussed over, never had to worry about one damned thing except shoving out babies and how her hair would be dressed for the next court ball; why should she deserve anyone's pity, now that we know she was a traitor in return for it all?"

"But to fall so far—" Aristide began.

"So what? So she's been locked up. Well, none of the precious royals lived so badly out there in the Temple tower, I hear. The grocer next door, he told me someone he knew sold the Commune supplies for them. They weren't living on bread and water, not on your life. Chicken every day! So just how, after a whole lifetime of luxury, does spending a year in a nice cozy prison, with your needs met, make you somebody to be pitied?"

"She's been in the Conciergerie since August," Aristide said, noting how pale and haggard Marie-Antoinette appeared. "I doubt it's as cozy as the Temple."

"So?" François glanced at him for an instant before turning his attention once more to the cart. "When you're the queen, or even the ex-queen," he continued, "even lodging in the darkest, dampest cell in the Conciergerie must be cushier than the life of your average peasant. They fed her, didn't they? Kept a fire going? Emptied her chamber pot? Gave her fresh body linen when she asked for it, I suppose? Well, Her Majesty still wasn't lifting a finger for any of it, was she?"

"I expect not," Aristide said, surprised by the normally easygoing François's vehemence.

"No, she was not. Don't make me laugh. What about the peasant who's never had one minute's taste of the luxuries that that useless bitch enjoyed all her spoiled, selfish life? She never spent fourteen hours a day out in the fields behind a plow, or wearing down her fingers in a weaver's workshop, all the while wiping the snotty noses of half a dozen brats, before she earned a few sous so she could eat a bit of moldy bread. Oh, dear, the insolent Jacobins didn't take their hats off in front of her, and called her rude names? Well, hard luck. I've had worse, and nobody shed any tears for me."

Aristide did not respond and François glared at the women standing near them, a few of whom were openly praying as they watched the cart's progress, before continuing.

"So now she's had it a bit rough, and they're going to cut her head off. What do I care? Why should anybody care? She still had it better all her life than everyone else." He spat on the ground and turned away as some of the crowd, pushing past the praying women, began yelling insults at the cart.

"Bitch!"

"They can't shorten you too soon!"

"Austrian spy!"

"Whore!"

"Down with Madame Veto!"

"Down with the Austro-bitch!"

One horseman in the escort spurred his mount toward the cart and its passenger. Astride his horse, he was on a level with Marie-Antoinette. Edging the horse as close to the cart railings as he dared, he leaned across the rail and shook a fist in her face.

"Austrian whore!"

The priest sprang to his feet and barked a sharp reprimand at the rider. Sanson, too, looked troubled and moved in front of Marie-Antoinette to shield her. Confronted with the unexpected tongue-lashing, the horseman drew back as some of the onlookers cheered him on, while others rebuked him for his cowardice and lack of courtesy toward a woman.

A second gendarme, gesturing to a few of his fellows, rode ahead and cleared the way so the cart could pass. A few shouts of "Death to Madame Veto!" rose from the crowd, but subsided as the procession turned left to continue down Rue de la Révolution toward the waiting guillotine.

"Come on," François said, tugging at Aristide's sleeve. "The crowds are only going to get thicker."

"Where?"

"At the square, of course!"

Aristide swallowed hard at that and stared at François for an instant. It had not occurred to him, despite his companion's bitterness, that he would be willing, even eager, to see the ceremony about to be carried out at the scaffold.

"No."

"Eh?"

"I'm not going," Aristide said. "Go ahead, if you must."

"Sure?"

"Yes."

"I'll meet you by Rue des Champs-Élysées, then, when it's over," François said, with a jerk of his thumb. "One street farther. Shouldn't be too long about it."

Aristide slouched westward until he reached the small street. Looking south, he could just see the fringes of the crowd that had gathered in the square beyond, reaching almost to the trees of the Champs-Élysées. The scaffold had to be just out of his line of sight. He leaned against the corner of the nearest house and stood brooding, arms folded and head down.

A common cart for the queen of France . . . the king, at least, rode to the

*scaffold in a closed carriage. A common cart for a queen, so the spectators
could spit at her.*

He caught a trace of movement from the corner of his eye. The
crowd in the square seemed to surge forward.

*My father, too, went to his death—that horrible death—in a manure
cart, with the crowd hooting and spitting at him. Crying foul names and
throwing filth at him as he knelt in his shirt, barefoot and bareheaded, to do
penance before the doors of the cathedral. Why should that woman deserve
better?*

*And the guillotine's lightning touch must be the soft kiss of an angel, when
compared with death on the wheel, broken and bleeding and gasping for
breath with lungs and limbs crushed beneath blows from an iron cudgel. . . .*

A few minutes later, as he stood scowling at the cobbles at his feet,
a faint cheer rose from the Place de la Révolution. He straightened and
glanced down the street, hoping François would not delay too long.

He appeared soon afterward, strolling along with hands in the pockets of his shabby redingote. "You ought to know I passed up more than
one offer of a free drink, in order to keep you happy," he told Aristide
when they were side by side again.

"I'm touched. Who was offering, for God's sake?"

"A couple of people wanted to go to the nearest wine shop and drink
to the Republic with everyone around them. But I said no, I needed to
meet a friend, and came away. Pretty damned decent of me, don't you
think?"

"Self-sacrificing," Aristide said. "Noble, even. Did the—did everything go smoothly?"

"Oh, yes, as smooth as they come. She stumbled a bit, but they
caught her, and the rest was bang, bang, swoosh, and it's over," François
continued, gesturing to illustrate the three swift movements of the
guillotine in action: the seesaw plank, on which the victim was strapped,
tilting to horizontal; the lunette clapping down to hold the victim's
neck in place; and the heavy blade falling in its grooves between the
twelve-foot uprights. "Don't you worry; I'm sure the Austrian never felt
a thing."

"Let's go," Aristide said. He turned to gesture François forward but paused as a horse and cart came abreast of them. Hamelin was sitting beside the driver. A few yards behind, a dozen ragged men and women trailed the cart, pointing.

"Is that—" He could just make out the long wicker basket within.

"Must be on their way to the cemetery."

As he watched, a woman ran a few paces ahead of the rest, dropped to her knees, and began patting at the cobblestones with a rag. The others caught up with her and huddled around her, jostling one another for space.

"They're wiping up the blood," François said, answering Aristide's unspoken question. "A bit of it must have dripped from the cart. They believe royal blood'll bring good luck."

"Old superstitions die hard," Aristide said absently, watching them. An acquaintance, back in January, had proudly displayed to all his friends a stained handkerchief that had wiped up a smear of Louis XVI's blood from the scaffold. A souvenir of a great moment in history, he had said; but even educated people, now and then, cherished objects with links to the sacred.

Old superstitions die hard.

He frowned. Where had he recently heard that phrase?

Without quite knowing why, he turned and followed the executioners' burial cart northward, across Rue du Faubourg Honoré. They would be going to the Madeleine cemetery, of course, to bury Marie-Antoinette in the same ground as her late husband. "Come on."

"Where are you going?" François said, trotting to keep up with him.

"Something that's bothering me—I can't yet work it out . . ."

"Eh?"

Sanson, Aristide realized ten minutes later, trailing the cart at a discreet distance as it neared the high, wooden cemetery gates on Rue d'Anjou. *Old superstitions die hard.* It was the master executioner who had said it, when referring to the ignorant folk, steeped in ancient, pagan peasant lore, who still believed that the fat of a hanged man could cure their ills. Would the fat of the guillotined do as well?

Something unexpectedly began to nag at him, a nebulous idea so unformed that he could make no sense of it except to know that he had to revisit the cemetery. He arrived at the gates, gesturing François along behind him, just as the cart disappeared beyond the wall and the guardsman on duty, turning, caught sight of him.

"No admittance here, citizens."

"I am an agent of the police," said Aristide, pulling out his police card. "I was here four days ago when the murdered man was found in the burial pit."

By God, yes, a murdered man found in the pit—

"The other guards will remember me. Or ask Citizen Hamelin. He knows me."

How on earth had the killer—or killers—dragged the dead weight of Echelard's corpse over the wall of this heavily guarded spot?

"I'm not allowed to leave my post, citizen."

"All right," Aristide said, "perhaps you recognize this handwriting?" He held up his pass to the prisons. "Or at least the names? Presumably you can read?"

The guardsman peered at it. "Yes, citizen. Sorry."

"As you can see, this document permits me to go inside any of the Republic's prisons and speak to any prisoner. Surely I may be allowed to pass the gates of a mere cemetery."

The guardsman hastily gestured him through. Aristide turned to François. "Go ahead and talk to Commissaire Conchon without me. Anything he can tell you about Echelard that might come in useful. And no stopping for drinks on the way!" he added, before turning and following the cart track.

The tumbrel stood well beyond the common burial pit. The long basket that contained Marie-Antoinette's remains lay, still shut, on the patchy grass beside a deep, open grave, but there were no gravediggers and no coffin in sight. Aristide surreptitiously glanced at his watch; it was entirely possible that, royal corpse or no, the sexton had gone off for his midday dinner break.

Neither of the Sansons was present, though Hamelin and a second assistant executioner stood conferring with a pair of men wearing sober suits and tricolor sashes, agents of the Revolutionary Tribunal or of the municipality, come to witness the burial of the former queen. They stiffened as they caught sight of Aristide, but Hamelin pointed to him and said something that evidently mollified them, for they shrugged and returned to their conversation.

He walked aimlessly on, unsure why he had felt compelled to return to that desolate acre of ground, circling the cemetery past the anonymous grave mounds along a path beaten down by countless burial processions. A few of the graves were fresh scars in the earth. The rest were sunken and overgrown with weeds and coarse grass, a bare handful marked with crude wooden crosses.

There was a clue there, he knew: something . . . something to do with his previous visit to the cemetery.

He could not grasp the idea that was teasing at him; it remained, like an elusive fly, maddeningly out of reach. At last he turned and tramped back to the gate.

François met him outside an eating-house on Rue de Suresne, a few houses down from the commissariat. "Isn't it time for a break?" he said, with a suggestive glance toward the noisy interior.

"What have you got about Echelard?" Aristide said, following him inside. He gestured François to a seat at one of the long tables, not too close to the fire or to other diners, and ordered bean soup from a sulky servant girl.

"Not a lot, but none of it good. The commissaire says he was a rascal and a drunk, and he'd sell his own grandmother for a bottle of brandy. He had his water cask, of course, which was a pretty steady income if you don't mind climbing four flights of stairs, with a bucket of water in each hand, twenty times a day, but he preferred easier ways of making a living."

"Any chance that those easier ways of making a living involved criminal activity?"

"Even money, I'd say," François said, seizing a bowl as the girl brought them a chipped earthenware tureen, and attacking the soup.

"What about criminal activity with a partner? Is it possible that a quarrel among thieves led to him being knifed?"

François shook his head, his mouth full. "Not likely," he said a moment later. "Conchon said Echelard worked alone when he was up to something. Didn't like to share."

Despite appearances, Aristide thought, as he served himself some soup, it looked more and more as if Pierre-Marie Echelard had been one more victim of the headsman.

So how much further did that get him?

17

Aristide paused for another visit at the Conciergerie the next morning, on his way to Rue Traversine, and found Mathieu and the others in good spirits, although Boyer-Fonfrède seemed more than usually subdued as they assembled around a table in his cell for a hand of cards. "It's Antoinette," he said, after a few minutes of Ducos's affable teasing. "I can't help thinking about her—about her trial, rather. It was so unnecessary."

"You think it was a foolish move, politically?" Aristide said. *So much for any real hope of peace with England. . . .*

He stared hard at his cards. They were from a new, patriotically republican pack, like those of the idlers who were forever playing in cafés or wine shops; in place of kings, queens, and knaves, the cards had figures representing winged Geniuses, classically robed Liberties, and virile but virtuous Equalities.

"Yes, and more than that," Boyer said. "Guillotining Antoinette is just a maneuver to pacify the sansculottes and make them forget that there's a war on and their bellies are empty. If the Jacobins can't manage to provide them with bread at two sous a pound—or any bread at all—at least they can keep the masses happy by chopping off the head of someone they hate."

"Well?" said Ducos. "I didn't think much of Toinette, either."

"Don't you see? You've got to admit that the sansculottes hate us almost as much as they hated her. Is chopping off *our* heads going to be the Jacobins' next attempt at keeping them happy?"

"Well, if it happens," said Mathieu, slapping down his cards and gathering up a handful of assignats, "you're going to go to Madame Guillotine a pauper, Boyer, because I'm going to win all you've got unless you pay attention."

"It's not a joking matter, Alexandre!"

"Isn't it? As far as I can tell, the whole thing's become a bitter joke."

"I don't mind dying for the Republic," Boyer began, "but—"

"Oh, come off it," said Mathieu. "Of course you'd mind dying for the Republic. We all have a strong objection to public execution when we're young, rich, healthy, clever, breathtakingly well educated, and—at least some of us—dazzlingly handsome. So don't pretend to be as noble as all that."

"As I was about to say," Boyer persisted, keeping his gaze on his cards, "I wouldn't mind dying if my death would somehow benefit the Republic . . . but dying simply to keep the rabble happy is something else again. I know we've made mistakes, but you can't say the Jacobins are doing much better than we were at keeping things from falling apart."

"But the difference is," said Aristide, as he tossed down two equalities, "that they're better at knowing what they want—and what the people want—from a republic."

Mathieu nodded. "Exactly. What did we want? Face it: We wanted a republic with ourselves, meaning the bourgeoisie, in charge."

"In other words," said Ducos, grimacing at a hopeless hand and dropping his cards, "the old regime, minus the king and aristocracy."

"Which is fine for the merchants and bankers," Mathieu continued, with a glance around the table, for he and his friends, save Aristide, were all sons of wealthy shipowners or importers. "They made even more money when the courtiers and their privileges weren't blocking their way."

"But the sansculottes," Aristide said, "who aren't stupid, have realized pretty quickly that a bourgeois republic isn't going to improve their lives one bit. No wonder they prefer the Jacobins, who are promising them all sorts of equality and prosperity, even if they never manage to provide it."

"You've put your finger on it there," said Ducos. "Perhaps you ought to go into politics yourself."

"Not on your life."

Mathieu snickered, with a glance about him at the narrow cell. "And end up here, with us?" He reached for the cards and began to deal. "Ravel's the smart one. He stays out of it. We've all read plenty of Roman history; we should have known that, in the end, the mob follows whichever demagogue promises the most bread and circuses."

"And when the Jacobins fail to deliver, and someone else promises them the moon, they'll turn on the Jacobins, I expect," said Aristide. "Too bad nobody ever learns from history."

"Well, we'll try our damnedest to avoid being thrown to the lions," Ducos began, but Mathieu slapped a hand down on the table.

"Enough of this dismal subject. Play."

"The commissaire's gone out," Inspector Chesnais told Aristide when he arrived at the commissariat. "A messenger was waiting here when he arrived at eight, and he went off right away with him. He left you this."

Aristide opened the note that Chesnais handed him, read the first line, and crumpled it in his fist, with a curse. One more murder for the tally—this one somewhere in the park of the Champs-Élysées.

The parkland extended a good half mile west of the Place de la Révolution and south to the Seine. There was no point in spending half an hour, at least, in a fiacre, in order to try to find Brasseur among several acres of meadows and groves. He trudged into the back room, settled himself at the table, and began to set his notes in order.

Brasseur returned at midday. Aristide, after sending a brief report off to Danton from the district post office, found him at his desk, pouring himself a glass of eau-de-vie.

"The same?"

Brasseur nodded. "The same. Throat cut, beheaded, lying in a pool of blood. They found the head hidden in some bushes about fifty feet away." He gulped down the brandy and slammed the glass onto his desk, with an oath. "How much more of this?"

Aristide remembered Mathieu's remark, that it was in the spirit of the times, but said nothing beyond, "Do they know who it was?"

"Some wretched boy-whore, about fifteen years old." The meadows of the Champs-Élysées, after dark, were almost as notorious for male prostitutes and covert homosexual encounters as were the gardens of the Luxembourg.

"A couple of the other queers found him around three in the morning. Nobody knew his real name, but they knew him, all right; he was one of the little catamites who cater to the perverts who like their boys dressed up as girls. He went by the tag 'Angélique.' One of them said he'd seen the boy going off with a customer an hour or two earlier. Same description as that *poule* from the Maison-Égalité gave you: tall, lean, black coat and hat. It was dark, of course, and no one saw much of his face."

He sighed and poured himself another brandy. "Well, there's nothing to be done. No clues anywhere, and we don't even know the boy's name; nor are we likely to learn it." The boy prostitutes who lurked in the parks were, like the street girls, the poorest of the poor, with no families, no resources, and often not even the money for a lice-ridden mattress for the night in a cheap lodging house. "No one'll be looking for him, the poor little rat."

"Random . . . it's got to be random," Aristide said, after some thought. "I can't imagine that any of these people knew each other, although perhaps Jumeau and Deverneuil might have been just barely on nodding terms at the Parlement—if a deputy royal prosecutor cared to condescend to a mere chief clerk. But the rest—they came from wildly different walks of life. I don't see how a mad patriot could have singled them out as enemies of the Republic. The only thing they share is the manner of their death."

"Which leads me to think that it's not a lunatic who's doing this, either," Brasseur mused. "I had an hour yesterday and I went to talk to a mad-doctor at the Bicêtre who, they say, is doing wonders with the patients. He told me that madmen who become violent, they often have the same story: that God or the saints told them to kill pederasts, or mountebanks, or Jews, or what have you. But this assortment of victims is so mad that it's sane, if you understand me."

"I think I do." Aristide glanced at his notes. "These victims are all so different that it looks as if the killer is choosing them carefully. A civil servant, a street peddler, a beggar, a retired army officer, a penniless bourgeoise turned prostitute, a water seller, a lawyer, a catamite . . . I think this headsman is sane, clever, and completely ruthless. So how do we catch him?"

"We wait," said Brasseur, "and we pray that he makes a mistake before he chops off too many more heads. What else can we do?"

Though he had managed a brief visit almost every morning or evening, Aristide had promised himself a full day with Mathieu and the other deputies from Bordeaux, in order to keep their spirits up. He spent Sunday in the prison with them, exchanging news, playing cards, discussing a certain friend's unfortunate tendency to throw away his money on greedy actresses—by tacit mutual consent, no one mentioned the Revolutionary Tribunal or the headsman—and sharing a lavish and excellent dinner that Mathieu and Ducos, as a surprise, had ordered in for the occasion from a nearby caterer. For a wealthy prisoner, he thought, as they finished the last of their third bottle of wine, life at the Conciergerie was not so bad.

He had just dressed on Monday morning, after returning home later than was usual, and was about to go out in search of a large portion of drinkable breakfast coffee when someone rapped at his door. He opened it to find Dautry, Brasseur's young secretary, outside.

"They've found another one," he announced, keeping his voice down, with a swift glance at the other doors on the landing. "The commissaire just got word of it, and sent me to fetch you. He'd meet you there, but a brawl in one of the brothels at the Palais-Égalité kept him up most of the night sorting it out, so he—"

"Wait a moment," Aristide said, raising a hand to stem the rush of words as he reached for his coat. "Slow down, Dautry! Where is it?"

"At the cemetery of St. Jean, a couple of streets from the City Hall. Patrol found the gate broken open and the corpse inside. Come on— I've a fiacre waiting below."

Aristide threw on his coat and followed Dautry down the three spiraling flights of stairs. Outside in the street, Dautry climbed into the waiting cab and gestured him inside. It was no more than a quarter hour's walk from Rue de la Huchette to the Hôtel de Ville, but time, he knew, could be precious.

The cemetery of St. Jean lay just east and north of the City Hall, half hidden amid the narrow streets of one of the oldest quarters of Paris, one of the few central, ancient cemeteries that had escaped the great clearances of the past decade. It lay dark and ignored amid a forest of dilapidated seven-story tenements that shut out the sun and turned blank faces to the dead. No building constructed within the past century and a half had been permitted windows on a side that overlooked consecrated ground; otherwise, the inhabitants were likely to consider the cemetery a convenient dumping spot for their chamber pots.

A few shabby passers-by stared incuriously at them as they arrived. Fiacres were rare in the quarter, once one left the immediate surroundings of the Hôtel de Ville.

A stocky, morose-looking man wearing a black suit and a tricolored sash approached him as he alighted. "You Brasseur?"

"I'm not Brasseur," Aristide said, extending his hand, "but I work with him. My name's Ravel."

"Commissaire Triboulet of the Maison-Commune section," the man said, without offering his hand. Even the innocuous term "Hôtel de Ville" smacked too much of the ancien régime, and soon after the fall of the monarchy the City Hall had officially become the Maison-Commune, or House of the Municipality, although only the most adamant patriots insisted upon using the cumbersome new name in everyday conversation.

"The body's that way," Triboulet continued, pointing past the gate from which a rusty, broken padlock hung. "Enjoy yourselves."

"Have you found the head?"

"No." He pulled out a grubby handkerchief and blew his nose before continuing. "Nice sort of killer you've got here. Glad I'm not the one looking for him."

"Have you or your men disturbed the corpse?"

Triboulet thrust the handkerchief back into a pocket. "Received orders, didn't I, from the Maison de Justice *and* the Maison-Commune? Any peculiar murders in my patch have to be reported at once to your Commissaire Brasseur, and nothing's to be interfered with. Well, I do as I'm told. And it didn't take a second look," he added, "to tell us that the fellow was beyond help. He's all yours." He pointed to the crudely carved, weatherbeaten wooden cross, twelve feet tall, that stood in the center of the cemetery. Something lay huddled, pale against dark earth and gray stone, at its base.

Aristide trod carefully across the patches of tough grass, recalling the first time he had encountered a murdered man in a cemetery. This graveyard was even drearier than the cemetery of St. André des Arts, where at least a few stone monuments to influential families of the past had broken the monotony of stony earth and tangled weeds. Here was nothing more than uneven, neglected ground that, across the centuries, had swallowed up twenty generations of the nameless poor, without a single visible tomb or marker, only the cross that loomed like a gallows over all.

The man lay prone, arms flung wide, one hand clutching at the cross's rough stone pedestal while the other clawed into the stony soil. The blood had fountained from the severed neck, drenched much of the linen shirt, and stained the gritty soil all around it a muddy red-brown.

"He couldn't have been outside during the night without even a coat," Dautry said, behind Aristide. He was keeping his distance from the corpse, Aristide guessed. "Look—over there." He darted forward, past the cross, bent, and returned with a bundle of crumpled fabric in his arms. "A coat, waistcoat, and cravat. And—look—there's his hat, over there."

Aristide shook out the coat. It was of dark red broadcloth, cut in a conservative style, but its wearer had embellished the lapel with a large rosette of tricolored ribbon. The old-fashioned three-cornered hat, too, bore a tricolored cockade. This victim was no counterrevolutionary, unless the man had attempted to make up for a royalist past with ostentatious displays of patriotism.

But why had he, like Deverneuil, been stripped of his coat, waistcoat, and cravat?

He gave the coat back to Dautry and turned his attention to the corpse. The backs of the hands, mottled and veined, betrayed the man's age. Gently he moved one arm back and forth, to see how far rigor had advanced.

The other hand came free of the soil at last. The man had clawed convulsively at the ground as he lay dying, digging his fingers deep into the stony dirt.

He examined the body again. Aside from the blood-soaked shirt, the man wore pale gray cotton corduroy knee breeches and high black boots.

"His watch is still here in the waistcoat pocket," Dautry said, feeling through the garments. "Robbery wasn't a motive. Though I can't find a pocket-book or any identity papers."

"Robbers don't take the time to behead their victims, Dautry—at least not in my experience." Aristide rose and turned to Triboulet, who was waiting just inside the gate, arms folded.

"Do you have more ethical vagrants in this part of town, Commissaire, than we do over by the Palais-Égalité?"

"What?"

"It looks as if nobody who was out in the streets at night noticed the broken lock and came inside to see what was up, or else this man's watch and boots would be missing, and probably most of his clothes. That rarely happens in the rest of Paris."

"Here?" Triboulet turned, spat on the ground, and advanced a few steps. "They bury criminals here. The locals don't come in, especially at night, no matter what. Think it's haunted, cursed, whatever you like.

Look, citizen, are you about done? My men've got more important things to do than hang about a burying ground all day."

"What about your police surgeon?"

"What about him? He'd take an hour to arrive, and I don't need a doctor to tell me that that man's dead. Just give the word and I'll have the body sent over to the Basse-Geôle."

"A few minutes more, Commissaire." Aristide stepped back from the corpse and surveyed the ground. Few footsteps were visible amid the weeds and stones, but he could discern two distinct sets of prints, both showing the broad heel of riding boots, which had been popular for informal dress among the middle and upper classes for more than a decade. One set clearly belonged to the corpse.

Swallowing his distaste, he knelt once again beside the corpse and examined what he could see of the stump of the neck beneath the thick crust of dried blood. The wound where the murderer had slashed the throat was invisible amid the ragged, unskillful hacking slices that had detached the head from the trunk.

He beckoned Dautry over and together they turned the corpse onto its back, which revealed nothing but a pair of muddy marks on the knees of the man's gray culotte.

"He was on his knees?" Dautry said. "Begging for his life?"

"Perhaps." Aristide gazed at the ground a moment longer, trying to imagine the scene. "Though the killer would have lost the advantage of surprise, wouldn't he?"

Something amid the grass reflected faintly in the pallid morning light as the sun, wreathed in clouds, crept above a nearby rooftop. Aristide leaned forward, probing with a finger.

"What's that?"

"Nothing—just some candle grease. Someone had a dark lantern, I suppose," Aristide added, with a glance upward at the high, windowless walls that surrounded the cemetery. The moon was just past full and would have given adequate light, though the houses would block most of it.

"I expect the lantern got knocked to the ground and spilled some melted tallow." He pulled out a handkerchief and wiped the grease off his fingertips before turning toward the gate. "Commissaire, we're done here. You can send the body to the morgue."

"A man," Aristide said an hour later at the Basse-Geôle. "That much is obvious, isn't it?"

Daude, peeling the blood-soaked shirt from the corpse, made no response to his feeble pleasantry.

First, identify him; that was essential to a murder investigation. When you knew who your victim was, you were on your way to knowing who might have killed him.

Usually.

"A man," he muttered, looking over the corpse, "of middle age or more, judging from his appearance . . . a man of easy circumstances, with a watch and good clothes."

"Dead eight or ten hours," said Daude. "Middle of the night. He's fairly stiff already."

"Yes. Let's see. Age, estimated somewhere between . . ."

"Fifty-five and seventy, I'd say."

"Middle height, approximately five feet seven or eight inches tall, give or take an inch, when his head was still attached. No hair or eye color to note, obviously, though the body hair is a graying medium brown. Medium-pale complexion, pockmarked but not badly, otherwise free of obvious disease, no syphilis sores and so on."

"My, my," said Daude, unbuttoning the man's culotte and pulling it deftly off, together with the underlinen. "This fellow's had an eventful life."

"Scars?"

"Here, and here: This on the upper arm looks like a bullet graze, and this," he continued, pointing to a puckered scar across the chest, "was some sort of glancing blow across the ribs. And I wouldn't be surprised if this slight crookedness in the leg is the result of a broken bone."

"A soldier?" Aristide said, examining the man's hand, which bore few calluses. "It would fit with the boots. Not a record-keeper or a professional man. There—see the little callus on the side of the middle finger of the right hand? Mine is far more pronounced than his, and yours must be, too, Daude, because you spend time taking notes and writing reports."

"One for every corpse that comes in, and full details on every stitch of the clothing," Daude said dolefully.

"And," Aristide continued, moving around the table and taking up the corpse's other hand, "there's a little scar on the side of the left forefinger, with a funny curve to it."

Daude pulled out a pair of spectacles and examined the hand. "I missed that. I regret the oversight. But if I may speculate, I should say that a penknife slipping at an oblique angle might have made this scar on his forefinger—while he was cutting a quill, perhaps."

"You'd agree, though, that he could have been a soldier?"

"Could be. It would account for the scars, and the broken leg might have come from a fall from a horse."

"An officer, then; a man of means. So there we have it: an ex-army officer—either bourgeois or noble—about sixty or sixty-five years old. And right-handed," Aristide added, with a sigh, "which leaves perhaps nine-tenths of the population of Paris."

"With a large mole at the base of his neck, near the left shoulder blade," Daude added, pointing to it. "The headsman just missed it. Well, I'll send word if someone turns up to identify him."

The Hôtel de Ville and cemetery of St. Jean were only a few minutes' walk from the morgue, and Aristide, as he left the Basse-Geôle, felt a sudden compulsion to return to the scene of the murder. He strode along Rue de la Tannerie, noticed out of the corner of his eye that workmen were constructing a scaffold in the Place de Grève for an impending execution, and hurried on. Lately the growing number of those condemned for political crimes, and executed at the Place de la Révolution, had overshadowed the more commonplace death sentences that were passed, from time to time, at the criminal court. The average murderer or bandit, however, was still routinely dispatched—just as criminals, great and small, had been for almost five centuries—at the Grève, in front of the City Hall.

The cemetery of St. Jean was bleak even in the full light of midday. The gate hung open; evidently the police or section committee had not thought it imperative to replace the broken padlock. The tall tenements loomed above him, the blank walls cheerless.

Someone had kicked loose dirt over the bloody patch at the base of the cross, but otherwise all remained unchanged since that morning. He gazed around him, frowning, wondering what it was that was nagging at him.

"The locals don't come in here," the commissaire had said. But someone had; a murderer, and also his victim.

He was groping at the same elusive feeling, he realized a moment later, that had teased him not long ago, when—by the saints, that was it—when he had stood in another cemetery. An idea, an instinct, that could not quite form itself into a theory, but which, he sensed, was significant. Something he had seen or heard, while examining the burial pit where Echelard's body had lain.

A murderer had come there, too, and disposed of his victim's corpse.

But if today's victim, he realized, like Désirée Marquette, like Deverneuil, had been murdered where his corpse was found, then why not Echelard? They had found no blood-soaked patch of ground beside the burial pit or anywhere around it—though that might be explained by the rain. But if Echelard had been murdered within the cemetery walls, then the pair of them, murderer and victim—unwitting accomplice? Struggling prisoner? Surely not!—had somehow crept inside, past the guards, without arousing the least notice or suspicion. And surely no one would have risked detection, at that heavily guarded enclosure, by doing something as irrational as drawing attention to himself by bringing his living victim there to be killed.

So why and how, once again, had the murderer, evidently at great effort and inconvenience, taken the time to transport a body, climb a wall, and dump the corpse in the cemetery of the Madeleine?

18

He strode for the third time into the Madeleine cemetery, wondering if he had come halfway across Paris on a wild-goose chase, and made a slow circuit of the ground, past the mass burial pit, past the older, individual graves, and finally past the spot, scattered with fallen leaves and twigs to disguise it, where they had buried Marie-Antoinette. The revolutionary authorities were determined, it seemed, to make the last king and queen of France disappear without a trace; republicans would not want the two royal graves to become sites of pilgrimage.

At last, still baffled, and frustrated at his own obtuseness, he turned back. Louis XVI, he thought, with a glance around him as he approached the gate, lay somewhere quite near him, in this lonely spot where no crosses or monuments stood.

Now how had he known that?

He stopped short, searching his memory. He had not seen the grave himself; that was certain. But somehow, someone . . . someone during their first visit—

That was it.

Hamelin had been speaking of the king's burial. *"We did have a coffin for Capet, nailed down well and buried deep . . ."*

And Hamelin had looked away, a quick glance toward the gate and the western wall of the cemetery, the sort of involuntary glance you made, without even realizing it, at something you were talking about. A quick glance toward the site of the king's anonymous grave, the site kept as secret as possible and known to no one but a few officials and executioners who had been present, and the men who had dug the grave and laid the coffin and scattered quicklime all around it.

"*. . . nailed down well and buried deep, so nobody can get to it, royalists and such hoping to get relics.*"

Louis XVI undoubtedly lay within a few yards of where he stood. The summer's weeds and rank wild grass would have covered the spot by now, of course, hiding the signs of disturbed earth to all but the most diligent searchers. But when Louis had lost his head, back in January, it would have been a raw wound in the sparse, stony turf.

The wall was only a dozen feet away. He stared at the gate, thinking again how difficult it would be to climb the wall unnoticed while burdened with a corpse.

How the devil had someone dumped Echelard's corpse?

Deverneuil's body, too, had been heaved over a nearby parapet. But the parapet edging the Bastille's dry moat had been only waist high. He stood close to the cemetery wall and stretched up an arm; it was at least a foot higher than his fingertips could reach, almost nine feet. The headsman had somehow managed, by himself—for two or more would surely have left obvious traces—to drag that deadweight up to the top of the wall and drop it over without leaving any marks in the grass and mud below.

Which is impossible.

He glanced about him. Above him stretched an unbroken expanse of sunless sky. No trees next to the wall to help you over; only a house southward on Rue d'Anjou, a street or two away at least, rooftop and garret windows clearly visible in the near distance.

No windows had directly overlooked the enclosure of St. Jean, but—

Windows?

From which an observer might have witnessed anything occurring here in the cemetery, from a secret royal burial to a killer dumping a corpse in the feeble moonlight?

"I wonder," he murmured.

The house he had seen from the cemetery was the northernmost of the row of handsome stone town houses on Rue d'Anjou. Neither the stench of ordure that tainted the atmosphere downwind from the open sewer at nearby Rue de l'Égout, nor the proximity of St. Lazare prison and the squalid, outlying district of La Petite Pologne to the north, however, had prevented prosperous aristocrats and bourgeois from building new houses all along the southern stretch of Rue d'Anjou between Rue du Faubourg Honoré and the parish cemetery.

A youthful footman, smart but not ostentatious in fawn-colored coat and neatly clubbed hair, answered the front door. "Monsieur?"

"I am an agent of the police; my name is Ravel," Aristide said, holding up his card. "Whose house is this?"

"This is the house of Maître Desclozeaux."

"Maître" was a title assumed by all lawyers, whether advocates or notaries, upon taking their license. A lawyer who was wealthy enough to own a town house, Aristide thought, and who still used "monsieur" rather than "citizen," at least within his own household, probably tended toward royalism. And a royalist whose upper windows overlooked the cemetery where the king had been buried would undoubtedly have taken advantage of the fact.

"What are the dormer windows in the attics that look northward toward the cemetery?"

The footman stared at him. "Monsieur?"

"This is a police matter. What are the windows that overlook the parish cemetery from the fourth floor?"

"That would be the maids' quarters," the footman said, after a little thought. "At least, I think so. Madame's strict about keeping men and women servants separate."

"I wish to speak with Maître Desclozeaux at once."

The footman began to protest that his master was not at home.

Aristide held up his police card again, repeating, "At *once*," and the footman yielded.

"This way, monsieur."

He led Aristide up two spiraling flights of stairs. Aristide took stock of his surroundings as he passed. What he could see of the furniture was at least three decades old, in the Louis XV style, and while of good quality, it seemed a trifle shabby, as did the Chinese-style wallpaper. He saw no other servants except for a manservant and middle-aged chambermaid. Desclozeaux, he suspected, preferred to live modestly, without undue display of wealth, during such uncertain times.

The footman stopped at a door on the second floor. "A visitor, monsieur," he said, opening the door for Aristide. "He insists upon seeing you."

"No matter, Baptiste," said the middle-aged man seated at a writing-desk, his back to the door. "You may go." He turned toward Aristide and rose to his feet, straightening his neat brown frock coat. "Monsieur? How may—ah!" Taking a step forward, he thrust out a hand in welcome. "I thought you might come again. I fear I have nothing more to tell you about their Majesties' resting places, but should you need assistance, money . . ."

For an instant Aristide wondered why Desclozeaux was addressing him as if they had met before. A moment later, with a sudden flash of understanding, he remembered that the woman at the Palais-Égalité, the *poule* who had seen Désirée Marquette go off with a stranger, had mentioned the superficial resemblance between the elusive killer and himself.

The room looked north and was spacious but dimly lit, and the lawyer had been sitting facing the window. A figure in the doorway would have been little more than a shadow to him, at least for a moment or two: easy enough to make a mistake at one's first glimpse of a visitor. And that, he realized, made all the difference: Desclozeaux had indeed seen the killer, but not from the height of his fourth-floor attics; he had seen him face-to-face, spoken to him, perhaps here in this very room.

"The man you were expecting looks rather like me, doesn't he?" Aristide said, moving forward into the light. "Tall, wearing dark clothes?"

"Forgive me," Desclozeaux said hastily. "I see I was mistaken. Who are you, mons—citizen—and how may I be of service to you?"

"Police," Aristide said, holding up his card once again.

"P-police?"

"I have some questions for you. Shall we sit down?" Forging relentlessly ahead, he decided, as if the full weight of police authority were behind him, was the best way to wrest information from a man who was likely to be uncooperative.

"Now," he continued, when Desclozeaux had warily gestured him to an armchair, "the man you expected to see, the man who resembles me, he visited you not long ago, didn't he? Right after the queen's execution, on the sixteenth or seventeenth of this month. And before that, a few weeks ago—late September, say? The first time he visited you he gambled on his instincts," he went on, before the lawyer could answer. "I think he guessed, as I did, from the look of your fine house, that you had royalist sympathies. He was desperate to pay homage to his king, and so he took a chance and asked you whether or not you knew where the king was buried. Yes?"

"I beg your pardon?"

"Please, Maître, let's not deny the obvious. Yours is the northernmost house on the street that's more than two stories high. I think it's possible—probable, in fact—that, back in January, you watched the burial cart carrying the king's remains go past your front door toward the cemetery. Then you hurried upstairs to the attics and looked out a window, and you saw where they were burying him. Being a loyal subject, and suspecting that the gravesite would be kept a closely guarded secret, you took care to make a note of the exact location."

Desclozeaux, like any good lawyer, was expert at concealing his reactions. The barest hint of unease flickered across his face.

"It's no crime to look out a window."

"None at all," Aristide agreed. "But this man who called on you back in September, this stranger, he told you enough to convince you that he was a faithful royalist, just like you, and he said he wished to pray at the king's grave. And you told him where it was. Am I right?"

"I saw no harm in it," he said, expressionless.

"You didn't fear he'd try to dig up the coffin in search of relics?"

"One man, in a spot so well guarded? No. They patrol the cemetery, and the grave was very, very deep; he would have been caught long before he succeeded. Besides, he spoke like a gentleman of high birth. He spoke with such sincere emotion, I felt sure he was speaking the truth, that he wanted to pray at His Majesty's grave and that was all."

"And then he returned on the day they executed the queen, because I'm sure you took care to note that burial site, also," Aristide said, with a glance out the study window. From the second floor, he could see no more than a stretch of the cemetery wall, but he could imagine the tiny figures of a couple of gravediggers, shoveling earth into the hole, and Hamelin standing at one side with the officials. "He returned to ask you where her grave was, didn't he? I don't suppose he gave you his name," he continued, without much hope. That would have been too easy.

"No. He didn't offer it and I didn't ask. But you're mistaken about one thing, citizen," Desclozeaux added. "He first approached me only ten or twelve days ago, not at the end of September."

"Ten or twelve days ago? You're sure?"

"Yes. He accosted us outside my front door, when my wife and I were alighting from a fiacre; he must have been waiting for me. It was certainly no more than a fortnight ago at most."

"Could it have been," Aristide said, consulting his notes, "the ninth or tenth of October?"

"Why, yes," Desclozeaux said, after a moment's reflection. "Yes. It was the tenth, Thursday."

"Certain?"

"Yes. I reserve Thursdays for social engagements. It was Thursday and we had been dining with friends in Auteuil, and he approached me when we arrived home in the evening, after dark. It was beginning to rain and I wanted only to get inside, but he was most insistent."

The tenth of October—the day before the murdered man had been found in the Madeleine cemetery. It had to fit.

"And he returned on the sixteenth, didn't he?" Aristide went on, trying to keep the excitement from his voice. "He came back on the night of the sixteenth, after the queen's execution, counting on your having observed that burial as well. And you told him what you'd seen, of course," he added, as Desclozeaux nodded. "Tell me, did he say anything to you—something about returning to pray at the graves, for instance? Did he give any indication that he intended to make it a regular pilgrimage?"

The lawyer compressed his lips. "Is this persecution necessary? Can a man no longer pray at a graveside without being arrested for treason?"

"If it were nothing more than a matter of simple royalism," Aristide said, "I wouldn't be wasting your time. But this man is a killer." He went on before Desclozeaux could protest. "He's murdering innocent citizens in order to dishonor the Republic. Is that the way you want to see the monarchy restored?"

Desclozeaux shook his head. "I can scarcely believe it."

"Have you heard the rumors of decapitated corpses turning up in the streets?"

"I—I suppose so, but really—"

"They're true. And your man, your mysterious stranger, is the one doing it."

"He? But he was a gentleman—an officer in the king's army, I'd guess, by his bearing. Such a man—"

"Such a man," Aristide interrupted him, "if he's an army officer, knows how to kill, when necessary. Such a man, hardened on the battlefield, also has the nerve and the stomach for killing, and the passionate devotion to the royal family that will drive him to committing such acts. Believe it, citizen."

"But—"

"You're an advocate; did you plead before the Parlement?"

"Yes, once or twice, but I don't see—"

"Did you ever know a man named Jumeau, chief clerk to the Grand' Chambre at the Parlement?"

"Yes, but—"

"Like him? Was he a decent sort of man?"

"Yes, he—"

"This man murdered Jumeau. And at least eight other people, including some with royalist sympathies as sincere as yours—the deputy prosecutor Deverneuil d'Estauran, for one. Murdered them at random, for no other reason than to stir up trouble and make Paris look like a den of vicious brigands. He hacked off their heads and left their corpses lying in the streets, in the muck. No matter how much you may weep for Louis XVI, is that the man you want championing his cause?"

"Gracious God," Desclozeaux said at last, making the sign of the cross. "I had no idea. . . . Yes. He did say something about revisiting the site."

"He's a royalist agent," Aristide declared, bursting into Brasseur's office forty minutes later. "No doubt about it. And we're going to trap him. Tonight, tomorrow, sometime soon."

"Eh? What's going on?"

"Our killer is a royalist, probably an émigré spy, one of Provence's men." Aristide thrust the door shut behind him and bent over Brasseur's desk. "He's a royalist spy, Brasseur."

"How'd you figure that?" said Brasseur. He rose, pushing his papers aside, and beckoned Dautry into the office from his own tiny room beyond.

"Ever since Echelard's body turned up in the cemetery," Aristide said, following him, too excited to keep still, "I've been trying to work out how on earth the killer got his corpse inside. It wasn't through the gate. There are too many guards and patrols about; you might climb the wall and get away with it unnoticed, if you were quick and careful, but imagine trying to drag the corpse of a full-grown man over it without attracting any attention! And I couldn't find any marks or smears of blood on the wall, or any cart tracks or hoofmarks outside."

"Two men, carrying it between them?" Brasseur said, turning to face him. "We thought—"

"Two men working together would have left more footmarks, crushed the grass, probably made more noise. It's impossible, when you think about it. No way to get the corpse in without being caught, and not even a way to get the corpse to the cemetery."

"So how'd he do it, then?"

"He didn't do it at all. Echelard got into the cemetery by himself, on his own two feet. It's the only solution that makes any sense."

"Accompanying the killer, you mean? But why would he—"

"No, no, no. That's where I went wrong. They came in separately." Brasseur and Dautry both looked blank and Aristide threw himself into a chair and continued. "Echelard had a bad reputation in that part of Paris. Remember? According to the local commissaire, he was a worthless scoundrel—a drunken layabout at the best of times, and a petty thief at the worst, when he'd drunk up whatever honest earnings he might have had. Just the sort of man to turn grave robber, to creep into a cemetery with the idea of stealing relics in order to make a profit from them."

"You think he wanted to dig up Fat Louis?" Dautry said, with a derisive snort.

"He probably wasn't that ambitious, but ignorant folk still believe that the blood and bones of executed men bring good luck. Perhaps he was just trying to take a bit of hair or some bloody rags from the open pit. In any case, he must have climbed the wall in the middle of the night—he had a tinderbox in his pocket, I saw it, and I expect he had a dark lantern with him that the killer took away. And once inside the cemetery, he encountered our royalist agent."

"But what was the other fellow doing in the cemetery?" Brasseur demanded.

"Making a clandestine pilgrimage, of course. Just a few hours previously, he'd been told the exact site of Louis's grave—I have a witness. I think one of them stumbled over the other, inside the cemetery, and the royalist, guessing what sort of man Echelard was, and that he might have intended to desecrate the king's grave, promptly killed him."

Dautry snapped his fingers. "That's why he was knifed, and none of the others were! It was an unplanned murder. The killer wasn't sneaking up behind this one or luring him off into a dark alley with some trumped-up story; he was struggling with him."

"Yes. But that didn't prevent our royalist from taking his opportunity to hack this corpse's head off, just like all the others."

"In the cemetery?" said Brasseur. "Wouldn't we have found some traces of that?"

"He was lucky; don't forget, it rained that night and the next day. Remember the puddles? I almost slipped once or twice on the wet grass. The pool of blood must have washed away, and the rain would have obscured most signs of a struggle." Aristide gazed from Brasseur to Dautry and back. "You see, don't you? All but one of the other victims, their heads were found well away from the bodies or never found at all. But Echelard's head was merely shoved into a corner of the burial pit, under another corpse, and covered with some quicklime and sacking. It was a spur-of-the-moment murder, done in haste."

"And you think he'll be back?"

"From all the evidence, this man is a fanatical monarchist. He'll come back at regular intervals to pray at both royal graves, or I'll eat my hat."

"It's just past the full moon," Dautry said. "Would he dare sneak in on a moonlit night?"

"If it was up to me," Brasseur mused, "I think I'd rather risk the moonlight than take the greater risk of bringing a light with me. The glow from a lantern's too noticeable."

Aristide nodded. "But it'll be soon, no matter what. Brasseur, you need to get together with Commissaire Conchon right away, and collect a party of half a dozen well-armed soldiers or gendarmes, and get them over there at least an hour before sundown. Be prepared to wait out the night and to return every night until you capture him."

"No fear," Brasseur said, returning to his chair and reaching for pen and paper. "We can't wait for him right at either grave, I suppose, even if I knew where they were—the bureaucrats would have fits if so many people learned about that—but we'll need to keep under cover nearby, where we can see him when he shows up. Dautry, have someone requisition an old cart, and take it over there now and leave it to one side—maybe with a broken wheel, that'll be convincing. Make it look as if the executioners had left it behind. That'll be a good enough hiding place." He turned again to Aristide. "Good work, Ravel. Don't worry; we'll get him."

19

Brasseur, red-eyed and irritable after two fruitless nights spent lurking behind a wagon in a damp cemetery, thrust a sheet of paper at Aristide when he stopped in at Rue Traversine on Wednesday morning. "Here."

Aristide glanced over the paper. "What's this?"

"Didier and François went around to a dozen sections yesterday and talked to the local police. So far, we've two men of the right age and social position who went missing during the past few days, and who might be the corpse from the St. Jean cemetery: Charles-Auguste Hanaud, speculator in the grain trade, of Rue d'Antin, Section de Le Peletier; and César Rainneville, man of property, of No. 16, Rue de Seine, Section de l'Unité, over on the Left Bank." He paused as Aristide finished scrawling down the names and addresses in his notebook. "But since neither of these men was from my section, I can't question the relatives for you without bringing the local commissaire into it. You'll do better if you inquire as a private citizen."

Rue d'Antin was near the Place des Piques, not far from Brasseur's headquarters, though in a section to the north. A few questions located the residence of Monsieur Hanaud, where a grim, elderly maidservant, after a suspicious stare, ushered Aristide into an ill-lit, overfurnished parlor and the presence of an even grimmer lady of sixty, in gray satin and a towering bonnet. Madame Hanaud was not inclined to be cooperative.

"Police?" she snapped, after he had introduced himself and shown her the card that identified him as an authorized agent of the police. "Have you found my husband, then?"

"It's possible," he began, but she cut him off.

"And which harlots was he wasting his money on this time, pray?"

"I beg your pardon?"

"Whores, monsieur. My husband is an incorrigible *débauché*. It's not uncommon for him to disappear for two or three days and return with the stink of the brothel on him. But after five days, I sent my maid to the commissaire to report him missing. Well? Where was he?"

"Citizeness," said Aristide, "locating straying husbands in brothels is not my business. What I am here for is to identify a dead man who was found in strange circumstances. Now, if you please, describe Citizen Hanaud."

"Describe him?"

"Is he stout or thin, fair or dark? Does he have any scars or moles?"

"His hair, what's left of it," said the lady, "is gray but once was a light brown, I suppose. He is of a medium build and is heavily pockmarked. Will that do?"

He did not need to glance at his notes; the unidentified corpse had borne only a few smallpox scars. "Yes, thank you; and I'm sure you'll be glad to know that the dead man who concerns me is not your husband."

She bade him farewell with a curt "Good day" and he left the apartment with the suspicion that Monsieur Hanaud had finally and understandably decamped with a sympathetic mistress.

No. 16, Rue de Seine proved to be a substantial private house, not large or imposing enough to be called a *hôtel particulier*, but the home of a person of means. An ancient manservant admitted Aristide and led him to an immaculate salon in which two women sat sewing beside a small fire.

"The police!" the elder of the two women exclaimed, when the servant had announced Aristide and retreated. She dropped her sewing on a footstool and rose to her feet. "Is it about Father?"

"You're Citizen Rainneville's daughter?" Aristide inquired. The woman who had spoken seemed about thirty-five and would have been attractive, he thought, if she smiled, though lines of bitterness or discontent were deeply etched from her nostrils to the corners of her mouth. The younger woman was perhaps half a dozen years her junior. Both wore their hair pinned beneath muslin caps, without powder or pomade, and were dressed in dowdy, well-worn calico gowns that bore no hint of the current fashions.

"I am Geneviève Rainneville and this is my sister, Lucienne. *Is* this about Father?"

"That's not certain—"

"Was he arrested?" Geneviève demanded. "Where is he? Why haven't we received any message from him? Won't they let us bring him some necessities?"

She seemed to be a levelheaded sort of woman, not one who would become hysterical and faint; Aristide chose to speak plainly. "A dead man has been found who may be Citizen Rainneville."

"Dead!" she echoed him. "How? That can't be right. His health is excellent."

"This man was murdered, citizeness."

They stared at him. "Oh, no," said Lucienne. "You must be mistaken. Why would anyone want to murder Father?"

"I can think of a few reasons," Geneviève snapped. Aristide glanced at her.

"Citizeness?"

"I exaggerate," she said coolly. "Please go on."

"Did your father have any noticeable scars, warts, or birthmarks?"

"Scars?" Geneviève echoed him. "I . . . he's sixty-six; of course he has plenty of age spots and freckles, but that's not what you mean, is it? Though he has a large mole or wart on his neck, on the left side," she added, after a little thought. "A broad, round, brown one, about half an inch across, toward the shoulder. You can't see it if he's wearing a cravat."

"He was a soldier for some time, an officer," said Lucienne. "He spoke of having some battle scars, though I wouldn't know where he bore them."

"A straight scar on his upper right arm," Geneviève said quickly, "and a narrow one on his chest. And he'd broken his leg once. The left one. He walked with just the slightest limp. Will that do?"

Aristide glanced at the copy of Daude's report that he had stuffed between the pages of his notebook. *Identifying marks: large dark brown mole on left side of neck, near shoulder blade; possible scar of bullet graze on upper right arm; narrow, glancing scar across breast; evidence of old break in left leg.*

"I fear I have bad news for you," he began. "I fear the dead man had the same scars, and the same mole on his neck—"

"Oh, God." She pressed her fist to her mouth and hid her face for a moment, bending her head, though she remained silent and still. Aristide looked away at the pair of family portraits that hung between the windows. The man—Rainneville himself, twenty or thirty years ago, he guessed, estimating the decade from the style of the clothing and wig—seemed proud and forceful, with something ruthless about the mouth. The woman, though possessed of a fragile prettiness, looked colorless and passive in comparison. Lucienne, he saw, strongly resembled her, though she had inherited a hint of her father's vigor as well.

"If you wish, citizenesses," he began, "I can return later; I don't wish to intrude upon your grief."

"Our grief!" Geneviève exclaimed, looking up again, with a harsh edge to her voice. She paused, with a sigh. "Citizen . . . Ravel, is it? You may as well know right now that neither my sister nor I will grieve for our father. In truth, it's a relief to know that he's dead."

"A relief—"

"He was a selfish beast. Tightfisted and selfish in everything."

"A self-serving, unfeeling man," Lucienne broke in, "who refused to allow either of us to marry or even to have any intimate friends, because he preferred to keep us at home, waiting on him. Do you blame us for not shedding any tears?"

An instant later, contradicting her words, she burst into tears and fled the room. Aristide was left alone with Geneviève, who drew a deep breath and gestured to a chair. "Will you sit down . . . and will you take some coffee?" she demanded, an instant later. "I feel the need of some."

"Your sister—" Aristide began, but Geneviève shook her head.

"Best leave her to herself."

"Shouldn't you at least send her maid to her?"

"We have no lady's maid."

Aristide raised an eyebrow at that, for rarely did a prosperous bourgeois or petty noble household not have at least one maid skilled in needlework and other feminine arts who attended the women of the house.

"Only a decrepit housemaid," she continued, "who's been with us for about a hundred years. She wouldn't be of much use in a crisis." She crossed the room to tug at a bell rope and returned to the sofa on which she had been sitting when he had first entered the salon. Her sewing—a much-mended man's shirt—was still lying on the footstool where she had dropped it. As if in a trance, she bent, picked it up, stood staring at it for a moment, and then, with a quick, decisive gesture, flung it into the fire, where it lay crumpled and blackening in the flames.

"I hated my father," she said, expressionless, turning to Aristide. "We both did. I expect that makes us look suspicious. How did he die?"

"I can't talk about that."

The elderly maid appeared in the doorway and Geneviève turned from him to order a pot of strong coffee. "Will the police suspect my sister and me of murdering him?" she said, when the maid had gone.

"At present, it's unlikely." He could think of few things less likely, in fact, than those two spinsters setting out in the middle of the night to murder and decapitate their father, when a royalist spy seemed a much better candidate for murderer.

"Will they have to go through all of my father's papers and personal effects?"

"I expect they may. It's routine. Why?"

"Because I never want to see anything of his again, ever. I'd like to take down that portrait on the wall behind you, right now, and throw it on the fire. And send the servants upstairs to his dressing room with orders to clear out every stitch of his clothing and burn it. Or at least to give it away to the poor," she added, with a wry twist of her lips at her own vehemence. "And then . . ." Her expression grew wistful, softened a little, and Aristide thought he could sense the traces of a gentle, smiling woman beneath her brusque manner. "Then I'm going to engage a maid for each of us, and call in the nearest dressmaker. Perhaps it's not too late to have lives of our own. Lucienne might even marry."

"Are you and your sister Citizen Rainneville's only heirs?" Aristide inquired.

"Yes."

"Did he have much to leave?"

She nodded. "You wouldn't think it to look at us, or at this household, but he had plenty of money, though we never had one thing that he hadn't approved first. Not a new pair of shoes, not a handkerchief. And he would tell us, when we protested, that we were grown women and we could leave whenever we wished, but that we would leave with nothing but the clothes on our backs." She paused, clenching her fists within the folds of her skirt. "I think he was the most selfish person I've ever known. He wanted attention paid him, and slavish devotion—always— and cared nothing for what anyone else wanted, or for anyone else's feelings. Do you blame me for hating him?"

Aristide shook his head, not knowing what to say. "You'd better come to the Châtelet with me now to identify him," he told her at last, "and get it over with. It's a formality, nothing more."

She answered his routine questions calmly. The citizen she was coming in to identify was Anne-François-César Rainneville, formerly de Rainneville, age sixty-six, man of property and retired lieutenant colonel in the army, born at Coucy-le-Château, near Laon.

"And yourself, citizeness?"

"Marie-Geneviève Rainneville, his elder daughter, age thirty-six, spinster."

"That's enough." He pocketed the notebook and rose to his feet. "Shall we go?"

Daude, he saw, had had the presence of mind to drape the headless corpse in more than the usual sheet. Aristide suspected that he had placed a cushion or a stuffed sack beside the stump of the neck, in order to give the illusion of a head. As Geneviève approached, Daude lifted away a corner of the sheet.

"Citizeness, if you'd be so good . . . hands are more distinctive than we realize. Do you recognize this man's hands?"

She gazed at them a moment. "Yes, I think so. Yes. There's the little triangle of moles on his wrist, and the scar on his forefinger where he cut himself trimming a quill."

"And these?" Daude twitched away other portions of the sheet, just enough to reveal the bullet scar on the arm and the mole on the neck.

"Yes," she said. "I'd know those anywhere." She turned to Aristide. "I can't see his face?"

"It was . . . disfigured," he said, after exchanging glances with Daude and Bouille. "It's better you don't see it."

Geneviève remained icily calm through the rest of the formalities. Only when he had led her back upstairs to the passage beneath the Châtelet, where the elderly maid, Bertrande, was waiting, did she pale and reach for the wall for support. Bertrande, with Aristide's help, managed to guide her out of the fortress toward the embankment and the fresher air at the river's edge.

"I'm quite well," she declared, after a moment and several deep breaths. "In fact, I've never been better."

"They'll inform you when the citizen's body has been released," he told her, "after they're done examining it. You can claim it for burial then."

"Do you think I care?" she said, turning from him to look out over the water, where a barge loaded with firewood and bales of hay was floating past. "He can go to the common pits, and good riddance. Lucienne and I are free now."

After sending Geneviève and her maid home in a fiacre, he walked westward, the length of the Île de la Cité, to clear the lingering stink of the Basse-Geôle from his senses. By the time he reached the Pont-Neuf, it was well past noon and he had regained his appetite. Michalet's was nearby and was always reliable for a solid dinner.

He was finishing his meal when he noticed the executioner Hamelin, two tables away, once again sitting opposite Sauvade. The two were talking and Sauvade refilled Hamelin's glass from time to time. A thought occurring to him, Aristide waited until Hamelin had reluctantly taken his leave, and approached Sauvade.

"Do you have a moment, citizen?"

"Of course."

"I asked you last week if you recognized any of the names I showed you. What about the name Rainneville?"

"Rainneville?" Sauvade echoed him, frowning.

"Our latest victim, it seems. Murdered two days ago."

"Wait a moment. Rainneville. That rings a bell. A Rainneville did come before the Tribunal two or three weeks ago." He snapped his fingers and looked up at Aristide. "And, by God, we acquitted him. I remember him now. He'd been arrested for incivism on the denunciation of a single citizen, who, it was obvious in court, held some private grudge. I made it clear to the others that the man had been falsely and maliciously denounced and ought to be set free."

"We're talking about the same man? A retired army officer of about sixty-five?"

"Yes, I imagine so."

"Then why the devil," Aristide said, half to himself, "didn't his daughters, when I questioned them this morning, mention the fact?"

Sauvade shrugged. "Some people prefer to keep such matters quiet. Being arrested on suspicion of incivism or counterrevolution, even if you're acquitted, is hardly a recommendation. And you can easily be rearrested, you know."

"You're probably right," said Aristide, though he was unable to dispel the feeling that something was not as it should be.

20

Geneviève, still alone in the salon, received him with surprise and not a little wariness.

"I learned an hour ago, after I'd questioned you," he said, watching her, "that Citizen Rainneville had recently been tried at the Revolutionary Tribunal. And I wonder why you didn't see fit to mention that to me?"

A faint blush crept into her pale cheeks, but she remained composed. "I didn't think it was relevant."

"This is a case of murder. Everything is relevant."

"Very well, then," she said after a moment's pause. She shivered and drew a chair closer to the small fire. "He was arrested in the middle of September, spent three or four weeks in St. Lazare prison, or the Maison Lazare as they call it now, and then went to the Tribunal. They acquitted him, he came home, everything was—" She stopped abruptly, then continued, with a bitter smile. "Everything was once again as it was. Perhaps I should admit, before you ferret it out for yourself, that Lucienne and I were not sad knowing he was in prison. It would have suited us if he'd stayed there."

"Or gone from the Tribunal to the Place de la Révolution?"

"Would you think me an unnatural monster if I said yes?"

"That depends."

"On what?"

"On why it is you hated your father so."

"I told you. He was selfish, unfeeling, tyrannical—"

"Is that enough to wish someone dead?"

"You live with that!" she flared, springing to her feet. "You live with a man like my father, and see how long it is before you're praying for his death." Shaking, she groped behind her and dropped once again into the chair.

"I apologize," Aristide said. "I didn't mean to distress you. I merely wanted to ask you why he had been arrested."

"He was denounced, I believe," she said, without looking at him. "Someone claimed he'd said something. 'Remarks advocating the reestablishment of royalty,' was what it said on the warrant."

Arrested in mid-September, he repeated to himself. Soon after the passage of the Law of Suspects, which more than a few unscrupulous people had manipulated in order to settle old scores.

"But he was acquitted," Geneviève added savagely, "and came home, and then—thank God—soon afterward he went away overnight without warning, as he sometimes did—or so we thought. That was the last we saw of him."

"When your father went away on these brief trips of his," Aristide said, "where did he go? To visit his property? Did he own estates outside Paris, or a manufactory or something of that order?"

"No, Citizen Ravel," she said, with a cold, direct glance at him, "I don't think that's where he went. The land he owned was rented; he had no need to make regular visits."

"Where, then?"

She paused, a slow flush creeping up her pale cheeks. "If you must know, I suspect he spent those days and nights in a brothel."

"Patronizing brothels isn't uncommon," Aristide said, watching her. "He was a widower, after all. If he needed to satisfy desires that couldn't be met at home—"

"You think not?" she said, her blush deepening to an ugly red. She looked away, her fingers clutching and fumbling with the fabric of her skirt. "Why do you think my sister and I don't have any female servants who are under sixty? Our last lady's maid left without warning, several months ago. I'd had my suspicions for some time, and I decided that we'd hire no more girls. Father was furious."

"I see." Young female domestics, usually alone, naïve, illiterate, and penniless, were often victims of unprincipled employers.

"Good day, citizen." She rose, tugged the bell for a servant, and swiftly left the room.

Margot let out a shrill squeak of surprise as she answered Aristide's knock at the door to Jumeau's apartment. "Citizen Ravel!"

"Good day, Margot. May I speak with you a moment?"

"What else have I got to do?" she said, with a broad smile, as she stepped back to let him pass into the little antechamber. The room was bare; Jumeau's daughters had evidently sent for his furniture.

"Have you heard anything from your mistress?" Aristide inquired. She shook her head.

"Not a peep."

"Found yourself a new situation yet?"

"No, not yet. Louise and I, we're friends, and we thought we'd try to find a household that was looking for a cook and a maid both, so we could stay in the same house. We've not found one yet, but we'll look a bit longer, until we have to clear out at the end of the month. The beds and such in the servants' quarters belong to the apartment," she added, with an ironic grin at the bare antechamber.

"I doubt Louise would come into it, but you might be able to help me find Citizen Jumeau's murderer."

"Help you?" she echoed him, blushing. "Yes, I'd like to do that. For poor monsieur's sake, of course," she added hastily. "What do you want me to do?"

"Take a position as personal maid for two ladies over on the Left Bank." He handed her a scrap of paper. "Their name is Rainneville. Go to this address right away, and tell them that you heard they were in need of a maid."

Margot nodded. "Where'd I hear about the job, then?"

"Oh, the Parisian grapevine; servants' talk. A friend of a friend."

"And what am I supposed to be doing once they engage me, if they do?"

"I don't know why they wouldn't engage you," he said, with a hint of a smile. "You're pretty, lively, and clever, and I'm sure you have an excellent recommendation from Citizeness Lépinay."

She blushed again and ducked her head, simpering. He would have to take care, he thought, that he did not inadvertently flatter Margot into falling in love with him, which would be awkward.

"Once they've engaged you, I want you to learn about the household. Innocent questions, of course: ordinary curiosity. Ask about the father, César, who was just murdered, evidently by the same man who killed poor Citizen Jumeau."

"You think they knew each other?" she said. "M'sieur Jumeau and this Rainneville fellow?" She paused a moment, thinking. "I don't ever remember hearing about anybody named Rainneville."

"It's just a hunch of mine. I'm sure the two ladies, Rainneville's daughters, are hiding something, and I'd like to know what it is."

"Oh, I can do that," she told him, with a dazzling smile. "I can gossip with the best of them! But how do I report back to you?"

"Why, you have a widowed old mother who lives not far away, and you'd like an hour, once or twice a week, to go and visit her. Appealing to their sentiment should do it. If they take you on, send me a message immediately, and meet me outside the Café Vachon, just off Rue des Cordeliers, on Saturday at five o'clock. Three days should give you enough time to gossip with the other servants."

"Yes, monsieur," she said, her eyes sparkling with excitement. "Let me just get my box together and make myself presentable, and I'll be off!"

"How are you progressing with your murders?" Mathieu inquired, late that evening, in his cell at the Conciergerie.

"Not well. We're up to nine. That we know of." Aristide dropped onto the edge of the bed and wearily rubbed his eyes.

"The headsman'll have to do better. The Tribunal's still outpacing him." Mathieu seized a bottle from the top of his chest of drawers and poured himself a splash of wine, which he tossed off in a swallow. "For form's sake, I'll ask you if you want some."

Aristide shook his head. "No, thanks."

"Have some anyway," Mathieu said. "Have a glass with me, all right?"

"If you wish," Aristide said, alert to the sudden harsh edge to his friend's voice. He peered at him, uneasy, but Mathieu's expression seemed no different, in the dim light of the candles.

Mathieu poured him a glass and refilled his own. "Well, here's to sanity," he said, throwing himself into a chair.

"Sanity?"

"Don't ever enter politics, Ravel."

"Me? You must be joking."

"I thought I could do great things," Mathieu mused, staring into his glass. "We all did. We thought we could set the world to rights simply by decreeing it, if only we—the educated, rational men, free of centuries of aristocratic prejudice and clerical superstition—if only we could have a voice in affairs. Well, we got our voice, and became the government, and—"

"And now you hate all the other educated, rational men who don't agree with you, just as much as you used to hate the aristos and the bishops."

Mathieu laughed, but his humor seemed forced. "God, what a botch. Thank the Lord you're not a deputy," he added, with a glance at Aristide.

"I couldn't imagine standing for election," Aristide said. He gazed at Mathieu for a moment. His friend's gloomy preoccupation, even bitterness, was not like him. "What's the matter?"

"Oh, you've been too busy, I expect, to read the newspapers."

"Newspapers? What's going on?"

"Our preliminary interrogation began a couple of days ago."

Aristide stared at him, his glass frozen halfway to his lips. "The Tribunal? You're going to the Tribunal?"

"Tomorrow."

"Which of you?" At least twenty of the best-known Brissotin deputies, he knew, were currently imprisoned in the Conciergerie.

"All of us."

"You're all to be tried together? But that's completely mad."

"It would seem we were all part of the same great conspiracy," Mathieu said, thumping his fist to his chest in a parody of the current oratorical style, "to destroy the Republic and trample liberty underfoot."

"But there are—"

"Twenty-one of us. Yes. It should be interesting." Mathieu leaned forward and gently touched Aristide's glass with his fingertips. "Drink up, and join the toast. Here's to sanity—she needs all the encouragement she can get."

21

I did tell her Saturday at five, didn't I? Aristide mused, as he waited outside the Café Vachon for Margot. He glanced again at his watch as pedestrians pushed past him and a fiacre rattled by. Ten minutes late.

Then again, perhaps this odd new republican calendar, which had been decreed into existence a few days before, was confusing everybody. They couldn't give the months new names and leave it at that: oh, no. It was going to be peculiar enough to speak of Brumaire instead of October; but when the twenty-sixth of October became, without warning, the fifth of Brumaire, in the middle of a ten-day week, how on earth were you to know where—or when—you were?

And the past few days, whether October or Brumaire, had not been at all agreeable. He had attended the first day of the Brissotins' trial, together with as many people as could manage to cram themselves into the spectators' gallery of the Hall of Liberty, only to hear a long, bitter indictment from Fouquier.

The first witness for the prosecution, Chabot—a former priest turned fanatical Jacobin, and a bitter enemy of Brissot—had swaggered into the chamber and Aristide had been close enough to the graded benches, where the twenty-one prisoners sat, to overhear Ducos exclaim to Boyer, "Oh, Lord, we're in for a devil of a sermon!" But the "devil of a sermon" had been, as Aristide expected, six hours of malicious, slanderous half-truths and outright lies, with no end in sight. He had walked out in disgust before Chabot finished.

Worst of all, two more decapitated corpses—of an aging, notoriously diseased prostitute, and a crippled old beggar woman—had turned up within a day of each other at opposite ends of Paris, while Brasseur and Conchon and their men grimly waited out the chilly nights at the Madeleine cemetery, with nothing to show for it. That morning, Brasseur, irritable with fatigue and frustration, had crossly demanded why Aristide was pursuing inquiries at the Rainneville household if he still believed that the headsman had chosen his victims without a personal motive.

"It's just a hunch," Aristide had said. "I'm sure I'm right about the killer being a royalist spy—but something's wrong at that house."

He glanced at his watch for the third time just as Margot appeared around the corner. Her cheerful smile did much to brighten his mood as he opened the door for her and gestured her inside the café. It was a slow hour of the day for coffeehouses and the server barely blinked at the unexpected presence of a woman.

"I've never been to a proper café before," Margot said, looking about her at the modest appointments. "Just coffee stalls on the street." Vachon's was far less elegant than the opulent and expensive establishments of the Palais-Égalité, with their mirrors, chandeliers, and gilded *boiseries*, but the brightly painted paneling was still a good step up from the smoke-grimed plaster walls of the average workingman's wine shop. She tried the coffee that the bored server set in front of her. "Can I have more sugar in it? It keeps me going during the afternoon."

Aristide beckoned to the server and pushed a coin his way. "Well?" he said, after Margot had taken a few more appreciative sips.

"What have I learned in three days?" She set down her cup and grinned at him. "Lots. Old Bertrande is a terrible gossip, and so is the cook. You wanted to know what the ladies were hiding? Well, I can tell you that already. Family scandals."

"Scandals?"

"To begin with, a traitor in the family!"

"I know Rainneville himself was—"

"Oh, no, not that. Long ago. They told me that the master had been up before the Tribunal just a little while back, all right, but that's not what I mean. It was somebody else, a relation of his dead wife. Bertrande said that he was a general or a colonel or whatnot in the army and he was executed for high treason, oh, years ago, because of something he did, or didn't do, during a battle. It was a frightful scandal, and madame's side of the family never really held their heads up again. It was back under the old king, Louis XV."

Aristide frowned. Louis XVI had been king at the time of the American war of the 1770s. "You mean, during the Seven Years' War?"

"Must have been."

"But that was thirty years ago, at least."

"Yes, it was when Citizeness Geneviève was just a child. The ladies never talk about it, nor did the master, Bertrande says." She leaned toward him. "Traitor, they called him, but Bertrande told me she heard it was all a plot, that he never was a traitor, that he had enemies and they betrayed him. And then," she added, lowering her voice, though her eyes glinted with excitement, "she said they botched the execution. A real mess of it they made."

"Delightful."

He could not help remembering his conversation with Hamelin over the table at Michalet's. Hamelin, a little tipsy, talking about executions gone awry.

"Is that all, then?" he said.

"No, something else . . . Bertrande—she's been with the family since she was a girl—she said that people think Monsieur Rainneville poisoned his wife."

"Poisoned his wife!" he echoed her. "I don't doubt he was capable of it, but is that just idle rumor, or do you think there's something to it?"

"Well, according to Bertrande, it was madame who had all the money. Monsieur was just a second son of some country lord who didn't have two sous to rub together. So he married madame, who was a sickly sort of creature, but she had plenty of family money. Some rich old relative of hers died sometime after she wed, and he left her a fat fortune. And then she died, herself, a few years later, not long after the younger sister, Lucienne, was born. Bertrande said the doctor had some doubts, but they couldn't prove anything, because she'd been ill for so long."

"That's interesting," he said, wondering if it was any help at all. A doctor who knew what he was doing might find traces of some poisons during an examination of the victim's stomach, but a long, wasting illness, especially one affecting the digestion, could disguise anything of the sort. "Well, they won't be pleased if you're late. Go back to Rue de Seine and keep your eyes and ears open."

"As you like, citizen." She finished her coffee and watched him while he drank the last of his own. He rose to leave, but she suddenly reached out and touched his hand.

"Citizen Ravel? I—I don't know where I'll go if I decide not to keep on working for the Rainneville ladies. Of course somebody always needs a maid, but I thought . . ."

"Yes?"

"I thought . . . well, you're a very pleasant gentleman, and maybe we could come to some arrangement."

Aristide stared at her for an instant. At last he summoned a smile and sat down again opposite her.

"If you intend to take advantage of your undoubted charms and become something more than a servant, Margot, as you ought to . . . you can do better than a fellow like me. I have little money to spend on a mistress, no matter how captivating she might be."

"I wouldn't ask for much—"

"Besides, I'm not very good company." He was silent for a moment, remembering Delphine and their last meeting, in August, before she had gone off with a wealthy protector. "I had a mistress, not long ago, and it ended rather badly."

Margot sighed. "Oh, well," she said, with an enchanting little pout, "it was worth a try. Who was she, that treated you so bad?"

"An actress."

"Oh."

"Now that it's a few months in the past, I can't blame her for leaving me the way she did. Theater folk have such uncertain lives. . . . A rich man fancied her, and she saw her opportunity and she took it."

"Like mademoiselle. Citizeness Lépinay, I mean. She was a singer once, you know, in the chorus, when she was just a girl. Then a gentleman, an aristo, took her under his protection, and she left the stage, because she said he was the great love of her life; but then he died young, so she went back to the opera for a time, until she found other protectors. She's really much more ladylike than most of those common theater folk." She giggled, with a demure glance at him. "There I go, rattling on again. Well, if you change your mind someday . . ."

22

Someone was making a terrible racket, hammering nearby. Bang, bang, bang. Couldn't they let a fellow get his sleep on a Sunday morning?

Aristide dragged himself out of a heavy, restless slumber to realize that the hammering was a quick, insistent rapping at the door, and floundered out of the bed and across the room in the dark to answer it.

"They got him, Ravel!"

"What?"

It was Dautry on the landing again, the candle he carried weirdly illuminating his boyish features. He stepped forward, pushing the door wide. "They got him," he repeated, in an excited whisper. "The murderer! He showed up at the Madeleine cemetery, just as you thought he would."

"They caught him?" Aristide said, rubbing the sleep from his eyes and hoping that he had heard Dautry correctly.

"Isn't that what I've been telling you? Come on, get dressed. The commissaire said you should be there. Commissaire Brasseur, that is, but they're not at Rue Traversine—"

Dautry had evidently been drinking coffee all night, and Aristide devoutly wished he could get hold of some for himself. He tossed his nightshirt aside and pulled on what he hoped was a clean shirt.

"They're at the République section, at the commissariat," Dautry continued. "The local commissaire insisted."

"What's he like?" He splashed a double handful of frigid water on his face, blinking. He badly wanted a shave and a bath. Perhaps later, at the public bathhouses—though they would be disagreeably cold in late October.

"The commissaire?"

"No, Dautry, the prisoner!"

If only he could get hold of a good, strong, milky bowl of breakfast coffee.

"Oh, of course—well, he put up a fight. I wasn't there; Brasseur knew I wouldn't be of much help in a scuffle, so he's kept me late at Rue Traversine all this week, in case any messages came in. But Didier said the fellow was strong, well armed, and determined. Just missed shooting one of the gendarmes right in the chest, and they're all nursing some cuts and bruises. Ready? There's a fiacre downstairs. Come on!"

A lamp was burning in the windows of the commissariat of the Section de la République when they arrived, twenty minutes later. Leaving Dautry to pay the cabfare, Aristide slouched inside, past a sleepy-eyed inspector who waved him through toward the room beyond, and stood a moment beside the closed door, listening.

"You may as well speak up."

Brasseur's voice, level, but with an edge of exasperation.

"We've got you, and that's that. We know you're the fellow who's carried out these atrocities. Now are you going to talk, or shall we just send you along to the Conciergerie and let the Revolutionary Tribunal deal with you in the morning?"

"This one's not going to spill anything," said a different, rougher voice. Commissaire Conchon. "Let's wash our hands of the bastard now and be done with it."

"You hear my colleague?" Brasseur continued. "He wants to be rid of you, citizen, and so do I, unless you start talking. Who are you and who sent you?"

No one spoke. Aristide formed a mental picture of a faceless prisoner, a pair of husky, armed guards flanking him, answering his interrogators with only a hostile stare.

He opened the door and strolled inside the tiny, ill-lit chamber without bothering to announce himself. "We already know who he is," he said, "or at least what he is. He's a royalist spy." A single glance at the lean, saturnine man seated on the hard chair between two gendarmes, arms tightly bound behind his back, was enough to confirm his guesses. "An émigré aristocrat, army officer, and passionate monarchist. An agent sent from Coblentz, or London, or some other haunt of the royalist riffraff, to save Antoinette if he could, or at least to stir up trouble in Paris. Isn't that who you are, monsieur?"

The man glanced up at him. Aristide could see the strong superficial resemblance between the prisoner and himself: gray-streaked dark hair, tall, long-limbed build, threadbare black coat that had faded to a muddy green. Despite the shabby clothes and undressed hair, however, the man had the bearing of one who had worn an officer's uniform on the field or brocade at the royal court, and who had stridden through life believing himself superior to other men.

"Well, monsieur?" he repeated.

The prisoner eyed him for a moment, then seemed to come to a decision, his shoulders relaxing.

"After all, what does it matter now?" His voice was crisp and cultured. "My family and friends who still live are out of your reach, thank God, and I know I'm a dead man. My name, messieurs, is Emmanuel-Marie-Auguste-Roch Favereau de Lorsanges, Comte de Saint-Dizier, colonel in His Majesty's armies. As for why I did what I did, I expect you know that as well as I."

"To discredit the Revolution and the republican government," Aristide said, "and, incidentally, to deter the English from making peace with France?"

"If you like to put it that way, though I do not, of course, recognize your so-called government as anything but a cabal of traitors and regicides. Long live the king!"

"Let's get this straight," said Brasseur, who had been pacing at the back of the room while Conchon sat hunched at the table and glowered at the seated prisoner. "You came to Paris with the purpose of committing a string of random murders and leaving the corpses strewn about, without their heads, in order to stir up terror in the city and destroy the Republic's credibility in the eyes of the rest of Europe."

"I am sorry for those who died," Saint-Dizier said. "But I believe my country and my king are worth the sacrifice."

"Your victims might have believed differently," Aristide said.

Saint-Dizier fixed him with a cold, unwavering gaze. "They died for their king, just as I've always been ready to do; as any faithful subject ought to be ready and willing to do. Take me to your machine straightaway; I'll die with 'Long live the king' on my lips."

"Well, we in our *republic*, Citizen Favereau," Brasseur said, deliberately omitting Saint-Dizier's title, "believe that French citizens aren't cattle for the slaughterhouse . . ."

Aren't they? Aristide said to himself, remembering that Mathieu and the rest, at the Tribunal, were still enduring the prosecution's countless vicious slanders and attempting to respond to the dubious testimony of shady witnesses.

". . . and ought to have a choice in the matter of who and what they're going to die for."

"Nobody volunteered to have his head hacked off so that your damned aristocratic privilege could be restored," Conchon growled, "and so that snot-nosed brat in the Temple could go and sit on a throne at Versailles."

"The sacred monarchy of France is worth any sacrifice," Saint-Dizier said, staring over Conchon's shoulder to the blank plaster wall beyond.

The commissaire slapped a hand down on the table before him. "For God's sake, let's take his statement and get this over with. I'm sick of this royalist rant. Your present residence?" he demanded, squinting through the wavering candlelight at Saint-Dizier after noting the initial formalities of name, age, place of birth, and condition.

"On the Île de la Cité, a lodging in the house belonging to one Raimbault, Rue St. Christophe, next to the foundling hospital."

Conchon pointed to an inspector who had been hovering in a corner of the room. "Parmentier—go to the Cité right away and search the lodging. Now, citizen," he continued, turning once again to the prisoner and clearing his throat, "you admit to committing the murder of the citizen Echelard on the eleventh of October in the cemetery belonging to the former parish of La Madeleine?"

A muscle twitched in the prisoner's cheek, but he said nothing. Conchon cleared his throat, spat on the floor, and began again.

"Citizen Favereau, you admit to—"

"I am a loyal subject of His Majesty Louis XVII," Saint-Dizier declared, still glaring at the wall behind the two commissaires, "and of the late, lamented Louis XVI before him. I am a Chevalier of St. Louis, and a nobleman of the sword, and no man's 'citizen.'"

Aristide stirred. "I think you'll do better, Commissaire, if you address your prisoner as 'monsieur.'"

"I don't address anybody as 'monsieur'!" Conchon growled. "The days of bowing and scraping to 'monsieur' are over, and good riddance to them."

"Suit yourself. But I expect Commissaire Brasseur and I have better things to do than to sit here, at five in the morning, yawning our heads off, while you two glare at each other and refuse to budge over forms of address. Do you want a statement or not?"

The commissaire and his prisoner stared at each other for a moment more in furious silence, during which Aristide could see Conchon's neck slowly turning brick red.

"Monsieur de Saint-Dizier," Conchon said, through gritted teeth, "you admit to committing the murder of the citizen Echelard, in the cemetery belonging to the former parish of La Madeleine, on the night of the eleventh of October last?"

Saint-Dizier inclined his head. "If that's the ruffian with whom I exchanged blows in the middle of the cemetery . . . yes. I relieved the world of his odious presence."

"You freely admit to murdering him, and cutting off his head, and leaving his head and trunk in the burial trench?"

"Yes."

"Why did you murder him?"

"As you said: I came to Paris with instructions to save Her Majesty if I could, or, if that proved to be impossible, to sow confusion amid the populace, and to confound the illegitimate, regicide republican government by any means whatsoever." Conchon scowled at the word "illegitimate" but restrained himself as Saint-Dizier continued.

"The lout was skulking around certain graves, trampling them underfoot—graves that ought to be held sacred and left unpolluted by such swine. He deserved no less."

Brasseur leaned forward. "Did the woman you murdered outside the Maison-Égalité—"

"The what?" Saint-Dizier said, bitter amusement in his voice. "You republicans, renaming everything. Do you think you can obliterate the memory of your God and your king as easily as that?"

"The Maison—the former Palais-Royal. Did Désirée Marquette, the woman you murdered and beheaded there, also deserve to die?"

Aristide thought he saw Saint-Dizier's hard features soften a trifle. "I pitied her," he said, "though I regret nothing. She had been the victim of misfortune. She had no money and no useful skills, not even those of the world's oldest profession, with which she could have earned her living in times such as these. No one could have helped her, short of giving her a home and committing himself completely to charity." He glanced from one to the other of the two commissaires, with a trace of a scornful smile on his thin lips. "In the old days, before your enlightened regime closed the religious houses, such women would have entered a convent and there found shelter and useful work, in God's service; now they starve on the streets. Is that how your revolution has improved the people's lot?"

"Did you kill her?" Brasseur said.

"She died quickly; she didn't suffer. None of them suffered."

"What did you do with her head?"

"I disposed of it."

"Why not leave it with the body?"

"I thought a corpse lacking its head would be a more unsettling discovery."

"Where'd you dispose of it?"

"I dropped it down a disused well in a courtyard nearby, where I saw the locals had been throwing their refuse."

"What about Citizen Jumeau?" Conchon demanded, glancing down at his own dossiers. "Did *he* deserve to die?"

"Who is that, pray?"

"The first man you murdered, a resident of this section. You murdered him outside the Maison de Justice."

"He died for the sake of restoring the monarchy," Saint-Dizier said, with a shrug. "They all did."

"And the others? You murdered them all for the sake of discrediting the Republic and restoring the monarchy?"

"Yes."

"You'll sign a statement to that effect?"

"Yes."

Aristide stepped forward and placed his notebook on the table. "Here are their names." Conchon took it and read off the names, squinting in the feeble lamplight.

"Louis-Michel-Rémy Jumeau, man of property; Jeanne-Louise Houdey, ink seller; Marc-Antoine Noyelle, ex-army officer; Désirée-Anne-Marie Marquette, spinster; Pierre-Marie Echelard, water carrier; Louis-Pierre-Auguste Deverneuil, advocate; Anne-François-César Rainneville, man of property; Marie-Madeleine Charon, prostitute; Agnès Vigne, of no profession; also a beggar and a young vagabond who've not been identified. You admit to committing these murders?"

"Yes, I do."

"How did you commit them?"

"I chose the victims at random," Saint-Dizier said, after a moment's silence. "I took my opportunity where I found it. I found them alone in the streets or the public gardens after dark, or lured them to a lonely spot, and I cut their throats with the knife I carried on my person." He glanced for an instant at a table at the side of the room, where a long, thin knife, a heavier butcher's knife that was almost a cleaver, and a pair of pocket pistols had been laid out, along with the rest of the prisoner's effects.

"You didn't cut Echelard's throat," said Conchon.

"The ruffian in the cemetery? No. He caught me unawares. I didn't dare shoot him, for fear of attracting attention, and I was forced to stab him. Not a neat job of it." He paused for an instant, brows drawing together in distaste, then continued.

"I cut the throats of the rest. I repeat, they did not suffer at my hands. I decapitated the corpses after death. I did so with the purpose of horrifying and panicking the populace in a city that has already seen an excess of decapitated corpses." He turned his head and stifled a yawn. "Your pardon, messieurs; my hands are bound. Is that all? This grows tedious."

"Oh, it'll be over quick enough," said Conchon. "You understand that this statement will be used as evidence against you at your trial?"

"I expect the Revolutionary Tribunal will want to try you," Brasseur broke in, "since you came to Paris as an enemy agent working against his own country. And the Tribunal doesn't waste time—"

"I do not recognize the right of any tribunal set up by this illegitimate government to try me."

"You tell them that," Brasseur muttered, "and see how far it gets you."

"I have no illusions, Commissaire," Saint-Dizier said. "I had none as to the risks of this mission, when a certain person close to the Comte de Provence himself asked me to take on this task, as a sacred duty, and I agreed. It will be an honor to die on the same scaffold as did His Majesty."

"And may you enjoy the honor," Conchon said, "and good riddance to you."

"God, how I loathe fanatics," Aristide said as Conchon and the guards led Saint-Dizier out and the door shut behind them. Brasseur glanced at him.

"Monarchists, you mean?"

"All fanatics. Royalist or Jacobin, take your pick. Extremism's an unlovely quality in anyone."

Brasseur grunted. "I'm inclined to agree with you." He paused for a moment, before nodding and offering his hand. "Well, thank God that's over with. Good job, Ravel."

They shook hands. "You, too."

"My brother-in-law's just sent us a couple of loaves of good country bread," Brasseur added with a conspiratorial wink, "and a crock of butter. Marie might even find some real coffee in the larder."

"Coffee?" said Aristide, brightening.

"What do you say we go to my lodgings and let Marie give us breakfast?"

23

Aristide spent much of the following day at the Revolutionary Tribunal, skulking in the rear of the Salle de Liberté. At last he could bear no more of the witnesses' calumnies against Mathieu and the others, particularly Vergniaud and Brissot, their leaders, and once again he strode out, seething, before the end of the session.

He slept restlessly on Tuesday for the second day in a row, waking finally as the single remaining bell at St. Séverin—the rest had been melted down months ago for cannonballs—tolled nine o'clock. He rose at last, went out in search of a halfway drinkable bowl of white coffee or something that resembled it, and settled down at a table at Vachon's, with his coffee and a slice of stale bread, to read the café's well-thumbed daily copy of the *Moniteur*.

He drowsily skimmed the news from abroad and the previous day's summary from the National Convention, avoiding the reports from the Revolutionary Tribunal altogether until a name caught his eye in a brief paragraph at the bottom of the page. The citizen Favereau de Lorsanges, ex-Comte de Saint-Dizier, suspected of murder and counter-revolutionary activities, was to be tried that day at the second section of the Tribunal. He glanced at his watch—just past ten o'clock—and, after a brief debate with himself, gulped down the last of his coffee and set out for the Palais de Justice.

As the principal division of the Tribunal, where Fouquier himself prosecuted cases, was occupied with the Brissotins' trial, the other three divisions were taking care of lesser matters. Saint-Dizier sat stiffly erect in a plain wooden armchair in the former Hall of St. Louis, now renamed Salle de l'Égalité, where the second division sat. During the past year the Salle de l'Égalité, like the larger Salle de Liberté, had been stripped of its former grandeur to make way for republican simplicity; carpets, tapestries, gilded woodwork, and, above all, royal crowns and fleurs-de-lys had given way to a chilly, austere marble chamber in which the speech of the judges, prisoners, and spectators incessantly echoed like the murmurs of ghosts.

The spy seemed composed, his face unreadable, as Fanchette, the prostitute who had witnessed Désirée Marquette's last wretched hour, came to the end of her testimony. The president of the court made a note and leaned forward in his seat.

"And do you see the man of whom you've spoken in this chamber?"

"Yes." She pointed at Saint-Dizier. "That's him. The prisoner. That's the man who talked sweet to her and lured her off."

"And you're certain of your identification?"

"Couldn't be mistaken, Citizen President. That's him, all right. The murdering swine!" she added, with a malevolent glance at him. The audience muttered.

The deputy public prosecutor rose from his table. "This concludes our evidence against the prisoner."

The counsel for the defense rose. Plainly aware that his client's case was hopeless, he made no more than a token speech and returned to his seat. The president turned to Saint-Dizier.

"Citizen Favereau," he began, but Saint-Dizier interrupted him.

"I do not recognize this tribunal's right to judge me," he said, without turning his stony gaze toward the judges' table. "I recognize only the courts established by the kings of France, by the grace of God, from time immemorial."

"God's death!" a red-haired man in front of Aristide exclaimed under his breath to the friend beside him. "Isn't he ever going to say anything else?"

"Why bother?" said the friend. "Look at him. He knows he's for it."

The president glanced at the defense counsel, who shrugged and shook his head, and turned back to Saint-Dizier. "Citizen, am I to understand that you refuse to speak in your own defense?"

"I do not recognize this tribunal's right to judge me."

"Citizen Lebeau, have you any witnesses for the defense?"

"No, Citizen President."

The president sighed and rang his bell. "This concludes the evidence. Remove the prisoner."

He rattled off the charges as a pair of guards escorted Saint-Dizier out of the chamber. The jurymen drew together and conferred. A few minutes later, when the spectators around Aristide had barely begun to fidget and whisper, the foreman rose to his feet.

"We find that the accused, Emmanuel-Marie-Auguste-Roch Favereau de Lorsanges, ex-Comte de Saint-Dizier, is guilty of all charges and did commit these murders with malice and premeditation; also with the intention of subverting the Republic by striking terror into the hearts of its citizens."

"As if we expected anything else," the red-haired man muttered to his companion, as the deputy public prosecutor rose and formally demanded the sentence of death. "Murdering swine, indeed."

"Come on, let's get over there early."

"Think it'll be today?"

"It's not yet noon. Of course it'll be today."

The two men turned and elbowed their way toward the doors, without sparing a glance for Saint-Dizier, whom the guards were marching back into the chamber. The president cleared his throat.

"Citizen Favereau, this tribunal finds you guilty of all the charges against you. Have you anything to say before sentence is passed?"

"I do not recognize your right to judge me," Saint-Dizier repeated, without a glance at him.

"Emmanuel-Marie-Auguste-Roch Favereau de Lorsanges, the Revolutionary Tribunal has found you guilty of murder and of crimes against the Republic, and sentences you to death, sentence to be carried out within twenty-four hours. Remove the prisoner."

Before the guards could seize his arms, Saint-Dizier dodged away from them and lunged for the rail that separated the spectators from the court. "People of France!" he cried. "If any among you still love your king, then come to my aid now! Seize this moment to rise up against this accursed revolution and strike down these murdering regicides!"

The audience paused in its milling and heads turned, astonished, toward Saint-Dizier. A few people tittered. No one moved.

"Aristocrat!" someone shouted from the rear of the chamber. "To the guillotine with you!"

"Will no one join me?" Saint-Dizier exclaimed, glancing from face to face. "Our murdered king's son is still a prisoner in the Temple—join me in rescuing him, and we will restore our sacred monarchy with Louis XVII and put our kingdom to rights!"

Aristide watched Saint-Dizier, expressionless. The ex-count, he thought, was realizing, for the first time, that Paris had little interest in rising up against the Revolution or in striking down regicides.

"To hell with Louis XVII, and all the rest of them!" a woman cried. "Long live the Republic!"

A dozen voices joined her, shouting "Long live the Republic!" and "Long live the Revolution!" Saint-Dizier fought to be heard above the cries but was drowned out. As the clamor died down, he leaned forward, gripping the rail, white-knuckled.

"I see you now for what you are. Traitors! Ingrates!"

"Long live the Republic!" a chorus of voices responded.

"You want your republic? Then you may have it! Take your republic and be damned!"

He raised his voice to be heard above the angry shouts and continued. "You worship your republic—but what has your republic done for you? War and famine—that's what it's given you! Look about you! This republic of yours has done nothing for the people in whose name you sacrilegiously murdered your anointed king and defiled your churches, and besmirched the name of France forever. Can you deny that the citizens," he continued, lacing the word with bitter irony, "the *citizens* of your precious republic, whom I killed, suffered less, at the moment of their deaths, than did the thousands who are dying of want in this city? Can you claim, without blushing for the manifest falsehood of it, that the people of France are better off without their king? It was an act of mercy to put those wretches out of their misery! I regret nothing and will cry with my last breath, 'Long live Louis XVII! Long live the king!' And may this accursed republic fall in infamy!"

A roar of outrage greeted his final words. A dozen spectators pushed against the barrier, shouting and shaking their fists, but the gendarmes who had stood silently at the sides of the courtroom marched forward and placed themselves in a row between audience and prisoner. Aristide saw his guards seize Saint-Dizier by the shoulders and hurry him out of the chamber.

Immediately the chamber began to empty. At last, as the crowd thinned, Aristide turned and followed the rest of the chattering spectators out into the corridors of the Palais de Justice.

The ancient clock on the tower at the corner of the quay was chiming noon as he reached the Salle des Pas Perdus. The midday dinner break had just begun and people spilled out of the Great Chamber across the wide hall from him, arguing and gesticulating. He shivered, thinking of Mathieu, and drew a deep breath, telling himself once again that when the Brissotins' turn came to defend themselves against the ludicrous accusations of royalism and treason, they would argue so skillfully that the jury would have no choice but to acquit them.

Between the crowds and the ubiquitous stallkeepers and peddlers who sold books, journals, trinkets, tobacco, and refreshments of all sorts to those who worked at or visited the Law Courts, the great hall was packed. Even in late October, the heat and smell of too many bodies pressing in on him from every side was oppressive and distasteful. He edged away toward a quieter corner, out of the stream, to wait until the rush was over.

He turned a moment later as he heard his name called. It was Sauvade, winding his way toward him through the mass of people and raising a hand above his head in greeting.

"I hope I'm not intruding," said Sauvade, as they shook hands, "by asking you which trial you've been attending?"

"I felt I had to be here for Saint-Dizier's trial—the murderer."

"I thought you might be. It was you who caught him, wasn't it?"

"Commissaires Conchon and Brasseur caught him. I merely tracked him down."

"But you felt it was your duty to see him judged."

"Yes . . . yes, I did."

"It's over?"

"A quarter hour ago."

"He was convicted, of course." It was not a question.

"No more than he deserved," Aristide said. "He confessed—he practically boasted to us of what he'd done. There was no other possible outcome."

Confessed? he repeated to himself, as he suddenly felt, with the instinct he had learned never to ignore, that he had missed something of significance.

I was there; I heard him myself. But something . . . something about his confession, something he said then, and just now, too . . . it doesn't quite add up.

"Good," Sauvade said, oblivious to Aristide's sudden preoccupation. "Such monsters shouldn't remain unpunished—justice should take its course." His expression, which had grown suddenly stern and hard, as quickly cleared. "Forgive me. Perhaps you'll do me the honor of dining with me, in return for telling me about the trial?"

"Dining?"

This man holds Mathieu's life in his hands, Aristide thought, with a flicker of revulsion. He thrust away the tiny, nagging doubts about Saint-Dizier, which were far too elusive to grasp, as he turned his mind to his more immediate concern. *Dine with a juryman who might, soon enough, choose to send them all to the scaffold?*

Sauvade, though, he sensed, would be scrupulous in all such matters; as an educated and evidently honorable man, Sauvade could see through the falsehoods and half-truths about the Brissotins that the Jacobins were trying to force upon the jury and the populace. At last he nodded.

"The dining room here is excellent, and you'd be allowed in as my guest." Sauvade gestured down a nearby passage. "This way, and down the stairs on your right. Of course, after we've dined, if you were planning to attend the execution—"

"No," Aristide said, so sharply that Sauvade turned in mid-stride.

"Forgive me. If I've caused offense—"

"No need to apologize. I have private reasons for loathing executions."

"So have I," Sauvade said, in a flat tone of voice that betrayed nothing. Aristide recalled the anecdote the Lemarchants had told him about the execution, decades ago, that the boys had so recklessly attended. Such a disturbing experience might indeed leave a sensitive child scarred. "Though I've seen the guillotine at work," Sauvade added, still without expression. "Once. I felt, before I applied for a place on the jury, that I ought to know what it was like. A man with the power to condemn others to death should be aware of the consequences of his decisions."

He said nothing more until they had reached the crowded private dining room on the ground floor, which was reserved for personnel of the courts, and chosen their dinners from among the half-dozen hot and cold dishes arranged on the buffet. Aristide glanced about him, curious, as they found seats. He recognized several faces, including the public prosecutor, and Herman, the president of the first division of the tribunal, who were seated together at a distant table.

"How much did Saint-Dizier admit?" Sauvade inquired as they waited for their server to arrive with the meal. "You say he boasted of committing these murders?"

"He couldn't disguise the pride he took in serving his cause. He's a zealot to the last possible degree, of course," Aristide added, suddenly fuming at the blinkered irrationality of mankind. "The sort who will never give an inch in his devotion to the royal family and to monarchy. As rigid and fanatical as the most fervent Jacobin at the Hôtel de Ville."

"Ah," said Sauvade, raising his voice to be heard over the noisy conversation all around them, "but keep in mind the important distinction between them. These fanatical royalists are clinging to a profligate, decadent, outmoded old institution, which all decent and forward-thinking men know ought to be obliterated for the sake of human progress. A fanatical Jacobin, at least, is looking toward a better future for his neighbors and his country. Don't you agree?"

"I scarcely know anymore." He dragged his gaze from the prosecutor and president. Herman, a handsome man of thirty-five, looked mild-mannered enough, for all his reputation as an inflexible judge, next to the irascible Fouquier. "I find extremists disturbing, whatever shape they may take."

"If they're willing to subvert what's right and just in order to achieve their desired ends."

Aristide felt a chill lance through him at Sauvade's words, for he had been suspecting that the Jacobin government was quite willing to do just that, in order to achieve final victory over the Brissotins.

The waiter arrived with carafes of wine and water and filled their glasses. "Your royalist agent, for instance," Sauvade continued as the man moved off. "He undoubtedly believes that what he was doing was for a great and good cause. But how can such evil and unjust means achieve good ends? Not that I believe the restoration of the monarchy would be anything but a tragedy, naturally, but *he* believes that it's a good and desirable end. Nevertheless, a worthy goal achieved through injustice cannot help but be corrupt."

Yes, there you've put your finger on it. . . .

"May I ask you a question?" Aristide said, more abruptly than he had intended. "What are the Brissotins' chances?"

"I feared you would ask that." Sauvade was silent for a moment, gazing at his wineglass. "It was you I saw among the spectators yesterday at the Tribunal, wasn't it?"

Aristide nodded, with another involuntary glance toward the prosecutor and judge, who were conferring earnestly together. "And I left when I could no longer tolerate the stink of the lies being told on the witnesses' stand. It's obscene, Sauvade—you, of all people, must know that. You and I both know that the prosecution's 'evidence' is nothing more than lies and vile rumors."

"If it were up to Antonelle and me and, perhaps, one or two others," Sauvade said at length, "I believe we would gladly acquit the Brissotins. We can recognize slander as well as you can, and I, for one, still believe that making poor political choices is not evidence of treason. But some of our fellow jurors are Montagnards through and through—creatures of Hébert and the Commune—fanatics such as we were just discussing. And I don't need to tell you how much the avid Montagnards of the Commune detest Brissot and everything he's stood for."

"You don't hold out much hope, then."

"I'm sorry. It's an ugly situation. A perfect example of evil means being used to promote a good end—the safety of the Republic. Of course," he added, "when it's finally put in our hands, Antonelle, being our foreman, could drag things out, while we do our best to argue the others into seeing reason, until they give in out of sheer exhaustion. I think that's the best we can hope for."

Their dinners arrived. Sauvade, ignoring the plate of veal tongue before him, gave Aristide a searching glance.

"Is a friend or relative of yours among them?"

"All the deputies from Bordeaux, and Alexandre in particular."

"I'm sorry," Sauvade repeated. "The whole affair offends me deeply. For me, the Revolution has always been about justice. It came about because of the blatant inequities of the old regime, and it was always about reform, from the very beginning. But many of our leaders seem to have forgotten that—as thoroughly as these royalists have, it seems!" he added, eyes blazing, evidently unable to dismiss Saint-Dizier and his crimes from his mind. "These narrow-minded, arrogant reactionaries—treating citizens like cattle, fit only to be slaughtered for the sake of restoring a rotten institution—" He reached for his knife and fork, with a token, self-deprecating smile. "Forgive me. Talking of politics, these days, would take away anyone's appetite."

Aristide said nothing. All at once, with a thrill of anger, he knew that he had to watch today's execution, however distasteful the prospect. Sauvade was not the only one with a consuming thirst for justice.

For the sake of his victims ... butchered with no more consideration than if they had been vermin ... you have to see for yourself, with your own eyes, that that pitiless bastard meets his end, that this horrible affair is done with once and for all.

They made small talk throughout the rest of the meal. Aristide toyed with his fricassée, not wishing to seem impolite in the face of Sauvade's generosity, but was barely aware of the food in front of him.

Why should I dread watching him die? It only takes an instant.

This man, this murderer who has taken the lives of eleven people, perhaps more, will die in the blink of an eye, without pain—almost more than he deserves. It will only take a moment.

They said my father took four hours to die. . . .

A twinge of nausea stabbed him and he swallowed down a mouthful of rabbit that tasted like ashes.

But you must see this one finished, said a small voice within him. *That is the least you can do to appease those ghosts—see him finished, know that the affair is closed and the city is rid of him.*

After they finished their meal, Sauvade pointed Aristide to an exit that would lead him to the courtyard of the Palais de Justice, and they parted without further discussion of politics or the Tribunal. Aristide strode out to the street, where he soon found an empty fiacre for hire and jolted through the hurrying pedestrians and street vendors on the quays.

The fiacre creaked finally into the Place de la Révolution, where a small, raucous crowd had already gathered around the scaffold. Aristide leaned out the window and slapped the side of the cab to draw the driver's attention.

"As close in as you can. I wish to stay inside and wait. I'll pay you for your time."

"Is it an execution, then?"

"Yes. Soon."

The driver chuckled, above him. "I don't get a chance to see many of those. Lord love you, yes, I'll wait. Is it a good one today? Some treacherous aristo?"

"Yes," said Aristide, "it's a good one today."

The driver whistled at his horse and maneuvered the fiacre toward the crowd until they were no more than thirty feet from the rail surrounding the scaffold. Aristide waited, feeling slightly queasy as he watched the two assistant executioners grease the grooves down which the great steel blade would drop, though he could not tear his gaze away from the sight. People drifted by ones and twos into the square. A bell tolled three in the distance.

The cart appeared at last, coming at a walking pace down Rue de la Révolution from the Madeleine, with a handful of jeering sansculottes trailing it. He could see Sanson, sitting in front beside the driver, and three men, shorn and bound, standing upright. A gendarme stood behind Saint-Dizier, keeping a firm grip on his shoulders; the authorities were taking no chances.

Saint-Dizier was the first of the three to climb the steep steps. He halted a moment on the platform, glancing scornfully around him at the avid, upturned faces of the crowd, before one of the executioners drew him away toward the waiting seesaw-plank. Aristide saw him turn swiftly to Sanson and speak to him.

Sanson replied, nodding. Immediately Saint-Dizier bowed his head and went down on one knee before the guillotine to lean forward and kiss the upright beam. Aristide could guess what he had asked the master executioner: *Is it the same as that on which Louis XVI died?*

The assistants hesitated, glancing at Sanson, who waited a moment, then nodded once. They hauled Saint-Dizier to his feet and pushed him toward the upright *bascule*. The plank tipped forward and the lunette banged into place.

"Long live the king! Long live His Majesty L—"

The blade thudded down and, an instant later, blood splashed to the boards of the scaffold with a loud, dull splatter, as if a bucketful of water had been dumped all at once from a height or thrown against a wall. Aristide quickly looked away.

Long live the Republic.

His heart was racing. He had been holding his breath, he found, and let it out in a long sigh.

His first execution . . . it had not been so frightful, really, he thought, as he stared intently at the grimy interior of the fiacre. Not when compared with the horrors the old regime had meted out from time to time.

My father, broken and dying in agony on the wheel . . .

And justice had been served—oh, yes, most certainly, justice had been served. Thank God the ghastly affair was over.

He permitted himself a brief, bitter smile of triumph and stared out at the sky above the river as he heard the second victim hustled up the steps amid the crowd's murmurs.

Crash.

Splatter.

Applause.

A brief pause, a few thumps, footsteps, voices, and then again: crash, splatter.

Thank God, it's done.

"You wait and see," said a man to a companion as they walked past Aristide's fiacre. "Next it'll be the Brissotins' turn to spit into the sack . . ."

His pulse pounded. *Oh, God—Mathieu—Ducos—Boyer—*

". . . any day now—wait and see!"

24

He waited a quarter hour more in the fiacre, lurking out of sight in the shadows as if he were the one who had committed a crime. When the square was empty, he paid off the cab and trudged toward the ruins of the Madeleine, hoping the walk would distract him.

Nothing he could do would help the Brissotins to cling to their lives in the face of a merciless tribunal. Yet the jurymen, he reminded himself, were not all as biddable as the public prosecutor would wish. Sauvade was a man of honor; perhaps some of the others would waver, in the face of the shameless falsity of the charges—and Sauvade, in his pursuit of justice, had persuaded the jury to acquit more often than once.

Justice . . .

Justice has been served. Sometimes the Revolutionary Tribunal does dispense real justice. Saint-Dizier—Saint-Dizier confessed his crimes, boasted of them, with a sort of hideous pride, and has paid for them with his life. No one can deny that justice has been served.

The tiny doubt began to prick at him again, like a stinging gnat.

What the devil about Saint-Dizier's confession, he thought once more, *doesn't seem quite right?*

He found himself on Rue de Suresne, near the commissariat of the

Section de la République, and paused, gnawing at his lip. What harm could it do to inquire?

"And what can I do for you today, Citizen Ravel?" Commissaire Conchon inquired, leaning back in his chair. He gestured to the brandy bottle on the desk before him. "Care for a shot?"

"Thank you, no. Do you have a copy of the transcript of Saint-Dizier's interrogation?"

Conchon shook his head. "It went to the Maison de Justice, along with his dossier. I expect I'll have a copy back in another day or two, when the clerks and the scribblers are done with it. Why?"

"Something's bothering me about it. Something he said, or something I've seen."

Conchon shrugged. "It sounded all right to me. Don't wake up a sleeping cat, I say! The affair's closed and the bastard's getting what's coming to him."

"He already has. Less than an hour ago."

"Well, that's done, then. Wish I'd been there. Long live the Republic, eh?"

"Nevertheless, something's not right—"

"Citizen Ravel," the commissaire said, rising from his chair and leaning across his desk, "I gather Commissaire Brasseur has a good deal of faith in you; and the word is that you're working for Danton and you're more important than you look. But I'm satisfied with how the affair turned out. Get that?"

Aristide shook his head. "I'm not sure *I'm* satisfied, Commissaire."

"Now look here. We got the bastard, and he's paid for his crimes, and there's an end to it! If you want to keep on nosing about like a bloodhound, I suppose I can't stop you; but don't you come to me, baying about some new scent you've unearthed in a matter that's over and done with. Because I've enough to do, here in my own patch, without interference from some glorified *mouche*. Understand?"

"As you wish, Commissaire," said Aristide, biting back the retort that had sprung to his lips. "Good day to you."

He stood brooding a moment in the street outside the commissariat. Where to begin?

Or was he chasing phantoms?

After the Tribunal's afternoon session ended at nine that evening, he went again to the Conciergerie, thrust his pass at the guards, and soon was standing in the open doorway of Mathieu's cell. Mathieu, a turnkey escorting him, appeared a moment later. He looked exhausted, the dark stubble on his jaw standing out sharply against his grayish pallor. His eyes, though, were still bright.

"It must be the elegant surroundings here that keep bringing you back," he said, as they clasped hands. "Faith, you look about as well as I do. Though I heard the headsman's been caught? The jailers were talking about it the day before yesterday—he was being transferred in for trial, and they were putting him in an extra secure cell somewhere downstairs."

"Yes. He was tried and g—" Aristide caught himself before he said the word "guillotined" and paused in mid-sentence.

"You can say it, you know," Mathieu told him, laying a hand on Aristide's arm for an instant. "I won't go into convulsions at the sound of it."

"He was guillotined today."

"Good job. Though you don't look too happy about it. Why aren't you as pleased with yourself as you ought to be?"

Aristide almost smiled. "You know me too well."

"So?"

"I can't help feeling that something's not right about it."

"Some little detail that doesn't fit in?"

"Exactly." Aristide crossed the cell to the table and leaned against it, scowling. "Ever since his trial. And I can't put my finger on it. It's maddening."

"You did promise, a couple of days ago, to bring me your latest notes on the affair," Mathieu said, sitting on the low bed and gesturing Aristide to the chair. "Come on, hand them over."

"I didn't—I haven't had time to copy anything else out for you."

"Well, whatever you have on you, then. Let's see."

"Surely you have more essential matters to concern you than—"

Mathieu interrupted him with a swift, jerky movement of his hand, as if he were unaware of it. "Such as?"

"This trial."

"I'm not worrying about it anymore."

"Can you be that confident that they'll acquit you?"

"No," Mathieu said, "you don't understand. I'm no longer concerned about the trial because, at this point, after hearing the slanderous clap-trap that the witnesses for the prosecution have been shamelessly spouting for a week, I'm convinced that it's all rigged. I'm quite certain they're not going to acquit us."

Aristide began to protest, but Mathieu shook his head, gesturing him to silence. "And if it's a foregone conclusion that we're all going to be a head shorter within the fortnight, then don't you think that accepting the fact, more or less calmly, seems easier on the nerves than raging against the inevitable?"

"Vergniaud still seems to believe that you have a chance," Aristide said, fighting the sudden nausea at the pit of his stomach. "This evening at the Tribunal—I didn't get to hear much, but when he—"

"He can believe what he likes. Come to think of it, despite his brilliance, you must recall that he's always been a bit of a Dr. Pangloss; after all, Vergniaud was one of the incurable optimists who thought that declaring war on the Empire was a marvelous idea. Face facts, Ravel."

Aristide said nothing. Though he would never have regarded himself as an incurable optimist—far from it—he had never truly allowed himself to believe that Mathieu and his associates could lose the political battle that was their trial. The thought that Mathieu's kindness, Ducos's black humor, their sharp intelligence, their irrepressible wit, could simply, suddenly, be gone, leaving behind them a void in the world, was too grim even to imagine.

"Look," Mathieu added, "I've already put my affairs in order as well as I can. I've written to my family, and to my father and brother, and to the notary who's in charge of my property, and handed over everything I could to my wife so that the government wouldn't grab it. I've written to every soul who means something to me, who ought to know what's become of me before they see it in the papers. I did it all days ago. There's nothing left for me to do. So how else should I occupy myself, if I don't care to spend my last few days on earth pondering my place in history, and thinking of something witty and memorable to say on the scaffold, just before they tip me under the blade?"

He sprang to his feet and turned away to face the whitewashed stone wall. "Damn it, Ravel; it sounds heartless, but the truth is that your visits—and your murders, despite the beastliness of it all—they're what has kept me sane. Don't you understand that? Now let me have a look at your notes."

Aristide silently handed over his notebook. Mathieu took up the candelabrum from the table and squinted at the pages.

"Your handwriting's still like hen scratches."

"Father Petitot never did manage to get me to write legibly."

"Do you have a list of all the murder victims, in order? Including the latest?"

"Two pages on."

"Good . . . that's good." He looked up. "Did you attend his trial? The spy, I mean?"

"Yes."

"Tell me about it. In fact, tell me everything you remember about him."

"Your typical inflexible, ultrareactionary aristocrat. Arrogant; ruthless; blinkered and mulish in his devotion to the monarchy." Aristide paused for an instant, searching his memory. "Proud to die for the sacred cause. Once we had him, and he knew he hadn't a chance, he was willing to talk."

"At his trial, too?"

"He denied their right to try him and refused to answer their questions. His trial lasted about five minutes. I don't think he said anything until he grabbed his chance to harangue the spectators."

"At the Tribunal?" said Mathieu, with a twitch of his lips.

"He could scarcely have expected a very sympathetic audience, I agree. But he was . . . well, self-righteous in his royalism. He actually declared that since conditions in Paris are so bad right now—it's all the Republic's fault, of course—he was really doing his victims a favor by killing them."

"You're joking."

"Sadly, no."

"Not even Fouquier would go that far. Evidently you're much better off if you die at the hands of a royalist fanatic than if you spit into the sack for the good of the Republic." Mathieu glanced upward, one hand on the notebook. "May I keep this? Until tomorrow?"

Aristide nodded. He already knew most of it by heart.

"Time, citizen," announced a guard, thrusting his head past the door.

Visitors had to leave by ten o'clock, when the prisoners were locked in their cells for the night. Aristide reluctantly rose. "I'll be back tomorrow, if I can."

The guards let him out into the deserted Cour du Mai and he strode northward, without any clear idea of where he was going, across the Pont-au-Change to the Right Bank. The weather had changed and a fine, cold drizzle began to spatter down as he passed the Châtelet.

He had meant, he supposed, to walk to the Section de la Montagne and stop in at Brasseur's lodgings, to enjoy a brief respite at his friend's cozy fireside and learn whatever was to be learned, but Mathieu's words kept echoing in his mind.

I'm quite certain they're not going to acquit us.

Inconceivable—and yet . . .

Abruptly he had no desire to call on Brasseur, who was of a pragmatic turn of mind, and who had no intimate, lifelong friends who dabbled in the ever more dangerous game of politics. Brasseur was a good fellow—the best—but he would not understand.

He walked on, adjusting his hat and pulling up his coat collar against the chill drizzle, toward the Palais-Égalité. Reaching the arcades, he turned into the first café he saw and threw himself down at an empty table in a shadowed corner. "Coffee," he said to the approaching waiter, and then checked himself. "No. Do you serve wine here?"

"Yes, citizen, we have a few selections. What would you care to order?"

"I don't suppose I'd get any drunker on expensive wine than I can on *vin ordinaire*?"

"No, I suspect not," the waiter replied, without blinking.

"The house red, then. A large glass."

The waiter returned with his glass and he gulped down a few swallows of it. Ordinarily he detested the effects of alcohol, but sometimes—just sometimes—the oblivion of wine was preferable to reality.

I'd like a little oblivion right about now.

"Don't you think that accepting the fact, more or less calmly, seems easier on the nerves than raging against the inevitable?"

Damn it, Mathieu—

He closed his eyes and took another swallow of the wine, grimacing at its acidity.

Mathieu knows his wines—a true son of Bordeaux—he'd loathe this vile local stuff.

Mathieu . . .

Oh, God, no. Please, no.

Raging against the inevitable . . .

. . . And there's not a damned thing I can do that will make a difference.

Halfway into his second glass, he sensed he was being watched through the shadows. He looked up from the ruby depths of the wine and studied the girl. She was, of course, a prostitute, but she was pretty in a bold, vulgar sort of way, and looked healthy and reasonably clean.

She smiled at him. "Buy me a glass?"

Oblivion, he thought. An anonymous encounter, a tumble in the dark, where you could lose yourself and forget the gnawing fear of catastrophe for an hour or two, or even the length of a night.

"Sit down." He tossed another three sous on the table and beckoned the waiter over. "Wine for the citizeness."

"'Citizeness'?" she echoed him, amused. "What are you, then, one of these Jacobins?"

He drained his glass and decided he wanted another. "Get used to saying it," he told her as he fumbled for coins in his pocket. "The Jacobins aren't going away."

25

The morning's everyday commotion of voices and wagons in the street outside woke Aristide and set his head to throbbing. He dragged himself out of the bed, leaving the girl stirring drowsily behind him, dressed, dropped a few small coins and assignats on the battered washstand, and slouched downstairs. The scrawny servant girl sweeping the hotel's foyer cast him an uninterested glance and said nothing as he slipped out the front door to Rue de Beaujolais.

Brasseur's commissariat was only a moment's walk away. He clapped on his hat and set out for Rue Traversine through the misty streets.

"What are you doing here?" demanded Inspector Didier, alone at the reception desk in the commissariat's antechamber, as Aristide entered.

"What?"

"The commissaire sent Chesnais off to fetch you as soon as we got the report. You were supposed to go straight there."

His head began to throb again and he rubbed cold fingertips across his forehead. "What report? Go where?"

Didier smirked, relishing Aristide's confusion. "There's been another one."

Aristide stared at him for an instant, regretting that he had not taken a moment to have a coffee, bad as it would have been—perhaps two or three coffees—along with the roll he had bought from one of the vendors near the Palais-Royal. "Another what?"

"Another *headless corpse*," said Didier. "What else are we talking about?"

"That's not possible," he said, after digesting the inspector's words.

"And yet it's happened. Funny, that."

"The royalist agent is dead."

"Fancy that. He must have had an accomplice, mustn't he?"

Aristide set his thoughts in order—*God, how I want some coffee*—and drew a deep breath.

"Where?"

"On the Cité, by the Palais de Justice, they said. That's why the commissaire went straight there: said he'd meet you there when he arrived, since you live around the corner. He took Dautry and left." Didier eyed him, his smirk widening. "Weren't you spending the night at home?"

"How and where I spend my nights is none of your damned business." Aristide threw the door open and strode out to hail the first available fiacre amid the heavy morning traffic.

It was apparent to him, as the cab drew near the Law Courts, where they had found the corpse. A row of guardsmen stood before an arched entry to a small courtyard at the north side of the Conciergerie, facing the quay. He paid off the fiacre and strolled past the guards, at a nod from Brasseur, who came striding across the courtyard to meet him.

"Where the devil were you? Chesnais said you weren't at home."

"I was out."

"I sent him over to fetch you an hour ago, but—"

"I wasn't expecting to be hauled out of my bed at the crack of dawn, Brasseur . . . since I believe we were all happily under the impression that the headsman had been captured and dealt with. Please, please tell me that Didier's got his facts garbled."

"Wish I could. We've got another one, and it's the same as the rest."

"No head?"

"No head." Brasseur gestured toward a cluster of inspectors and guardsmen who milled in front of the door that led to the Conciergerie's towers and the stairway to the public prosecutor's office. "Found the body lying at the foot of the steps."

"Did Fouquier trip over it?" Aristide inquired, with a flash of malicious interest.

"No such luck. They say he spends the night in his office when he's got an extra heavy load of work. The first of the clerks in discovered it. Want to take a look?"

"Frankly, no. I've seen enough blood already to last me a lifetime."

"Haven't we all." Brasseur led the way to a cart, waiting at one side of the courtyard, and drew back the coarse sheet that covered the corpse within. Aristide glanced at him.

"You moved it."

"Didn't know when you were going to turn up, did I?" Brasseur said, with a tinge of annoyance. "I did send for you first thing."

"Never mind." Aristide swallowed his own irritation and glanced over the corpse. The victim wore a shirt that, though drenched and stiff with blood, seemed of good quality, and a neat pair of broadcloth knee breeches, with silk stockings and silver-buckled shoes. A blood-spattered coat, waistcoat, and cravat lay next to the corpse, as well as a stylish hat. "Any clues to his identity?"

"We were lucky this time. His papers were on him." Brasseur opened a slim leather case to reveal a civic card and identity papers bearing the seal of a distant *département*, both heavily bloodstained. "This is bad, Ravel; worse than bad. His name was Gaillard, and he was a member of the Convention, from the Allier."

"A deputy?"

"We'll have to confirm it, of course. But the murder of a member of the government—this isn't going to go away quietly. Especially when we thought we'd gotten the right man."

"We did get the right man," Aristide said as he glared at the corpse.

"Then there were two of him."

"Well, who's to say there weren't? There are plenty of fanatical royalists knocking about Coblentz—why send only one enemy spy, when you can send a dozen? Perhaps they were working together. Perhaps this one's picking up where Saint-Dizier left off."

"Death of the devil," Brasseur muttered, as Aristide strode toward the cluster of guards.

The blood lay in vast, sticky pools over the cobbles at the bottom of the steps. Had Aristide not witnessed the guillotine in action, he would never have believed that so much blood could spill out of one man's body.

Nothing to be learned from a puddle of blood. He returned to the cart and looked the corpse over again. "If it is an accomplice of Saint-Dizier's," he said, glancing at Brasseur, "do you think he's progressed to making targets of the government itself?"

"Might be."

What on earth am I supposed to find here? he asked himself. The identity papers had solved the most pressing question but gave him no clue to the identity of the murderer. He pulled the sheet farther down. The corpse's hands, particularly the fingertips, seemed scratched and raw, the scrapes fresh and barely scabbed over; he made a mental note of the fact for later consideration. He could see little else beneath the muddy red-brown stain that had soaked the body to the waist, but one detail caught his eye.

"Brasseur—he's got smudges on the knees of his culotte."

"Is that supposed to mean something?"

"It might. And—look—his shoes are scuffed and scratched here, on the toe and instep. I'd venture that this man was kneeling soon before he died—probably right here on the cobblestones. I've seen that before."

"A pattern?"

"It's not much, but it's something. Brasseur, I'm going to the Châtelet. I'll wait there for delivery." He clapped Brasseur on the shoulder and hurried out.

"Is Rainneville's body still here?" he demanded, throwing open the door to the antechamber of the Basse-Geôle. Two cups of muddy, chicory-laden coffee from a dubious handcart on the way, while vile-tasting, had at least cleared his mind and conquered his headache, and he felt much more prepared to take on this new, perplexing problem.

Daude looked up, squinting, from a record book and reached for a rag to wipe his inky fingers. "Rainneville?"

"Last week. I need to take a second look at him. Don't tell me those crows from the Security Committee took him away already," he added, alarmed.

"No, that one's still here, together with Charon, the whore from the other day, presumably because they were identified. I signed the order for release the day before yesterday, but nobody's claimed either of them."

No, Geneviève and Lucienne Rainneville wouldn't willingly take on the expense of burial; they'd probably dance at his funeral.

"Go ahead," said Daude, gesturing to the iron grille and the stairs beyond to the cellars. "Bouille's taking inventory from a suicide, but he won't be in your way."

"Where's Rainneville?" Aristide said as he hurried down the steps. A foul, sweetish stench, laden with decay, assaulted his nostrils from a nearby table: an unclaimed corpse that had probably been pulled out after a week in the river.

Bouille, scarcely looking up from his examination of a limp, tattered homespun gown, pointed to a stone table at the far corner of the cellar room. Aristide strode over to the sheeted body, flung back the grimy linen covering it, and glared down at it, wondering what it was that was teasing at him.

"Fingers," he said suddenly.

"What's that?" said Bouille.

"His fingers." He lifted the corpse's left hand in both his own, to stare at the thin line of grime under a fingernail. "His fingers—they were digging into the dirt when I first examined him. They said he hadn't been moved. He'd been clawing at the dirt as he died, as if he were trying to drag himself away."

Bouille turned at that, with a puzzled frown on his melancholy clown's face. "He would have had little chance, or strength, to do that after his throat was slit. Once the great vessels are cut, death's almost instantaneous. The body may twitch, but without conscious thought or action."

"I know. I think that's what was nagging at me. That, and . . . of course!" Aristide exclaimed, snapping his fingers. "Today's corpse—the hands were scraped. He was lying on cobbles, so he couldn't have clawed at the dirt, but those rough stones would have scratched his hands and broken his nails if he'd been lying prone and struggling to get away. . . . Look here, Bouille, can you see any clear sign that this man actually died of a cut throat before he was beheaded?"

Bouille sighed and trudged over to him. "Hmm . . . stump of the neck uneven, hacked away rather amateurishly: certainly no doctor or surgeon did this."

"I'm not looking for a doctor or a surgeon," Aristide said impatiently. "But can you tell if his throat really was cut first?"

"No obvious sign of it at either side," Bouille said, after a moment's examination. "Do you remember the Neuville murder, or the Saint-Landry murder back in 'eighty-six? Well," he continued, as Aristide nodded, "those were typical. The murderer stands behind his victim, grabs hold of him from behind, like so, taking him by surprise, and slashes his throat."

He shambled over to another table, beckoning Aristide along, and pulled back the sheet. "Here's the woman Charon. See the bottom of the slash, just there, crossing the deep cuts that took her head off? With a slit throat, the cut generally starts rather high, just beneath the ear, and proceeds at a downward angle toward the other side of the neck. In other words, the victim of a right-handed murderer, or a right-handed suicide, will have a cut that commences beneath his left ear and angles downward across his neck to his right ear."

"So?"

"Well, I don't see any trace of that on Rainneville. There's no sign of a diagonal cut slicing through his flesh from either side. Either your headsman managed both to cut Rainneville's throat with a perfectly horizontal slash, and then, in decapitating him, to cut through the neck in precisely the same spot . . . or else he never slit that throat at all before taking his head off. Damned careless of me not to notice that. Though it's been a bit hectic here lately," he added dryly.

"And yet," Aristide said, searching his memory, "when they questioned him, Saint-Dizier declared that he'd cut their throats. All of them. All but Echelard, that is, whom he'd stabbed in the hand-to-hand struggle in the cemetery. Why would he lie?"

"So that he wouldn't be thought a monster?" Bouille suggested, returning to Rainneville's body to bend and squint at the raw stump of the neck. "Any alternative to a quick throat-slitting would be pretty brutal."

"He wanted to be thought a monster. The more shocking, the better. And he freely admitted everything to us. Except this."

"He said explicitly that he'd cut their throats? Look at this, then." Bouille heaved the corpse onto its side and pointed at the back of the neck stump and two wounds that bit into the flesh but which had barely sliced into the bone. Aristide stared at the cuts.

"Why the devil did I miss that?"

"He was beheaded, Ravel; he would have bled like a slaughtered ox. Ever see the guillotine at work?"

"Yes, in fact I have," Aristide said, a sudden, irrational rush of shame leaving him hot all over.

"Then you've seen how much blood can come out of a man in the space of a breath, when his head's off. You did the best you could," he continued, before Aristide could respond, "when examining a corpse in poor light and hindered by a mess of dried blood."

"This means he might have been attacked from the back, doesn't it?"

"Those wounds, certainly. With a heavy blade—an axe, a cleaver, perhaps even a saber."

Would Saint-Dizier, that cool, ruthless assassin, have been reckless or foolhardy enough to attack from the back and try to kill a man by chopping at his neck?

It would be utter madness—unless the victim were not standing but bending . . . or kneeling. . . .

"If I remember correctly," Aristide said, "he had dirt ground into the knees of his culotte. Let's see it."

Bouille vanished into the back room and soon returned with Rainneville's clothes. Aristide snatched up the culotte and examined the muddy marks.

"Look—he was kneeling. No question about it. Dautry and I

thought he might have been begging for his life—but if his killer attacks him from behind . . . why?"

"The element of surprise?" Bouille suggested.

"The killer gets in a couple of blows to the neck from behind, without warning, and Rainneville . . ." Aristide closed his eyes, trying to envision the scene. "Rainneville falls forward on his face, half stunned, losing blood, feebly trying to get away, *groping at the ground*, where his murderer finishes the job by hacking his head off. My God—"

The new corpse's arrival interrupted him. As soon as the two litter bearers had heaved the corpse onto the nearest table and departed, Aristide turned to Brasseur, who had accompanied them, and gestured to Bouille. "There's a pattern—I'm sure of it. Bouille, you have to examine this one right away. Look at the neck and tell us if his wounds are similar to Rainneville's. Was his throat cut, or was he attacked from behind, as Rainneville was?"

Bouille sighed, with a backward glance at the heap of tattered clothing he had been inspecting, and trudged over to them. "No diagonal slash," he said as he bent over the corpse, while Aristide concentrated on the corpse's hands. "No evidence of it at all." He adjusted the body and peered at the back of the neck. "Oh, yes. Yes. There's a deep wound here, on the side, just below the point where the neck was severed, and it's bled copiously. This man was killed with more than one blow to the neck, no doubt about it. Just like Rainneville. Dead no more than twelve hours, by the way. If you'll give me ten minutes to undress him—"

"Hold on a moment," said Aristide. Something had caught his eye, something pale under the man's neatly trimmed thumbnail, partly obscured by the dried smear of blood that had oozed from the scraped flesh on his fingertips. "Give me a small knife, would you?"

He teased the substance from beneath the nail and looked at it in the palm of his hand. "Fat," he said, after he had smelled it and rubbed it between his fingers. "Hardened fat. Candle grease? Come to think of it, look, Brasseur, there's a greasy spot on his right hand, as well. Let's get a better look at his shirt."

Bouille stepped back as they examined the sleeves, stiff with drying blood, and found a few grease spots near the cuffs.

"If he frequently wrote letters," Bouille suggested, behind them, "he may well have been working at a desk and moved a candle closer and, in the process, spilled a bit of candle grease on himself. My wife often complains that all my shirts have grease stains at the cuff."

Aristide nodded. "Possible. He's got a few ink stains on his fingers—see?—and a slight pen callus on his third finger."

"If he was a deputy," Brasseur said, "he'd have written a few speeches. I think we can agree that this man is who his papers say he is."

"You don't have the head, I suppose?" Bouille inquired, looking from one to the other of them. "If you had the head, perhaps I could tell you more about how he died."

"No head," said Brasseur. He added, with a grimace, "What in God's name do they want with the heads?"

"Saint-Dizier didn't take all of them, remember," Aristide said. "He left a couple behind."

Bouille tut-tutted. "Slack of him."

"Although," Aristide said slowly, "Saint-Dizier was the last person I'd describe as slack."

"I scarcely like to say it," said Bouille, after a moment's silence, his voice echoing hollowly from the stone walls, "but could your royalist have had a confederate?"

"Easily," Brasseur growled.

"Or did either man have any enemies?"

"I haven't the faintest idea. Ravel?"

"We'll have to find out about Gaillard," Aristide said. "But as for Rainneville having enemies—I could safely say that two of them were living in his own house."

26

Lucienne Rainneville was looking better than she had the last time Aristide had seen her; the figured afternoon gown she wore, though a few years out of fashion, suited her and her cheeks were pink. "You're looking well, citizeness," he told her, after exchanging commonplaces. The fire in the hearth, too, he noticed, was considerably larger than he remembered from his previous visits.

"Oh, it's a whole new life!" she said, smiling at him and spinning about so that her skirts flared. "No more living like a nun. Soon I shall have some new gowns, and we've already engaged a lady's maid for ourselves! Now, what questions do you have for us today, citizen?"

"You said, when I first saw you, that your father couldn't have had any enemies. Are you quite sure about that?"

Her smile faded. "I expect Father had some enemies. He was that sort of man. But a deadly enemy, who would have murdered him . . . no. No one hated him that much."

"You think not?" Geneviève said, entering the room and overhearing. Her gaze flicked to the opposite wall; the portrait of Rainneville, Aristide noticed, had disappeared, leaving behind only a dark, less faded rectangle on the flowered wallpaper.

"No, it was a stranger!" Lucienne cried. "I heard about it just this morning, at Rataud's, while they were taking measurements. A man—a lunatic, or a spy, or some such man—had been murdering people around the city, chopping their heads off—ugh!—and they caught him. That's true, isn't it?" she added, turning to Aristide for confirmation.

"We did capture a royalist agent," he said, nodding.

"Surely it was he who murdered Father?"

"You mentioned, when I spoke with you last," he said, watching Geneviève, "that you didn't hire young maidservants because you feared that Citizen Rainneville would abuse them."

"What has *that* to do with anything?" Lucienne demanded.

"That's true, isn't it?" he said, still looking at Geneviève and ignoring Lucienne.

"Yes."

"And you also said that your last maid had left your service without warning?"

"That's right," Geneviève said, color creeping into her cheeks.

"Do you know if she had an admirer, a sweetheart, even a fiancé?"

"I'm not interested in the servants' affairs. Why do you ask?"

"Because I wouldn't be at all surprised if the person who denounced your father to the authorities in September was someone connected to her. It's the sort of thing an angry fiancé would do, now that almost anyone can be denounced as a suspect under the new laws, often with baseless accusations."

"But—"

"And isn't it possible," he continued relentlessly, "that a man who denounced a personal enemy out of a desire for revenge, and then saw him go free, despite all his efforts, might exact justice by other means?"

"You mean, could someone connected to Sophie have murdered our father?"

"Yes. It's possible that your father's murderer was someone who had heard the lurid rumors going around the city, and tried to disguise the murder as the work of a royalist assassin."

"Oh!" Lucienne exclaimed. Aristide turned to her, curious. She really was quite pretty in a fragile, pallid way, he thought, when her cheeks had turned pink with pleasurable excitement and her eyes sparkled.

"I've just recalled . . . Sophie was Parisian, wasn't she?" she said to Geneviève. "Not from the countryside."

"That's true," Geneviève said. "Usually Father let us hire only girls fresh from the country, who didn't have anywhere else to go when he— took advantage of them." She paused, drew a deep breath, and continued, still without looking at Aristide, her cheeks flaming. "But Sophie was a local girl, and she must have had some kind of family here in Paris."

"Her name?" Aristide said, noting Geneviève's color and wondering what could have brought it on; it was not Lucienne's rosy blush, but a scarlet flush of embarrassment.

"Capelle, Carpeaux . . . no. Caniot. Sophie Caniot. She came from the faubourg St. Marcel, I think. I don't know of any sweetheart, but she did mention a young brother, and that her parents were both living."

"Anything else?"

"No. Nothing I can think of. Good afternoon."

As the elderly maidservant led Aristide out to the foyer, he stole a quick glance backward, in time to see Geneviève sink into a chair, face in her hands. He paused a moment, watching her, as Lucienne fluttered about the salon, chattering about her dressmaker, oblivious to her sister's distress.   ～

An ugly suspicion began to form in his mind. He strode back into the parlor, saying to Lucienne, "Would you kindly leave us alone for a few minutes." She backed out of the room and shut the door behind her as he planted himself in front of Geneviève.

"It wasn't just the maidservants whom your father abused, was it?"

She turned a white face up to his, the hot angry blush ebbing like an outgoing tide. "What?"

"His own daughter—it's a vile notion, but it happens more often than anyone would want to think. And not just among poor folk who all sleep in one room. It happens among the gentry, too."

"How dare you suggest—"

"I think, in the end, you allowed him to keep on with it, for Lucienne's sake, and even for the sake of all those servant girls. You never let him touch Lucienne, did you?"

Her shamefaced silence was enough to confirm his suspicions. He waited, certain that she would speak.

"I told him, years ago," she said at last, clutching white-knuckled at the arms of her chair, "when he began looking at her . . . *that way* . . . that I would kill him if he touched her. And I meant it. I told him I was already soiled and ruined by what he'd done to me and I didn't care anymore; moreover, that I could get a knife from the kitchen any time I pleased, and I wouldn't give a damn if they hanged me as a parricide."

"How long?"

"Am I under suspicion now?"

He seated himself in the chair beside her. "How long?" he repeated quietly, ignoring her question. He reached across the arm of the chair and placed his hand over hers. She jerked back, shrinking from him, but then yielded with a sigh, like a tired child.

"Over twenty years. I was thirteen when it began." She raised her eyes to his and he winced at the depth of bitterness and pain in them. "He was very practical about it; he told me what to use, and whom to go to, to keep from conceiving. And often he—he took his pleasures in ways that didn't risk pregnancy."

"Why not just go to the nearest brothel, in the name of all the devils?" he demanded, half to himself. Revulsion roiled his stomach and he tasted a nauseating sourness at the back of his mouth.

"But it's so much more convenient if you don't even have to leave your own house," Geneviève said, her voice heavy with contempt. "And why pay for a whore, who might be diseased. . . . Oh, yes," she added, as Aristide gave her an incredulous glance. "Father was like that. Why pay for a whore when you could get the same service from a wife . . . or a terrified daughter?" She gulped a deep, shuddering breath. Aristide sat silently, scarcely daring to budge, for fear that she would take fright at his least word or movement and the moment of unexpected intimacy between them would be irretrievably shattered.

"Understand, citizen, he never cared a fig about any of us; we mattered nothing to him, except in how he could profit from our presence. He married Mother for her fortune—and everyone suspects, though nobody talks about it, that he murdered her for it."

"Why didn't it go to you when she died?" Aristide inquired. The property of a married woman with children normally went to her children, not her husband, at her death.

"Father made sure of that in the marriage contract," she said, with a bitter smile. "Mother, you see, together with her first cousin, was due to inherit a large fortune from a childless old uncle. And Father wanted to get his hands on that fortune. So he insisted that the contract state that he, not any children of the marriage, would inherit her property at her death. Then . . . then Mother's cousin died, leaving her the only heir, and then the old uncle died, so she inherited all of it; and, within a few years, *she* died, after a long illness. Do you blame me for believing that Father poisoned her?"

A man who was capable of repeatedly raping his own daughter across a span of decades, Aristide thought, was probably capable of anything. Enemies? Rainneville must have collected enemies the way other men collected stylish waistcoats.

"It seems rather convenient that your mother's cousin died when he did," he said. "Is it possible that your father could have had something to do with his death, too, in order to clear the way to that fortune your mother was to inherit?"

She glanced at him and quickly looked away. "I've no idea."

"But he couldn't have been terribly old?"

"He was . . . about forty. I don't really know. I was only a child then. He was away with the armies in America. I never knew him."

"Armies?" he said, remembering what Margot had told him about old family scandals and a relative, an army officer, who had been condemned to death for treason decades before. "This cousin of your mother's—"

She snatched her hand away from his. "I will not talk further about this."

"Citizeness—" he began, startled, but she cut him off.

"Get out of my house this instant!"

"As you wish." He bowed and went to the door, cursing himself for raising an ill-chosen subject at the moment when he thought he had gained her trust. Why had he not remembered what Margot had told him, that the Rainnevilles never spoke of their dead cousin? The shamefully executed traitor in the family was plainly a forbidden topic in the household.

"We'll speak again."

Aristide sent a message to François by way of a loafer on a street corner, requesting him to meet him at the Palais de Justice. Two hours and five livres in silver later, he emerged from the record rooms where the dossiers of recent trials at the Tribunal were kept, with a suspicion growing in his mind.

Anne-François-César Rainneville had, indeed, been tried on the twelfth of October, barely three weeks previously, for incivism and counterrevolutionary remarks, by the principal division of the Revolutionary Tribunal; the denunciation had come from one Louis-Gabriel Caniot, journeyman butcher. The accusation had been imprecise and transparent and a competent defense counsel had easily undermined it.

"I want you," he told François, who was straggling behind, after lingering a moment with a pretty tobacco seller in the corridor, "to take yourself to the faubourg Marcel and find this Caniot. When you've found him, make friends with him or with someone who knows him well. Learn about his family, especially a girl named Sophie, probably his daughter. It's possible that Caniot previously lodged a complaint against our Citizen Rainneville for taking advantage of the girl—"

"Nice fellow, Rainneville," said François.

"Yes, he was a fine specimen of humanity. Find out just how much of a grudge Caniot held against Rainneville over the matter. Get going."

"What about you?"

"I'm staying here," Aristide said, with an involuntary glance at the doors to the Salle de Liberté, where the Brissotins' trial would be proceeding as usual, still with witnesses for the prosecution.

François raised a forefinger to his battered hat and was gone. Aristide pushed open the great door to the court chamber, seeking out Mathieu among the others on the prisoners' benches, only to find neither prisoners, judges, lawyers, nor jurymen. A few determined spectators waited out the interval in the empty chamber by perching on a high windowsill, legs dangling, as they discussed the trial between bites of bread and sausage and the occasional swallow from a pocket flask.

"What's going on?" he asked the first guard he saw, who was leaning against the door that led to the restricted corridors in back of the court chambers. "Why—"

"Why is the place empty?" said the guard, shifting position. "Extra long dinner break, I suppose. Herman kept them at it for hours, after that business early on. Maybe he was expecting the jury to pipe up right away like he wanted them to, but they didn't, so finally, when you could hear stomachs rumbling across the room, he declared a recess at two, and—"

"What 'business early on'?" Aristide echoed him. "What do you mean?"

"Haven't you heard? They came in this morning with a new decree from the Convention. Seems like, now, a trial doesn't have to take as long as it takes. The Convention—or rather the blasted Jacobins, I'll wager—" he added, with a contemptuous curl of his lip, "they've made it official that three days is long enough for any trial at the Tribunal, and after three days, the jury can stop the whole affair and make up its mind whenever it likes."

"Stop . . . the trial?"

"Stop the trial. Just like that. What are we coming to, citizen, I ask you? Wasn't the Tribunal supposed to be about real justice?"

It was icy in the unheated chamber, he thought, as he struggled to catch his breath. The Brissotins' trial had, of course, taken far longer than three days already. At any minute, with an oblique threat from Fouquier or Herman ringing in their ears, the jurymen could declare themselves satisfied, mull over their verdict without even hearing the prisoners' defense, send twenty-one men to their deaths with a few words. . . .

He relieved his feelings, though only slightly, with a sharp obscenity and strode from the chamber. It was no more than five minutes' walk across the bridge to the Left Bank and back to his room on Rue de la Huchette. He climbed the three flights, barely aware of bruising his shin as he slipped on a spot in the wooden treads that decades of footfalls had scooped out until it was treacherously smooth. Once in his room, he stopped short, wondering why he had come there and staring out at the windows opposite his own across the narrow, noisome courtyard. Above the rooftops, the pale sun had vanished, veiled once again in heavy autumn clouds that promised rain.

"No," he whispered, and then louder, "No," and once again, "No—no—*no!*" He pounded his fist once against the wall between the two windows, wanting to batter it down, to smash the windows, to break something, anything.

Or perhaps murder. Yes, it would give him a fierce satisfaction to commit a murder. To do away with Fouquier, or Robespierre, or whichever ruthless, resentful Jacobin—Hébert, Collot d'Herbois, Billaud-Varenne?—had been instrumental in deciding that it was not enough to unseat and discredit the Brissotins and lock them away, but that they had to be eradicated, like a plague, from the face of the earth.

He spent a moment savoring the notion, the image of dapper little Robespierre or sour-faced Billaud-Varenne cringing beneath the cocked pistol thrust in their faces, before dismissing it with a soft, bitter laugh. He was no murderer. Even when provoked almost beyond endurance, he was not a killer.

Not like my father.

Am I?

He lost track of time as he sat hunched over his writing table, staring at the cracked plaster on the wall. The neighbor's cat mewed outside his window, as usual, and pawed at the glass, but the sound seemed to come from a long distance away, as if from the far end of a long, long tunnel.

At last, hearing a distant bell, he rubbed his eyes and pulled out his watch. Quarter to six.

The trial—this travesty of a trial—may be over already—

Please, someone tell me this is just a bad dream.

27

The Salle de Liberté was packed to bursting point when he returned to the Palais de Justice, but the trial had not yet recommenced. He edged his way in to the rear of the chamber, at last finding a space in the corner where a young man was skulking, face averted, as if ashamed to be seen there.

The young man's glance slid over him and then darted away, but not before Aristide recognized him. Camille Desmoulins and he had first met in 1786,* when they were both living the hand-to-mouth life of the struggling writer, and had continued to stumble upon each other from time to time; most of Paris's literary men and women knew each other at least slightly.

Desmoulins had risen considerably in the world since his days of garrets and second-rate cafés; four years after he had made himself famous by calling Paris to arms in 1789, he was a popular journalist, a deputy from Paris to the National Convention, and a close personal friend to both Danton and Robespierre. Moreover, he was still writing screeds against the enemies of liberty with a brilliant,

---

* *The Cavalier of the Apocalypse.*

devastatingly witty and trenchant style that Aristide, his own literary ambitions long forsaken, could not help envying. Desmoulins's
Brissot Unmasked, however, though published a year and a half previously, seemed to have been written to order for Robespierre and the
most intransigent of the Jacobins, for it had skewered Brissot and,
by implication, his followers, with venomous precision; some said it
had contributed not a little to their eventual downfall and denunciation.

"G-good day, Ravel," Desmoulins said at last.

"Good day." He winced at the banality of the greeting. It was enor-
mously far from being a good day.

Desmoulins seemed so ill at ease that Aristide abstained from small
talk and contented himself with staring at the empty tables and graded
benches. Would it never begin?

"Wh . . . what time is it?" Desmoulins inquired, as Aristide stole a
glance at his watch.

"Just past six."

"That's a long dinner interval. Two to six. Normally it's only two
hours."

"You think something's going on?"

"I think they finished their d-dinner hours ago and now they're in
the jury room, all of them, and Herman or Fouquier is breathing down
their necks."

"You're a member of the Convention," said Aristide. "How'd they
push that decree through?"

"You know what they're like. The M-Montagnards' official line is
that they hate Brissot and the federalists and everything about them,
and most of the rest are just spineless. They'll vote for anything put in
front of them."

"Did you vote against it?"

"I wasn't there."

"How convenient," Aristide said, under his breath, as Desmoulins
looked away.

The five judges entered the chamber and took their seats, the jury following. Next would come the accused, lining up on the gradines like spectators at a theater, although they themselves were the play.

Herman turned and gestured to a guard, only to pause, hand in midair, as the jury foreman rose to his feet in the silence.

"Citizen President."

Antonelle seemed perceptibly discontented, as if following orders against his better judgment.

"After conferring with my fellow jurymen, it's my duty to declare that this trial need not proceed further. The minds of the jury are sufficiently enlightened."

"Christ," Desmoulins muttered. Aristide caught sight of a hard, triumphant smile on Herman's lips, instantly suppressed, as he rang his bell for silence.

"You are prepared to deliberate the guilt or innocence of the accused?"

"Yes, Citizen President."

"Very well. The jury will retire and deliberate upon the following—"

Aristide did not stay to hear the rest of Herman's speech. He hurried toward the doors, wondering if he could bluff his way into the corridors beyond the two court chambers and find Mathieu, warn him that soon, for good or for ill, it would be over.

His pass to the prisons, he soon discovered, was, in the Palais de Justice, of no more use than a false assignat. The chambers where the accused waited, a guard patiently explained to him, were not, strictly speaking, prison cells, and therefore a document that allowed a citizen to visit the prisons was not relevant. The accused were allowed no visitors, besides their advocates, so long as they were held within the Law Courts, and that was that.

At last he gave up and trudged back to the Salle des Pas Perdus, where members of the public hung about the book and refreshment stalls, passing the time. No verdict yet. He told himself that the longer the jury deliberated, the better the prisoners' chances were, and continued out to the top of the great staircase, to stare bleakly across the torchlit May Courtyard in the evening chill.

"Thought I might still find you here," François said, hurrying up the stair to meet him some time later. "Saints, I'm famished! Can we go get a bite to eat? You look like you could use something yourself," he added, eyeing Aristide.

"Perhaps." How long was it since he had eaten? He led François to a cheap eating-house just off the quay and waited until his companion had shoveled away a few mouthfuls of thick soup. "Well?"

"Found Caniot, all right. Lives on Rue du Fer à Moulin. Your average sansculotte: works hard when he's not drunk, complains about his pay. Father of a family. Neither a devil nor a saint, by all accounts; doesn't beat his wife more than once a week. And right now he's grousing to all and sundry about how Marat was right and the damned rich get away with everything."

"The girl, Sophie?"

"His daughter. Pretty thing with big blue eyes, seventeen, and out to here." He held his cupped hands a foot away from his belly, indicating pregnancy. "Rainneville's, according to her. Neighbors and the local police say Caniot was roaring mad about it. First complained to his section, and to Rainneville's section, and didn't get too far; then clumsily denounced Rainneville with the first story he could think of, which was, since imagination's not his strong suit, the crime of saying 'Long live the king' in a public place, but with no witnesses and no proof to back him up—"

"Of course it was fabricated." Aristide looked down with vague surprise at his own bowl of soup, as if it had appeared in front of him without warning, and tried a spoonful. It was mostly turnips, of which he was not particularly fond. "I'm sure Rainneville, no matter what his actual political opinions, was smarter than to say anything compromising in public."

"Right. Well, Rainneville got off at the Tribunal and Caniot's been raising hell about it ever since."

"Still?"

"When I walked into the wine shop where he usually spends his evenings, he was shouting about aristocrats who ruined the respectable daughters of good sansculottes, and making a few boozy threats."

"He doesn't yet know, then, that Rainneville is dead?"

François shrugged. "Apparently not."

The clouds that had promised rain had made good their promise. Above them, a soft pattering gave way to the drumming of a steady rainfall. A few tables away, a handful of comrades let out surprised yelps as they were spattered from a leak in the roof above.

"Though if he'd killed Rainneville himself," Aristide mused, picking at the hunk of bread in the basket between them, "he'd have to pretend he knew nothing about it, and keep on threatening Rainneville until the murder was common knowledge. Do you think he has the brains to work that out?"

"He's a loudmouthed oaf, but I suppose he has brains enough for that, at least. You're thinking he did it, aren't you? But what about today's corpse?"

"It depends upon whether or not he has the wit to come up with the idea of disguising the murder by committing a second that's similar." The bread was heavy, gritty, and tasted faintly of mold. He quickly swallowed it and took another few spoonfuls of soup. "Although," he added, "he may have been only the brawn, and someone else the brains. I've rarely seen such hatred. . . ."

"Who do you mean?"

"Rainneville's daughters," he said reluctantly, "or at least one of them."

He could not help pitying Geneviève; she had suffered terribly at the hands of a selfish and callous man. But the law demanded that murder, no matter how justified, could not go unpunished.

"Geneviève Rainneville, in collusion with Caniot . . . it's possible. They both loathed Rainneville, for their various reasons, and Geneviève is quite intelligent enough to come up with such a scheme. A man like Caniot would go along with it, don't you think?"

François nodded. "Especially if she sweetened the agreement with a little gold."

"Yes." He slid his half-finished soup toward François, who had been gazing hungrily at it after wolfing down his own. "Here, finish it. Go back to Caniot's neighborhood tomorrow morning and find out if he's had more in his pockets than usual lately and, if so, where people think he got the money." He thrust a few assignats across the table. "For your expenses. Try not to get so drunk that you can't remember what you hear."

"Me? When I'm working, I *don't* get *drunk*," François said, indignant, as Aristide left.

Desmoulins was still skulking in his dark corner at the rear of the court chamber when Aristide returned to the Palais de Justice, shaking rainwater from his hat and overcoat. "Nothing, yet," he said, when Aristide glanced at him.

Most of the lamps in the chamber were unlit. Shadows loomed and wavered in the dim light as people drifted in and out, pointing, chattering.

"I know Souberbielle, on the jury; he's a d-decent man," Desmoulins said abruptly. "A physician, for G-God's sake. He'd see through the lies. So would Antonelle."

Desmoulins seemed pitiably anxious. Perhaps, Aristide thought, the gifted, but often heedlessly cruel, pamphleteer was regretting the too caustic words that had flowed so easily from his pen in 1792. Surely he had never imagined that a petty personal feud with Brissot could have fueled a sequence of events that might soon lead to judicial murder.

Nine o'clock.

The rain fell steadily, spattering the tall windows at either side of the chamber. Spectators continued to straggle in and out of the Salle de Liberté, some debating the affair, some yawning. The coffee and brandy stalls outside in the great hall did a brisk business. Aristide recognized a few acquaintances, including Lemarchant, the notary, and his sister, amid the crowd that was slowly assembling once again as the quarter hours passed: a crowd composed of well-groomed bourgeois as well as of the usual journalists, sensation seekers, and unemployed laborers. The upper bourgeoisie of Paris, he guessed, had begun to fear that when wealthy, sophisticated men like themselves, men who shared their conservative republican sympathies, could be tried for treason on the basis of their too moderate political opinions alone, the Revolution was skirting dangerous territory.

Ten o'clock.

An usher appeared from the rear corridors and relit several of the lamps. "They're coming back," someone whispered, and all around Aristide the murmur arose like the wind sweeping across a meadow, "They're coming back. . . ."

The jurors appeared and trooped to their benches. Desmoulins pushed his way through the crowd to the front, to speak to Antonelle. The jury foreman looked troubled, as did Sauvade, two places away from him.

Troubled, and . . . defeated.

Oh God.

The five judges took their places and the chamber fell silent.

"Are the members of the jury sufficiently convinced of the guilt or innocence of the accused?"

Antonelle rose to his feet. Aristide heard a slight hesitation and a catch in the foreman's voice as he spoke.

"Yes, Citizen President."

"And are the accused innocent or guilty of the charges against them?"

Again the infinitesimal pause.

"We find the accused citizens, namely the ex-deputies Brissot, Vergniaud, Brulard-Sillery, Fauchet, Dufriche-Valazé, Alexandre, Ducos, Mainvielle, Lauze-Duperret, Duprat, Boyer-Fonfrède, Lacaze, Gensonné, Carra, Duchâtel, Vigée, Gardien, Boileau, Lehardy, Lesterpt-Beauvais, and Alba, called Lasource, guilty of all the charges of treason and conspiracy against the Republic."

You expected anything else? Aristide said to himself, even as a queasy pang lanced through the pit of his stomach and his heart pounded until he thought his chest would burst. A soft astonished murmur rippled across the chamber like a racing flame.

Fool! You expected the Jacobin government to let them go free?

"That is your own verdict, Citizen Antonelle?"

"Yes."

As Herman polled the jurors, one by one, Aristide watched Sauvade. He looked as though the entire proceeding had left a nauseating taste in his mouth. Evidently he was now finding his duties as a juryman less to his liking.

"Citizen Sauvade?"

A mutter, scarcely audible.

"Guilty."

"Citizen Trinchard?"

"Guilty, Citizen President."

Guilty . . . guilty . . . guilty . . . guilty . . .

The murmur swelled to uproar, echoing in the marble chamber, and Herman rang his bell. "Silence! Bring in the prisoners."

The prisoners and their defense counsel filed in and took their places. Mathieu turned and murmured something to the man next to him. They looked, all of them, nervous but hopeful; they could know nothing of the new law that had already condemned them.

Herman rang his bell and importantly squared the papers on the table before him into a neat stack before speaking.

"Citizens, the verdict of this tribunal—"

"Verdict!" Boyer exclaimed, half rising from his bench.

"This tribunal has found you guilty of conspiracy against the Republic."

"No!" someone cried. "What are you saying?"

The men on the benches stared at each other and began to shout at the judges. Fouquier shot to his feet, raising his voice in the clamor.

"In the name of the Republic, I demand the sentence of death, within twenty-four hours."

"Sentence?" Vergniaud cried. "There's been no trial!"

"We've barely spoken! Our defense counsel—"

"Murderers! *Butchers!*"

"To hell with you and your republic!"

"No!" said another man among them, with a deep, resonant voice. "Never say that. The Republic is worth dying for, isn't it?"

A noble gesture, but what use are your deaths to anyone?

The shouts of angry protest from the benches would have doubled if one man, on his feet like the rest, had not clutched at his chest and swayed, knees buckling. The prisoners beside him bent to his aid, crying for help. A jeer went up from the crowd nearby.

"Can't take your medicine?"

"Ooh, look, he's fainted!"

One prisoner climbed onto a bench, amid the melee. "Valazé's stabbed himself!"

"Dead!" one of the spectators nearest to the barrier cried over his shoulder. "He's killed himself!"

"Better to take that way out, citizens, than let yourselves be murdered by tyrants!"

The commotion continued. A shower of papers—someone had flung away his notes for his defense—rose from the benches and drifted to the floor. Aristide managed to locate Mathieu among the others on the gradines who were still shouting protests and insults at the judges. He seemed composed and pensive, neither agitated nor fearful.

Herman shouted, "Remove the condemned!" above the uproar. Guardsmen converged upon the prisoners and surrounded them, manhandling them toward the doors. Valazé's body remained behind, sprawled across a bench, a great crimson stain vivid on his pale fawn waistcoat. Mathieu disappeared from Aristide's view amid the crush.

Around him, a few spectators stifled yawns as the excited chatter swelled. Mechanically he looked at his watch. Half past ten.

Death, within twenty-four hours.

He turned about and roughly shouldered his way through the milling crowd.

Halfway to the doors, he came up against Desmoulins, who was staring as the prisoners, still shouting, were shoved out of the chamber. He was tempted to snap "Had enough?" but held his tongue and contented himself with a chilly glance as he passed. Desmoulins shrank back as if slapped.

"It was I who k-killed them, wasn't it? My *Brissot Unmasked . . .*"

"What do you want me to say?" Aristide said, pausing. "Do you want me to make you feel better by telling you, 'No, no, this would have come about whether or not you'd had a hand in it'? It's not that easy."

"I k-killed them," he repeated. Aristide caught the first glint of tears in his eyes in the fitful lamplight. Perhaps it was the first time that Desmoulins had truly realized that careless, venomous words, in a time of crisis, could do terrible damage. "M-my work—killed them."

He turned and fled the chamber. Desmoulins had disappeared by the time Aristide reached the Salle des Pas Perdus.

So late in the evening, the hall was mercifully empty, the stalls shuttered. Like a great church, its cool, candlelit, echoing space was oddly soothing. He floundered away from the crowd spilling from the court chamber and stood a moment by a pillar, head bowed, pressing his palms against the cold marble and willing himself to be calm, as rage and nausea flooded through him like a wave of heat.

28

Voices sounded near Aristide, on the other side of the pillar, two men and a woman, one of the men speaking so softly he was scarcely audible. The woman seemed to be offering words of comfort. Aristide recognized the voices and whipped about.

"After all your fine words about justice," he said. "Is this justice, then? Twenty-one honorable men dying because they and the Jacobins can't agree?"

Sauvade looked away for an instant as Julie Lemarchant took his hand in hers.

"He had no choice," she said. "None of them did."

"There is always a choice!"

"Let me tell you about the choice we were given," Sauvade said, turning back to Aristide and steadying himself with one hand at the pillar while avoiding Aristide's gaze.

"One of Herman's flunkies came into the jury room, polled us, and told us straight out that any juror who dissented from the guilty verdict would find himself before the Tribunal himself within a matter of days. Eight or nine of them were already voting guilty—naturally, because we were never allowed to hear a defense—and they were going to vote that way until Judgment Day. Nothing I could have done would have saved the Brissotins. Nothing. Do you blame me for choosing not to throw my own life away?"

"Let him be," Julie said as Aristide took a step closer to them.

"I'm sorry," Sauvade added. "It offends me deeply, how—how perverted this process has become. I joined the jury to serve justice and—and now—I'm truly sorry." He brushed past Aristide and hurried away, Julie following him, their footsteps loud on the stone floor.

"Justice!" Aristide echoed him, as they disappeared at the end of the great hall.

"He really does mean it," said a voice behind him. Aristide jerked about, startled; he had forgotten Bernard Lemarchant's presence.

"He tried his best, citizen; but it seems that events are passing out of anyone's control." Lemarchant paused, adding earnestly, "Sauvade's a good man. Don't blame him for this. He blames himself enough already."

Aristide said nothing and Lemarchant hurried off, toward the foyer, after his sister and his friend.

So late in the evening, the guards were slow in answering the door in the sunken courtyard below, but Aristide's police card and prison pass finally let him into the Conciergerie once again. The jailers left him in an unheated Gothic antechamber to brood and fume for half an hour more. Somewhere in a nearby office, a clock chimed eleven.

Voices raised in argument echoed outside the antechamber. He caught the words "corpse" and "completely improper" and guessed the debate was of what to do with the body of Valazé, the prisoner who had killed himself. A quick and discreet burial had evidently not been an option.

At last a turnkey appeared and led him through the stinking ground-level corridors to one of the small clerks' offices, where Mathieu was already waiting in the murky twilight that a few candles barely dispelled. A key grated in the lock behind Aristide as he entered. *They've never before locked us in*, he thought, and then realized, with a sickening jolt, that the jailers were sure to take extra precautions with the condemned.

"Well, Robespierre," Mathieu said, after a dreadful moment of silence. "What does one say, I wonder. Except, I suppose, 'adieu'?"

Standing so close to Mathieu, Aristide could see the dark circles under his eyes and a few fine lines around his mouth that he had never before noticed.

"I—" His voice sounded harsh and strange in his ears. "I shouldn't have come. . . ."

"No—I'm glad you came." Mathieu reached out and grasped his forearm, as if to prevent him from fleeing. "It's all right."

He threw his arms around Aristide and clutched him in a fierce grip. Aristide returned the embrace as well as he was able, though he could feel the tautness in his friend's body, like a violin string about to snap.

Mathieu at last let him go and turned away for an instant, adding, "Why are we standing?" He pulled the clerk's chair away from the desk. "Why don't you sit down? That stool will do for me."

He dragged the stool away from the wall and perched on it as Aristide sank onto the chair. "I'm glad you came," he repeated. "Truly. Because I've been thinking about your little problem."

"My what?"

"These murders." He extracted Aristide's notebook from a coat pocket and held it out to him. "Here: This is yours."

"There was another one," Aristide began, as he took the notebook.

"Yes, this morning, right here outside Fouquier's door. The jailers were all talking about it. Were you there?"

"Yes."

"Who was it? Do you know?"

"As far as I know, it was a member of the Convention named Gaillard."

To Aristide's surprise, Mathieu grinned. "Perfect."

"Perfect? Do you mean you know him?"

"Don't know him from Adam. I don't mean to rejoice in the gruesome murder of a fellow creature," Mathieu hastened to add, the grin fading, "even a Jacobin, but it fits. It fits the pattern. And there *is* a pattern."

222 Susanne Alleyn

"A pattern? What do you mean?"

"A pattern in where the bodies were found. If you clear away the others, the ones your royalist murdered."

Aristide shook his head. "We know a second murderer must be out there, either one with a private agenda or one of the spy's confederates, but we're not entirely sure—"

"Which ones the spy murdered? I am." He leaned forward, his gaze fixed on Aristide through the gloom. "Tell me again what his last words were at his trial. How he justified himself."

"He . . . he claimed his victims had suffered less, in dying, than most of the people who are suffering through the shortages . . . and that he had done them a favor, that they were better off dead. Words to that effect."

Mathieu drew a deep breath and leaned back with a sigh and a smile. "Oh, Ravel, it's obvious. Clear away his victims, the wretches he felt were better off dead, and a pattern remains. Have you not seen it?"

Aristide thought for a moment but could not make sense of his words. "Sorry. I—I can't think."

"The Palais de Justice," Mathieu said, ticking off the names on his fingers. "Nôtre-Dame. The Bastille. The cemetery of St. Jean. And now the Conciergerie. Don't you see it?"

Aristide shook his head. Mathieu let out a little impatient sigh and sprang from the stool, to perch restlessly on the edge of the clerk's desk.

"All right, think about home instead. What about the Fort du Hâ, the Palais de Justice of Bordeaux, the principal doors of St. André, and the Place Dauphine? What particular meaning do those have for you, and what do they add up to?"

Aristide felt himself grow cold for an instant as Mathieu listed those familiar landmarks of their home—the prison where criminals were held, the law courts where they were tried and condemned, the cathedral doors where they were forced to kneel and make formal penance before their brutal deaths on the scaffold in the Place Dauphine. All the places where his father—

"You know damned well what they add up to!" he exclaimed, his voice louder than he intended.

"Good," Mathieu said, indifferent to his outburst. "Now turn your mind back to Paris. The Bastille, the Conciergerie, the Palais de Justice, Nôtre-Dame, the cemetery. What does it add up to, Ravel? Think!"

All at once Aristide understood. "Imprisonment . . . trial . . . penance . . . execution?" he said. "At least, as it was before the Revolution: imprisoned at the Bastille, then at the Conciergerie, trial at the Palais de Justice, penance at Nôtre-Dame—"

Penance.

The condemned man led barefoot, bareheaded, clad only in shirt and breeches, through the streets to the cathedral, where he would kneel, clutching a great lit taper two feet tall, on the steps below the carving of the Last Judgment and ask pardon of God, of the king, and of Justice, before his execution at the Place de Grève—

Clutching a lit taper—in shaking hands . . .

So that he might get a smear of candle grease on his shirt and under his thumbnail?

"Of course, I've been acutely aware of such details lately," Mathieu added, with a flash of a bitter smile. "It didn't take me long to see it."

"But the Grève—no corpse has been found at the Place de Grève. At the Place de la Révolution, but not at the Grève."

"But the cemetery of St. Jean is the burial ground closest to the Place de Grève. Just as they now bury—" His voice caught for an instant, and he paused, drew a breath, and began again. "Just as they now bury those who . . . those guillotined . . . at the cemetery nearest the Place de la Révolution. It's simple expediency. The churchyard of St. Jean-en-Grève is where they would bury someone who'd been executed at the Grève."

"But it's closed now, probably hasn't been used for years—"

"Closed to regular parish burials, perhaps, but I expect they could always squeeze in a few more cadavers from the Grève if they had to. They still execute common criminals there, don't they?"

"Yes, of course they do," he said, remembering the scaffold he had seen some days earlier, in front of the Hôtel de Ville.

"Then that's where the bodies are going to go, whether or not the cemetery's officially open. You went there yourself—it's only a few steps from the Hôtel de Ville, isn't it? *Think*, Ravel. Look at the pattern. Imprisonment, trial, penance, execution."

"These murders—they all have something to do with justice."

"Or possibly the lack of it."

It can't be a coincidence, can it, Aristide realized, *when Rainneville was murdered at St. Jean and his body left there where it fell, that the Rainnevilles had a relative who died on the scaffold?*

"And I'd wager that your murderer," Mathieu continued, "if he sticks to his pattern, sooner or later is going to leave a corpse at the Place de Grève." He sat down again on the stool. "Does that help?"

"Yes. Yes, it does. Quite a lot."

"Good. Because, you know, I wanted to—to—accomplish something, something useful, anything at all, before—"

Suddenly he bent and hid his face with one hand, his other arm huddled against him.

"Alexandre?" Aristide said softly. "Mathieu?"

"We put a brave face on it, you know," Mathieu said, raising his head, his voice unsteady. "Because it's the thing to do. 'You're dying for the Republic—don't let the people see you flinch—someday they'll understand it was for their sake.' It's the sort of resoundingly noble thing Brissot would say. But I don't mind admitting to you that I'm scared."

"It's all right . . . it doesn't matter."

"Damn it," he continued, "I've had a good life—wealth, a career, a child, friends, a chance to see progress made at last—and I'm not ready to leave all that. I'm thirty-seven years old. Yet, in another twelve hours, it'll all be gone, done, *over*. And I did want to do some good in the world."

"You played your part in the Revolution," Aristide said. "And I, for one, still believe that the Revolution was necessary."

"Yes, we all played our part in making a mess of it, didn't we? Face it, Robespierre; we've been feeling our way, all this time, like blind men at the top of a cliff, and half the time we've been walking right over the edge." He paused, drew a deep breath, and sighed.

"That's why I said I wanted to have accomplished at least one useful thing. Because I'm not sure that our deaths are going to mean anything. And that scares me, too, that Boyer was right, that we're dying for nothing at all, nothing but—but a show for the mob."

Aristide could think of nothing to say, and soon Mathieu continued. "I'm babbling now. I know it. We all are, to keep the fear at bay. Back there—" He gestured at the door. "The rest are in the old chapel, just down the corridor a ways. It seems they don't take you back to your cell after sentence has been passed; they herd you all together in one place, in order to keep better watch over you. Some wealthy partisan of ours paid to have supper sent in for everyone, did you know that?"

Aristide mutely shook his head.

"It's good. Generous. He didn't spare any expense. Fine dishes, fine wine. Back in the chapel, they're eating and toasting the Republic, those who can stomach the idea of it, and they're all talking, talking, talking between every mouthful, as if it would do some good to talk. That's all we ever were, I think—just a lot of pretty words. Talk, talk, talk. Trust me, they're just as scared as I am. Ducos—he's been cracking jokes all day, even in the Tribunal. Keep on laughing, and you won't have time to weep. Perhaps I'll try laughter. It seems as good a way as any . . ."

He fell silent, staring at the floor between them. Aristide waited for him to speak again, not knowing what he could say that would not be unbearably trivial, and unwilling to leave Mathieu until he was dismissed. At last Mathieu looked at him again, brows drawn a little.

"Ravel."

"Yes?"

"Aristide . . . I . . ."

"What is it? Something you want me to do for you?"

"Yes," Mathieu said hastily, looking relieved. "Yes. A letter—I'm not sure they'll post our final letters if we leave them with the jailers. Please take this and post it for me. That's all." He felt in a pocket and handed the letter over. Aristide glanced at it. It was addressed to an unfamiliar name, in care of a grocer's shop on Rue de la Tisseranderie.

"Who's this?"

"No one you know. Just some unfinished business."

Aristide slipped it into his pocket. "I'll post it tomorrow morning."

"No—not in the morning."

"No?"

"They'll be coming for us in the morning. It'll probably be over by noon. Promise . . . promise me that you'll be there tomorrow, at the Place de la Révolution."

Aristide swallowed. "You want me to—"

"Yes. As a friend."

How did one refuse the last request of the dying? Reluctantly he nodded. "If that's what you want."

"I'm sorry," Mathieu said. "I'm so sorry. But it occurred to me, recently, that every soul in Paris whom I still count as a friend—a real friend—is here in this place with me, and sharing the same cheerful prospect for tomorrow. Except you. I wanted . . . I wanted someone to tell my father and my wife and son, someday, that I died well . . . or at least decently . . . that I didn't disgrace myself. You're the only one I can ask. I'm so sorry. I know you're the last person I ought to—"

"I went to the Place de la Révolution yesterday," Aristide said, without meeting Mathieu's eyes. The shame flooded through him again like the tide. "I've seen it. I can stomach it." He glanced up to discover that Mathieu was watching him with an odd combination of pity and curiosity.

"Why, for God's sake?"

"I wanted to know for myself, without any doubt at all, that Saint-Dizier—the spy—would no longer trouble us."

"How'd he take it?"

"As I expected. Proud to die on the same spot where his king and queen died."

Mathieu let out a short, nervous bark of laughter. "A privilege less meaningful for some of us. Well? Is it as quick as they say?"

"It's quick. They know their business."

"That's good. Not much time to think about it."

"No."

Mathieu asked, after an awkward moment of silence, "Do you want to see the others? Boyer, Ducos?"

"I . . . I'd rather not."

"No, perhaps it's better you don't." He rose to his feet and rapped on the heavy door, calling "Pascal! Let me out of here!" before turning back to Aristide and gazing at him for a long moment with mingled affection and regret.

"I ought to go back to them." He thrust out a hand. "Adieu, Ravel."

"Alexandre."

They shook hands. It was an oddly formal, schoolboyish parting, as if they were merely going home at the end of the summer term and might not see each other for a few weeks; but Aristide could not bring himself to say the word "adieu."

The turnkey let them out of the office. Aristide watched Mathieu stride away at the man's side, hands thrust in pockets, shoulders a little hunched. An instant later he paused and glanced backward, a smile teasing the corners of his mouth.

"Don't be late for our appointment, hear?"

29

Aristide was at the gates of the Palais de Justice an hour after dawn. The morning was damp and cool, with an overcast sky. The thirty-first of October . . . All Hallows' Eve . . . the night of demons and goblins, the night when the doors of Hell lay nearest to the world of daylight. Hell had never seemed so close.

By the time the great clock on the quay chimed nine o'clock, a fitful rain was spattering down once more. A dozen mounted gendarmes had gathered inside the May Courtyard and at least two dozen guardsmen were milling about, keeping the crowd back from the five carts that waited near the gates that led to the Conciergerie.

Sanson and a pair of his assistants appeared shortly before the clock chimed ten. The executioner seemed composed, as always, but grimmer than usual. Twenty-one—twenty, rather, Aristide realized, remembering the suicide—twenty executions in a single morning: surely Sanson had never before been faced with such a bloody task.

"Look there!"

"They're coming!"

The murmur rose all around him. Unwillingly he turned toward the prison door with the others. Two men led the way up the steps, lugging a sheet-draped litter between them.

"They're going to chop Valazé's head off with the rest!" someone exclaimed behind him. "Serves him right."

"That's disgusting," said another voice. "It's not the Republic's job to guillotine corpses. Look at old Sanson—he looks like somebody gave him a cup of vinegar instead of good red wine."

"Nobody's guillotining any corpses," a third man said. "I heard Fouquier ask for it last night—"

"He would, the swine!"

"—but Herman said the same, that it wasn't decent to behead a corpse. They'll take the body to the Place de la Révolution with the rest, but no more, and then bury him in the same grave with them when it's over."

The voices continued to buzz. Other figures had appeared at the top of the steps, hands bound behind their backs, shirt collars cut off, long hair shorn away. Aristide recognized one face, then another. Vergniaud, Boyer-Fonfrède, Fauchet. And Mathieu, looking like a stranger with his hair cut short about his ears.

Twenty-one . . . some he did not know, some he knew only by sight. Twenty-one seemed an immense number when it counted out deaths.

Sillery, limping painfully without the canes he habitually used, two of Sanson's men helping him along. Brissot, Gensonné, Carra. Ducos, behind them, disdaining a hand up the stairs, now slippery with the rain. The four friends from Bordeaux moved toward each other in the confusion and were gestured into the same cart.

Ducos noticed him first. He held Aristide's gaze for a moment before winking and turning to Mathieu, beside him. Aristide gave them an infinitesimal nod—it was not wise to show too much sympathy for the condemned—as Mathieu glanced his way, with a fleeting smile.

I can't do this, he said to himself. *Follow these accursed carts for an hour through Paris, in the midst of a jeering mob—and what good can I do by it?*

He would not be breaking his promise to Mathieu, he decided, if he preceded them to the Place de la Révolution, avoiding the eager, merciless curiosity and glee of the bystanders along the hideous journey. Mathieu was among friends; none of them was truly alone.

A dozen voices began to sing the "Marseillaise" behind him as he elbowed his way toward the tall, gilt-tipped gates. It was not the crowd singing, he realized, glancing over his shoulder, but the condemned men, standing defiantly upright as the five carts began to jolt forward.

The procession would invariably make its way from the Cité to Rue Honoré, so it could complete the journey through the heart of Paris. Such ceremonial processions to the place of execution had, for centuries, made a deliberate show of the state and the law at work; it was no different under the Republic.

The rain continued to spatter down as he hurriedly crossed to the Right Bank, under the shadow of the Châtelet, and went on along the quay, past the Louvre and the Grand Gallery and the high riverside wall of the Tuileries gardens beyond. A thick fog had gathered over the river and drifted to the shore.

He was drenched with sweat in the clammy air by the time he reached the Place de la Révolution, the lank, wet hair clinging to his forehead and neck. A hundred or so idlers already clustered near the scaffold, where Hamelin and another of Sanson's men were making final preparations. A great stack of the coffinlike wicker baskets waited below the platform.

It was the sight of the baskets, more than his first glimpse of the guillotine, that sent a pang of nausea stabbing through him. Like hampers of fish at the market . . . one minute they would be alive, breathing, thinking, speaking; by the next, no more than a load of dead flesh to be heaved into the baskets and carted away. He turned his back to the sight and hurried to Rue de la Révolution, where the procession would enter the square.

A quarter hour later, the first of the mounted gendarmes appeared at the top of Rue de la Révolution. The carts and their escort turned down the short street, for the last few turns of the wheels before the journey's end. As Aristide watched, the condemned men began to sing the "Marseillaise" again, a few voices at first, then all twenty. He saw Mathieu pause a moment and say something to Vergniaud, next to him. They both smiled before resuming the song.

Mathieu . . . look at me; I'm here, as I promised. . . .

The cart creaked past him. Unwillingly, he followed it back into the

square. The executioners busied themselves with assisting the condemned men down to the ground and sorting them into a line, backs to
the scaffold so they would not have to see the guillotine at work.

They took Sillery first, helping him up the steep steps. Aristide
quickly looked away as they led him toward the blade.

Mathieu would be sixth. Only a few minutes more, before—

The blade fell and the gush of blood splattered, as the crowd let
out a hiss and sigh of excitement.

Look at me, Mathieu. . . .

Mathieu turned to Ducos, near him, and murmured a few words.
Ducos laughed before leaning out from the line to Boyer, who was a few
places away, and passing along the jest. Boyer smiled weakly, wincing
as, above them, the blade fell for the second time.

Look at me—I'm here, just over here—

At last their eyes met. Mathieu gave him a nod—*Thank you*—and
shrugged his shoulders, as if to say, *What now?*

Three.

Just a few minutes more, if Sanson's men worked swiftly. His heart
was thudding in his chest, as fiercely as if he were the one waiting in
the line beneath the scaffold.

*What do you say to your oldest friend when they're the last words you'll
ever exchange?*

A pool of blood was collecting beneath the scaffold, growing with
each crimson shower from above. A rivulet began to trickle away between the cobbles, along the gentle slope toward the Seine, dissolving
beneath the fine, pattering rain.

Perhaps there was nothing to be said. It was not the time or place
for speaking, though Aristide saw Mathieu's lips move, murmuring a
few words that he could not make out. He shook his head, trying to
make it clear that he had not understood, but Mathieu merely gave
him a quick grin—the ghost of that easy, boyish grin Aristide knew so
well—and the slightest of nods, then swallowed and looked away.

Four.

The rest were still singing the "Marseillaise," their voices drown-
ing out the crowd's taunts.

And all of a sudden Mathieu was at the head of the line, now a little pensive, perhaps regretful, though still composed. Above him an assistant executioner was guiding a man up the steep steps while another sponged down the seesaw-plank and the lunette, washing away the worst of the blood. A third, with the list in his hand, approached Mathieu, reached for his arm.

Aristide turned away, trembling, tasting acid bile at the back of his throat, and pushed his way past those behind him. A moment later he heard the blade fall once again—*five*—and he increased his pace through the fringes of the crowd toward the stony road that led out to the Champs-Élysées, anything to avoid hearing the sound of the blade as it fell for the sixth time.

Rage and pain gave him strength he did not know he had. He walked blindly, the west wind and the cold rain in his face, straight out through the parkland and meadows to the customs wall and the Étoile barrier where half a dozen roads converged at the city gate, as if he might escape the misery through sheer exhaustion.

He did not remember the long walk back, into the center of Paris, though somehow he avoided the Place de la Révolution. Finally he came to himself on Rue Honoré, not far from the Tuileries, dizzy with nausea, his head throbbing, and a chill sweat soaking his shirt.

His room was another half hour's walk away, but Rue Traversine was mercifully near. Inspector Didier was not on duty in the antechamber of the commissariat, for which he was vastly thankful; nor was Brasseur in his office. He blundered his way into the back room, stumbled into a hard chair, and collapsed upon it, leaning on the table and dropping his head onto his arms. His chest ached and his head felt as if it were about to burst.

He sat alone for a long time, losing himself in the everyday noises of wheeled traffic and street criers from beyond the windows, as the muted chimes of the clock in Brasseur's office rang the quarter hours one by one. Blessed ordinary everyday noises . . . and yet it was obscene, horrible, that life should go on just as usual, hour after hour, as if what had happened at the Place de la Révolution that morning mattered not at all.

"Ravel?"

He turned and found François standing in the doorway. His face must have reflected the misery devouring him, for François stepped forward, staring.

"Are you ill? You look like you just lost your best friend."

Wildly he began to laugh at the foolish commonplace. François uttered a resoundingly blasphemous oath and pulled out a chair opposite Aristide.

"I'm the world's worst imbecile."

Aristide sucked in a few deep breaths and willed himself into an icy calm, though he dared not look at François. At last he went to the water jug in the corner, dampened his handkerchief, and pressed it against his aching eyes.

"Anything I can do?" François said, some minutes later.

"Do?" Aristide echoed him, his voice strangely steady, his expression settling into an impassive mask.

"Old Sanson," he remembered Hamelin saying, *"he just goes silent and formal and polite, like he's hiding behind a mask."*

Odd, that I should behave, after witnessing my friends' deaths, exactly as does the man who butchered them.

Yes, he wanted to say, *yes, there is something you can do. Start a riot, murder all the members of the Jacobin Club, poison the vicious mad dogs who rule Paris, burn the guillotine. As if it would do any good.*

He pressed his hands flat on the table, to keep them from trembling, and looked up at François. "We still have work to do."

30

He scribbled a note to the clerk who had assisted him previously in his search for Rainneville's dossier from the Revolutionary Tribunal. "Take a message to the Pal—the Maison de Justice for me."

François glanced dubiously at the note. "The Maison de Justice? What's this about?"

Keep talking. Keep talking and perhaps, for a minute, you could forget.

"If we're right in guessing that these last murders could be a personal matter and not the work of a second spy, then it seems, somehow, to all come down to Rainneville and his family. Rainneville was a monster; we know that. He raped his servant girls and even his—and even poisoned his wife for her money, if the rumor is true. It's also possible that he first had a hand in the death of his wife's cousin, who may have been falsely accused of treason, so that his wife would inherit the whole of a great fortune. I want to know more about that cousin, and why Geneviève Rainneville might want to avenge him."

"Sounds reasonable. When was this?"

"Thirty years ago, more or less."

"Thirty years!" François exclaimed. "Pardon me for saying so, but your brains are addled for sure. How in the name of all the devils are we ever going to find—"

"He was an aristocrat!" Aristide interrupted him. "How many noblemen can have been executed during the half century before the Revolution—four? Five? He'll be in the records. Have them send me a reply with the essentials. Go."

When François had loped off, Aristide retreated to one of the better cafés in the gardens of the Palais-Égalité, where they still served real coffee for a handsome price, and drank three demitasses in rapid succession to clear his mind. He returned to the commissariat and planted himself in Brasseur's office to await a message from the Palais de Justice.

The message, delivered by an odd-job man, arrived an hour later. Aristide read it over a few times and at last went outside and walked south, across the river to Rue de Seine. Geneviève and Lucienne, who had just risen from their midday dinner, received him warily and did not invite him to sit down.

He looked from one to the other of them. Lucienne was wearing a new, striped afternoon dress, cut in the latest style, but Geneviève's gown was as drab as ever, an old two-piece calico, its flower print fading, that probably had been altered at least twice in the past dozen years in an attempt to fit prevailing fashions.

"Citizenesses, what does the name Montjourdain mean to you?"

"Montjourdain!" Geneviève echoed him. Lucienne clapped a hand to her mouth, staring at him as she flushed a deep pink.

"I see it has some significance for you."

"We never had anything to do with him!" Lucienne burst out. Geneviève turned on her like a tigress.

"Lucienne!"

"We never knew him," Lucienne protested. "I wasn't even born yet."

"I see," Aristide said. "A relative, was he?"

Lucienne's only response was to gasp and hurry out of the room, leaving Geneviève alone with Aristide. "Montjourdain," Geneviève said, in the stony silence that followed, "was a family name of our mother's."

"The Vicomte de Montjourdain was your uncle, then, on your mother's side?"

"Our cousin," she said. "First cousin, once removed."

"This is the cousin you mentioned before, the one you merely said had died?"

"I told you, I don't wish to talk about it."

Thirty years ago, Aristide thought, Geneviève would have been about six or seven, far too young to understand the uproar. Nor would she or Lucienne have learned much of the family scandal as they grew up, beyond hints of a shameful kinsman who was not to be spoken of; properly reared young girls of good family would have known nothing of politics or of corrupt, sordid intrigues.

Though they could not, he knew, have been spared the disgrace that would have blighted the entire family of anyone even remotely connected to a state criminal. That, he knew firsthand.

He strode to the nearest armchair and flung himself down in it. "Sit down, citizeness," he told her. "Sit down this instant!" he repeated, when she did not move. Startled, she backed toward the sofa and dropped onto it.

"Listen to me," he continued. "I don't have the time or patience left to deal with your fastidious aversions. I couldn't care less if you'd rather not admit kinship with a man who was beheaded for treason . . ."

"How would—" she began, but he pressed onward.

". . . even though some people insisted, then and afterward, that he had been the victim of a great injustice. Citizeness, at this moment I don't give a damn about your sensibilities. I need to know whatever it is you know—"

"How dare you?" she interrupted him again. "How would *you* like to be related to a criminal?"

"I know perfectly well what it's like to be related to a criminal," he said. He let that sink in for a moment and rose to his feet, standing over her as she shrank back into the shabby brocade of the sofa.

"My father was executed for shooting my mother and her lover when I was nine years old," he said, watching her shocked reaction. "Just a common murderer. There's no possible taunt or humiliation you may have been subjected to that I haven't suffered myself. I have been through everything you can imagine, and worse, and today saw some of my best friends on their way to the scaffold, and let me assure you I'm in no mood for nonsense or genteel squeamishness! Now, will you tell me what I need to know, or must we sit here like fools and glare at each other until New Year's Day?"

She stared at him. He brought a hand to his eyes as his head began to throb again. "That was uncalled-for and ill-mannered. I beg your pardon."

"You needn't apologize," she said at last. She rose and diffidently took his hand in both her own. "I'm so sorry. I—my own troubles—I may not have led a happy life, but it's all behind me now. I can't begin to imagine how you suffered today, but . . . I think we understand each other better."

He pressed her hand, a gesture of sympathy, and felt her flinch. It would be a long time, he thought, if ever, before she was ready to allow any tenderness or intimacy into her life.

"What do you want to know?" She drew away from him and gestured to a chair, but he remained on his feet, rigid, and clasped his hands tightly behind his back.

"You earlier mentioned a cousin who died and left your mother the sole heir to a fortune. Was Hippolyte-Gilles-Aimable Courbonnet, Vicomte de Montjourdain, this cousin?"

"Yes."

"So your mother eventually inherited twice what she would have, had the vicomte not died when he did."

"Yes."

He turned and paced toward the mirror that hung above the pink marble mantel. "Your father was an army officer himself, back then," he said, without looking at her. "Did he have a hand in making the initial accusations against Montjourdain?"

"Are you suggesting that Father might have deliberately tried to get him out of the way, so that he could get his hands on all of Great-uncle's fortune?"

"Do you think it likely?"

"It wouldn't surprise me for a moment," she said. "You see, I heard rumors . . . whispers . . . years later. That Father was known to have been connected with one or two of the officers who did accuse Monsieur de Montjourdain of treason. It would have been just like him, to stay out of the mess himself but pull strings in the background like a puppeteer with a marionette."

"Do you recognize the names Gaillard or Noyelle?"

"Yes, Gaillard. A man named Gaillard de Cauville used to call on Father."

"Could they have conspired together against Montjourdain?"

"I don't know," she said, after a long silence. "I was a child. No one ever talked about it in front of me, except the servants gossiping."

"Let me get this straight," Aristide said. He strode to the bell by the door and tugged at it, then pulled out his notebook. "Your mother and the Vicomte de Montjourdain are first cousins. They are joint heirs to a substantial fortune belonging to an elderly, childless relative."

"Our great-uncle Frédéric-Louis Courbonnet. He was very clever. He owned some land that proved to have a rich vein of copper, and made a fortune mining and smelting it, even though people said it was unsuitable for him to be in trade like that. But none of his children lived to grow up."

"Your mother marries your father, César Rainneville, while Montjourdain—did Montjourdain have any heirs of his own?"

Geneviève shook her head. "His wife died in childbirth with their first child, and the child died, too. He remarried eventually, but they lived apart from one another and had no children. I hear he was devoted to his mistress."

"Just so. Your mother marries Rainneville, and the marriage contract stipulates that if your mother predeceases your father, all her property will pass to him and not directly to any children she might have with him."

"Yes."

"Some years later—did your great-uncle show signs, perhaps, of infirmity?"

"I really don't remember. It was decades ago."

The elderly maid, Bertrande, sidled into the room. "Mademoiselle rang for me?"

"Come in, Bertrande," Aristide said. "I want you to think back to when your late mistress was young. Do you remember, long ago, if old Monsieur Courbonnet, your mistress's uncle, perhaps fell ill not long after your mistress married Monsieur Rainneville?"

The old woman glanced, puzzled, at Geneviève, who nodded. "Tell monsieur whatever you know."

"Yes, m'sieur, that he did," Bertrande said, after a moment's thought. "I remember madame telling me about it. She said her uncle had had an apoplexy, like he'd had once before, and she was worried about him. I didn't know what that was, but I remembered the funny-sounding word. That's a kind of fit, isn't it?"

Geneviève cast her a swift glance. "Dear Lord, yes, you're right. An apoplexy. I remember it now, thinking what a funny word it was. Great-uncle didn't die of it, but it wasn't long after that when the war ended and all the uproar about—about the vicomte began, and then Mother talked only about him."

"Madame had a soft spot for Monsieur de Montjourdain," Bertrande said unexpectedly. Geneviève glanced at her.

"What do you mean?"

"Why, she was always a little in love with him all her life. A crush, you know, like girls have on good-looking gentlemen what they see a lot of. Monsieur de Montjourdain was handsome as an angel, and a fine man on a horse, and enough older than what she was to captivate her when she was just a young thing. She went all to pieces when that nasty business began and they were calling him a traitor."

Aristide scrawled a few last notes and closed his notebook. "Do away with Montjourdain," he said, as Geneviève dismissed the old maidservant and turned back to him, "and your mother becomes the sole heir of a wealthy man who might not be expected to live long. Do away with Montjourdain, and a self-seeking, self-centered man is no longer competing for his wife's attention with a dazzling rival whom she's known since girlhood. As neat a couple of motives for judicial murder as I ever saw."

Brasseur found him at seven o'clock in the evening in his own office on Rue Traversine, meticulously laying out cards across a small side table. He paused, eyeing Aristide, a fist at his hip.

"Thinking something out?"

"Yes," Aristide said, without looking up from the cards. "I'm grasping at straws here, Brasseur, but so far it's the best lead I've got. Does the name Montjourdain mean anything to you?"

"Not a thing. Why? Did you get a tip about Saint-Dizier's accomplice?"

"He had no accomplice." He took another card from the pack and stared at it, quickly placing it on one of the tableau piles before his hand began to tremble. "I think we've been racing off in the wrong direction."

"But the royalist plots—"

"There's no great, wide-reaching royalist plot. Oh, probably some fanatics are cooking one up somewhere, but not in this. We're all letting ourselves believe the hysterical rumors—which is what Saint-Dizier, and those who sent him, wanted. There's no plot." He turned over the three of diamonds, placed it on the two, and added a four, five, and six to the foundation pile. This round of patience might yet come out properly.

"All right," said Brasseur, settling himself at his desk, "tell me why. And if you're right, then who's taken over from where Saint-Dizier left off? Don't tell me his ghost is chopping off heads!"

"It's not a second royalist taking up Saint-Dizier's task. He had no confederates." He paused, wondering why he was so certain of the fact, and added, "A man like him works alone. I saw enough of myself in him to know that."

"Eh? Then who—"

"I believe, now, that there was always a second murderer, with no connection whatsoever to Saint-Dizier." Eight on the seven, nine on the eight. Ten knave queen king, and it was done, the cards sorting themselves out.

"Or rather," he continued, still staring hard at the cards, "a *first* murderer. There were two murderers from the start—"

"Two!"

"Yes—it's the only way this all makes sense. Two murderers, not one. I doubt the two of them ever had anything to do with each other, or even knew who the other was."

"But I'm damned if I'll believe it was just chance that two people, without any connection, should both be chopping off heads in back alleys—"

"No, of course it's not chance. The other killer started it. Saint-Dizier seized upon the idea—face it, Brasseur, beheading strangers in alleys isn't something a sane man, however fanatical, would conceive on his own—and he was just adding to the total, hurrying things along, to stir up trouble." He paused, sorting out his ideas as he gathered up the cards into a pack and rapped them down against the desk to square the edges. Most of the cards were grubby, bent, and frayed; it was time he replaced them with a fresh pack, free of royalty and full of patriotic geniuses, liberties, and equalities.

"You'll agree, first of all, that the killer we caught was a royalist provocateur who chose strangers at random, easy prey; their deaths were simply a means to his goal of disrupting and discrediting the Republic."

Brasseur shrugged. "That much, we know."

"We know most of what Saint-Dizier did, and I think I can guess the rest. He came to Paris and took a lodging in the Cité, among the foulest, seediest slums in town, where he could lie low and move unnoticed, where the police scarcely dare to go. And, perhaps not coincidentally, not far from the Conciergerie and his queen's prison cell."

"Go on."

"I expect he learned, soon enough, that any attempt to rescue Antoinette would be hopeless; she was far too well guarded. But, living in the Cité, he would have heard a juicy rumor about a headless corpse discovered just a few streets away, behind the Palais de Justice."

Brasseur slapped the desk with an open palm. "Of course!"

"Wouldn't such a lurid murder strike your fancy, if you were a bitter enemy of the Republic?"

"Headless corpses littering the streets of Paris!"

"A fitting symbol, in his mind, of what had happened to France. So he began his own campaign of terror in the streets."

"We know that," Brasseur said impatiently. "But what makes you think that Saint-Dizier didn't murder the first one—what's his name—Jumeau?"

"Jumeau himself." Aristide paused for a moment, recalling what Mathieu had said to him the night before. "I heard what Saint-Dizier shouted out at the Tribunal, just before they hauled him away. He said, 'Your republic has done nothing for the people. Can you deny that my victims suffered less, at the moment of their deaths, than thousands who are dying of want? It was an act of mercy to put those wretches out of their misery!'"

"Wretches?"

"That's right. 'It was an act of mercy to put those wretches out of their misery.' Would you have called Jumeau a wretch? Or Rainneville? Or Gaillard? They weren't poor men; they weren't starving. They were well dressed, prosperous, clearly bourgeois or petty ex-aristocrats."

"Yes, whoever murdered them would have seen that in an instant."

"Men of that sort weren't Saint-Dizier's targets; on the contrary, he seems to have felt, in some twisted way, that he was doing the down-and-outs a favor by slitting their throats."

"You're saying that Saint-Dizier knew perfectly well that he hadn't done all the murders, though he was content to let us think he had, and to take all the credit for stirring up panic."

"Yes. Any opportunity to confound us, you see. But I think he tripped himself up at the Tribunal. At the last instant, his last chance to proclaim his devotion to the monarchy, he let his emotions get the better of him, and he let it slip that his own victims had been wretches who, in his mind, were better off dead anyway."

"Faith, you may be right. Two unconnected murderers . . . that makes all the difference. If we can separate the murders, and know which Saint-Dizier actually committed—"

"It's clear as day. First of all, he only murdered people who had gained nothing from the Revolution—in other words, beggars, whores, the destitute, the working poor who were always only just scraping by." Aristide reached for a quill and began crossing off entries in his notebook. "Désirée Marquette was a respectable woman reduced to selling herself at the Palais-Égalité; we know, from the witnesses, and his own detailed admission, that he killed her. That's one."

"Jeanne Houdey—a poor ink seller—Saint-Dizier's work," Brasseur said, craning his neck to look at the list.

"He stabbed Echelard; we know why. Then some beggars and street whores of both sexes. All ordinary folk, poor all their lives or reduced to poverty, familiar with hunger, cold, disease, thankless, endless toil, whose lives have certainly not improved much—and may have grown worse— since the beginning of the Revolution. Take those seven away and what do we have?"

Brasseur took up the list again and ran a finger down the names. "Jumeau, retired clerk of the Parlement; Noyelle, retired army captain; Deverneuil, ex-deputy prosecutor to the high court of the Parlement; Rainneville, retired army officer and man of property, ex-noble; and Gaillard, deputy to the National Convention from the *département* of the Allier." He checked himself and flipped through a dossier on his desk. "Didier just questioned Gaillard's servant; his family's back at home in the provinces, of course. Here we are. He was a retired army officer, according to his man; from a minor noble family, formerly known as Gaillard de Cauville. I'll be damned."

"Five men, all middle-aged or old, all of a certain class, professional, military, or minor nobility: three soldiers, and two men connected to the Parlement of Paris. And all their bodies were left at locations across Paris that have something to do with justice as it was carried out before the Revolution."

Thank you, my friend . . . this, at least, is your legacy.

"The Parlement?" said Brasseur. "You think that's the link? Or the army?"

Aristide shook his head. "I think it's all connected, through the Parlement and the army, to the name I mentioned before: Montjourdain."

31

M ontjourdain," Brasseur repeated, brow furrowed.

"It was during the American war," said Aristide, with a glance at the page of notes that the helpful clerk at the Palais de Justice had sent him. "Not the Americans' war of independence: the earlier one, during the Seven Years' War. He was an officer, a colonel, and he lost a battle to the British." He set down eight cards to begin a new round of patience as he spoke. "It was one of the final battles in North America. Rumors began to spread that he had retreated far too quickly, and lost far more men than he should have, and he was eventually tried for high treason before the Grand' Chambre of the Parlement. I don't know the details; I'd have to study the dossier. But he was found guilty."

"And executed," said Brasseur, nodding. "Yes. I remember that, now that I think about it. Montjourdain . . . wait a minute. . . ." He snapped his fingers. "The army. That's it. It wasn't my regiment, but some of the old career soldiers were still arguing about him when I was in America myself, even though it all happened when I was a kid, long before I joined up. It was a dodgy affair, wasn't it?"

"Evidently."

"And all this has to do with our murders . . . how?"

Aristide continued to lay down the cards, one by one. Somehow, miraculously, his voice was calm and his hands steady. "Montjourdain was condemned to death. As he was a nobleman, they couldn't hang him. He was beheaded at the Place de Grève. But they made a botch of it and he died a lot more painfully and horribly than he should have; it took three or four blows to take his head off."

"Three or four blows?" Brasseur said. "Just like ours. I see where you're going."

"As I said, I'm grasping at straws. But now someone murders a former chief clerk to the Grand' Chambre and hacks his head off and leaves his corpse behind the Palais de Justice. And three retired army officers, one of whom was related to Montjourdain by marriage, and an elderly deputy prosecutor from the Parlement, are found decapitated near the Bastille, Nôtre-Dame, the Conciergerie, and the cemetery nearest the Grève, where Montjourdain's body would have been buried. Found murdered by someone who hacks their heads off with three or four blows, while at least two of them, as we saw, were still alive and feebly struggling to get away—which is one thing Saint-Dizier never claimed he did. It may be a bizarre coincidence . . . but, then again, it may not."

"Retired army officers . . ."

"It's only the work of a few hours to look through the court records. What if Deverneuil had prosecuted the affair, and the officers who gave evidence against Montjourdain at his trial happened to be friendly with Rainneville? Geneviève knew the name Gaillard right away."

"Let me get this straight," Brasseur said, leaning forward. "You think someone—a relative, perhaps—is taking revenge for Montjourdain's death, years afterward? That the murderer blamed Jumeau and Deverneuil because they were officials of the Parlement that condemned him, and blamed Rainneville, Noyelle, and Gaillard because they were enemies . . ."

"Or somehow directly benefited from his death."

". . . and had given false evidence against him?"

"Isn't it possible?"

"Who, then?"

"Montjourdain had no children of his own," Aristide said, wishing that the conclusion was not springing so easily to his mind, "but I think, after enduring a living hell for two decades, Geneviève Rainneville is capable of almost anything. Perhaps, besides pure hatred of her father, she feels duty-bound to avenge both her mother and Montjourdain, who, after all, was her mother's cousin, her own flesh and blood."

"But why go into the revenge business *now*? Saints above, it's been thirty years."

"Flesh and blood," Aristide repeated, scarcely hearing Brasseur. *Flesh and blood . . .*

"Oh, Lord." He began to bite his nails, thinking it out. "Perhaps that's it. She didn't even know him, but—could he have been more to her than a cousin once removed?" He tried to envisage the portraits that had hung in the Rainneville salon. Lucienne had been the picture of her mother, but Geneviève—Geneviève resembled neither of her parents. Weak, circumstantial evidence at best, he reminded himself, but still . . .

"They told me—their servant told me that Madame Rainneville, their mother, had once been in love with her handsome cousin."

"What are you getting at?" said Brasseur. "That the lady was indiscreet and passed off Montjourdain's child as her husband's?"

"Well, I can't imagine that life with Rainneville was a bed of roses. What if Geneviève isn't Rainneville's daughter at all? And sometime not long ago, perhaps finding an old letter or what have you, she finally realized it?" He sprang up and paced back and forth across the room. "Brasseur—the swine Rainneville—he'd been raping her repeatedly for the past twenty years or more. His own daughter. But perhaps he always suspected she *wasn't* his own daughter. Perhaps that was his twisted way of punishing his wife for cuckolding him. Take it out on the bastard child, over and over and over again, long after his wife is dead and past caring. Plot the downfall of the lover, poison his wife and watch her die by degrees, and tyrannize and terrify both girls, never allow them lives of their own, punish them for their very existence. All because an adulterous wife bruised his pride thirty or forty years ago."

"And now the daughter knows it, too—"

"And is killing two birds with one stone. Ridding herself of the man she hates more than anything on this earth—"

"And at the same time avenging her real father, by murdering Rainneville and all the rest who conspired against Montjourdain?"

"She's also, of course, getting hold of that fortune at last, that should have been hers."

"It's a stretch. Got any proof of all this?"

"No idea. It's only just come to me—but it seems to make more and more sense." Aristide bent over the table where the cards lay and with a quick savage gesture pushed them together into a heap and gathered them up. "And I do know, without a doubt, that if anyone who was connected to Montjourdain—anyone who had cared for him as a friend, a brother, and who knew the vile circumstances that led to his death—if anyone felt half the rage that is boiling inside me right this minute, then they would be quite capable of a brutal murder if offered the opportunity. Perhaps more than one murder."

"Rage?" Brasseur said. He smacked the desk again. "Mother of God. I heard the newscriers—it had clean slipped my mind. I'm sorry, Ravel. It's—it's a damned shame."

"Thank you." He did not know what else to say.

"The Rainneville women," Brasseur continued, after a brief, uneasy silence. "You can't be thinking that a couple of upper-class spinsters did all this themselves, can you?"

"No, this was the work of a man—and I'm sure the servants could provide them with alibis for all the murders. But if Geneviève had found a man who bore a violent grudge against Rainneville, and who wasn't too particular about who else he killed, so long as he was well paid for it . . ."

"Have someone in mind?"

"Oh, yes. A man whose daughter Rainneville raped when she was a servant in the house. And he's a butcher by trade. If he can gut a pig and hack it apart, I expect he can chop off a human head."

"Did Montjourdain have any other family who'd want to see Rainneville dead?"

"No children, and probably no siblings, if he and Madame Rainneville were the only heirs to their uncle's fortune." He pushed the note he had received half an hour earlier toward Brasseur. "Nicault at the Palais de Justice sent me the bare facts, but I expect I can learn more from the trial transcripts."

He dropped into the chair again, feeling all at once immensely weary, and hid his face in his hands. Brasseur said nothing and Aristide finally glanced up at him, meeting his gaze for the first time that afternoon. "Or do you think I'm raving mad?"

"No," said Brasseur, "I don't think you're mad."

Aristide put up only token protest when Brasseur insisted he take some supper. He shared a silent meal with Brasseur and his wife and at last fell asleep in sheer exhaustion, fully clothed, on the daybed in their small parlor.

He went straight to the Palais de Justice at first light and spent four hours in the archives, poring through the files relating to the trial of Hippolyte-Gilles-Aimable Courbonnet, Vicomte de Montjourdain, in November of 1763. Brasseur sent Dautry to join him in mid-morning and they returned to Rue Traversine as the clocks were striking one o'clock, to find Brasseur and François waiting for them.

"Well," Aristide said, when they had gathered around the table. He opened his notebook. "Has Brasseur brought you up to date, François?"

François nodded. "About this aristo, you mean? Someone, maybe a daughter who never even knew him, avenging dirty work thirty years later? Seems a bit far-fetched."

"But it's the only lead we have," Brasseur said, interrupting him. "Go on, Ravel."

"All right." He closed his eyes for a moment, marshaling his thoughts, grateful for the distraction the records had provided him for the past hours. "Montjourdain came from an old noble family of modest means on his father's side—his mother was an Englishwoman of similar background—and went into the army as a career. He was a colonel in 1760, when his regiment was sent to America to fight the British. To make a long story short, one day a party of British and Indians surprised him and his men, out in the wild country near one of the big lakes, well beyond any settlements. They fought a brief battle, in which they were vastly outnumbered by the British reinforcements, and eventually retreated, leaving a large number of men dead or captured.

"That defeat led to a British advance and to the last, decisive battle of the war. The British captured Montjourdain during the initial skirmish and held him prisoner for three years, until the peace treaty was signed, although the British commander initially offered to release him, as a gentlemanly gesture."

"Release him?" François said.

"The British officer was a distant relation," said Dautry. "Pure bad luck. That became another black mark against him."

"But half the nobility—the ex-nobility—of France is related to foreigners, in one degree or another," Brasseur protested.

"Certainly," Aristide said, "but Montjourdain had made some enemies during his career. He had a reputation for high-handedness, apparently, and was talented and knew it. And he had no patience for strutting aristocratic fools who had purchased their commissions because they enjoyed looking dashing in an officer's uniform but didn't know which end of a cannon was which."

"What happened, anyway," Dautry burst in, "is that several officers accused him of treason, because he had retreated too quickly and lost too many men."

"Now wait a minute," François said. "Anyone who's ever worn a uniform knows that every commander makes a mistake now and then. They don't accuse you of high treason because of it."

"Circumstances were against him," Aristide said, glancing back at his notes. "Including his own capture, which, his accusers suggested, was merely a ruse for him to spend some time behind enemy lines, revealing French military secrets to the British commander who was his own second cousin on his mother's side. And everybody wanted someone to blame for losing Canada. That, in the end, was enough to have Montjourdain arrested for treason as soon as the British released him in 1763. He was tried a few months later, found guilty, and executed."

"In the most ghoulish of circumstances," Dautry added. "It took a few chops to behead him."

"So you think all these men were mixed up in Montjourdain's trial," François said, "and now somebody's getting back at them by chopping *their* heads off, too, and making sure it's just as gruesome?"

"Precisely. Rainneville, naturally, benefited the most from Montjourdain's death: that's one. And according to the records, Deverneuil was the deputy royal prosecutor at the tribunal of the Grand' Chambre at the time—"

"Hold on, wouldn't it have been Joly de Fleury himself who prosecuted a case of high treason?" Brasseur said, referring to the royal prosecutor-general who had held the position for decades under the monarchy.

"Joly de Fleury was absent, probably due to illness, so Deverneuil was in charge of the affair. Two. And the chief witnesses against Montjourdain were Noyelle, who was a captain in his regiment, and Gaillard, who was a senior officer and friendly with Rainneville. Three and four. And, of course, Jumeau was chief clerk at the Parlement. He'd have been there at Montjourdain's trial. That's five. It all fits."

"And you think this woman, Rainneville's daughter, who might really be Montjourdain's little by-blow, is behind all this revenge."

"What do you all think?"

One by one, the other three nodded.

"It makes a good case," said Brasseur.

"I wish to call on Citizen Danton," Aristide told the porter who answered his ring at the house on the Cour du Commerce. "My name is Ravel; he knows me—"

"Citizen Danton?" the porter repeated. "But he's not here, citizen."

"I'll leave a message, then, if I may. When do you expect him back?"

"Nobody knows."

"I don't understand," Aristide said, with an uneasy feeling that all was not as it should be.

"Why, he packed up and left, with his family, a fortnight ago, the day Antoinette's trial began. They've gone to the country. Everybody knows Danton's been absent from the Convention," the porter added, with an incredulous glance at him.

"I've been occupied with other matters," said Aristide, thinking sourly, *The bastard could at least have told me he was leaving town.* He thrust his hands in his coat pockets, scowling.

What now?

As much as he detested the idea, perhaps a visit to the public prosecutor was in order.

32

He turned his steps northward to the Cité and the Palais de Justice. As he passed Michalet's, he saw two familiar figures ahead of him: Sauvade, returning to the Tribunal after dining with Lemarchant.

No matter how disillusioned Sauvade may be with revolutionary justice, Aristide brooded, *he's still dispensing it. Or have things gone so far that men fear they'll be suspected of incivism if they resign from the jury in disgust?*

Sauvade and Lemarchant paused at the great gates to the May Courtyard and Aristide was abreast of them before he realized it. They exchanged chilly nods before Sauvade turned away and hurried into the courtyard, toward the grand staircase.

Sauvade was not looking well. The juror's handsome features seemed to have grown sharp and haggard over the past few days, as if the strain of the Brissotins' trial and its moral dilemmas had worn him down. Just like—

Aristide stopped short and gazed after Sauvade's retreating figure. Just like . . .

Why did Sauvade remind him so strongly of Geneviève Rainneville?

He mulled it over. Geneviève and Sauvade both showed outward signs of having carried an intolerable burden—hers of shame and misery, his of guilt in acting against the demands of his conscience—but it was more than that.

It was Sauvade's fierce singlemindedness, he realized a moment later, that he thought Geneviève shared; it had even given them the same look in the eyes. In Sauvade, it was that hard, blazing, adamant thirst for justice. And if Geneviève shared that craving, she could well have chosen to exact justice at last, as Aristide had suspected, for all of Rainneville's victims: justice for herself and for her sister, justice for her mother, justice—why not?—for Montjourdain.

Though a mere opinion, he reminded himself once again, was very far from being evidence.

"Citizen Ravel," Lemarchant said, behind him, "might I have a word with you?"

Aristide came to himself with a start, guessing what Sauvade's friend was going to say to him. "I understand that Sauvade is your best friend," he said, without looking at Lemarchant, "and you want to see the good in him, but *my* best friend died yesterday because Sauvade said 'Guilty.' "

"That's not fair. You know there was nothing he could have done."

"No?"

"Give me five minutes, I pray you. Let me tell you a little about him," Lemarchant continued, when Aristide said nothing, and drew Aristide aside to a corner of the courtyard, out of the thin stream of foot traffic. "He's the most honest man I know. And I've never known anyone who cares as passionately about fairness and integrity as Sauvade does, no matter what you may think."

He was silent for a moment, his round, cheerful face unusually grave. "Do you remember that story my mother told you, that evening when you called on us?"

"Story?"

"About when he and I were schoolboys and played truant to—"

"Yes."

"His desire for justice—I think it began then. We were only twelve or thirteen."

"Well?" Aristide said, half listening, still thinking of Geneviève.

"You mustn't think too harshly of us," Lemarchant added. "We were just silly boys. As Mother told you, he and I and another boy sneaked out of school one day to go to the Place de Grève, to an execution."

Aristide could not help wincing, but Lemarchant did not seem to notice. "You see, it wasn't just another hanging or breaking," he continued. "That wasn't worth being whipped for. But that execution was special. It was the execution of a nobleman, and of course he was to be beheaded."

"Beheaded?" Aristide echoed him. Suddenly Lemarchant had his full attention.

"Back when we were boys, how many times would you expect to get a chance to see that? Once in twenty years, maybe. We were close enough so we could see everything. A whole procession of magistrates in their fine coaches, and soldiers, and a few priests, and the executioner with half a dozen assistants, and finally the condemned man himself, in a carriage."

Yes, once, not so long ago, the riffraff had been hauled away to the gallows or the wheel in a dung cart, while "gentlemen" had ridden to the scaffold in their own carriages, to be honorably beheaded while the spectators prayed for their souls.

Now everyone was equal: the lowest beggar and the queen of France all traveled in the same cart.

Lemarchant went on. ". . . And they blindfolded him and bound his hands behind his back, and helped him to his knees. But I glanced over at René, and I was shocked to see how pale he was. He looked as if he'd seen a ghost."

"He was regretting having come to the execution?" Aristide said.

"He must have been. I thought he was going to faint."

"Didn't he?"

"Not right then. Maybe he'd have been all right if the *bourreau* hadn't bungled the job."

"Bungled it!"

Could more than one nobleman have been executed for high treason—executed so gruesomely—during the past half century?

"I nearly fainted, myself. He began the swing well enough, but his aim went wrong. Instead of the sword slicing through the man's neck, it only caught him across the jaw and wounded him. The assistants grabbed the sword and tried to finish the job, but of course it didn't work, and they had to do it with a hatchet, blow after blow, while he was still moaning from the pain. Blood everywhere. It was the most horrible thing I've ever seen. That's when René fainted. And from that day forward—"

All at once Aristide felt as though he had just been spun about a dozen times and left reeling.

"The victim," he interrupted Lemarchant, "what was his name? Was it Montjourdain?"

"Yes, that's the one. Everybody was talking about it. It was the scandal of the season, what had happened." Lemarchant took a step forward and gripped Aristide's arm. "Do you see now? From that day forward, Sauvade has never spoken a word about what we saw, but that absolutely uncompromising desire for justice of his has become his whole life. I know that as well as I know my own name. So please, citizen, please believe him, and try to understand him."

"I do understand," Aristide said. He turned away from Lemarchant to stare up at the Palais de Justice, its columns and squared dome looming above the grand staircase.

The Palais de Justice . . . where the Parlement had once sat in convocation in the Great Chamber. The Palais de Justice, where a merciless court had judged the Vicomte de Montjourdain. The Palais de Justice, where the Revolutionary Tribunal, seated in that same chamber, doled out justice even more rigid and merciless.

The Palais de Justice . . . where Louis Jumeau had once been a fixture and where his headless corpse had been found.

Louis Jumeau?

A mere record keeper, a man who had had no control over any verdict given at the court. Why, why, of all the numerous staff at the courts, had Jumeau been singled out, he asked himself, as the answer began to unfold before him. Why had Jumeau been the first to die, when Clarisse Lépinay had insisted that her harmless, amiable, middle-aged protector had been the most generous and conscientious of men?

"Where's François?" he demanded, rushing into Brasseur's office. "Is he here?"

Brasseur jerked his head toward the adjoining room, where François, his booted feet up on the desk, was idling with Dautry. He swung his feet off Dautry's desk as Aristide strode in, and gazed at him in mild alarm.

"François—thank God—I want you on the next coach—no, hire a postchaise—that'll be quicker—"

"Eh? What did I do?"

"I've got a job for you. I need you to find someone right away." He scribbled down the particulars on a scrap of paper that Dautry pushed at him and thrust it at François, together with a handful of silver and crumpled assignats. "Go prepare for a few days' journey, and hire a postchaise, and damn the expense."

"What's this about?" said Brasseur, as Aristide returned. "Got an idea?"

"Yes. I know—I know everything." He paused and took a deep breath. "Or perhaps I'm completely off my head. But I'm sending François out to Rambouillet to find—I pray to God he succeeds—to find Citizeness Lépinay."

"Lépinay? That's the courtesan, isn't it?"

Even I, Aristide thought, scarcely hearing him, *though I may be the son of a man who died on the scaffold—until yesterday, even I never saw someone I loved butchered before my eyes . . . probably she never knew . . . never guessed at the truth, until I told her myself how Jumeau died—*

"What's a middle-aged fancy woman got to do with all this?" Brasseur demanded.

"Everything. That's why she packed her bags and fled Paris. She suspected . . ."

"Suspected what? Or who?"

"Why did Jumeau die first?"

"Eh?"

"Why was Jumeau the first one to be murdered?"

"Because he was at Montjourdain's trial."

"As a clerk. Little more than a spectator. Yet something about him made it vitally important that he die first. If you suddenly go on an insane spree of revenge, thirty years after the injustice that you're avenging took place, something has to set you off. I think it was Jumeau—and Citizeness Lépinay." Aristide glanced at the clock on the mantel. It was past three o'clock. "Brasseur, I need you to come with me to the Palais de Justice this evening, after the Tribunal's done sitting for the day. I need you to help me convince the president and the public prosecutor that Geneviève and Lucienne Rainneville, and their confederate, Caniot, have to be arrested and tried as soon as possible."

"But I thought you just said that Lépinay has something to do with it—"

"She does. She knows the truth. But I've no hard evidence, no proof—none at all. We'll have to startle it out of her. This is the only way it's going to work."

33

"I can give you five minutes," Fouquier snapped, striding with a whirl of black robes into his office, Aristide and Brasseur following him from the antechamber. The evening session of the Tribunal had just ended. Fouquier squinted at them in the candlelight and pushed aside a litter of papers and bread crumbs as he settled himself at his desk.

"It's about the headsman murderer," Aristide said. He clasped his hands tightly behind his back and hoped the revulsion he felt in the presence of the prosecutor who had demanded his friends' deaths was not visible in his face.

"He's been dealt with, has he not?"

"Yes, Citizen Prosecutor, but are you aware that a similar murder was committed soon after Saint-Dizier was executed? The corpse was left right here, near the door you use yourself."

"I had heard something to that effect," Fouquier said, with an infinitesimal nod. "Well?"

"I believe that this other killer committed at least one of the murders that Saint-Dizier confessed to, that of Citizen Rainneville. Moreover, I have a strong suspicion who's behind it."

"Splendid." The public prosecutor rang a bell, barked out an order for coffee to the clerk who appeared at the door, and turned back to

Aristide. "What has it to do with me, pray? That's a matter for the criminal court—unless this other murderer is also a royalist agent?"

"It would be a criminal matter only, citizen," Brasseur said, looming out of the darkness and speaking for the first time, "but it ought to be brought to your attention, if it hasn't been already, that the victim found here at the Conciergerie, Citizen Gaillard, was a deputy to the Convention. That's a political issue, the murder of a member of the government."

"Yes. Well?"

"And the perpetrator of such a crime should properly be tried before the Revolutionary Tribunal and not the criminal court," said Aristide. "Isn't that correct?"

"Correct."

"You see, it's most important, when we have the persons responsible in custody—"

"Persons?" Fouquier interrupted him, with a flicker of interest in his black eyes. "More than one, you say? A plot?"

"Commissaire Brasseur and I believe that this secondary affair was actually a conspiracy to murder one man for personal reasons."

"You do see, Citizen Prosecutor," said Brasseur, "that the murderers, when we have them, must be tried by the Tribunal, and as soon as possible."

"Certainly." The unforgiving shadows in the room molded Fouquier's harsh features into a caricature as his lips curved into the semblance of a small, bitter smile. "The murder of a representative of the people cannot be ignored."

"It's also essential that you prosecute it yourself," Aristide continued, repeating the argument he had rehearsed to himself many times during the past few hours. It was absolutely vital, for his plan to unfold as he prayed it would, that the Rainnevilles' trial take place before the first division of the Tribunal. "Only you, citizen, are capable of pursuing this tangled affair to its proper end. Besides, the whole city must know about these murders by now, despite our best efforts. A trial before the most important division of the Revolutionary Tribunal, in the Hall of Liberty, before the public prosecutor himself, will impress it upon the people that such an abominable crime is worthy of immediate attention by the most important officers of the court."

Fouquier's smile grew infinitesimally wider, though his eyes remained cold. "You intrigue me, Citizen Ravel. Bring me the particulars of the case, once you have the wretches in custody, and I will, indeed, prosecute it myself, with all due speed. I want this affair over and done with."

Herman, unlike the tireless and singleminded Fouquier, went home every evening after the day's session at the Palais de Justice. Aristide and Brasseur found the president of the Revolutionary Tribunal reading beside the fire in his comfortable apartment on the Right Bank. Without the judge's menacing uniform of black cloak and plumed, wide-brimmed black hat, he seemed almost commonplace, no more than a good-looking, if austere, young lawyer: scarcely the pitiless magistrate who had, within three months, sent more than fifty men and women to the guillotine.

"Ravel, is it?" he inquired, when they had introduced themselves. "Possibly I've heard your name mentioned?"

"Perhaps, citizen." Aristide could feel his expression settling once more into the familiar mask of impassivity, as he gazed at the man who had sentenced Mathieu to death. "Aristide Ravel; I often work for the police."

Unaccountably, a sudden smile illuminated Herman's features. "Aren't you working for Danton these days?"

"Not exclusively."

"Please sit down, citizens," he said, gesturing to armchairs. "Well? What pressing errand brings a commissaire and a very able police agent to my door at this hour of the evening?"

"The affair of the headsman murderer, Citizen President," Brasseur began, and repeated to him what they had already told Fouquier.

"This is all most interesting," Herman said, when Brasseur had finished, "but it's the public prosecutor's duty to bring suspects to trial, not mine."

"We've already spoken to Citizen Fouquier," said Brasseur, "and he's ready to prosecute the case as we've presented it to him. But there's more to it than that. For us to get at the real truth, we've hatched a plan, but we need your cooperation, citizen, and perhaps the approval of the Minister of Justice as well."

"Indeed. What's really going on here?"

Aristide, who had been silently staring into the fire, glanced for an instant at Herman. The president, in person, seemed temperate and reasonable. How could one reconcile the soft-spoken man before him with the icy, remorseless judge?

"I believe this affair began thirty years ago or more," he said, still gazing into the fire, "when a greedy and unscrupulous man named César de Rainneville decided to seize a great fortune for himself, by hounding an innocent man to his downfall and death. . . ."

Herman listened, now and then interjecting an astute question or remark into the narrative. "I see," he said, at length, when Aristide had concluded. "And you wish my collaboration in this scheme of yours, in order to set things right."

"Yes, citizen."

"You're certain of your conclusions?"

"All the facts point in one direction. And I should have proof shortly, with luck. Or rather, not proof, but—with your help—final evidence that should lead to the truth."

"Very well," said Herman, after a moment's thought. "If the Minister agrees, I'll go along with your plans. But if you are wrong, citizens," he added, with a sharp glance at them, "I can't be responsible for the consequences, especially to the two of you. Is that understood?"

"Yes, citizen. Thank you."

"You bear a fine republican name, Citizen Ravel," Herman said unexpectedly as they rose to take their leave.

"Pardon me?"

"The great Athenian lawgiver: 'Aristides the Just.' You share it with my own son."

"I regret to say that I was named after, not the lawgiver, but the less illustrious saint."

"Nonetheless . . . it's a name one can aspire to, is it not?" A trace of regret, or even uncertainty, seemed to flicker in Herman's expression for an instant.

That man isn't a monster, Aristide said to himself, as Herman's man-servant showed them out. *He's no monster, even though I'd like to think of him as one, because then it would be so easy to hate him for it.*

He and many like him, they've chosen to believe that anything—even despotism—is justified in the name of preserving the Republic. Evil means to a good end . . . though how can you have a republic founded on justice and liberty if you ignore justice and liberty while you're creating it?

I wonder if he ever has his moments of doubt?

Geneviève Rainneville, as Aristide expected, did not react calmly when he pushed past the servants into the salon and warned her, as gently as he could, that the police were about to summon her for questioning in the matter of her father's murder.

"This is too much!" she exclaimed, backing away to the hearth, though no fire was burning there, and resting one hand on the stone mantel. Aristide suspected that she was longing to snatch up a poker and defend herself with it. "You now believe that my sister and I had a hand in our father's death? That we went out and attacked him in the middle of the night, and then did the same to a man we hardly know?"

They both twisted about toward the door of the salon as a loud rapping sounded from the foyer. "What the police believe," said Aristide, "is that you and your sister conspired with Louis-Gabriel Caniot, Sophie's father, in the murder of your father and of at least one other man. That the victims died by Caniot's hand, and not yours, is immaterial."

Geneviève glanced again at the door that led out to the foyer, from which they could hear old Bertrande protesting in shrill tones against the intruders, but stood her ground. "Citizen Ravel, do you honestly think that Lucienne and I would connive at murder with such a man?"

"What *I* believe," he continued, moving closer to the hearth, "is a different matter. Now, please, listen to me. That's Commissaire Jolivet at the door, coming to take you in. The justice of the peace is going to question you all, and on the circumstantial evidence we have, he'll order your arrest."

"But—you're quite mad. I thought we understood each other. What can you be thinking?"

"Please, citizeness—Geneviève—trust me. I will visit you as soon as I can, and explain everything to you. You're going to have to help me, in order to clear yourself and your sister. Will you trust me, and follow my instructions?"

She stared at him, brow puckered. "You want us to go along with some plan you've devised?"

"Will you promise to follow my instructions?" he repeated. "You and your sister both?"

"And if I don't?" she said, as Jolivet strode into the salon, imposing in black suit and tricolored sash, half a dozen men behind him. Abruptly she drew closer to Aristide, lowering her voice. "All right, if we're to be arrested—then I must trust you, I suppose. What choice have I? But leave Lucienne out of it, as much as you're able. She'd go to pieces and spoil your plans."

"As you wish."

"Tell me what you want me to do or to say: I can do it."

Swiftly he raised her hand to his lips and gave her an encouraging smile. "Yes, I believe you can."

34

Revolutionary justice, Aristide thought as he paced up and down the length of the Salle des Pas Perdus, was, if not lenient, at least swift. Four days from arrest to trial. But it had been time enough for Geneviève, with his help, to master her part.

He glanced once again into the chamber. They were concluding the formalities with each of the accused. Name, place of birth, age, residence, condition. . . . Caniot, a hulking ruffian with a heavy three days' growth of black beard, sat slumped on the prisoners' bench, looking as if all the bluster had been knocked out of him. Lucienne perched on the opposite end of the bench, hands tightly clasped in her lap, gazing at the floor, as if, by looking at no one, she could become invisible. Only Geneviève, beside her, seemed calm.

Their defense counsel shuffled his papers. *Just do what I asked you to do,* Aristide said to himself, as if the lawyer could hear him. *Just stall them, if you have to; keep it going as long as you can.* He backed away, with a quick glance at Herman, who was proceeding as if nothing was out of the ordinary, and resumed his pacing.

He was biting his nails again, he realized, and balled his hands into fists as he strode the pillared length of the hall for the twentieth time.

"Thank God," he said aloud, as, half an hour later, he made out

François, pushing his way through the milling crowd that had gathered around one of the newspaper stalls. Clarisse Lépinay was beside him.

"Just in time," he said as they hurried toward him. "The trial's just starting. Citizeness, come with me."

"Please," said Clarisse, "please tell me what this is about. Citizen François could tell me little."

"Did he tell you that we were close to capturing the murderer of Citizen Jumeau?"

"He said that much, yes."

"I want you to come into the court chamber with me to identify someone. Not as a formal witness; just look at everyone—officials, prisoners, audience—and tell me if you recognize anyone there."

"If you wish," she said, bewildered. He led her into the Salle de Liberté, François trailing them, and escorted her through the crowd until they stood near the barrier. Fouquier was just concluding his indictment. "Who should I be looking for?"

"Just tell me if you see anyone you know, or even think you know."

He watched her, as she scanned the mass of faces, the prisoners' bench, the judges' and lawyers' tables, the jury benches, the fidgeting spectators, and caught her tiny start of surprise, soon concealed.

"No," she said at last.

"Are you sure?"

"I don't—wait," she added, turning toward Fouquier. "Did that man say the name Rainneville?"

"Does it mean something to you?"

"My—someone I once knew . . . he knew a man named Rainneville."

"Anne-François-César Rainneville?"

"It might have been. It was a long time ago. I think . . . I think he was a relative of some kind. But you said that this was to do with Jumeau. What has this Rainneville to do with me?"

"Patience, citizeness."

Herman, ominous in cloak and tall, plumed hat, glanced over the notes before him and cast a severe eye at the prisoners.

"You stand accused, citizenesses, of conspiring in two most frightful and brutal murders: First, the horrible assassination of your own father; and then the slaughter of a blameless citizen, a representative of the people, in order to divert the public attention and the guardians of the law from the true object of your crimes.

"You, Citizen Caniot, are accused of committing these frightful crimes with your own hand, for the sake of avenging an injury done to your daughter. Any extenuating circumstances must be ignored in the face of the abominable manner in which you committed these murders, and most especially in your choice of one of the people's deputies as your victim.

"What have you to say for yourself, citizen, citizenesses?"

Geneviève rose, with an encouraging touch to Lucienne's arm, and a swift, contemptuous glance at Caniot. "I am innocent of these crimes."

"Innocent," Lucienne said, her voice scarcely audible.

"I didn't do it," Caniot mumbled. "Didn't do any of it. I wish I'd killed the bastard who ruined my daughter, but I didn't. And you've no proof that I did!"

Aristide shifted his position, behind a group of excited bourgeois women whose immense "pouf" bonnets provided excellent concealment. He glanced at Clarisse, beside him. Her gaze kept darting between the prisoners and the jury benches, and a little puzzled frown had gathered between her brows.

One by one, witnesses spoke for and against the prisoners. At last, as the afternoon light began to fade and an usher lit lamps around the chamber, Herman turned to Geneviève.

"Citizeness, it is the public prosecutor's contention, borne out by the testimony of several witnesses, that you had a motive several times over for this horrible murder of your father. Is it not true that you hated Citizen Rainneville?"

He saw her swallow and clench her fists before replying. "That's false, Citizen President. My sister and I loved our father. Why would we have hated him? He was the best of men." Lucienne glanced up at her at that, bewildered, but soon returned to sniffling into her handkerchief.

"The best of men?"

"Yes, he was stern but fair. He would never have done us, or anyone else, any cruelty or injustice."

"Is it not true that Citizen Rainneville forced his attentions upon the unfortunate Sophie Caniot, as she claims, and left her with child?"

"I can't believe it for a moment," she said coolly. "Perhaps Sophie got herself into trouble with a young man who refused to marry her, and so she chose to accuse my father of rape in order to conceal her own indiscretions. Dishonest domestics have made such slanderous accusations before now."

"Is this true, citizen?" Herman said, turning to Caniot.

"I only know what my daughter told me," Caniot said sullenly. "Could have been the master, could have been she made a slut of herself with some young stallion who wouldn't do the right thing by a girl. How's a man to know? She swore up and down that it was her master who took advantage of her."

"My father would never have done such a thing," Geneviève declared. "He was honorable, principled, and virtuous in all matters."

Good work, Aristide said to himself, watching her. *Lay it on thick. Rainneville was a saint!*

He glanced again at Clarisse. She was staring at Geneviève and now seemed visibly worried.

"And what of the witness Fruchard, your neighbor," Herman continued, "who repeats a circulated rumor that, many years ago, Citizen Rainneville poisoned his own wife, your mother, in order to inherit her fortune? Why should this court not believe that you avenged your mother's death with the murder of your father?"

"Citizeness Fruchard is mistaken. Our mother died of natural causes, after a long illness. Besides, Father loved her. He would never have hurt her, just as he would never have hurt anyone, or done anyone a bad turn, for the sake of gain or any other such petty motive. He was beyond such underhanded dealings. He was, in fact, a model citizen; one whom many other citizens of the Republic could have emulated—"

"A model citizen!"

Heads turned toward the jury benches, where one man had sprung to his feet. Clarisse gasped.

"That's a lie," Sauvade cried. "A lie! And you know it!"

Geneviève glanced at him, startled, then at the president, who promptly rang his bell.

"Silence, citizen. It's not your place to offer an opinion at this time, before all the evidence has been presented to you."

Sauvade slowly resumed his seat, as Herman turned to Geneviève. "Citizeness, in searching your house, the police found a most illuminating letter among your papers. Tell the court the substance of that letter."

"I will not," she retorted. "That is a private matter—you have no right—"

"The clerk of the court will read the letter aloud," Herman declared.

"'My dearest Émilie,'" read the clerk, in unemotional tones, "'I read, with astonishment and concern, your last letter to me. If what you tell me about your daughter Geneviève is true, then I pray you, my beloved, to take care. I have had much opportunity, as both a kinsman and a fellow officer, to observe Rainneville's character, and I fear, should he learn your secret, that he might exact his revenge upon both of us, but most heavily upon you.

"'I wish with all my heart that I could return to France to protect you, but my duty to my king must come first. I pray you, should you ever fear for your safety at your husband's hands, take the child—dare I call her my daughter?—and flee to my property at St.-Martin in the Dordogne, where Rainneville has never been and where, it is to be hoped, he cannot find you. I remain, as ever, your most loving cousin and dear friend.' The letter is initialed 'G. de M.' and dated the third of March, 1760."

"Well, citizeness?" Herman demanded. "What have you to say to this? Is this letter not compelling evidence of your late mother's infidelity?"

"You may interpret it as you wish," she retorted.

"May it not now be surmised that your alleged father, Citizen Rainneville, suspected this betrayal and did, indeed, cause your mother's death, many years ago? And did you not, finding and reading this letter from the man who believed he was your true father, now have a most convincing motive to murder Citizen Rainneville, to avenge your mother's death?"

"This is all surmise!" Geneviève cried. "You have no proof!"

"Furthermore, citizeness, Citizen Rainneville was a wealthy man, yet witnesses have testified that he was miserly and that he deprived you and your sister of many common comforts. I put it to you that you wished to enjoy his fortune, the fortune that ought to have descended to you and your sister at your mother's death, but which, instead, was denied you. I put it to you that you conspired with your sister and with Citizen Caniot to murder Citizen Rainneville for the sake of your inheritance."

"It's not true," Geneviève said, but her voice seemed to waver.

"I put it to you that Citizen Rainneville, together with denying you your inheritance, was a hard and cruel man, and you murdered him to be free of this domestic oppression. Did you, and your sister, not make a statement before a representative of the police that you hated the citizen, because he was, and I quote, 'a selfish beast; tightfisted and selfish in everything'?"

"The citizen must have misunderstood us," she said. "It's true that our father was frugal and exacting and gave us little in the way of allowances. But it was, of course, our duty as his daughters to obey him in all things and to love him." She paused, glanced uneasily about the chamber, and continued, her voice unsteady. "These allegations you bring against his character are false, citizen. My father, Anne-François-César Rainneville, was a model citizen and an excellent patriot."

"Can you deny that he was tried, himself, here at this tribunal not long ago?"

"No, Citizen President; but you yourself know that the accusations against him, of making counterrevolutionary remarks, were untrue, and he was released."

"They were brought by Citizen Caniot, your fellow accused, were they not? Speak up, Citizen Caniot."

"Damn right I accused the bastard!" Caniot snarled. "He said—he said, 'Long live the king!' I heard him myself!"

Geneviève shrugged. "The denunciation was patently false. Citizen Caniot maliciously denounced Father because he bore a grudge against him for the reasons he's repeated here—he believed that Father had taken advantage of his daughter. But this jury, here before us, acquitted my father of all charges of incivism, as you must recall. And it's the duty of all juries," she added, turning to face the spectators, "but most particularly of the jury at the Revolutionary Tribunal, which safeguards the Republic itself, to bring the full force of the law against the guilty. If my father was acquitted here of all wrongdoing, is that not proof that there wasn't the slightest stain on his character or his patriotism?"

"Enough!"

Sauvade was on his feet again, now white and trembling.

"That swine Rainneville got off because I argued them into letting him go! Because the guillotine was too good for him!"

Herman's bell rang in the startled silence. "Citizen, control yourself. Are we to understand—"

"I persuaded my fellow jurors that Rainneville was innocent of those ridiculous charges. No doubt he was—though he was guilty of far worse, throughout his life, than a few reckless words. *I* made certain he wasn't sentenced to the guillotine—he didn't deserve such an easy death!"

Sauvade looked swiftly over at the Rainneville sisters and gazed at them for an instant before turning back to the judges. "End this now, citizens," he said, his voice steady, though Aristide thought he could hear a note of hysteria in it. "These women are innocent. It was I who murdered Rainneville."

35

Y ou, citizen?" Herman echoed him, as the spectators gasped.
"Yes! And Gaillard also. And no man deserved it more than they!
Rainneville was a Judas and a murderer! A betrayer who bore false witness against the best, noblest man who ever lived, for the sake of gain, and advancement, and his petty resentment!"

Aristide glanced at Herman. Their eyes met for an instant before the president gave him the slightest of nods and then turned once more to Sauvade. "Citizen, be so good as to explain yourself."

"He was a murderer!" Sauvade cried, his voice rising to a shriek as he continued. "He deserved to die! He and all the others—they conspired against an innocent man, cowards who couldn't advance themselves except by bringing down a better man who stood in their way, like mangy dogs tearing at a lion's flesh—they conspired and lied and brought him down—the most honorable, noble man who—who—"

Clarisse Lépinay plunged forward, clawing her way past the gawking spectators, to throw herself at last against the railing by the jury benches. "René! *René!* Dear God, René, calm yourself!"

He turned, astonished, at the sound of her voice. "You?"

"René—"

"You know what they did! *You*, of all people! You know the lies they told about him! You must have known!"

"No, no, I never did!" She reached over the railing to him, but he jerked away from her touch. "I never knew all that happened. We had parted—when he left France—you know that. Believe me, I never knew!"

"Tell me you didn't know about the swine you took up with—the swine I saw you with in September—a man who had a hand in my father's death!"

She froze, staring at him, her face as white as his.

"*Jumeau?* No!"

"Can you deny he was part of the Parlement that condemned him to death?"

"Order!" Herman shouted, the bell jangling over the uproar that had arisen. "You will address the court, Citizen Sauvade. You, too, citizeness, stand back! We will have order in the Revolutionary Tribunal!"

Sauvade remained standing in the midst of his astonished fellow jurors, just far enough from Clarisse to avoid her touch. Aristide forced his way forward through the pressing crowd.

"Citizen President," he said, when he had reached the railing, and stood in clear view of the judges' table, "may I have leave to speak? Citizen Sauvade is speaking the truth. It's he who murdered Citizen Rainneville and also the citizens Jumeau, Deverneuil, Noyelle, and Gaillard."

"No!" Clarisse cried. "No! You're wrong!"

"You know I'm not wrong," Aristide said, turning to her. "You knew the truth, or guessed at it, the instant I told you about the manner of Jumeau's death. You guessed it couldn't be a coincidence that both your lover of long ago and your present protector had died in the same frightful manner. And you suspected, though you were loath to believe it—for who else could be linked, even remotely, to both deaths?—that Jumeau's murder might involve your own son."

"Her son!" Fouquier exclaimed.

"Yes. René Sauvade is the bastard son of this citizeness, Clarisse Lépinay, and of Hippolyte-Gilles-Aimable Courbonnet, Vicomte de

Montjourdain, colonel in the king's army, who, thirty years ago, was condemned to death for high treason in this very chamber."

"And what," Fouquier demanded, "has that to do with any of—"

"My father," Sauvade interrupted him, leaning forward and looking from the judges' table to the spectators and back again, "the Vicomte de Montjourdain, my *father*, was betrayed to his death by those swine: Rainneville, Noyelle, Gaillard, who stood in this chamber and poisoned the air with their lies and their malice, and Deverneuil and Jumeau, who let them perjure themselves until they befouled the name of justice! They murdered him, and got away with it, and profited by it—they lived free for thirty years with the fruits of their betrayal. Why should I not take their lives in return?" He glanced from side to side once again, at the judges, at the crowd, at the speechless prosecutor, at last fixing his gaze on Clarisse, who was weeping.

"And *you*!" He thrust the jurors aside as he scrambled across the benches and lunged forward, reaching across the rail to seize her by the shoulders. "You whore! How could you? Sleeping with a man—*living* with a man—who took part in that vile travesty that sent my father to a horrible death! How could you do it?"

"He had no part in it!" she cried. "Jumeau was no magistrate, he had no part in the Parlement's decisions. He was a good man!"

"He was *there*! He worked for them—for the judges who condemned him!" Now Sauvade was weeping, too, as he clutched her and violently shook her. "He was *there*—everyone who was there is guilty!"

"No, René, no! I would never—I could never have formed a liaison with Jumeau if he'd had any hand in poor Gilles's death. He was innocent of that!" She reached for him, trying to clasp him in her arms. "Believe me, my darling, he was innocent! Oh, please, please, believe me—my poor darling boy—"

"Do you know what they did to him, Mamma?" he demanded, thrusting her away. He straightened and glanced about the chamber, locking eyes with each staring spectator in turn. "Do you know? Who among you—which of you vultures was there in the Place de Grève that day? Thirty years ago—who else here remembers it as if it were yesterday? They cut his head off—they hacked it off, as if they were chopping firewood! Because the *bourreau* couldn't do his job! The sword slipped—and instead of letting my father die like a gentleman, honorably, quickly, they had to hack his head off while he lay in the straw, writhing, screaming from the agony—"

"Oh, God!" Clarisse cried, and went so pale that Aristide feared she was going to faint. He pushed his way through to her as Sauvade, oblivious, continued to rage.

"He did his part—he was brave and noble and knew how a gentleman should die, even one falsely condemned as he was—he held himself steady for the sword, as he had to, he never flinched—and then the fool missed and struck him on the cheek and he went over and he was bleeding and . . . and . . ." He began to choke on his hysterical sobs. "They tried again—they tried to chop at his neck with their sword—there was blood all over—the sword couldn't c-cut through . . . they—they had to—to use a *hatchet* to t-take off his head at the end . . . a barnyard goose would have fared better . . ."

At last he paused, breathing hard, tears streaming down his face. "They deserved it—all of them," he said. "Do you hear me?" He turned to Herman, who was standing frozen, just as he had risen from his table, as if shocked into immobility by such a display of raw and unbalanced emotion.

"They *deserved* it. It was justice. Only justice."

Herman recovered himself and beckoned the nearest guardsmen toward the jury benches, but too late. Sauvade hurtled forward and vaulted over the railing into the crowd, thrusting them aside. Clarisse stretched out a hand to him, but he took no notice of her as he plunged past the petrified spectators and disappeared out the door into the great hall beyond.

Aristide reached Clarisse, just as she swayed and clutched at the railing before her. At his touch she turned and stared at him with wide, horrified eyes.

"He—how does he *know*?"

With difficulty, Aristide escorted her out of the chamber and to a bench in the Salle des Pas Perdus. "That—that—frightful day," she continued, after she had sunk onto the bench and a little color had returned to her cheeks. "I only learned about it from rumors—and—and I never told him his father's real name. . . . How did he know?"

"He witnessed it."

"*Witnessed* it?" she echoed him, her voice cracking as she raised it to be heard against the excited clamor that was rising from every side as the crowd spilled out into the hall and a dozen guardsmen rushed to the exits.

"He and his friend Lemarchant played truant one day, when they were boys, to see an execution—"

"Oh, dear God—"

"An important execution, of a nobleman, a state criminal—a trial and sentence everyone was talking about. Something exciting for a schoolboy to boast about having seen."

"Oh, God," she repeated. "Oh, may God forgive me. So he saw that horror, with his own eyes, and I never knew. . . ."

"He went expecting a gruesome thrill, and instead saw the last person in the world he could have expected to see on the scaffold—his own father—"

"On the scaffold, preparing to die—and then to see him die so horribly. And René adored his papa. Oh, sweet Jesus, I never knew!"

She was silent for a moment, pressing a crumpled handkerchief to her lips. "I saw so little of him, once he was old enough to go to school. We—Gilles and I—we had decided, together, that it would be better that René didn't know who his father really was, until he was old enough to understand what it was to be a bastard. Gilles used an assumed name when we visited René. He—he never knew his papa's real name."

No, a twelve-year-old schoolboy couldn't possibly have known that the notorious traitor whom everyone was talking about was his own father.

"He scarcely shed a tear when I told him, much later, that his father had died in battle," she said suddenly. "I thought he had forgotten Gilles, after all those years Gilles spent in the American wars, and like a fool I thought it was better that way . . . but of course he already knew that his father was dead, and how he had died. . . ."

"Such a harrowing, horrific experience—thrust upon him without warning—it would have stayed with him for years," said Aristide. "Believe me, I know." *And at least I was spared the sight of my father's death; what Sauvade must have seen is beyond comprehension.*

"Citizeness," he said, taking her hands and lifting her to her feet, "we have to find him."

36

He—he owns a little property in Montsouris," she said. "It's the house where he grew up, with his nurse. We visited him every week, before Gilles went off to the war. Gilles made it over to René when he was still a boy, just before he left for America."

"Montsouris—yes." The Lemarchants had mentioned Sauvade's little house at the edge of the city. "He lives there still?"

"I—I think so, though he often lodged with his friends, the notary and his family—"

"I know them. But I doubt he'd go there. Come with me—perhaps Sauvade will listen to you, when he would listen to no one else." He gestured to François, who had hurried up behind them from the chamber, along with one of Brasseur's men. "François, Chesnais, go get us a fiacre that'll take us to the southern barrier and beyond. Quick!"

"Do you really think he will pay heed to me?" Clarisse asked him, as he guided her through the hall, between the stalls and the clusters of excited bystanders. "He always knew, once he was old enough, that his mother was a woman of no reputation, though I think he had come to terms with that—but for me to become the mistress of one of the men whom he blames for Gilles's death—what an unnatural monster he must think me!"

"It's worth a try. Come."

He led Clarisse outside and down the great staircase to the May Courtyard, where François came running to meet them. "Come on— I've got a willing driver. What's more," he added to Aristide, "he told me that a driver ahead of him in the queue took off hell-for-leather a couple of minutes ago, with a single passenger inside who might have been Sauvade."

"Which way did he go?"

"South, looks like. Made straight for the bridge."

"To Rue de la Harpe," Clarisse whispered, as Aristide handed her into the fiacre. "Which leads to Rue d'Enfer and the Orléans road—"

"South to the barrier, quick as you can," Aristide ordered the driver. "Follow the driver who was ahead of you—ten livres if you can catch up with him!"

The driver needed no further encouragement. The cab leaped forward as he cracked his whip and urged the horse on with a shrill whistle.

It was all falling into place, just as Aristide had suspected. He stared out the window as carriages and peddlers' carts slipped by. What was it Sauvade had shouted at Clarisse, at the Tribunal? *Tell me you didn't know about the swine you took up with—the swine I saw you with in September.*

Sauvade was a notary, with a plausible excuse for spending hours upon hours at the Palais de Justice, examining the records of old cases. He had had time; he had searched for and found them all—had known, perhaps for years, the names and histories of every soul, guilty or blameless, connected to the shameful Montjourdain affair. For thirty years he had lived with their hated names haunting his dreams, as he brooded over his revenge against the men who had murdered his father.

Would he ever have carried out his lethal fantasies, if nothing had happened to fan that low-burning ember of hatred into an inferno?

But the sight of his own mother arm in arm, openly affectionate, with a man who had been present at the affair—even though he had taken no part in the verdict and sentence—that sight might have been enough to wrench Sauvade from a precarious sanity into madness. Enough to launch him on a brutal campaign of carnage that had begun with Jumeau and would not end until he had hacked off the heads of all the men he believed most responsible for his father's frightful death.

"That was some sharp deduction there," François said as they jolted along past houses, shops, boarded-up monasteries, and market gardens. He glanced at Clarisse, sunk in her own thoughts, silent and immobile, and continued. "I was sure those women were guilty as sin. That letter was a bit of luck—how the devil did you find it?"

Aristide permitted himself the faintest of smiles. "I wrote it myself."

"You mean you planned—" François began. "Death of the devil. Of course you planned the whole thing. They were never in any danger, were they?"

"No."

"And Citizeness Rainneville was in on it. D'you think she's really Montjourdain's bastard?"

"I've no idea. But I've felt that she and Sauvade resembled each other, somehow, and after seeing the two of them together in the same room . . . Geneviève Rainneville shares more physical traits with him than she does with her sister."

"And you guessed that Sauvade wouldn't let them condemn his own half sister for a crime that he'd committed?"

"In the end, despite the madness that has taken hold of him, I think Sauvade is still an honorable man." Clarisse gave him a quick, grateful glance as he continued. "I took a chance in believing that although he could commit murder in the name of justice, he could never have permitted himself to let an innocent person be condemned in his place."

Heavy traffic on Rue de la Harpe slowed them. They arrived at the barrier forty minutes later, without overtaking Sauvade's fiacre. Clarisse, stirring to life, directed the driver half a mile farther, through the sparsely populated suburban district of Montsouris to its outskirts. "There," she said, as their fiacre rolled to a stop in front of a modest but well-kept stone cottage that stood a good distance away from its neighbors amid trees and vegetable gardens. "That's the house. Gilles bought it when—when I gave him a son, and set him up here with his wet nurse. René spent his whole childhood here."

Beckoning François and Chesnais on, Aristide scrambled from the cab and hurried to the front door. It was unlocked. He stepped inside, glancing about him in the gloom.

"Sauvade?"

"René?" Clarisse called, behind him, as he proceeded cautiously through the cottage. "Are you there? It's Mamma . . ."

"Sauvade? This is Ravel. I have armed men with me. Please don't try anything foolish."

"René, darling, please come out," Clarisse said, her voice trembling. "I understand now. Please, darling, please forgive me."

Silence greeted their words. Inspector Chesnais emerged from the room beyond, shaking his head. "No one here, not even servants."

Clarisse shook her head. "The last I knew, he had only an old woman who lives in the village, who comes in a few days a week to cook and clean."

"That's conveniently private," Aristide said under his breath. No inquisitive servant sleeping in the house, who might notice that occasionally Sauvade would return to his home at two or three in the morning, spattered with blood. . . .

"Nobody upstairs," said François, trotting down the steep staircase.

"Only one place he could be, if he's here," Chesnais added. He led the way to the small kitchen at the rear of the house. "Cellars," he said, pointing at a low, arched doorway in a corner. "Look at the hearth; the fire hasn't been built up for days, but there are some warm ashes, just enough for someone to have lit a stick or two, not long ago, in order to light a candle."

"Oh, Lord," Aristide muttered. He did not like the notion of pursuing anyone into a cellar, where he would doubtless turn on them like a cornered rat.

"I could fetch a few men from the guard post at the barrier," Chesnais suggested.

"Go. And take the citizeness with you and make sure she gets safely back to town."

François occupied the time, while they waited for the inspector to return, by searching the kitchen and pantry. He returned in triumph with a handful of candles and settled down to producing a new fire from the striking steel of his pistol, using a tinderbox he found above the kitchen hearth. By the time Chesnais returned with four men in National Guard uniform, two of them with lanterns, François had a small flame going and was lighting candles for everyone. Aristide drew in a breath and lifted the latch of the cellar door.

He was half prepared to find the door barred from the inside, but it gave way. At last he reached the bottom of the narrow, curving stairs. The cellar was dark and silent. Chesnais held his own candle high overhead and passed it about shelves that held a few bins of root vegetables and a dozen earthenware crocks, keeping cool in the chilly stone-walled chamber.

"Just a storeroom—nobody here. You two, see what's behind that door."

"Nothing," one man said a moment later from the darkness beyond the heavy door. "He's not here."

"D'you think he could have made fools of us," François suggested, "and dashed off or doubled back as soon as he passed the barrier, where he knew they'd recognize him?"

If he did that, by now he could be anywhere, Aristide thought glumly. He was about to order them back upstairs when another man spoke up.

"Citizen! There's a trapdoor here! In the back room."

"A subcellar?" Chesnais said. "Why would you need one of those out here?"

"Why, indeed?" said Aristide. Dual levels of cellars were not uncommon in the heart of Paris, where houses were narrow and space was at a premium, but out in the rural suburbs it would be far easier to construct outbuildings than to dig a second level to the cellar. "Will it open?"

His answer was a crash as someone pulled the trap up and let it fall backward. He hurried past the door, its heavy padlock hanging open from a hasp, into the room beyond and found François and the guardsmen clustered about an irregularly shaped, dark opening.

"This isn't any subcellar, by the look of it," one of the men said, lowering his lantern into the gap. "I'd guess it's an entrance into an old tunnel in the quarries. Maybe once was just a crack in the tunnel ceiling that fell in."

Aristide bent over the hole. A steep ladder led down to a narrow passage far below, its walls of uneven, buff-colored limestone still bearing the chisel marks of long-dead quarrymen.

"Two of you men, wait here," he said, straightening. "The rest of you, stay close and, for God's sake, take care with your candles. You don't want to get lost down there without a light."

He clambered down the ladder and cautiously stood upright in the passage. The stone ceiling was little more than an inch above his head. He glanced about him, passing the candle along the walls, and, to his delight, discovered a smudged dark line in the center of the ceiling that someone, long ago, had made with greasy candle smoke. The line began at the ladder's base and went off down one end of the tunnel.

The others soon joined him and they set off down the passage, following the sooty guideline. The tunnel, sloping steeply downward, soon intersected another, and then another, but the black line did not falter.

After some time, and a long flight of steps that led them still lower into the depths, the passage widened into an empty gallery and then, beyond, into a roughly hewn, round chamber. Aristide glanced upward. The chamber had no ceiling; high above them, the walls receded into darkness.

"One of the quarrymen's pits," said the guard, who evidently knew something of the ancient underground limestone quarries that riddled much of the Left Bank. "This is where they'd hoist up the blocks, I'd guess. But all this hereabouts must be part of the abandoned workings."

"Ravel!" François said sharply, from farther down the passage. Aristide followed his voice and found him standing outside a crude archway about thirty feet away, shining his light within. He edged beside François, holding out his own candle, and peered inside, straining to see in the gloom.

It was a small chamber with a bare rock ceiling that had once— long ago, Aristide thought, glancing at the layers of candle soot that had blackened it—fallen away in a dome, suggesting the vaulted roof of a church. At the far end of the room, a cross carved in low relief in the wall stood over a simple altar. Quarry workers of past centuries, it seemed, had hollowed out a simple chapel for themselves, for use during their long days and nights fifty or sixty feet underground.

On the altar, half a dozen thick candles burned before a small, black-draped portrait of a man who strongly resembled Sauvade.

Montjourdain . . .

A dark smudge on the altar caught his attention. He brought his candle to the smear, close enough to tell that it was a dull reddish-brown, and touched it with a fingertip, but it was dry. Something had lain on the altar, something that had once had fresh blood on it.

"Ravel," François said, behind him, "you'd better turn around. Mind your candle—don't burn yourself."

"What do you—" he said, turning. His hand jerked and droplets of hot tallow splashed on his fingers as the words caught in his throat. On a shallow shelf cut into the wall, arranged so that they were opposite the altar and portrait, sat six glass jars with lids, of the sort an apothecary might use for herbs, two feet high and a foot in diameter.

Five of the six jars contained human heads.

37

The heads rested on the stumps of their necks, tilting to one side or the other, in a clear liquid that Aristide supposed was spirits of wine or some other preservative agent. The eyes, cloudy and alcohol-burned, were open and faced forward, toward the portrait.

"Holy mother of God," François muttered. "What kind of madman *is* this?"

"One who, at a most vulnerable age, saw his own beloved father butchered before his eyes," Aristide reminded him, "and who must have spent his adulthood searching out those who were responsible for it."

Five heads, he said to himself, *but six jars*.

"Oh, God. One more. He needs a head for that last jar."

"Eh?" said François, startled out of his horrified daze.

"He must have planned it . . . or at least he formed his final plans after he killed Jumeau. Half a dozen people whom he blamed the most for Montjourdain's murder." He ticked them off on his fingers, one by one, with the horrid feeling that the cloudy eyes were watching him.

"Jumeau . . . he was just the chief clerk to the court of the Grand' Chambre, but he must have been present at the trial, and that was enough to put him on Sauvade's list. Then, when he realized his own mother was actually Jumeau's mistress, that must have done it. That was why Jumeau had to die immediately, because Sauvade wanted to punish her for betraying Montjourdain's memory, or because he had some confused idea that Jumeau's evil presence was tainting her, whatever you like. And the rest: Deverneuil, who prosecuted the case against Montjourdain, and must have profited from his success. Rainneville and Gaillard, the original conspirators who betrayed him with lies, in order to advance their own fortunes or careers. Noyelle, who served under Montjourdain and probably shared in the blame of that defeat in America, but managed to put it all on his commander. That's five. But who's the sixth?"

"One of the judges from the Parlement?"

"Perhaps . . ." Lemarchant, he remembered, had mentioned a former magistrate whom Sauvade had tried to acquit, though the other jurors had overruled him. But could Sauvade have found many more of them, thirty years later? Quite a few must simply have died of old age during the intervening decades. And of the magistrates still living, men who had enjoyed such power and influence in the old regime, most would have emigrated, or gone into hiding, or were already in prison, awaiting their turn at the Tribunal.

He turned and looked over the altar again, at the dry bloodstain where something had lain: a bloody knife, perhaps, laid reverently before the portrait after each kill. Like a pagan, he thought, brandishing his sacrificial blade to the gods. An offering to the dead, just as Sauvade had left the corpse of Rainneville, of the man who bore the most guilt for Montjourdain's fall, lying headless and bleeding at his father's grave.

Had Sauvade snatched up his blade within the past hour as he fled through the labyrinth of quarry tunnels—tunnels which, growing up here, he must have explored and known intimately?

His feverish imagination could feel the cloudy eyes staring at him, the sagging, half-open mouths ready to accuse him. He turned and left the chamber, pulling François along with him.

"What's in there?" said Inspector Chesnais.

"His victims."

"His victims?"

"Pieces of them," said François.

"Sweet Jesus."

"Don't go in there."

"We're going on," said Aristide. "We're following Sauvade."

"Following him where?" François said, trotting at his heels. "You haven't the least idea where he's got to. He could be anywhere, or already up some shaft he knows about and we don't."

Aristide shrugged, pointing to the smudged line on the ceiling that continued down the corridor. "We follow that as long as we can. Then—I don't know. We'll work it out when we have to."

The murky corridor snaked on, at random intervals branching into a labyrinth of different routes with cryptic directions and dates carved into the walls, but always the guideline led them forward. The narrow passages sometimes widened without notice into broad, empty galleries with crude pillars of limestone blocks supporting the ceiling, some so vast that the light of their candles was not strong enough to pierce the gloom all the way to the walls. A beautifully chiseled staircase off to one side of their path, lined with blocks of masonry, led down another twelve feet to a brimming well that once must have provided drinking water for the quarrymen.

They had walked nearly an hour when François, who had gone a few yards ahead, stopped as if transfixed.

"Holy—"

"What is it?" Aristide demanded. "More of Sauvade's trophies?"

"No. At—at least . . . well, you tell me."

He swiftly made the sign of the cross and raised his candle to eye level, its flame trembling. François, Aristide thought, despite his swagger and bravado, was still very young.

"What do you make of *this*?"

The tiny flame reflected feebly off the ivory-pale surface of a death's head, the vacant eye sockets black pits in the darkness. Aristide took a step forward with his own candle and the skull, illuminated, became one of many, one of hundreds of bones, large and small—no, not hundreds, thousands of jumbled bones in a solid heap six feet high, a scant foot short of the ceiling, thousands of bones spilling out to their feet from where they were piled pell-mell like carrots and turnips at harvest.

"They're *everywhere!*" François said in a hoarse whisper.

One of the men behind them laughed, the sound echoing with a cackle off the stone around them. "So *that's* where we got to."

"I'd forgotten you're not a Parisian," Aristide murmured to François. "You don't know about the ossuary, do you?"

"Ossuary? Isn't that a kind of crypt?"

"Of a sort. For bones. In 'eighty-six, they emptied the Cemetery of the Holy Innocents—which was the foulest place you can imagine—and transferred all the old bones over here, to the quarries. They're no longer excavated hereabouts, because the land is so riddled with tunnels that the houses above might collapse."

He paused a moment, remembering the eerie sight of black-shrouded carts trundling away, southward across Paris to the quarries, to the sound of priests chanting the offices for the dead. It had gone on every night for months.

"At least a dozen galleries, like this one, were consecrated for burial and are full of bones. They're still emptying the old cemeteries of them, especially where the church property has been sold off and people want to build on the land. These aren't Sauvade's work; some of these bones are probably three or four hundred years old."

"But—but how can you fill entire huge rooms with bones up to the ceiling?"

"You've been to the market at the Square des Innocents, haven't you?"

"Sure."

A memory stirred. Who was it who had spoken to him of Les Innocents recently?

"Well," he continued, "that whole square—the whole marketplace—was the cemetery, the oldest, most overcrowded one in Paris, until seven years ago. Think how many corpses must have been buried in it, in the common pits, over the course of five centuries, as they reused the trenches. It took them almost two years to empty it of bones, and even then, I doubt they found all of them." He glanced up at the ceiling, following the line of soot. It continued, as far as he could tell, straight across the chamber that was now filled with thousands of cubic feet of bones. If Sauvade had made the guideline, he had made it long before the city and church authorities had chosen the quarries of Montsouris for their dumping ground for the remains of long-dead Parisians.

"There must be an exit over that way," he said. "But I don't think we can reach it." He stepped forward, boots crunching on small finger and neck bones despite his best efforts to avoid them. The underground room, fifty or sixty feet across, was filled almost to the ceiling, with no space by the walls for them even to edge past. The route was impassable, save by crawling, inch by inch, across the top of the solid mass.

They explored the adjoining corridors as far as they dared, keeping within earshot of each other, but none of the tunnels seemed to lead them in the direction they wanted to go, and they found no sign of Sauvade.

"What now?" François said, when they were all together once more in the corridor beneath the soot line. "This looks like a dead end, Ravel. I'm not crawling over those bones, even if we were able to."

"Count me out!" one of the men exclaimed, crossing himself.

"There are old quarries where I come from, too," François continued, "right beneath the town hall and the market square. They're not so much different from this, saving the bones, of course. But you can get lost in them easy as winking. I've heard stories about one or two people who went down and never came out again. I wouldn't like to take the chance."

"Nor would I," another man said. "Our captain has a report of a man missing right now, name of Aspairt. They think he went into the tunnels a few days ago to break in and lift some brandy from the cellars at the old monastery, but if he lost his light, he'll never find his way back. I'm not going any farther down here."

Aristide sighed. Sauvade undoubtedly knew a portion of these tunnels intimately, while he—and the men with him—could easily lose their way and wander for days in the dark, perhaps until they dropped of starvation and exhaustion, as soon as they diverged from the marked path. If it hadn't been for those cursed bones . . .

Bones . . . cemeteries . . . Les Innocents . . . What was it that was teasing at him?

Someone who had mentioned Les Innocents, not so long ago—

"Oh, my God," he said.

François peered at him through the murk. "Ravel?"

"We have to get back," he said. "Now. Back the way we came, quick!"

Fragments of memories surfaced as he strode back through the tunnel, his candle flickering wildly before him in the breeze of his passing.

Sauvade was curious . . .

Who had said that?

Hamelin—of course, Hamelin.

Too much chance of something going wrong—

That was Hamelin, also. But who was it who had said . . . who had said something about . . . forty years?

Something going wrong . . .

Man and boy, forty years—

God—yes—that's got to be it—

"Hurry!" he repeated, for the fourth time.

"What is it?" François demanded, catching up to him at last as he reached the ladder that led upward to Sauvade's cellar. "What's up?"

"I know where Sauvade's gone. Or—at least—where he'll be later."

"What? What're you talking about?"

"The sixth head," Aristide said as they scrambled up the ladder. "The final head, for that empty jar back in his shrine."

"But he's on the run—he knows we're on to him—he *confessed*—"

"Do you suppose that really matters? He took his knife with him. I think he's too far gone to care about anything else. All he'll want now is to get that last head before we catch up with him—to complete the task he's set himself."

Chesnais and the remaining National Guards joined them in the cellar storeroom, its mundane darkness familiar and almost comforting after the horrors that lay below in the tunnels. Aristide glanced at his watch, in the light of their candles; it was past eleven o'clock. Time had seemed to stand still, down in the eternal night of the quarries.

He gestured the men upstairs. "Out, everybody out! Don't waste time looking for him—he's gone."

"Gone where?"

"Back to the city, I expect." Undoubtedly the maze of quarries extended northward; a man who knew the system could go underground to bypass the barrier and the city walls.

A light rain was falling outside as they returned to street level. He thought furiously as they left the house and headed back to the barrier along the muddy, unlit road. It would be impossible to find a public carriage out here in the suburbs at this late hour; he would have to requisition something, a carriage, a cart, a couple of horses, from the guardhouse or a nearby dwelling. Then back to the heart of Paris, and—what next?

He had no idea where Sauvade's intended victim lived. He could ask them at the Palais de Justice, of course—someone was sure to be there still, working into the night, keeping the wheels of revolutionary justice relentlessly turning—but that would take time, and time was short. And the man was sure to live somewhere at the sparsely settled edge of the city, in an area with few neighbors to point and stare. That would be another hour spent in travel and searching, while Sauvade pressed inexorably forward with his plans—had perhaps already tracked down his prey. No time to find the information and trail the murderer's footsteps.

"I don't know where Sauvade may be right now," he told François at last, as they neared the barrier and the guardhouse, "but I can guess where he'll be before the night is over, and that's where we're going. The Place de Grève."

38

Pinpricks of lamplight gleamed from upper windows of the Hôtel de Ville—the officers of the Paris Commune kept late and wearying hours—but did little to pierce the darkness beyond. Only a sputtering torch at a sentry box illuminated the Place de Grève, its cobblestones wet with rain. Farther away, at the corner of Rue de la Tannerie, a single street lamp flickered from its notorious iron bracket, from which victims of "popular justice" had also dangled in their time.

"Are you certain about this?" François whispered once again, as they settled in to wait, skulking in the concealing shadow of one of the two high, gated archways that led into the Hôtel de Ville's central court-yard. It was almost half past one and the chill midnight breeze from the river swept, sighing, across the empty square before them as the steady, sullen rain continued to fall.

"As certain as I can be." Aristide continued to watch the streets that led to the Place de Grève. "It's the obvious place. The Palais de Justice, the steps of Nôtre-Dame, the Bastille, the Conciergerie, St. Jean cemetery—this is the only place missing. And Montjourdain died here. He'll come."

An insanely hazardous thing to do, to bring—by force or trickery—the man you intended to murder to such an open, public place, even during the small hours of the night; but Sauvade, evidently, was no longer even close to sane.

Both the traffic along the nearby streets and the stream of messengers who hurried in and out of the Hôtel de Ville had dwindled to a trickle. How soon before he would make his move?

"I still don't understand," François whispered again, at his side. "*Who?* Who's the last one?"

"Sanson, of course."

"Sanson? You mean the *bourreau?*"

"Hush! Yes. The master executioner. I've seen Sauvade myself, talking with one of Sanson's men, plying him with wine, probably pumping him for information—Sanson's address, the hours he keeps."

"Why him, in the name of heaven?"

"He's been executioner of Paris for decades," Aristide said, keeping his voice low. Of course, François, not having lived in Paris long, could not be expected to know that. "The master executioner had to perform the execution himself, when a nobleman was condemned to death by the sword—that was the rule before the Revolution."

"I know that much, but—"

"Isn't it likely that he was the one who botched Montjourdain's beheading?"

"Holy—" François exclaimed, before remembering the need for silence.

"Thirty years ago, he'd have been in his early twenties. I expect you could count on one hand the number of nobles who'd been beheaded during the previous fifty years. Decapitating a man with a sword would require skill and nerve, and he'd probably never done it before, or even seen it done. It's got to be Sanson—the man whom Sauvade saw hacking his father to death. In Sauvade's eyes, he'd be as guilty as the men who betrayed Montjourdain. That's the sixth head that he wants for that hellish collection of his."

"Why would you want to save *him?*"

"Executioners are human beings, too, François."

"This one executed your friend."

Aristide squeezed his eyes shut for an instant at the raw memory, then thrust away the vision of blood and rain at the Place de la Révolution and stared out at the cobbles, watching them feebly glitter in the faint light of the sentry's struggling torch, forty feet away.

"That shouldn't matter," he said, keeping his voice level. "He didn't order it. I hope I'm more forgiving than Sauvade is, and saner."

They said nothing more for a time, as the rain fell and the water sluiced away across the cobbles toward the quay, carrying the accumulated filth of the past days down to the river.

"There," said François, leaning forward. "Coming from Rue de l'Épine. Two men, on foot."

Aristide could see nothing yet in the darkness. "Your eyes are sharper than mine."

"One's a little behind the other—might be pushing him along with a blade stuck in his ribs."

"Or a pistol. Careful."

"Not in this rain; he can't have kept his powder dry."

Sauvade, Aristide realized, could have brought him most of the way without rousing his suspicions at all. He could envision it: the executioner, at home, out at the edge of Paris where rumor and the latest news did not penetrate so quickly—a knock on the door at midnight—the visitor whom he must have recognized, the polite, well-spoken, clean-cut juryman from the Tribunal, with a plausible excuse for his presence—a message, an extraordinary directive summoning him at once to the Palais de Justice or the Hôtel de Ville. Sanson would have come with him, unsuspecting, until, without warning, he felt the point of a knife at his back and heard the harsh whisper ordering him to walk to a spot he must have known only too well.

Now he could make them out in the gloom. The taller man in front, walking with measured step, hands at his sides but held out a little from his body; the other behind him, keeping close.

The two figures paused. The one behind prodded the other with his weapon, speaking a few words that were lost in the heavy spatter of the rain. The taller man sank to his knees and brought his hands before him in an attitude of prayer. There would be no lit candle in the ritual, Aristide thought wildly, not in this torrent.

The man with the blade spoke again, his voice rising.

"Say it! Bareheaded—take off your hat and your coat! Now! Say it!"

The man on his knees doffed his hat and coat and began to speak, the words unintelligible. The other man moved about until the point of his dagger was at his victim's throat.

"Say it again! Louder! I want to hear you! 'I have taken part in the foul and brutal murder of an innocent man, and have most grievously and wickedly offended God and Justice'—*say it*!"

"I have taken part in the foul and brutal murder of an innocent man, and have most grievously and wickedly offended God and Justice."

It was not quite the formula of penance that condemned criminals had once repeated before they went to their execution, but it undoubtedly satisfied Sauvade's own craving for justice. Sauvade shook his weapon, his voice rising to a shriek.

"Again! Say it again!"

He edged behind Sanson as his other hand stole inside his overcoat.

Aristide opened his mouth to give the order to the guardsmen lurking behind him, but the words caught in his throat. How easy it would be, to be just an instant too late, to let Sauvade raise his blade and take his final revenge, to have the fierce satisfaction of offering up blood for blood to Mathieu's ghost.

And yet—

If I can't bring myself to call Herman and Robespierre and the rest of them monsters, those who murdered my friends in the name of their undeniably worthy ideals, then how can I condemn this man, who was no more than a weapon in their hands?

François was grasping his shoulder, shaking him.

"Ravel!"

"Go."

They charged from beneath the archway and rushed the two men in the middle of the square. Sauvade whipped about, waving his dagger wildly at arm's length.

"No!"

François knocked the blade out of his hand and grabbed his wrist. "No you don't!"

"No—no—you mustn't," Sauvade shrieked as the guardsmen seized his shoulders. "Not yet! Not until I have him!"

The guardsmen surrounded him. He screamed once more, "No, I have to have him!" as he went down beneath them.

A moment later, it was over. The guards rose one by one, keeping tight hold of Sauvade, as one of them drew a long, heavy butcher's cleaver from the prisoner's belt and another bound his hands behind his back. He collapsed onto his side, weeping.

Sanson, surprisingly, had remained on his knees, bareheaded, throughout the commotion. Aristide moved aside, after satisfying himself that Sauvade was securely bound, and approached him. The executioner, he discovered, was praying, with bowed head and closed eyes.

"Are you unhurt?"

Sanson slowly raised his head. "Yes. Thank you. I'm unhurt."

Aristide reached out a hand to assist him to his feet, then snatched it back as he remembered with whom he was speaking. "We have him. You're in no danger now."

"Thank you," Sanson repeated, as he rose. He turned and looked at Sauvade for a moment, who was still shaking with frenzied sobs.

"The poor man. I shall pray for him."

The executioner seemed so composed, after such a harrowing ordeal, that Aristide felt compelled to probe further. "Do you know who he is, then?"

"I recognized him from the Tribunal. He's one of the jurymen, isn't he? He must have concealed his true feelings for months," he continued, as Aristide nodded. "Does it matter?"

"I—I thought it would be of some concern to you."

"I've been expecting this day for some time now," Sanson told him, with another glance at the weeping Sauvade, as François and the guardsmen escorted him away to the Hôtel de Ville. "In January, when they sent me my orders . . . for the king, I received dozens of threats. 'If you lay a hand on His Majesty, you will die.' But, in the end, no one had the courage to rescue him." He sighed, picked up his dripping hat and coat from the cobbles, and wiped the rain from his face with a handkerchief.

"Every day since the twenty-first of January, I've resigned myself to the chance that someone, somewhere, may at last avenge the king's death by murdering me, just as Deputy Le Peletier was murdered. I'm prepared; I go to Mass and confession as often as I can."

Aristide shook his head. "It wasn't for the king. Sauvade was no royalist."

"No?"

"He didn't tell you why he wanted you dead?"

"He said only something about my being guilty of the murder of a great man. Perhaps he's lost someone dear to him to the guillotine."

"Not even that," Aristide said. Tears pricked his eyes and he hoped, absurdly, that they were invisible in the rain and the dark.

What a bitter joke . . . I've just saved the life of the man who watched Mathieu die, whose hand let the blade fall.

Rage surged in his chest for an instant and he forced it away. Sanson had taken pains to treat his victims, no matter who they might be—Marie-Antoinette, Mathieu, even Saint-Dizier—with kindness and respect.

"His wounds were older," he said. "Sauvade was the son—the illegitimate son, but passionately devoted to him—of the Vicomte de Montjourdain."

He could see the faint start that Sanson gave, even in the feeble light of the torch. "I see you remember the name."

Sanson made the sign of the cross before replying. "God forgive me. Yes, I remember it, far too well."

"Sauvade's lifelong obsession with the men who hounded Montjourdain to his death at last drove him mad. I fear he blamed you as much as he did them—"

"As he should have," said Sanson. "Citizen, that name and that day have haunted me for thirty years." He glanced about him, brow furrowed. "I could tell you, within an inch, where the scaffold stood. The steps were just beyond that mounting block and post. I stood just there. . . ." He turned away, strode to the quay, and stood looking out over the Seine, where the waters were rising with the rain and lapping at the boats pulled up on the gravel beach below the embankment. "I was young, I was inept in performing my duty to my patient, and a brave man—an innocent man, as I understand it—suffered hideous torments because of it. Do you think I wouldn't remember?"

"My best friend—and others of my friends—were among your 'patients' not long ago," Aristide blurted out, and an instant later wished he had not, as Sanson turned a stricken face to his.

"I am truly sorry. I imagine, then, that you can understand that wretched man's bitterness." Sanson drew himself up to his full height, two or three inches taller even than Aristide, and turned his hands palm outward with a tiny, resigned shrug. "As I said, I'm prepared for whatever may happen. It may be that some unhappy man or woman who has lost a loved one will take my life in return, perhaps a year from now, perhaps tomorrow. And I can't say that I find the prospect especially terrifying."

Aristide gazed at him for a long moment. *No*, he said to himself, with a sigh, *I can't hate this man for what he's obliged to do; it's clear he loathes it, and perhaps loathes himself, for remaining in the job at such a time. How can I feel anything but pity for such a victim of circumstance?*

"If I could resign my position," Sanson continued, echoing Aristide's thought, "I would. But my brothers and I have fifteen mouths to feed at home now, and we all bear an age-old stigma; no one else will employ an executioner. To be honest, were I not a good Catholic, I might have done away with myself long before this. To be obliged to lay hands on royalty . . . and these constant death sentences for trivial offenses or political differences, they disgrace what has always been an honorable trade." He mopped at the rain on his face again and gave Aristide a brief, awkwardly formal bow.

"I'm most obliged to you for your aid. I must go home now; my wife will be worrying about me. She fears I'll be assassinated every time I leave the house." He paused. "I think I'll keep tonight's incident from her. She would fret."

"I'll walk you to a cab," Aristide said. "These streets can be dangerous at night."

They walked in silence along the quay, huddling into their overcoats against the rain, as far as the Châtelet and the Pont-au-Change, where a late-going fiacre stopped for them. Aristide saw Sanson off in the cab, heading swiftly northward, then turned and crossed the bridge to the Île de la Cité, toward home.

The rain had cleared the streets of foot traffic and he paused alone in front of the Palais de Justice. The vast courtyard was silent and empty, the paving stones and the gilded tips of the spikes in the high iron fence glistening wetly in the faint light of a street lamp.

Tears sprang to his eyes again, hot on his cheeks. He pulled off his hat, letting the tears mingle with the cold rain that spattered his face, feeling the downpour wash over him until he, like the city around him, for a fleeting moment was clean once more.

HISTORICAL NOTE

Palace of Justice was suggested, in part, by the case of Thomas Arthur, Comte de Lally and Baron de Tollendal (1702–1766). Lally-Tollendal, a career soldier, was governor of the French possessions in India. After several disastrous military defeats during the Seven Years' War, ending in his capture by the British, he was at last accused of high treason against the French crown.

As he had made enemies during his career, and his family background was Irish rather than French, he was an easy scapegoat for all the French losses of the war and was condemned to death. His atrociously bungled beheading by sword at the Place de Grève, on May 6, 1766, by twenty-seven-year-old Charles Sanson (who had never before beheaded a man), made news for weeks. Lally's execution was even described in lurid detail as part of the argument twenty-six years later, in 1792, for adopting the more efficient and foolproof guillotine:

> He was kneeling and blindfolded. The executioner struck him on the back of the neck. The blow did not separate the head from the body, nor could it have done. . . . [The victim] toppled forward, and the head was finally separated from the body by four or five saber blows. This hacking, if we may use the term, was witnessed with horror.

Lally's legitimized bastard son, Trophime-Gérard, Marquis de Lally-Tollendal (1751–1830), only discovered the truth about his parentage on the day of his father's execution, when he was fifteen years old. He spent much of his early life unsuccessfully attempting to clear his father's name, though he never turned to murder as a final resort.

Pierre-Louis-Olivier Desclozeaux, the royalist lawyer whose house overlooked the Madeleine cemetery, bought the land when the city put the cemetery up for sale in 1802, and surrounded the two royal graves with weeping willows and cypresses. In 1815, at the Restoration, he informed King Louis XVIII that he knew the exact spots where the late king and queen were buried, and the remains were excavated and transferred to the royal crypt at the basilica of St. Denis.

A small public park, Square Louis XVI, now occupies the area of the former cemetery. The altar of the Chapelle Expiatoire, a chapel completed in 1826 and dedicated to the memory of Louis XVI and Marie-Antoinette, stands directly over the spot where Louis was buried.

Those who have visited the Municipal Ossuary of Paris (traditionally, but inaccurately, known as the Catacombs) may wonder why this story does not mention the macabre but imaginative arrangements of bones into decorative patterns and retaining walls. The millions of bones were, in fact, initally left in vast heaps in the disused quarries, and were not arranged into patterns of skulls and femurs until about 1810, when the Catacombs were opened to the public and soon became a popular tourist attraction.

An additional skeleton, that of Philibert Aspairt, the Parisian who lost his way in the quarries in 1793, was discovered in the tunnels in 1806; the unlucky Aspairt may be the only individual out of the six million in the ossuary to still have his own grave marker. Old human bones are still occasionally discovered, in the remnants of ancient cemeteries or family crypts, during construction projects in Paris, and are sent to the ossuary to mingle, far beneath the city, with the rest.

A WORD FROM THE AUTHOR

Would your book club, class, or writer's group like to discuss *Palace of Justice* and/or any of Aristide Ravel's other adventures? Visit www .susannealleyn.com for some suggestions for discussion topics (no spoilers!), or to contact me and schedule a live chat with your group (in the United States, Canada, or the UK), in person or via your speakerphone. I look forward to our conversation.

SELECT BIBLIOGRAPHY

Christophe, Robert. *Danton: A Biography*. Garden City, N.Y.: Doubleday, 1967.

Christophe, Robert. *Les Sanson: Bourreaux de Père en Fils Pendant Deux Siècles*. Paris: Librairie Arthème Fayard, 1960.

Cobb, Richard. *Death in Paris, 1795–1801*. Oxford: Oxford University Press, 1978.

Dunoyer, Alphonse; A. W. Evans, translator. *The Public Prosecutor of the Terror: Antoine Quentin Fouquier-Tinville*. New York: G. P. Putnam's Sons, 1913.

Emsley, Clive. *Policing and Its Context, 1750–1870*. London: Macmillan, 1983.

Fierro, Alfred. *Dictionnaire du Paris Disparu: Sites et Monuments*. Paris: Parigramme, 1998.

Hillairet, Jacques. *Connaissance de Vieux Paris*. Paris: Éditions Payot & Rivages, 1993.

Lacroix, Paul. *France in the Eighteenth Century: Its Institutions, Customs and Costumes*. New York: Frederick Ungar, 1876.

Lenôtre, G. [Théodore Gosselin]; Mrs. Rodolph Stawell, translator. *The Guillotine and Its Servants*. London: Hutchinson & Co., n.d.

Lenôtre, G. [Théodore Gosselin]; Frederic Lees, translator. *The Tribunal of the Terror: A Study of Paris in 1793–1795*. Philadelphia: J. B. Lippincott, 1909.

Levy, Barbara. *Legacy of Death*. Englewood Cliffs, N.J.: Prentice-Hall, 1973.

Massin, Jean. *Almanach de la Révolution Française: Des États Généraux au Neuf Thermidor*. Paris: Club français du livre, 1988.

Restif de la Bretonne, Nicolas-Edmé; Linda Asher and Ellen Fertig, translators. *Les Nuits de Paris or The Nocturnal Spectator*. New York: Random House, 1964.

Sanson, H.C. *Sept Générations d'Exécuteurs, 1688–1847: Mémoires des Sanson, Mis en Ordre, Rédigés et Publiés par H. Sanson, Ancien Exécuteur des Hautes Œuvres de la Cour de Paris*. Paris: Dupray de la Mahérie et Cie., 1862–63.

Wallon, Henri. *Histoire du Tribunal Révolutionnaire de Paris*. Paris: Hachette, 1880.

Wills, Antoinette. *Crime and Punishment in Revolutionary Paris*. Westport, Conn.: Greenwood Press, 1981.